Praise for

BLACK SALT QUEEN

"Centered within a whirling battle between love and power, *Black Salt Queen* is an epic tale of female ambition, court intrigue, and betrayal that is sure to keep you on the edge of your seat. Bansil is a writer to watch."
—O.O. Sangoyomi, author of *Masquerade*

"Richly immersive with political intrigue as sharp as a blade, *Black Salt Queen* is a triumph of a debut. This precolonial Philippines–inspired fantasy is a vivid portrayal of love and power and what happens when one is forced to choose between them. Skillfully epic yet splendidly intimate."
—Maddie Martinez, author of *The Maiden and Her Monster*

"Complex matriarchs in a vivid setting. A marvelous addition to the growing multitude of voices in Filipino fantasy fiction."
—K. S. Villoso, author of *The Wolf of Oren-Yaro*

"*Black Salt Queen* is a superbly gripping tale of love, mortality, and the intergenerational effects of trauma. With lush and evocative prose, Samantha Bansil brings to life a Filipino fantasy world of mythic proportions that is bursting with historical and cultural details. If you want intrigue, passionate romance, and a delicious dose of yearning, *Black Salt Queen* is a must read."

—Gabriella Buba, author of *Saints of Storm and Sorrow* and *Daughters of Flood and Fury*

"Samantha Bansil crafts the perfect storm in *Black Salt Queen*. Crackling with magic, the prose is as soft as a summer rain but packs the punch of an unrelenting monsoon. The plot—steeped in equal parts love and betrayal—is utterly addicting. Moreover, the three main characters offer a clever and varied exploration of femininity, motherhood, and power. This book kept me reading late into the night and [made me] never want to leave Maynara."

—S. Hati, author of *And the Sky Bled*

BLACK SALT QUEEN

BLACK SALT QUEEN

Letters from Maynara
BOOK ONE

SAMANTHA BANSIL

Published by Violetear Books, an imprint of
Bindery Books, Inc., San Francisco
www.binderybooks.com

Copyright © 2025, Samantha Bansil
All rights reserved. Thank you for purchasing an authorized copy of this book and for complying with copyright laws. No part of this book may be reproduced, or stored in a retrieval system, or transmitted in any form or by any means, except in the case of brief quotations embodied in articles and reviews, without express written permission of the publisher.

Acquired by Kevin Norman
Edited and designed by Girl Friday Productions
www.girlfridayproductions.com

Cover design by Charlotte Strick
Cover and map illustrations by June Glasson

ISBN (hardcover): 978-1-964721-00-2
ISBN (paperback): 978-1-959411-98-7
ISBN (ebook): 978-1-959411-99-4

Library of Congress Cataloguing-in-Publication data has been applied for.

First edition
10 9 8 7 6 5 4 3 2 1

This is a work of fiction. Names, characters, places, and incidents are either the product of the author's imagination or are used fictitiously and not to be construed as real. Any resemblance to actual persons, living or dead, organizations, events, or locales is entirely coincidental.

Printed in China

For my father, who gave his goddesses everything.

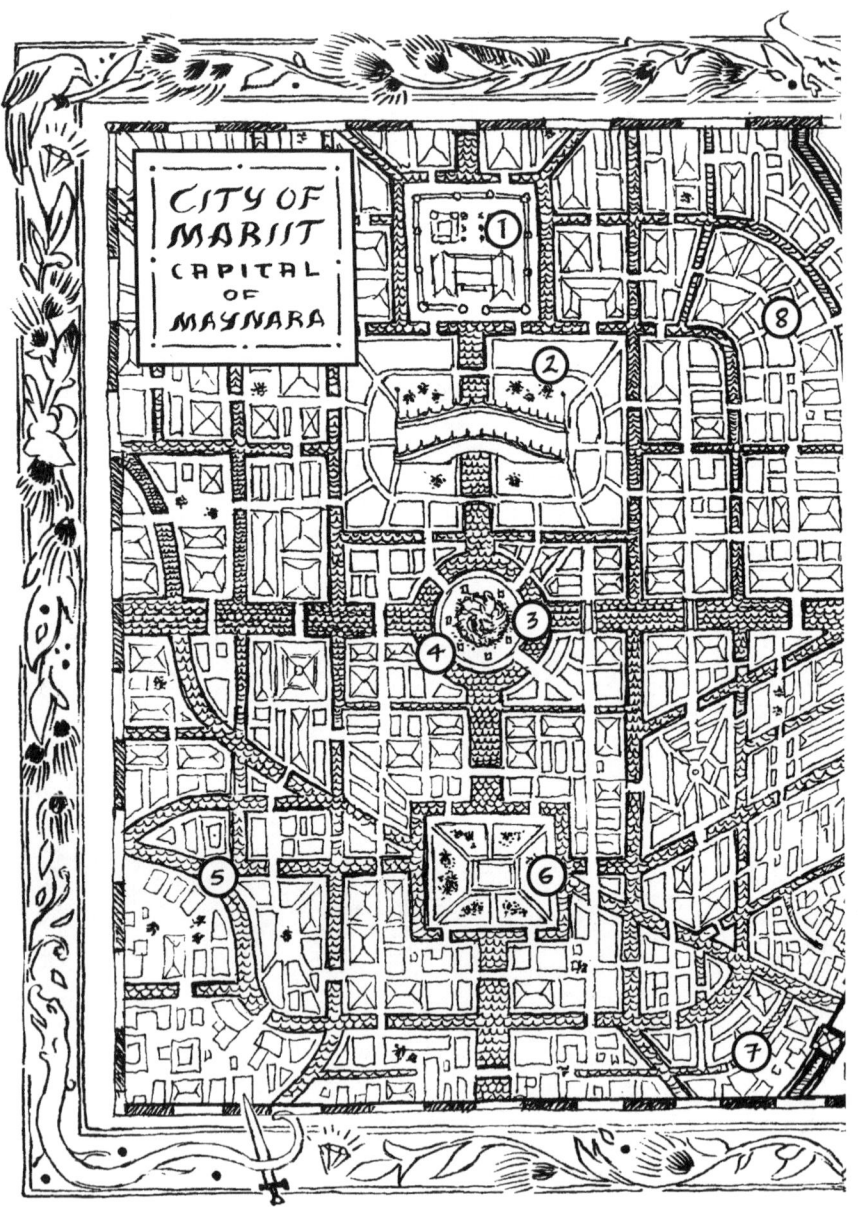

One

TWO INVITATIONS

Dear Luntok,

My sources have informed me that you arrived safely in Mariit, and that you were awaiting this letter with bated breath. They did not need to inform me of this latter detail. Seeing as over a month has passed since your last visit, I had assumed your impatience.

You will have to wait a while longer, darling. The feast days are about to commence, and my sister tells me there is an urgent matter at the port. She begged me to come immediately, but first I thought of you. Urgent matters to attend to, and all I can picture is you scampering to the palace without a worry in your lovely head. However excited you are to see me—wait.

It pains me to caution you against the passions to which you are so inclined. After all, you sent heart-stirring elegies in your last letter. How could a warrior wield such a gentle pen? When we meet again, you'll hang your head and beg me not to be so brisk. To this I say, Wait, my darling. What I promise will ignite your soul far more than some paltry poem. When you are in my arms, you will forget all else.

Come see me tonight, but no sooner. You know the way, perhaps better than myself by now. You mustn't come before the usual hour. I'll leave the window open for you, as I always do.

You accused me of apathy in your letter, alongside your poems. I wonder, Luntok, What do you expect me to confess?

I would tell you I missed you, if that's what you want to hear, but when I said it last time, you didn't believe a word of it.

Until tonight,
Laya

One

LAYA

Few things displeased Laya more than impromptu appointments. She was doubly displeased when such appointments were demanded of her before noon.

She drew back the carriage window shade with an impatient sigh. Bulky blocks of limestone loomed in the corner of her vision—the city's ramparts, a relic of past wars, now a modern eyesore. The royal carriage lumbered through the ramparts' imposing gates, slowing as it entered the port on the outskirts of the city.

"What took you so long?" Her older sister's voice, crisp as the ocean breeze, greeted Laya as soon as her carriage rolled to a stop on the warped planks that lined the wharf.

"I had scarcely woken up when you sent for me," Laya said, shoving open the door. Bulan jumped out of the way. The hilt of her sword scraped against the carriage's lacquered surface—a piercing sound that made both girls wince.

"*Laya,*" Bulan hissed as she regained her footing.

"What?" Laya asked, unperturbed. She gathered her skirt with one hand, the glossy indigo silk creasing in her fingers, and grabbed the doorframe with the other.

"Allow me, Dayang Laya," one of the guardsmen muttered—a

new recruit, judging by the pristine shine of his armor. He stole a glance at Laya, his beady eyes shimmering with curiosity, then offered his arm to help her down.

Laya ignored him and stepped out of the carriage on her own. She cast her gaze beyond the mouth of the harbor, squinting at the pale dawn light that rippled across the Untulu Sea. If given the choice, she would not have left her bed until midday, but Bulan's messenger had been persistent.

"You truly have no sense of urgency, do you?" Bulan said, pursing her lips. With her arms crossed in disapproval, Bulan could not have looked more like their mother.

Laya's nostrils flared in annoyance. "I came, didn't I?" she said, waving Bulan's attention back to the port.

The port was the gateway to the capital of Maynara. Over half the goods traveling in and out of the kingdom went through these very docks. No matter the hour, the murky harbor was teeming with activity. Dozens of ships with hulls large enough to transport entire villages squeezed into the crowded channels. Gauging by the flock of sails billowing on the horizon, dozens more were on their way. But, according to Bulan's messenger, those ships wouldn't get anywhere without Laya's help.

"Now," Laya said, "tell me about this emergency."

Bulan's brow furrowed, and Laya couldn't help but bite back a smug grin. Her sister wouldn't have summoned her here if she'd had any other choice. Whatever the problem may be, Laya was the sole person who could fix it. Her talents were as useful as they were rare. Yet she was seldom given an opportunity to use them.

"Follow me." Without another word, Bulan turned on her heel and hurried Laya away from the carriage.

Laya struggled to keep up with her sister's long, steady strides. Bulan marched them over to the other end of the main pier, her boots striking the planks at an even staccato. No matter the task, Bulan moved with manic precision. Much of that stemmed from her sword training. Bulan awoke before sunrise every morning to perfect her form. Laya would have gone mad if she'd had to rehearse the same slash sequences and foot patterns for the rest of her life. For whatever reason, her sister found pleasure in it, in the sweat and drills that were part of her relentless quest for self-mastery.

As Bulan pressed forward, she didn't notice the number of heads turning in their direction—but Laya did. She held her head higher, slowing her pace to an elegant glide, as uniformed guardsmen and wind-battered sailors froze where they stood to stare after the princesses in awe.

Bulan glared at her over her shoulder. "Laya, keep up, will you?"

Laya scowled and slowed down further just out of spite. "You're my sister, not my handler," she called back.

"According to Mother, I am both," Bulan said curtly. "I'm to be your high counselor."

Laya bit back a retort. Though Bulan was only fulfilling her duties as counselor to the future queen, Laya wanted nothing more in that moment than to smack her sister across the face.

Thankfully, Bulan didn't give her another order until they reached the water's edge. Laya leaned against the brass railing. Her nose filled with the scents of rusted metal and crusty salt. Under the uneven slits between planks, coral-tinged waves splashed up against the wooden beams holding up the pier.

"Do you see the problem now?" Bulan pointed several hundred feet across the water at the entrance to the harbor. Its opening was flanked on either side by rocks that gnashed at passing ships like sharks' teeth. Laya followed Bulan's finger with her gaze. Her eyes widened when she saw the source of all the fuss.

"What on earth . . . ?"

Bulan nodded. "Last night, one of the ships got blown off course. Now it's blocking half the entrance. Only the smaller boats can get in."

"How strong were those winds?" Laya asked, incredulous.

The ship in question was one of the largest cargo vessels Laya had ever seen. Its hull would rival the belly of a whale, and its masts shot straight up to the heavens, disappearing into the clouds overhead. The bow had gotten lodged between the jagged rocks at the mouth of the harbor. Laya counted several rowboats tethered to the sides of the hull, sailors straining with their oars as they struggled in vain to free the ship.

"Didn't you hear the storm last night?" Bulan said. A shadow of recognition crossed her face. Her gaze hardened. "Ah—the Kulaws must have arrived early for the feast days. I'm guessing *that's* what kept you occupied."

A deep flush crept up Laya's neck. Her knuckles whitened against the railing. "I don't know what you're insinuating. I haven't seen Luntok in weeks," she said testily. It wasn't a lie.

Bulan hummed a note of disbelief and turned back to the beached ship. No matter what excuse Laya gave, her sister would never believe her.

Doubt churned in Laya's gut. *She can't prove anything,* she thought savagely. Rather than press Bulan on the subject, Laya swallowed her worries and focused on the task at hand. Her eyes fell once more on the men in the rowboats—their meager oars could do little to free a vessel of that size. A powerful gust had entrapped the ship between the rocks, and only a powerful gust could blow it out.

"Stand back," she told Bulan as she raised her palms to the sky. The air rushed down to meet them in winding currents. Laya grinned as the invisible threads of energy wrapped themselves around her fingertips. She balled her hands into fists, cementing her grasp. With a deep breath, she gave the threads a harsh tug. The air above their heads split with a mighty blast that almost knocked her and Bulan off their feet.

Laya steeled her jaw, firming her stance on the pier. At her summons, dark, gray storm clouds barreled in from across the Untulu Sea. She whisked the wind to a violent speed, relishing the way it whipped her hair back and rushed past her fingers. Its energy coursed through her veins, at once exhilarating and familiar. She closed her eyes, wishing for the wind to lift her along with it. Laya had tasted power like that once, years earlier. Power so strong, it shot her skyward and gave her wings. How long before she would taste that kind of power again?

"Laya, be careful!" Bulan's fearful scream pierced through the roaring in her ears. Bulan had seen what Laya became when she got swept up in the throes of Mulayri's power. She, too, remembered.

Her sister's voice brought her back to the earth. Laya blinked, the wind stinging her eyes. She trained her gaze once more on the ship. Another breath, and she shifted the angle of her wrist. One mighty gale would do the trick. With a grunt, Laya hurled it straight at the sails.

At the mouth of the harbor, the ship lurched. The bottom of its hull scraped against the rocks with a metallic groan. Powerful waves rippled out from the ship, threatening to overturn the surrounding rowboats. Agitated shouts echoed from the water below as the men scrambled to steer themselves out of harm's way.

"Yes! Hold out a bit longer, Laya. It's starting to move," Bulan cried.

For once, Laya was happy to obey. She tautened her hold, her arms shaking as she tugged harder on the threads. When she opened her fists, the air burst from her palms in relentless gusts. The sails ballooned as they filled, propelling the ship forward.

She had never sustained a hold on the wind for longer than a few seconds before. The power tore at her aching muscles. The threads pulled through her fingers, fighting their way free. Laya willed herself not to panic. She sagged against the railing, battling the urge to collapse. The clouds continued to buck against her hold, like horses jerking at their bridles, when one of the rocks beneath the hull gave at last. A final jet of air, and the bow of the ship slid back into the water with a resounding splash.

Laya's arms dropped to her sides, limp as noodles. She crumpled as the threads of energy ripped free from her grip. Across the harbor, sailors broke out into triumphant cheers. Laya did not pay them any heed. Her storm clouds dispersed as quickly as they had appeared. The sun emerged, higher above the horizon than when Laya and Bulan had arrived, beating down on the wharf once more. She wrapped her arms around her knees, teeth chattering despite the renewed heat. Power liked to make its absence known; deprived of its embrace, Laya felt cold.

Bulan knelt beside her, brow furrowed in concern. "Are you all right?" she asked, resting a tentative hand on her sister's shoulder.

An old memory flickered in Laya's mind. Another sunny morning, over a decade earlier, they had been racing in the palace courtyard. Their youngest sister hadn't been born yet, and it was just the two of them. Laya, desperate to keep up with Bulan's longer legs, had tripped on a loose tile and skinned her knees. Bulan forgot about winning. She rushed to Laya's side and wiped the tears from her cheeks.

Don't cry, Bulan had told her. *I'm right here.*

They were children then. They hadn't known that their fates had already been decided. Had been before their mother, Hara Duja, named her heir. Before Laya discovered she could summon the wrath of the skies at her fingertips.

"I'm fine," Laya said, her throat tight. She stood, brushing Bulan's hand and the memory aside.

They walked back to the carriage in silence. This time, Laya accepted the guardsman's arm as she climbed inside. She collapsed against the cushioned bench, feeling like her muscles had dissolved into gelatin. Bulan slid into the seat across from her. At the front of the carriage, the driver gave the command. The wheels shuddered into motion, rolling over the creaking planks as they pulled away from the harbor.

Laya gazed sleepily out the window as the towering walls of Mariit came into view. Members of the Royal Maynaran Guard stood in straight, unbroken lines before the great wooden doors that led to the heart of the capital. Laya recognized a few of their faces, and if she cared enough, she could ask Bulan about the name of their regiment. With their chain-linked armor and menacing lances, they looked ready for war. Much of their presence was ceremonial, as no one had dared attack Mariit in decades. These days, the guardsmen mainly served to stamp travel papers and keep all suspicious elements at bay. Laya Gatdula had brought no travel papers with her. She needed only show her face at the checkpoint—Maynara's highest-ranked princess required no further explanation.

At the sight of her, the guard at the front of the line snapped to attention. He barked an order up the ramparts, and the gates groaned as they opened. The carriage rolled through the rusting gates, continuing alongside the long, narrow canal that flowed from the harbor all the way to the bustling center of Mariit. It wasn't long before the royal banners, strips of Gatdula green fluttering from the roof of the carriage, caught the city's full attention.

The glittering Maynaran capital, Mariit, was home to half the kingdom's population. The streets were busy enough on a normal morning, packed with fishmongers and rice brokers and orphans with featherlight fingers and mud-streaked knees. With one week until the start of the feast days, the capital was bursting at the seams. Chaos swept through the cobblestone alleyways snaking between buildings, spilling onto the arched footbridges that soared over Mariit's shimmering canals. Noise rang out from every street corner—southern villagers, far from home, pestering innkeepers for room and board; weavers from the northern Skylands, hawking their hand-spun baskets and textile bolts.

The clamor grew as Laya and her sister approached. In the poorer, outlying districts, the royal carriage stuck out like a gold-encrusted thumb. Hara Duja's subjects flocked to them from all sides. Before long, the crowd swelled across the entire street, blocking the carriage's path. People stumbled over one another, most of them shouting in the heavily accented Maynaran of the provinces. They stared, wide-eyed, through the open windows of the carriage, hungry for a glimpse.

"Your Highness!" they called, their hands slapping at the carriage's gilded doors. "This way, Your Highness!"

At the front of the carriage, the driver grew incensed. He roared at the passersby to move out of the way, pushing them back with his buffalo whip.

"Awfully excited to see us, aren't they?" Laya said dryly.

Bulan snorted, pulling the hemp shade down over her window. "Awfully excited to see *you*."

As always, Bulan spoke from the glaring chip on her shoulder.

Laya was in no mood to reason with it. "They say jealousy is unbecoming," she said. "And frankly, Bulan, now is not the time to argue—"

"I imagine Luntok is excited to see you too." Bulan's gaze snapped to hers, sharp as the laminated steel of her blade—she hadn't forgotten.

Laya tensed. She lifted her chin in defiance. "I wouldn't know anything about that."

"I think you do, Laya," she said, her frown deepening. "And if Mother finds out—"

Laya's hands balled into fists, and the air outside her window crackled. "But Mother won't find out, will she?"

"If she does, I will not have been the one to tell her." Bulan didn't stir at Laya's thinly veiled threat. Quietly, she added, "I'm your sister. Don't you trust me?"

"No," Laya said in a flat voice. "I don't."

Bulan stared back, unable to conceal the hurt that stretched across her face. Laya tore her gaze away, but not fast enough. She couldn't look at Bulan for long before the guilt unfurled, swift as a lizard's tongue.

Laya loved her sister, but how could she trust her? Bulan had always resented her for her lot in life: Laya was a true Gatdula and held the power of Mulayri at her fingertips. One day, Laya was going to be *queen*. And Bulan, who was born in the wrong year under a godless moon; Bulan, who wielded nothing but a broadsword and an empty title; Bulan, who was Hara Duja's eldest but not her heir—where did that leave her?

Laya knew her sister, knew that her bitterness burned stronger than any power she herself might have possessed. Bulan might not steal the throne, but she would find a way to take Luntok away from her, celestial alignment be damned.

When Bulan didn't answer, Laya turned back to the window and rested her forehead against the cool glass. Freeing the ship had exhausted every ounce of strength she possessed. She closed her eyes, succumbing to the fatigue washing over her like a tidal wave.

Sisters or not, Laya could not bridge the divide that grew wider between them with each passing year. No promise she made could change that. Silence was a far greater comfort than any words she could share. She pretended to sleep, and Bulan didn't talk to her for the rest of the ride through the city.

Laya kept her eyes shut until they rolled to a stop in front of the palace gates. By the time she opened them, the carriage door was swinging on its hinges, and the seat across from her was empty.

It was better this way, she reminded herself, as she made her way up the marble staircase and into the palace. She crossed the central courtyard, weaving through the throng of servants furiously scrubbing the tiles before the opening feast. From the courtyard, she retreated to the privacy of her chambers. No one was waiting for her when she arrived. She kicked off her shoes and sat down hard on the edge of the bed. A maid had left the balcony doors open to let in fresh air.

Laya stared past the fluttering curtains at the blue sky beyond the palace, half expecting a man's head to appear over the balustrade. But no one was coming. She had ordered Luntok to wait until nighttime. A weight dropped on her shoulders when she realized he had heeded her request. Doubt leaped from her gut to her throat. She ought to have sent a kinder letter. What if she had angered him, and he'd never come again?

An absurd idea. Luntok could not keep away from her for long. He'd come to her, just as he promised.

Laya glanced up at the round giltwood clock that hung above her wardrobe. Hours to go before Luntok's next visit. Her heart sank when she wondered how she might fill them.

Two

LAYA

Laya was prone to moments of melancholy, but she was not one to wallow in darkness for long. She allowed a full hour to feel sorry for herself before deserting her room in search of someone to bother. By the time she emerged, a rare stillness had settled over the palace grounds. Most of the servants had broken for an early lunch; some, she suspected, were already taking advantage of the festive atmosphere. Next week, the faint buzz of excitement would build to a lusty uproar. Laya tried to relish the quiet as she made her way to the main stairwell. Peace was a privilege, and she wouldn't see it again until the end of the feast days.

It was important for sovereigns to have these moments of solitude, she'd been told. Laya didn't know about that. In solitude, her mind filled with the stormy thoughts she tried ardently to ignore. The silence consumed her.

She didn't see Eti until she almost tripped over her younger sister's outstretched feet. Laya gasped, saving herself on the banister.

"Watch where you're going!" Eti cried, indignant, as if it were acceptable behavior for young princesses to lie sprawled across the palace stairs.

"Haven't you got another place to practice your wielding?

Your private chambers, perhaps?" Laya drawled as she stepped over Eti's legs.

The tiny golden pellet Eti had been tampering with fell into her palm. Where Laya wielded the wind and the rain, Eti's affinity was for metal. And while Mulayri's power burst from Laya in raging torrents, it trickled from the younger girl in a gentle stream, which suited Eti just fine.

"I was going to turn this into a bracelet and give it to you for your coronation, but I think I'll keep it for myself," Eti said loftily, in near-perfect imitation of Laya's tone.

Laya chuckled—for a child, Eti was a talented mimic. "Do whatever you wish with that bracelet. I don't care."

Eti stuck her tongue out at her. Unlike with Bulan, there was no malice between Laya and her younger sister.

Laya stuck out her tongue back, tousling Eti's hair as she continued up the steps. She paused when she reached the landing. On the flight below, Eti had stretched out to occupy the full width of the stairwell. The younger girl kept her gaze trained on the golden pellet, which now floated a few inches above her nose. Her brown cheeks were still as round as steam buns. Between them, Laya could make out the beginnings of a woman's chin. A bittersweet warmth burst in Laya's chest when she realized how much Eti had grown.

Laya knew this time with Eti was fleeting, like everything else in her life. At the moment, all Eti wanted was to get lost in her world of pretty shapes and shining things. She didn't care for fancy titles or Maynaran politics. Eti was content with what she had. It had not yet occurred to her to want more. In a few years, that would change. Eti would either grow up to fear Laya, like their mother did, or resent her, like Bulan. Laya couldn't decide which prospect she hated more.

She tore her gaze away from Eti as she made her way to the upper floor. The passageway leading to the queen's chambers was long and narrow, with a high, coved ceiling. Deep-mahogany panels lined the walls, interspersed with latticed window screens that overlooked the palace courtyard. A few feet from the landing, a pair of servants were hunched over an ancient Xitai vase. Both were busy replacing the wilted flowers inside with a gigantic white-orchid arrangement as high as Laya's waist. They bowed to Laya as she walked by. She gave them a cursory nod, then breezed past them to the end of the hall, where Hara Duja was waiting. When Laya opened the door, her nostrils flooded with the thick, heady smells of honeysuckle and burnt wood.

Laya wrinkled her nose and stepped inside. "Mother?"

She found her mother lying in the dark. The window screens had been drawn tight. The only light that penetrated the white-shell panels pooled across the floor in wavering strips. The queen was still in bed, her eyes closed and her black hair unkempt. Shadows danced across the dusky hollows of her cheeks. She barely stirred when Laya settled on the chair beside her.

Slowly, her mother opened her eyes. "Laya, is that you?"

"Yes," Laya said. "It's only me."

On shaking arms, the queen pushed herself up to a seated position. Her tremors had gotten worse over the past year. Mornings, she said, were the toughest. Her muscles were the last to wake up. For now, the queen managed to run the palace and corral the court into submission. But Laya could see better than anyone that Hara Duja was fading, far more quickly than she said she would.

A lump formed in Laya's throat as she watched her mother struggle to prop herself up against the pillows. The same fate befell each human; only it befell descendants of the Gatdula bloodline faster than most. It was no secret that the Gatdulas' ability to wield the elements was equal parts blessing and curse. Their bodies hosted celestial gifts, but their human muscles were not built to withstand powers of divine magnitude. Gatdulas burned brighter than any other being on earth—and they burned out twice as quickly. This was the price of being a god.

"Strange to see you up and about this early," Hara Duja said, voice scratchy from sleep.

"There was an emergency down at the port."

Hara Duja quirked an eyebrow at her. "Oh? What sort of emergency?" she asked, suspicion edging her tone.

Laya tensed. She could see the thoughts swirling in her mother's mind—the beginnings of a lecture. "A ship got stranded on the rocks. It was blocking the entrance to the harbor. No one else could move it. And I—"

"You what?" Terror flashed in the queen's eyes. "You moved an entire ship?" she demanded.

Frustration flared at the base of Laya's throat. "I've moved bigger things before. I'm strong enough, you know."

Stronger than you. Laya stared back at her mother, her hands balling into fists. Sometimes she wondered if the queen had any intention of stepping down from the throne. Even though Hara Duja's days in power were numbered, she was more determined than ever to keep any true responsibilities out of Laya's reach.

Her mother's mouth flattened into a tight line. She gazed at Laya as though she were a batch of kindling that was ready to explode. "I've seen you exercise the full extent of your strength, Laya. *That* is what worries me."

A stone dropped in Laya's stomach. Bitter tears threatened to spill out of the corners of her eyes. "Why are you blaming me?" she cried. "I freed that ship. I helped those people. You speak as if that was a bad thing."

"Nonsense, Laya. What you did with the ship—it isn't a *bad* thing. What you might have done, however . . ." The queen fell back against the pillows, pinching the bridge of her nose. In the shadows of her bedroom, she looked wearier than Laya had ever seen her. "We have a long week ahead of us," she said, in a voice like broken porcelain. "Please, darling. Let me rest."

Laya swallowed hard. Hara Duja wished to hold her at arm's length, and she had no choice but to let her. Dejected, she rose and made her way out. She paused when she reached the doorframe, unable to bite back a retort.

"If you want to blame anyone, blame Bulan," she said. "Because of you, she thinks she's in charge of me."

"Laya—" the queen said sharply before Laya slammed the door behind her.

The rage surged inside her chest, rising, up and up, like a cresting wave. She barreled through the corridor and down the stairs, stomping on her sister's feet on the way.

"Hey!" Eti whimpered.

This time, Laya ignored her sister. She rushed through the palace's cavernous halls, her sandals slipping across the freshly waxed floorboards. She did not stop until she was back in her chambers, where she let out a desperate scream. Her cry, harsh as the monsoon winds, echoed across the vaulted ceiling of her bedchamber. What had possessed her to tell her mother about the ship? Laya should have known she would react that way. In the queen's mind, Laya could do nothing right.

For all her strength, Laya could not ignore the pain blossoming in the nethermost corner of her soul—the part of her that still craved her mother's warmth. It stretched miles deeper than her peaks of rage, this raw and tender ache.

The tears Laya had been fighting since she'd spoken to her

mother splashed over the front of her dress. She leaned her forehead against the cool wooden panel that spanned the door. She sucked in a breath, ready to sob in earnest, when a muted thump behind her drew her attention.

An intruder. Laya whirled around, palms outstretched.

The man on her balcony held up his hands in surrender. His dark hair was pulled away from his smooth, handsome face. He wore a scarlet vest that exposed the mesmerizing swirls of tattoos on his chest. A sword twice the length of Laya's arm hung at his hip, its curved brass hilt melded into the beak of a hornbill.

"Luntok?" She lowered her arms. An incriminating smile spread across her face.

"I believe you summoned me," he said, grinning.

Laya remembered herself, drying her tears on her sleeve. She didn't allow anyone to catch her in a moment of weakness—Luntok Kulaw was no exception. A defiant spark wound through her as she slinked across the room and draped her arms around his neck. The queen would give Laya far more than a lecture if she learned the true nature of this dalliance. With every visit, she and Luntok danced closer and closer to the razor's edge. The guardsmen had nearly discovered them over a dozen times in the past, and the head of the royal guard, General Ojas, had doubled the patrol in light of the upcoming feast days. Luntok knew to take better care.

"Dolt." She pretended to chide him. "You weren't supposed to come until later tonight. I ought to throw you in the prison hold for this."

By now, Luntok was accustomed to her empty threats. "If I begged, would you look past my impertinence?" he asked, reeling her in by the waist.

Laya's breath caught in her throat. The fatigue from her excursion at the port faded as giddy longing flooded her veins. She resisted the urge to melt into his arms. Instead, she squared her jaw and leaned closer. "Dolt," she said again. "You don't deserve clemency."

Luntok chuckled and pressed his lips to the crown of her head. "I came as soon as I heard of your heroics with the ship. Submit me to your ire if you wish. That is how badly I missed you," he said. The deep rumble of his voice sent a cool shiver down the column of Laya's spine.

Oh, but Laya knew far too well what he meant. Her heart sang whenever Luntok showed up at her balcony, and a small piece of it died each time he left.

"Lovesick fool. Have you not an ounce of sense?" Laya said crisply, more to herself than to him.

There are worse mistakes I can make, she thought as she appraised Luntok. He had grown into a beautiful man over the many years she had known him. What his family lacked in repute, he countervailed in passion. He could have his pick of the loveliest brides in the kingdom, but he burned for the one woman to whom he'd been forever barred. The truth had never mattered to Luntok Kulaw. When he fell, he fell deeply. And Luntok loved Laya more than air—everyone knew this.

The court liked to whisper about the pair of them. Not even joyless Bulan could deny Luntok's devotion. Laya could not help but love him back. Unlike the rest of Maynara, Luntok didn't stare at her in envy or horror or cowlike worship. When Laya met his eyes, she saw nothing but desire there. He adored both the woman and the god in her. He treasured even the ugliest parts— the parts her own mother refused to love. Luntok was the sole person who would accept whatever storm she sent his way and love her more for it. Although Laya would never admit it, her heart belonged to no one else but him.

"Sense," Luntok echoed, his breath tickling her ear. "What good ever came from that?"

Laya's eyes darkened at the hint of a challenge. She kissed him in response, losing her breath against his lips.

They were fools, the pair of them. Laya and Luntok, a Gatdula and a Kulaw. History ordained that they hate each other forever, yet their jagged edges fit together so easily. But Luntok was different. Luntok was nothing like his ancestors. He belonged to *her*, not to history. The court could chatter as much as they liked. Whenever she was with him, her heartbeat drowned out whatever warnings she'd been told.

Sex was a song they learned from each other—how wrong it felt to sing it with anyone else. They first succumbed to the music three years before, when they were old enough to know better. Each time, they made love to the same harried rhythm, as if the sky would suddenly crack open above their heads and the earth were about to swallow them whole. If Laya had been half the fool her mother thought she was, she might have allowed herself to get swept away in the swells and the motions and the beats she knew by heart. But she kept one hand tangled in Luntok's hair, the other firmly pressed against his collarbone. Laya was ready to push him back at any moment—despite the queen's disparaging remarks, Hara Duja had taught her well.

"You ought to go now," she said afterward, when they were lying together in bed, their limbs entwined beneath the sheets.

Luntok bristled at her sudden coldness. He reached for her, annoyance rising in his tone. "Laya—"

"Luntok, I'm serious." Laya withdrew from his side and

reached for her dressing robe. She yanked it on over her shoulders, almost tearing the fabric. It was hand-stitched from imported lilac pongee, more delicate than any other garment she owned.

He didn't budge from the bed. Pain flickered in his eyes. His gaze burned. She felt it on the side of her neck even as she turned away.

This wouldn't last either. The reminder left an acrid taste in Laya's throat. None of this was Luntok's fault, but she wanted to punish him anyway.

The mattress creaked when Luntok at last got up to dress. Regret sank in as she watched him slide his vest over his broad, muscled shoulders. He thought her haughty and cruel. It wasn't fair. She didn't want this any more than he did. She resisted the urge to reach across the bed and shake him. *Can't you see how I ache?*

"All of Mariit is talking. They suspect you'll choose a husband soon," he said as he laced up his shoes.

"Let them speculate," she said coolly. Marriage was a dangerous subject. She knew better than to provoke Luntok's jealousy.

With a weary sigh, he headed back to the balcony. Laya followed him, impatient to see him out. He paused, bracing his weight against the balustrade.

Laya's eyes darted to the palace grounds. A passing guard could spy him in an instant and toss him into the hold. "What are you waiting for?" she hissed.

"For you to make up your mind," Luntok said, tilting his gaze to the cloudless sky above. Much to Laya's chagrin, he appeared blissfully unbothered by the threat of imprisonment.

"Make up my mind about what?" she demanded.

"About running away with me." He turned to her with a cheeky grin.

Laya scowled and waved him off. "Go on, then. Don't you have swords to sharpen? Fish to catch?"

Luntok's mouth twisted in annoyance. He was among Maynara's highest-born sons, and he hated nothing more than her gibes likening him to a common fisherman.

But as she pulled away, he grabbed her hand and held it to his lips. "I'll catch you a whale shark, Laya. How about that? Then I'll string you a necklace out of its teeth, and we'll carve our wedding bed from its bones."

"Sharks don't have bones," Laya said. Her fingers twitched in his hand, but she didn't jerk them back. He needed to leave now, before his promises left her breathless.

"An elephant, then. Or a wild boar." Luntok looked up from her knuckles, hope glistening in his eyes.

Her heart broke then. She couldn't give him what he wanted. She couldn't ask him to stay.

"You really should leave. Someone will catch you," she said, this time a touch less cruelly.

Luntok sighed once more. He planted a last rueful kiss on the back of her hand before releasing her. Wistfully, she stared as he swung one leg over the balustrade.

"I'll come back," he vowed, "whether or not you send for me."

Too cheeky. Laya frowned. "You'll come back when I send for you, and not a moment sooner," she told him. The fatigue swept through her once again, and his promises became too heavy.

Luntok chuckled in return as he heaved himself atop the balustrade. In a flutter of scarlet, he disappeared over the side of the balcony. Halfway down the wall, he fell, landing with a groan in the bushes beneath Laya's window. She bit back a laugh as he dusted himself off. Luntok stopped once more to salute her, flashing her a final disarming grin. Laya gazed at his back as he retreated into the gardens, through patterns of blossoms and fruit sprawling northward behind the palace. From the gardens, he would head for the thick stone ramparts encircling the complex. Then he'd slip beneath them through a long-forgotten drainage tunnel, which emptied into a narrow alleyway that oft evaded the Royal Maynaran Guard's view.

No soul apart from the two of them knew of this tunnel. Laya was the one who'd shown Luntok its entrance, a rusted grate scarcely visible beneath a thicket of tangled vines. He must have taken it over a hundred times by now. This was the only path to her he was allowed.

When I am queen, Laya thought sadly, *all this will change.*

The false hopes she fed Luntok were trite compared to the lies she told herself.

She remained on the balcony long after he left. She stayed there until the sun disappeared and fat droplets splattered against her brow. She looked up in alarm. Rain clouds swirled above her head, casting shadows on the gardens below. They descended upon the palace's tiered roofs, thicker than mountain mist. Laya had summoned them unintentionally.

She closed her eyes, then exhaled slowly through her nose. The tension ebbed from her shoulders. The clouds dispersed as the threads of power slithered from her grip. A light breeze whooshed past her ear, tender as Luntok's lips along the side of her neck. When she opened her eyes, Luntok was still gone. Sunlight shone brightly overhead, glaring off the golden finials lining the rooftops, blinding her.

Laya shouldn't have fallen in love with Luntok Kulaw. She had always known better.

"Fool," she murmured, even though there was no one around to hear.

To His Royal Highness, Hari Aki,

Twice now, you have rejected my offers of assistance. I implore you, old friend, to reconsider. Please forgive my terseness. You favor a gentler hand, but you know as well as I do that subtlety was never my strong suit.

You made your reservations abundantly clear in your previous letter, and I will not challenge them. You have every reason to doubt me. My words alone cannot convince you.

Instead, would you listen to the words of an honest messenger? Despite your many rejections, I have brought him to Maynara as evidence of my goodwill.

You must speak to him, Aki. For he is a man many on this side of the Untulu Sea call an alchemist. He holds the key to abiding glory. I believe he is the answer Duja has been searching for.

I dare not lie to you, old friend. If you refuse to accept my messenger, what more proof can I give? Know that I pen these words with steady fingers. And, should you decide to meet me, I will stand and greet you on sturdy legs.

If you love the queen, as I believe you do, you will meet him. I beg you to meet him. After I receive your reply, I will send him to you. He can help Duja more than you or I ever could.

My previous letters did not convince you.

Let me tell you this: I care not for myself, but for my sister. A lifetime has passed since I left Maynara—everything I've done in the years since, I've done for her.

This is the truth, Aki, whether or not you choose to believe me.

All my love to Duja and the children,
Pangil

Three

DUJA

The queen hadn't meant to pry.

Duja trusted her husband more than she did anyone in the world. She would not have thought to riffle through his correspondence, but never before had Aki been so careless with his personal items. Carelessness was not a trait anyone associated with her husband. If he had not been so occupied with feast-day arrangements, he might not have left the letter inside one of the tomes stacked beside his pillows. Duja discovered it while she was getting dressed that morning, a task that grew more cumbersome each day. A Gatdula of her age and rank was entitled to attendants who could assist her. Duja had dismissed them years earlier. She was determined to dress herself as long as she was able. But that morning, she'd struggled to fasten her earrings, tiers of golden disks inlaid with freshwater pearls, which she had inherited from her mother. One earring had slipped from her trembling fingers and disappeared beneath her husband's bedside table. When she'd bent over to retrieve it, she noticed the letter.

It wasn't the letter that caught her eye so much as the swirling symbols that peeked out over the top of the book—*To His Royal Highness, Hari Aki*. Duja recognized, with blistering intimacy, the hand that looped them together.

Her heart hammered in her chest as she tore the letter from the book and pored over its contents. She didn't budge for what felt like hours. She read and reread the letter. If she could commit the words to memory, maybe they would make sense.

But nothing about this letter made sense—none of it. What on earth might have possessed her husband, the Maynaran king, to contact Duja's exiled brother?

With a ragged breath, Duja folded the letter and slipped it into the pocket of her skirt. She finished dressing and headed to the central courtyard. The king was not there orchestrating the final preparations with his pipe sticking out of the corner of his mouth, as she had hoped he would be. Perhaps it was for the best. She had a hundred questions for him, but she wasn't yet ready to hear the answers.

"Your Majesty." At the soft thudding of Duja's footsteps, the handful of servants buzzing about the courtyard promptly dropped to their knees.

"Please, continue," she said, offering them a thin-lipped smile as she passed.

A tall, slender shadow appeared in the arcaded walkway that ran along the sides of the courtyard. Duja froze in her tracks, the smile melting from her face. Her hands twitched, and a low rumble rippled beneath the tiles. When the shadow emerged from behind one of the marble pillars, sunlight glinted off the brass clasps of a breastplate. She let out a shallow breath—it was merely one of the royal guards patrolling the palace perimeter. Her fingers trailed to the letter, which felt hot enough to burn a hole through her pocket.

Duja's brother, Pangil, had not set foot in the palace in many years, but it wasn't the first time she had imagined seeing him there.

She crossed the courtyard and stared up at the eastern wing, thrice rebuilt now. Her hand shook as it hovered over the stone walls of the wing, which stood a half-shade lighter than the others. During her mother's reign, the eastern wing had been the grandest in the palace complex. Its red-tiled roofs still sloped toward the heavens, its spires piercing the clouds like crocodile teeth. The reconstruction had changed little, but the gold-encased finials and latticed windows, in their third incarnation, had lost their luster.

For Duja, there had always been a certain romance about the place. After her father passed, it was where her mother had housed her new consort, a younger man with kind eyes who always brought Duja something from his travels. She remembered his gifts, the bitter chocolate and yellow-haired dolls. She could no longer remember his name, but she had cried for him, as well as for her mother and the other poor souls who'd perished in the fire.

She had watched the eastern wing crumble twice in her lifetime. Two decades had passed since the first incident. Time could not wash away the taste of ash in her throat, could not smother the towers of flames that continued to chase her from the courtyard with their bloodcurdling heat. *His* laugh echoed over the sound of crackling doorframes, cold and remorseless. She couldn't outrun him, and she'd been more powerful then.

Sister, he'd called her, his voice either sweet as coconut flakes or thick with drink. She heard it in the silence between prayers, in the rustle of narra leaves. She heard it as if the eastern wing had never fallen, as if no time had passed at all.

Some days, it shocked her how strongly she remembered.

The dull thumping of a walking stick against the tiles jolted Duja from her thoughts. She turned around to find that an old woman had entered the courtyard. Her simple, handwoven clothes clung like seaweed to her slight frame but left her arms bare where tattoos spiraled over the leathery skin. Her graying hair, threaded with red glass beads, glowed silver under the morning sun, as did the medallion on her neck, which was engraved with the image of the raptor god, Mulayri, the mark of a high shaman.

"Hara Duja." The old woman bowed her head when she noticed Duja's presence.

Duja nodded in greeting. "Hello, Maiza. Do you mind if I speak to you alone?" Maiza wasn't her husband, but maybe she was the person Duja needed to see.

The shaman raised her eyebrows and nodded toward the main building. Maiza had known Duja since she was Eti's age. She knew when something was bothering her.

"Let's go somewhere quiet, Your Majesty," Maiza said. "Then you can tell me everything that's on your mind."

Duja led Maiza back to her private chambers. The shaman sat beside her at the foot of the bed. She took Duja's hand and rubbed slow circles into the fleshy heel of her palm.

"The tremors," Maiza said. "Have they gotten worse?"

With a weary sigh, Duja nodded. "Much worse. And faster than we anticipated."

"I see." Maiza pursed her lips as she kneaded the gracelessness from Duja's hand.

With these hands, Duja could wield sand and stone and send shocks deep into the yolky center of the earth. With these hands, Duja protected her family and her people from harm. She could erect mountains with a flick of her wrist and topple them just as easily. The power of the gods wound through her fingertips. She needed her hands to be steady and sure enough to bear the weight of the mantle. *Hara*—queen. But for the strength of her bloodline, no hands were built to sustain power of this magnitude. Not even the mightiest Gatdula could bear the mantle for long. The power of Mulayri meant shorter lifespans and even shorter reigns. It bore a hefty price, and Duja was not yet ready to pay it.

"How have the girls progressed?" Duja asked, keen to distract herself from the stabbing pain that radiated from her fingers. She couldn't remember the last time she'd watched her daughters train. She'd hired the best teachers in the land—Ojas for Bulan, Maiza for Laya and Eti. When they were younger, she used to marvel at how fast the girls learned, at the wealth of power concealed in their tiny bodies.

"Eti has come a long way since last season," Maiza told her proudly as she reached for Duja's other hand. "Her affinity for metal is impressive. She needs to work on her precision, but when she does—Hara Duja, you will be very pleased."

Duja nodded, relieved. The youngest and most timid of her three daughters, Eti had been slow to develop her abilities. Duja was content to see her blossom under Maiza's watchful tutelage. However, Eti's chief interest lay not in combat, but in embellishment and filigree. She had inherited her father's indefectible eye for beauty, over which Duja could hardly complain.

"And Laya?" she asked.

"Oh, Laya." Maiza drew in a sharp breath, and Duja already had her answer. "Her power is at once raw and limitless. I need only explain once, and she grasps everything I say by sheer intuition. She is Mulayri incarnate, perhaps the most powerful Gatdula we've seen in centuries. But she's—"

Duja completed her thought. "Callous. Unthinking."

Dangerous.

The high shaman sighed, setting the queen's hand down lightly on the bed. "I haven't seen such a power since . . ."

Him. Maiza didn't need to say it.

Duja swallowed hard. "Laya will learn. I'll teach her."

Maiza hesitated. She said carefully, "Since the accident, the princess has shown more of an interest in practicing control. That's a good sign, at least."

The accursed accident. Three years before, and Maynara still spoke of nothing else. In the council room, Duja's critics hammered on her regime's negligence and waste. How could she justify herself? Twice in twenty-two years, an entire wing of the palace had to be rebuilt. Both times, they'd paid for the reconstruction from the funds allotted to shipbuilding and the rice harvest and the kadatuans' dedicated chests. The blame fell, as it always did, on Hara Duja. Laya had been a child of fifteen then, wide-eyed, remorseful, and easy to forgive.

If the council had allowed them to move on, it was because they'd gotten lucky. Since the first fire all those years before, the eastern wing had stood uninhabited, and no one had been hurt in the second wreckage. Laya claimed to have learned her lesson, but sometimes, Duja wasn't so sure. Her daughter was eighteen now, and she was expected to take Duja's place frightfully soon. She could no longer afford to make such irreparable mistakes.

If Laya wanted to inherit the throne, to call herself Hara Laya one day, she had so much left to learn.

Duja set her jaw. She had known of her daughter's callous nature since she'd been a little girl, yet how many years had she wasted? "I should have taken greater care with her. After all, I knew better. I saw firsthand what happened with Pangil." She often avoided saying his name, as if the slight omission would keep the memories at bay.

Maiza shook her head vehemently. "You mustn't think that way, Your Majesty. Laya is nothing like him."

Him. Pangil, Hara Duja's older brother. The fire starter, the spirit who haunted the palace, the man who was once Maynara's beloved heir. He'd laughed as the eastern wing burned, not yet knowing that his own mother had been trapped inside it. Another accident, he'd claimed, back then.

Subconsciously, Duja rubbed the faint scar on the side of her neck, dark specks that stood out against her brown skin in the morning light, the ghost of a burn Maiza had healed many years earlier. Her brother was prone to accidents.

"Yes, Maiza, you're right."

She closed her eyes, and Maiza began chanting in the low, somber cadences of Old Maynaran. The pain in her muscles subsided, flushed out of her body in a great wave. The stiffness wouldn't trouble her for the rest of the day, and the enchantments should stem the tremors until the following evening. Any reprieve the shaman could grant her was only temporary.

Meanwhile, the tremors would not wait for Laya to learn control. The power of the gods would continue to wear away at Duja's body at alarming speed. For her daughter's sake—and for the rest of Maynara—the queen needed to maintain her hold on the throne for a while longer. But how?

Duja's thoughts flitted to the letter in her pocket. Her husband knew of her misgivings when it came to Laya. He loved their daughter, but even he agreed that Laya was not ready to ascend to the throne. For months, he had been searching for a way to buy Duja the time she needed. He wouldn't have contacted Pangil without good reason. At least, that's what Duja wanted to believe.

Twenty-two years since her brother had last roamed the

island. He couldn't be allowed to return—not after what he'd done. Duja's mouth flooded with bile at the mere prospect.

Nothing like him, Maiza had said.

Duja wanted to believe her, but the memory of her mother's death was still fresh in her mind. Between her brother's flame and Laya's wreckage, she could not wash away the haunting resemblance.

Duja did not see the king until it was nearly suppertime. She happened upon him in the library, where the peppery scent of pipe cloves announced his presence. She made out his distinguished profile as she rounded one of the tall mahogany bookshelves that stretched to the gilded ceiling.

Hari Aki carried no despotic airs. If anything, he radiated intelligence—more scholar than king. He was a surprising breed of handsome, with attentive eyes and warm brown skin, and a pleasant face that grew more bewitching the longer you gazed at it.

He hadn't been Duja's first love, but she had always admired him. Before they'd courted, Aki had been the gentlest man she'd known. His intelligence and political acumen, she gleaned much later. She fell in love first with his hearty laugh, which sent pleasant vibrations throughout every inch of her body. After their daughters were born, she saw how tenderhearted he could be. He was the sole man she would have chosen to father her children, and now he was the only soul whose counsel she could trust.

Until that morning, when Duja had found the letter, that was. The damned letter. She still did not know what to make of it. She frowned as she studied her husband—her clever, gentle husband. A memory flashed of two young men strolling in the courtyard, Pangil's arm slung around Aki's shoulders. Aki had been her brother's friend long before he'd become her king. What had Pangil promised him, exactly?

Duja could hear from the murmurs echoing across the quiet library that Aki wasn't alone. She craned her neck. Curled up on one of the window benches next to a stack of books was Bulan, their eldest. A faint smile spread across Duja's face when she peered at the title in Bulan's hands: *The Art of Maynaran Swordsmanship.* Even when Bulan wasn't in the courtyard sparring with General Ojas, she was busy training.

The queen watched as Aki leaned over their daughter's shoulder. He pointed at the page she was reading, whispering something that made Bulan laugh—a rare sound, like crinkling paper. It filled Duja with a tenderness she often didn't feel for her other daughters. Beneath those sturdy muscles built up from hours and hours of sword training, Bulan suffered from the sting of comparison. She tried to drown it in sweat and sacrifice and duty, but Duja saw the envy in Bulan's eyes when she gazed at her younger, more powerful sisters. Over the years, Duja tried to console her. The power of Mulayri may not flow through Bulan's veins, but that did not make Duja love her any less.

Those words meant more coming from the king, a normal man who drew from a deeper source of strength. Aki understood Bulan's insecurities more than anyone else in their family. Duja's heart swelled when he planted a kiss on Bulan's forehead.

Duja cleared her throat. Aki and Bulan looked up in surprise. Before the queen could speak, Bulan clapped her book shut and shot to her feet.

"Mother, about the ship—I can explain," Bulan began, worry creasing her brow.

Duja raised her hand to silence her. Her heart had nearly

stopped when Laya had told her about the ship. At the moment, however, she had more pressing worries to address. "Never mind that, darling," she said. "Would you mind if I spoke to your father alone?"

Bulan nodded and gathered her books in her arms. She cast a curious glance at the king on her way out of the library. Duja didn't speak until she heard the door creak shut behind her daughter.

"You've been awfully busy, my love," she said.

Aki was an observant man. He picked up on the sadness laced in her tone. "I take it you don't mean with feast-day preparations?" he said.

Duja took Bulan's place on the window bench. Her hands quivered when she rested them in her lap. "I'm worried, Aki."

"About the tremors?" Aki sat down across from her. He laid a hand on her arm and lowered his voice. "I promise you, darling, we will find a solution."

"It appears you already have," she said.

Duja pulled the letter out of her pocket. Her brother's distinctive scrawl glowed in the afternoon light. She thought of Pangil's words—*old friend*—intimate enough to make her question her husband's intentions.

Aki's expression darkened. "It isn't what you think, Duja," he said calmly. But she could tell by the tightness in his shoulders—he was ashamed.

"Isn't it?" Duja asked. *I love you. I trusted you.* She swallowed her accusations.

"Pangil—he wrote to me years ago. I ignored him. I would have gone my entire life without speaking to him again. But then—Laya's accident." He rubbed his chin and reached into the pocket of his vest for his pipe.

Duja watched as he struck a match against the windowsill. The tobacco cloves sputtered when he drew the flame to the pipe bowl.

"Pangil had written to me around that time. Claimed to have found a way to suppress the body's degradation. At first, I dismissed it as mere rumors. But then, I began to read things—terrible, fascinating things." Aki drew in a deep breath. When he exhaled, puffs of smoke wafted from his mouth to the library's high coffered ceilings. "I meant it when I told you I would explore every avenue, Duja," he said, meeting her gaze. "And while I hate your brother as much as you do, there is hope."

Anticipation bubbled in Duja's stomach—anticipation and dread. Her husband would not have hidden the letter from her if he didn't have his reasons. He was loyal to Duja, to his family—not to her brother, the exiled prince. But what if he and Pangil had struck some perverse agreement? Would Aki renege on the vows he'd made her based on nothing more than the empty promises of an old friend?

"This man," she said, thinking back to the letter. "Pangil mentioned a man who can help me. A kind of . . . alchemist."

The word felt foreign on Duja's tongue. Alchemy had no place in Maynara. It was more science than sorcery, and it lay beyond her realm of comprehension.

"The key to abiding glory," the king said, quoting Pangil's letter. Judging by the faint frown at the corners of his lips, a large part of him doubted it. "I *was* going to tell you, Duja. I wanted to wait until after the feast days," he added, a wrinkle of regret between his eyes.

Doubt twisted in her stomach. She *wanted* to believe him. While the king was clever, he was no match for Pangil and his nose for weakness. She couldn't believe any promises either man made her. Duja needed to meet with this alchemist herself.

"No. We shouldn't wait. How fast can you get word to him?" she asked. The words flew from her mouth before she could stop them.

Aki's eyebrows rose in surprise. "Duja—are you certain?"

No, she wasn't certain. But what choice did she have? Her body's clock was ticking at an alarming rate. Duja's control over her powers faded with each passing day. If a solution was lying out there, awaiting her discovery, she couldn't afford to ignore it. Even if the solution had come from her brother's lips.

"Write to him tonight," she said, sounding more confident than she felt. "Let us see what this messenger has to say."

Who was he, this so-called alchemist? And how could she know whether to trust him? Her nerves lit up when she thought back to Pangil's claim: *He can help Duja more than you or I ever could.*

The king's eyes softened. He leaned over and kissed her on the cheek. "Of course, my love."

He would move heaven and earth for her, her husband. Duja closed her eyes and breathed in his familiar scent. The cloves calmed her nerves, but nothing Aki said could quell the doubts swirling in her head. Duja's concerns had grown far greater than her daughter's readiness to inherit the throne. Laya's accident appeared trivial wherever Pangil's shadow loomed. If there was any truth to Aki's words, her brother held the secret to long-lasting power. For all they knew, he could be stronger than Duja, or even stronger than Laya. This realization didn't sit well with the queen.

The decades-old fear twisted in her gut when Duja stared out the window at the eastern wing. She could still picture, with heart-pounding immediacy, the last time she'd seen it aflame.

Duja. Pangil's voice reverberated across the rifts of time.

This time, he wasn't alone. No, Duja had not forgotten—another ghost, another threat. Amidst Pangil's laughter, she could still hear the echoes of another girl's screams.

four

LAYA

Needlework is a special kind of magic, Laya thought as she twirled in front of the mirror. Her new skirt fanned out around her ankles, the delicate blue threads sparkling in the midday sun. It was nearing lunchtime, and the dressing room adjoining her bedchamber was basked in yellow light. The royal seamstress, a stout woman with graying hair and spidery fingers, had arrived that morning with Laya's wardrobe of feast-day gowns, each grander than the last. With the opening procession in just three days, they had little time for adjustments.

"Arms up, Dayang," the seamstress said, holding up the skirt's matching blouse.

Laya complied. The dressing room disappeared in a cascade of lapis—a far cry from the Gatdulas' signature green. She didn't care for her family's colors. After all, the court knew who she was. Laya chose instead to stock her wardrobe with every shade of blue known to the human eye—a rainbow of sea and sky ranging from the dark monsoon waters to the pale horizon at dusk.

As the seamstress helped her into her sleeves, Laya turned to face her reflection. The ensemble had cost a hefty sum, but it was worth every coin. Luntok would not be able to keep his eyes off her now.

The seamstress frowned as she added a pin to Laya's waistline. "You've lost weight, Dayang. We'll have to take this in."

"You wouldn't know with all the yam cakes she eats," a voice chimed from the hall.

Laya looked over her shoulder. Bulan was leaning against the doorframe, garbed in a threadbare tunic and a pair of trousers, which hung loosely from her hips. Her curly hair sat in a sweaty pile atop her head. Judging by her disheveled appearance, she had been training since daybreak.

"What are you doing here?" Laya asked with a grimace. Her sister was in desperate need of a bath.

"Maiza is looking for Eti. She's hopelessly late for her lesson. Have you seen her?" Bulan took in the sight of Laya in her feast clothes, envy flickering in her expression. "Pretty dress," she added.

Laya glanced pointedly at the shifting pile of silk in the corner of the dressing room. Eti was small and light-footed, with a talent for hiding in plain sight. Yet she'd revealed herself with a muffled sneeze about a quarter of an hour before. Laya had pretended not to notice.

Bulan followed Laya's gaze. They exchanged a tiny smile. Bulan turned back to the hallway and called, "Maiza! I think we've found her."

Uneven thuds echoed from the hall, and High Shaman Maiza appeared at Bulan's shoulder. "Come along, child. We've wasted enough of the day as it is," Maiza said. Her voice was scratchy and stern, but her eyes glimmered with affection.

At last, Eti peered out from beneath the sheet of amethyst silk that made up Laya's midnight feast dress. "No fair," she said, pouting. "Laya always gets the loveliest clothes."

The high shaman trudged into the dressing room, leaning

heavily on her walking stick. Although hard to tell by Maiza's simple clothes, she was one of the highest-ranked members of the court. She was the guardian of Maynaran traditions as well as the bridge to the spirits. Like the lower shamans who served beneath her, she dealt primarily in healing incantations and blessings—petty sorcery compared to the Gatdulas' might. Maiza had been a close friend of the royal family since before Eti was even born, and she had always appeared as ancient as Maynara's sacred texts. She would never die, the old crone.

"Very lovely, indeed," Maiza said, gazing at Laya with a rare shade of tenderness. "You are the spitting image of Hara Duja on the day of her wedding ceremony."

Laya met Maiza's eyes in the mirror. "You will officiate my own wedding soon if the rumors are to be believed."

The leathery corners of Maiza's lips folded into a grin. "Ah yes, but first you must find a husband befitting a daughter of Mulayri. When that day comes, I shall be waiting for you on the Black Salt Cliffs."

"I remember the stories," Laya said dryly.

When Laya was a young girl, Maiza had taught her all about Maynara's founding myths, including the story of the Black Salt Cliffs. The cliffs lay hours outside Mariit, at the base of Mount Matabuaya. Centuries earlier, a battle had taken place there. It had ended when the first Gatdula king plunged a spear into the chest of a foreign invader and threw his corpse into the dagger-like rocks below. As a reward for his bravery, the Supreme God Mulayri gave the king his own daughter for a bride. They were married on the cliffs amidst the fallen bodies of their enemies. From their union, a mighty kingdom was born. Maynarans never forgot this story, and every Gatdula since had been married on those cliffs.

In the doorway, Bulan snorted. "That day will never come, Maiza. Have you seen the miserable cads parading about court? Laya is better off ascending the throne alone."

Laya laughed. She didn't mind entertaining a few cads. She craved their attentions, no matter how contrived, and flirtation was among her favorite pastimes. Bulan was the opposite. She had no interest in suitors nor plans to marry. In one of those rare moments when the sisters had gotten along, Bulan had confided in Laya that she never felt any attraction to anyone and was quite content without pleasures of the flesh. She was glad to leave Laya her pick of the cads. Courtship was one of the few realms in which they never had to compete.

Eti shrugged on one of Laya's sheer walking shawls. It was too big for her, and the embroidered hem pooled at her sandaled feet. "If I were you, Laya, I'd marry a sun god and mother a million stars," she said, staring wistfully at her reflection.

"A sun god?" Laya echoed. "Where do you propose I find that?"

"Laya is likelier to marry the sun itself," Bulan said, chuckling.

Laya's heart fluttered when she thought of Luntok. He was no god, but each time they lay together, Laya was sure she caught a glimpse of divinity.

She imagined her wedding day often. In her dreams, Luntok was kneeling beside her, his broad shoulders glowing beneath his white marriage vest, his fingers intertwined with hers. But, unlike Maiza, Luntok would never be waiting for her on the Black Salt Cliffs. Laya sighed as she fiddled with her sleeve. The hem fell past her wrist in an elegant butterfly wing of silk—beautiful, but inconvenient.

"These are too long," Laya barked at the seamstress. "How many times must I tell you? They'll get in the way of my wielding."

The seamstress bowed her head, her cheeks reddening in

shame. "My apologies, Dayang. I will have this ready before the dawn feast."

"You'll have it ready tomorrow, at the very least," Laya said with a sniff of disdain.

The grin slid from Maiza's time-battered face. She held out a hand to Eti. "Follow me, child," she said. "It's time we begin your lesson."

Mournfully, Eti complied, slipping out of Laya's shawl with a dramatic sigh. Laya reached out to tweak her nose. "Don't fret, Eti," she told her. "When I am queen, I'll buy you a trunkful of pretty dresses."

"You'd better," Eti said. She hung her head as she followed Maiza out of the room.

Laya stepped out of her blouse and skirt to try on her next ensemble. Bulan watched her, her brow knitted in uncertainty.

"Why are you looking at me like that?" Laya asked.

"All this talk about weddings," Bulan said. "I hope you're not truly listening to the rumors."

"Of course not," she said. "You know me better than that."

"I know. But as high counselor—"

Laya gritted her teeth in impatience. "As high counselor, you will advise me when I ask you to, and not a moment sooner."

She could hear in her sister's tone that Bulan was one sentence away from lecturing her about Luntok and bloodlines and political matches. The last thing Laya wanted was another reminder of the failed rebellion led by Luntok's relatives three decades earlier. The Kulaws' war had slashed an ugly wound through the island, and their family had been granted clemency to keep it from festering. But as punishment, no Kulaw could come near the Maynaran throne.

To wed a Gatdula was a privilege granted only to descendants of the kingdom's most loyal families. According to myth, the oldest bloodlines in Maynara once practiced magic of their own. There were the Lumas, who were believed to have had the ability to commune with beasts. And the Tanglaws, with their bygone talent for soothsaying. Most nobles believed that marriage to a Gatdula—and mixing their blood together—would allow their long-lost magic to one day reawaken. Such a phenomenon had yet to occur, but the nobles' faith in the possibility held fierce. That faith grew stronger with each generation—too strong even for the mighty Gatdulas to ignore. Despite their uncontested abilities and rank, faith that powerful demanded at least a modicum of appeasement. Laya hadn't forgotten. The gods knew she received enough of those lectures from her mother.

Bulan huffed but stepped back, lowering her gaze. "I'm only saying, Laya, you don't need to bow to the pressure. With your power, you're strong enough to reign without a marriage alliance."

Her sister spoke not out of jealousy, for once, but out of concern. A bolt of excitement ran down Laya's spine at Bulan's words. From the window on the opposite wall, the sun rose above the tiered rooftops, casting light across the mirror's polished glass. She stared at the mirror, unblinking, until the seamstress left the room and returned with a bundle of indigo and gold.

"Arms," the seamstress said.

Wordlessly, Laya raised them.

Bulan ducked out of the doorway, letting Laya carry on with the gown fitting in peace. Laya stood stock-still while the seamstress draped the fine silks over her body, pinning them to perfection. Her sister's claim echoed in Laya's ears long after Bulan left the dressing room.

Laya didn't believe Gatdula blood could revive a nobleman's lost bloodright. But she knew that to take a husband would be to share the throne. Although Laya grew up with two siblings, she didn't care for the idea of sharing one bit. Ruling without a marriage alliance, however—that was a prospect she had yet to consider.

"Almost done, Dayang," the seamstress murmured. She reached toward the table behind Laya for the last ensemble—a day dress of cerulean pongee, which floated down to her knees—and a royal sash tumbled from the pile. It was a simple column of viridian silk, bearing the Gatdulas' curled-crocodile insignia. This was the queen's sash, meant for Laya's mother.

"I apologize," the seamstress said. "I don't know how that got in there."

"No matter," Laya told her. "I want to try it on for myself."

She knelt so the seamstress could lift the sash over her head, draping it over her white cotton camisole. The sash hung from her left shoulder, gathering at her opposite hip. Laya traced the hemline, and the thin fabric slipped between her fingers. She looked back at the mirror. The sunlight had shifted since the start of their fitting. Its rays glared off the glass, outlining the crown of Laya's head in piercing light.

"You look beautiful, Dayang," the seamstress said, bowing her head.

The corners of Laya's lips quirked up into a smile. "Like a queen?" she asked.

The seamstress met Laya's gaze in the glass. "More than that," she said in a low, heavy whisper.

No one ever looked at Hara Duja the way the seamstress was looking at Laya now. Smugly, Laya committed the woman's expression to memory. When she was queen, she would see the same expression echoed across a thousand faces. No longer would they gripe about Laya's untamed power. No longer would they question her readiness to rule. All would fall silent the moment they saw her sitting high above them on the Maynaran throne. Whether they liked her or not, the entire country knew Laya belonged there.

Hara Duja, Maiza—they were always telling Laya she was too young, too fickle, to understand the responsibilities awaiting her. But she understood far better than they did what it meant to reign over Maynara. Although centuries had passed since the first Gatdula king had rid the land of invaders, foreign ships still lingered on the horizon. One by one, the invaders had vanquished the neighboring kingdoms. Maynara was the last sovereign nation left for miles—and their sovereignty hinged on the Gatdulas' very existence. For the Gatdulas were the one thing standing between them and conquest. They stood for safety and prosperity. They were freedom made flesh. That was why their people worshipped their monarchs more than their ancestral spirits, more than Mulayri himself.

Laya knew that a Gatdula's reign was about more than ruling a country. To become queen of Maynara was to become a god.

Unlike her mother, Laya had never shied away from her destiny. She donned it like armor. And soon, she would slip into her rightful title like a glove. In her imagination, they called to her, thousands of Maynarans chanting her name—*Hara Laya*.

That bolt of excitement rushed through her again, and she thought back to Bulan's claim. Her sister was right—all this marriage talk was nonsense. Laya was stronger than her mother. Stronger than any Gatdula who'd come before her.

Strong enough to sit upon the throne alone.

five

IMERIA

The last time Imeria Kulaw arrived in Mariit alone, she was ten years old. Her jaw had dropped to the ground when she'd first laid eyes on the kingdom's capital city and the towering buildings with their sloping, red-tiled roofs and saber-like spires puncturing the heavens. The capital had been unreachable back then, looming above the rest of Maynara in a nebulous haze. In the provinces, people whispered of the magic permeating Mariit. It glowed brighter there than in the countryside, spilling through the twisting roots of the giant balete tree that dwelled in the capital's sacred center, leaking through the cracks in the cobblestones and the canals, which crawled across the city like veins.

Imeria never cared much for these myths. Even when she was a child, she had seen past Mariit's sparkling veneer. It was as ugly a city as any, bloated with half-civilized laborers who squabbled over whatever crumbs the noble families left behind. Its canals did not stream gold with power, but rather ran rust-colored from the highland runoff. And the Gatdulas, its sovereigns, were not the gods' mighty descendants, as so many Maynarans proclaimed.

Imeria's father tried to free the island from its ignorance. But when he was alive, he lacked the power to make himself heard.

He'd died when Imeria was a girl. What she knew of him, she'd learned from her mother's stories and from the damning testaments of recent history. He was more myth than memory, yet her thoughts wandered to him more and more as she aged.

"Datu Kulaw! They told me they saw your sails approaching."

Imeria turned at the sound of a deep voice. Vikal, the captain of her family guard, had come on deck. He was an imposing man, with trunk-like biceps and a boxy face, who came from a long line of warriors who had served the Kulaws for generations. He had been teaching her son, Luntok, to fight since he'd been old enough to walk. Vikal loved Luntok—of this, Imeria was certain. Unlike with dozens of other individuals under Imeria's command, she'd never had to buy Vikal's loyalty.

"You have no idea how good it is to see you, Vikal," she said. He was one of the few souls in Maynara whom she greeted with a smile.

"My lady." Vikal bent low at the waist, planting a chaste kiss on her knuckles. "You must be tired from your journey."

"Exhausted." It took several days to sail to the capital from her ancestral lands in the south. She would have arrived earlier had they not hit choppy waters crossing the Untulu Sea.

Same as the dirt-streaked provincials Imeria saw milling around the docks, the most important members of Maynaran society flocked to the capital for the week. This included the other highborn datus, who no doubt had been counting the days until their next opportunity to eat Imeria alive. Every one of them relished the feast days; for Imeria, they were a bloodbath of a subtler, more sinister kind.

"Where would you like me to put this, my lady?" another voice called. A young man emerged from belowdecks, hauling behind him a heavy mahogany trunk packed with Imeria's finest clothes. He was younger than Luntok and sturdily built, unlike most serving boys his age.

Vikal blinked in surprise. For the past few months, he had been giving this young man sword lessons at Imeria's instruction. She had failed to tell Vikal she would bring him, along with a dozen other battle-trained serving boys, to Mariit. He cleared his throat. "I see you brought, uh, reinforcements."

Imeria cut him a sharp look. "The town house was horribly understaffed last year, as you recall," she said airily. "And I need not tell you, Vikal, that beyond the south, well-trained servants are impossible to find."

He gave her a tactful nod, then rushed to the serving boy's aid. "Let me help you with that, son," he said, heaving the other end of the trunk in his arms.

Imeria followed them off the deck and onto the wharf, where the carriage was waiting. Vikal helped the boy hoist the trunk onto the roof of the carriage. She saw Vikal making calculations. Imeria had brought twice as many trunks as the previous year.

"Traveling light, are we?" he said, amused.

His remark brought a dry grin to her face. She knew what he was thinking. Imeria had arrived in the capital armed to the teeth, and she had been awfully clever about it. The Royal Maynaran Guard would not blink at Luntok's impressive collection of weapons; he was competing in the feast-day tournament, after all. Imeria spared no expense on additional arms—convincing replicas of antique swords with engraved blades and ivory hilts, each too precious to appear useful. If the guards troubled her, Imeria need only say the swords were part of her generous tribute to the queen.

Hara Duja. Imeria looked up at Mariit's skyline. The sloping, tiered roofs of the palace peeked out over the outer walls.

Her stomach twisted when she remembered the first time she had met the queen. That had been three decades earlier. Duja, only a princess back then, had not allowed Imeria to kneel too long.

Rise, Duja had said in that soft, gravelly voice of hers. She'd given Imeria a shy smile as she pulled her to her feet. *Don't trouble yourself,* she'd added, noticing how Imeria's eyes had widened in apprehension. *There will be no need for that with me.*

Duja had not smiled at Imeria that way in years. She did not acknowledge Imeria if she could help it. The Kulaws' disgraceful legacy aside, Imeria could trace much of the court's hatred of her back to the queen.

Imeria remembered a time when she'd hungered for any opportunity to see Duja again—to beg for her forgiveness. That was when Imeria had been a desperate girl, with a broken heart and without the slightest care for her own dignity. So there she stood, twenty-two years later, a bitter woman plotting the Gatdula queen's demise.

"Do you believe this year is *the* year, then?" Vikal asked, lowering his voice to a cautious whisper. He helped Imeria into the carriage and climbed into the seat across from her.

"I believe in preparedness," Imeria said blithely.

She glanced over Vikal's shoulder. The driver had finished strapping the last of the trunks to the top of the carriage. He took a seat at the front bench with the serving boy at his side. For months now, Imeria had been making promises to the battle-starved servants under her employ. Like Imeria, they harbored their own hatred for the Gatdulas. Vikal had warned her more than once about their growing impatience. How much longer could she count on their loyalty?

If Imeria was going to act, it must be soon. But for her

schemes to come to fruition, she needed every star in the universe to align.

The carriage wheels groaned beneath the weight of Imeria's trunks as they pulled away from the dock. She looked at the empty seat beside Vikal. Maybe the key to the Kulaws' success was closer than they realized.

"Luntok didn't accompany you?" she asked, raising an eyebrow. She had sent an earlier ship to the capital—kitchen staff and scullery maids to prepare the town house for their sojourn. Luntok insisted on departing with them.

Her son spent half the year in Mariit, far longer than any future datu had a right to. His frequent stays in the capital did not go unnoticed. Imeria, along with the rest of the court, knew precisely whom to blame.

Vikal cleared his throat. "Luntok was occupied this afternoon. He didn't say where he was going, but, well . . ."

"That Laya Gatdula." Imeria let out a dry laugh. The princess was pompous and impulsive and vain. It didn't help that she was beautiful the way a limestone statue was beautiful—high-nosed, untouchable.

"He's awfully devoted. I'll give him that," Vikal said with a shrug.

Imeria raised an eyebrow at him. "To the princess, or to the cause?"

Vikal chuckled in response. "To be frank, my lady, I believe Luntok has yet to figure that out."

She sighed. Laya was not the core of the Kulaws' plans, as Luntok claimed, but a distraction. Imeria might not be able to save her son from heartbreak, but maybe she could grant him the power he desperately craved.

At the great stone walls that protected Mariit, the guardsmen barely glanced at Imeria and her traveling party. All she had to do was play the role of the bored noblewoman, unable to part with her luxuries for more than a week. One look at her dour expression, and the guards waved them through the checkpoint.

Imeria gazed out the window as the carriage trudged deep into the heart of the city. It was dusk, and the market canal had long since emptied. Boats crowded its lanes during the day, laden with green cabbages and dried fish and unripe mangoes. Hundreds of baskets exchanged hands over the water each day—food and wares as far as the eye could see. Silence, rarer than snow in the capital, had settled over the market canal when Imeria rolled past. The only boats docked to the moorings drifted empty, thudding against the wooden planks of the walkway as they swayed.

The carriage followed the canal west before crossing the nearest bridge into the central district. The buildings there stood tall on sturdy coral stones. The Kulaws' town house stood the tallest, with slanting, gold-tipped roofs that mirrored the architecture of the royal palace. After the carriage rolled to a stop, Vikal popped open the door and helped Imeria to the ground.

"Welcome back to Mariit, Datu Kulaw," one maid chimed. She and a handful of servants had been waiting to receive Imeria in front of the veranda.

"I'm parched," Imeria said by way of greeting. She shrugged off her traveling shawl, which smelled of brine and rotting seaweed from her journey, and handed it to the maid.

"We've prepared wine for you, my lady." The maid bundled up the shawl in her arms and gestured to the veranda. Imeria spied a pitcher waiting for her at the center of the rosewood tea table beside a platter of sticky-rice balls wrapped in banana leaves. It was one of Luntok's favorite dishes. He would have been sitting on the veranda sampling them had he waited for Imeria at the town house as he promised.

"I don't suppose any of you have seen my son lurking about," Imeria called, when the front gates swung open. In stormed Luntok. His hands were balled into fists at his sides. Hard lines creased his young, handsome face. It was too early in the day to invite himself into Laya's bedchamber. No doubt he'd tried. If allowed, Luntok would spend every spare moment at her side. But that afternoon, the ghastly Gatdula girl must have refused him.

At the sight of Imeria's carriage, Luntok looked up in surprise. "Mother, you're here." He swept over and kissed her on both cheeks.

"Is something bothering you?" she asked. The golden bands on her wrists jingled when she reached up and brushed a thumb across his jawline. The sound echoed over the hollow walls of the veranda. Imeria thought of those first few months after her husband had died. Luntok would curl up beside her in bed, and she'd lay a palm on his temple to soothe away the nightmares. Those moments stood out among her untainted memories, which were few and far between.

Her sweet, foolish boy—if only he knew how much she loved him.

Confusion flickered in Luntok's eyes. He shook his head and drew back. "No," he said. "Nothing's bothering me."

She pursed her lips. A wall had sprung up between them since Luntok had taken up with Laya three years before. Imeria knew this stemmed from Luntok's fervent desire to have Laya to himself. But politics, not passion, dictated the princess's decisions. The entire court suspected, even if Luntok was too blind to see it, that Laya would choose another man for her husband—no doubt one of Hara Duja's preselected bores—within the next year.

Instead of subjecting her son to a lecture, Imeria took a seat on the veranda. She gestured for Luntok and Vikal to join her. Luntok sauntered over to the tea table. He removed the scabbard from his belt and leaned it against the capiz-shell screen that walled off the veranda from the rest of the house. Vikal watched him, a small smile on his boxy face, and followed suit.

"Oh my. Has she tired of your company already?" Imeria drawled as she poured them each a glass of wine.

His gaze snapped to hers. "Dayang Laya sends her regards," he said sarcastically.

"I don't like how she toys with you," she said, taking a sip of her drink.

"Laya doesn't toy with me. She's very fond of me, you know." This time, Imeria could detect a hint of uncertainty in his tone.

She barked out an unkind laugh. "Fondness," she said. "Surely you can inspire something stronger than that."

Across the table, she and Vikal exchanged a knowing look, but Luntok didn't notice. He crossed his arms and slouched further in his seat. To avoid an argument, Imeria turned to Vikal. They went over the schedule for the week of the feast days while Luntok stormed silently between them. Imeria resisted the urge to hold him to her chest. He was a man now, and a sensitive one at that. She wished she could soothe his angry thoughts as she had when he was a child.

Luntok deserved not the princess's mocking, but a throne of his own. *This, too, is temporary,* she wanted to say. For now, it was the sole comfort Imeria could give him. Instead, she laid a hand on his shoulder and squeezed. His brow was still knitted in frustration, but his shoulders softened at her touch.

Rage now, my boy. Soon, the Gatdulas would toy with them no longer. Once Imeria's plans came to pass, the Kulaws would be the ones laughing in the end.

Six

LAYA

At the first glimmer of light, the royal guard drew open the palace gates to make way for the procession. Laya stood wedged between her sisters on top of the great marble steps and watched their subjects flood in. The procession stretched through the pebbled ground of the forecourt and along the full length of the main canal, its water glittering a preternatural shade of turquoise thanks to the cone-hatted workers who'd spent the past week fishing out debris.

At least a hundred Maynaran nobles had already professed their devotion to Hara Duja and presented the Gatdula family with lavish gifts. Laya lost count of the imported porcelain, rare stone vases, and pongee-wrapped parcels they received.

The best tributes came from the Council of Datus, who arrived at the end of the procession. Second in rank only to the Gatdulas, these were the highest-born members of the royal court. Their gifts, intended as small tokens of their loyalty to the queen, were but an excuse for the datus to flaunt their wealth before the rest of the court. Often, they reflected the datus' personal tastes.

Datu Luma, as was custom, mounted the great steps first. The oldest datu, with stern eyes, wisps of white hair, and a kadatuan that encompassed the lush forests of the northern highlands, he liked to shower them with extravagant furniture carved from native Maynaran timber.

"A gift to adorn your private chambers, Hara Duja," Datu Luma murmured, bowing low at their feet. It was a towering commode of lacquered mahogany with mythical scenes engraved in the facade. Laya made out Mulayri's raptor as he swooped between the swirling vines chiseled into the wood. She watched enviously as servants hauled Datu Luma's tribute up the steep palace steps. Her mother received the finest gifts. But, like the mantle, everything would pass to Laya soon.

Next in line stood Datu Gulod, who had a flair for pageantry and never failed to delight. He waved his hand and called up his servants to present his tribute—a trio of emerald-green peacocks that blinked up at them with beady eyes, the delicate bars of their cages too sparse to contain their many-eyed plumes.

"*Oh!*" To Laya's right, Eti let out a gasp of wonder, which told Datu Gulod he'd chosen well.

"Please accept my tribute, Hara Duja." Datu Gulod bowed theatrically, his greasy nose brushing against the freshly polished tiles, a smug smile on his waxy, youngish face. He nodded in Eti's direction—the most precious of the Gatdula sisters, she had always been the datus' favorite.

"I'm glad the birds please you, Dayang," Gulod told her, then took his place along the marble railing.

The Kulaws were next. Once, they, too, had boasted gods-given powers, but their infernal abilities were lost to history, stamped out by the Gatdulas themselves. And while they were no longer the mightiest foes in the land, the sight of the family still rendered Maynara speechless. An expectant hush swept over the waiting crowd as Luntok and Imeria mounted the steps.

He kept to his mother's side, a triumphant warrior in full ceremonial dress. His vest, woven from fine, scarlet silk, revealed the web of tattoos etched across the broad planes of his chest. A few highborn women, clustered at the base of the stairs, tittered behind their hands, no doubt noticing how much Luntok had grown since the previous year.

"No longer a boy, is he?" Laya thought she heard one of them whisper.

Annoyance flared beneath her ribs. *Let them stare*, she thought to herself savagely. Luntok had belonged to her since he'd been nothing but a reed. They were reeds together, she and him. The rest would have to fight for their piece.

"Your Majesty," Imeria Kulaw said as she got to her knees, golden bangles clanking on her slender wrists, her face absent of its customary sneer. Sunlight glinted off her headpiece, which was shaped like a bird midflight, its brassy wings fanning out above Imeria's temples like a pair of flames. Luntok bowed beside her, raising his head slightly to give Laya a smirk.

Their tribute was far more lavish than Laya had expected: a dozen cases overflowing with jade pots from Xitai, king quail eggs, and a number of other exotic delicacies—all this, perhaps, to make up for Imeria's many insults toward the queen.

The Kulaws' generosity did not end there. "In addition to our tribute to you, Hara Duja, we are honored to present the princesses with a token," Imeria said, "each carefully selected to reflect her unique gifts." She nodded to Luntok, who got to his feet.

First, he presented Bulan with the most impractical sword Laya had ever seen—the blade a rich cobalt blue inlaid with gold-foil motifs. The hilt had been carved into the snapping jaws of a crocodile, the Gatdula family's symbol.

"Thank you," Bulan said when she accepted the sword, mesmerized as she ran her finger over the tinted metal.

For Eti, Luntok handed over a sculpted figurine of the Weeping Goddess. The gold of her hair had been melded by a delicate hand into the tiniest tendrils, an expression of both agony and cunning etched onto her face. Beauty moved Eti more than anyone Laya knew. When she took the figurine from Luntok, she appeared too stricken by the craftsmanship to express any words of gratitude. She simply stared open-mouthed at the treasure in her hands.

Luntok approached Laya last. "For you, Dayang," he said in a low voice. Luntok was her lover, but she was still a princess; he addressed her by her proper title when they were in public.

But called her Laya when they were alone.

A faint blush spread over her cheeks when she remembered how he whispered her name like a prayer, like a curse, whenever they were together. He reached out with her gift—a handwoven fan of soft ivory and pineapple silk, the featherlight fabric embroidered with the tiniest jasmine flowers far more delicate than any breeze she could summon. The carrier chain pooled in Laya's hands, made of seven coins linked together to depict Maynara's primordial moons.

"It's lovely," she said, folding the fan shut as gently as she could. Her gift didn't glitter as much as Eti's and Bulan's presents. It kept half of its beauty a secret, but that was what made it grander.

Luntok inclined his head once more, waiting to be dismissed, but Laya couldn't let him leave yet. She knew what she was doing when she held out her hand to him.

Luntok grinned as he bowed to brush his lips over her knuckles. "Not half as lovely as its owner," he murmured when he met her gaze. He tightened his grip on her hand before he released it, letting his fingers linger.

Laya bit back a telling grin. She didn't notice how her heart was thumping until she heard her father's knowing chuckle behind her.

"I'd be careful with that one," he joked to the queen, softly so Luntok couldn't hear.

Hara Duja stiffened in her seat. "That will be all, Datu Kulaw. Thank you," she said, dismissing them more coldly than the others.

Laya frowned, watching Luntok's back—his strong, lovely back—as he retreated down the palace steps. She understood her mother's coldness with Imeria, a selfish, horrid woman, but she couldn't forgive Hara Duja for sending Luntok away so brusquely.

To her right, Bulan scoffed.

"Not a word from you," Laya hissed.

"I wasn't going to say a thing."

"Please," Eti pleaded under her breath. The most sensitive of the three, she cried pitifully when they fought. For her sake, Laya and Bulan ignored each other.

Laya turned back to the procession. It was nearly over, with only three families left in line to present their tributes. Her stomach rumbled. She thought greedily about the platters of food waiting for them in the palace. And, if they could sneak away, the prospect of Luntok waiting for her in her bed.

As Datu Tanglaw and his son mounted the steps, their servants lugging what looked like a chest of antique Maynaran instruments behind them, General Ojas swept over to the queen. He wore ceremonial armor, a silk sash of Gatdula green, and an even stonier expression than usual. *Curious.* Laya craned her neck to listen.

"Your Majesty, a man just arrived at the palace," Ojas whispered. "My men tried to send him away, but he insisted."

"What kind of man, General?" the queen asked in a hushed voice.

"Not *our* kind, Your Majesty. I would have sent him on the first ship out of Maynara, but he . . ." For the first time, Laya heard Ojas hesitate. "He bears an invitation from the king."

Laya's ears perked up in interest. Her father often received a wide range of eccentric guests at the palace—thinkers and artists and exotic beast tamers. Something in Ojas's tone told her this guest was unlike any of them.

"Did he . . . come alone?" the queen asked.

"Yes, Your Majesty," Ojas said.

For one sharp moment, Hara Duja remained silent. Her sleeves rustled as she reached for the king's hand. "Aki . . ."

The quaver in her voice caught Laya's attention. She had never heard her mother sound so anxious before. She looked over her shoulder, no longer pretending she wasn't listening.

Her father leaned in toward the queen, uncharacteristically tight-lipped. "When this is over, you must speak with him. Take Ojas with you so you're not alone," he whispered. He cast a wary glance at the procession, at the hundreds of Maynarans gathered beyond the palace gates, and added, "Be careful, Duja. Go as quietly as you can."

Speak with whom? And why the secrecy?

Laya's skin tingled with anticipation. She fidgeted, impatient, as the remaining families took their time climbing the great steps. Would the procession ever end? She stifled a groan. When Laya was queen, she would order the datus to deliver their tributes to the palace several weeks ahead of the feast days and be done with it.

"What on earth is the matter with you?" Bulan demanded under her breath.

Laya ignored her. She stared hard at Datu Patid, flanked on either side by his daughters, young girls around Eti's age with forgettable names and sallow cheeks, until he at last rose from his knees. Hara Duja gave him a regal nod, accepting the last of her tributes. She stood and gestured at General Ojas. Together, they disappeared through the enormous doors atop the great stairs. Moments later, the forecourt erupted into a flurry of movement as the nobles streamed into the palace for the opening feast.

On either side, Laya's sisters gathered their skirts. They, too, made their way inside. Laya glanced between them. She didn't want to spy on their mother alone, but who should she take with her? Eti couldn't keep a secret to save her life. But Bulan, with her sharp mind and soldier's tread—

"Hari Aki, if I might have a word." One of the nobles, Datu Tanglaw, caught up with the king. Laya had scarcely exchanged words with the man over the years, but she remembered his thick black eyebrows and obsequious tone.

Laya's father turned to the other man, a winning smile on his face, ready to fend off whatever request Datu Tanglaw planned to make of him.

Perfect. They could slip away while the king was distracted.

Laya grabbed Bulan's wrist. "Follow me," she whispered.

Bulan stared at her, incredulous. "What are you—"

She whisked her from the throng of nobles before Bulan could finish her sentence. They darted down the long corridor leading to the great hall. Laya refused to stop until they reached the passageway that linked the great hall to the palace kitchens.

"Now will you explain where you're taking me?" Bulan asked.

Laya silenced her with a look. Servants passed them with

trays of food in their hands, not bothering to conceal their curious gazes. Laya glared at them until they diverted their eyes. To Bulan, she leaned forward and whispered, "It's about Mother. Weren't you listening earlier? She's meeting someone in secret."

Bulan raised her eyebrows. "She's meeting someone? *Now?*"

Laya nodded and lowered her voice even further. "If I wanted to speak with someone out of sight of the prying eyes of Mariit, where would I take them?"

Recognition flashed in Bulan's eyes. She pulled Laya to the end of the servants' passageway, where stood a narrow window overlooking the central courtyard.

"Look," Bulan said, pointing.

Laya scanned the grounds. She spied a handful of guards on patrol, gardeners tending to the flower arrangements the king planned to unveil later in the week, and—*there*. Marching along the arcaded walkway was their mother. Laya recognized her straight back and brisk pace. When the queen wasn't suffering from her tremors, she moved like death itself was chasing her, which wasn't far from the truth.

"She's heading to the eastern wing," Bulan murmured.

"The eastern wing?" Laya echoed. Guilt boiled in her stomach when she thought about her accident. She had apologized over a hundred times. But it hadn't been the first time a Gatdula had destroyed the eastern wing. The building was cursed. After watching its gilded facade crumble beneath her gusts of wind, Laya knew that better than anyone. Who on earth could Hara Duja be hiding there?

Bulan cast a wary glance over her shoulder. Wave after wave of servants poured out from the kitchens. Spirited music reverberated through the walls. Back in the great hall, the feast had already begun.

"We should get back," Bulan whispered.

Laya scowled. "But—"

"Drop it, Laya," she said with a terse shake of her head. "We'll only draw attention to Mother if we try to slip away now. Obviously, she wants to keep this meeting a secret. I say we keep it that way."

Laya glanced back at the window and saw no trace of the queen. Their mother must have disappeared into the eastern wing.

"Stay behind if you want," she told Bulan. "I will see for myself."

Bulan grabbed her arm. "And how do you suppose Mother will react when she finds out you're spying on her? You never think things through."

"I do," Laya said with a huff.

"Then, by all means, fly to the eastern wing," Bulan retorted. "I'm sure the queen will be more than pleased."

Laya scowled. Bulan was right, of course, but that did not deaden Laya's interest.

Grudgingly, she followed her older sister into the great hall. Dozens of heads turned toward her as they entered. Beside her, Bulan shrank back at the onslaught of attention. Laya gave her a small, triumphant smile. Bulan shied away at the slightest beam of scrutiny. Imagine the horror if, in a different life, Hara Duja had chosen her for her heir. Laya, on the other hand, was no wilting flower. Standing in the great hall, under the heat of the scrutiny of a pit of snakes and admirers, Laya bloomed.

"Happy feast days," Laya said languidly to her sister as she strode into the room. She plucked a wineglass from a passing tray and wove through the throng. If anything, she was doing the queen a favor. No one would notice Hara Duja's absence as long as her dazzling daughter held their attention. Laya smirked at the nobles as she breezed by, inviting them to stare.

One by one, they flocked to her side. "Dayang," they called, each in that same kowtowing tone. They bowed low at the waist, offering to fetch her food and drink, showering her with silk-spun compliments.

Laya thanked them demurely. She was only half listening as she looked past their heads. Most of her admirers were young noblemen, who no doubt had traveled to Mariit from across the island to fawn over Laya and her loveliness. But Laya kept her ear trained on court gossip. Half of those men thought her snotty and vile; the other half did not know her well enough to care. A pit formed in her stomach when she thought back to Luntok's words before he'd jumped from the balcony a week earlier. Each of the men there expected her to select a husband soon.

Laya didn't want to think about that. She continued to nod and smile as she sipped her drink. Over a hundred pairs of eyes on her, and not one of them mattered. It was foolish, she knew, but she could not help herself. Laya glanced over her shoulder every few moments, hoping to pick out Luntok's gaze in the crowd.

Seven

DUJA

The alchemist was not what Duja had expected. She spied his outline through a crack in the doorway. He was as tall as General Ojas, but half his width. He had a gangly, almost malnourished frame so unlike the brutish guards who once trailed Pangil as he terrorized the palace. Duja wondered, What in Mulayri's name did her brother see in him?

General Ojas had him brought up to the guest chambers in the eastern wing, far away from the prying eyes of Mariit. No one, not even the servants, went up there anymore. The air that hung in the corridor was stale. Above Duja's head, dust particles drifted along in slow, lazy currents, reflecting the faint light streaming in through the white-shell window screens.

Duja had scarcely set foot in the eastern wing in over two decades. She remembered, with heart-pounding immediacy, the last time she had made it to the upper floors. How could she forget that fateful afternoon? The air seeping into the guest chambers had been heavy with the promise of torrential rain. It was red-hot and suffocating, but they needed to keep the screens drawn for fear of being seen. The eastern wing—whose idea had it been? Duja would have been too reticent, too skittish. As she stared down the darkened corridor, Imeria's laughter, soft as orchid petals, echoed in her ears. Reaching through memory's haze, Imeria's slender fingers left trails of gooseflesh across Duja's skin. Oh, yes, the queen remembered. The air had been thicker than honey that day, but that hadn't been the reason she couldn't breathe.

"Are you all right, Your Majesty?" Ojas's deep voice jolted Duja back to the present, resonating through her bones like a gong.

She blinked. The general watched her, his stoic eyes hard with concern. Duja gave him a small smile of gratitude. Beneath his stern exterior, Ojas was undeniably loyal to the Gatdula family. It didn't matter to Ojas who the man in the guest chambers was. If Duja or the king gave him an order, he would follow it without hesitating. His left hand rested on the doorknob, awaiting her instruction.

Duja nodded, smoothing down the thin fabric of her skirt to collect herself. "Go ahead, Ojas," she said. "I'm ready to speak with him."

Ojas opened the door and strode into the guest chambers. He announced her presence, as if she were receiving any other visitor. "Her Majesty, Hara Duja, daughter of Mulayri and protector of the Maynaran throne."

But the alchemist wasn't some highborn son or foreign dignitary. He was standing at one of the closed windows, lost in thought, when Ojas's voice startled him. He whipped around. His spectacles, crooked wire-framed glass, slid down his nose; like his starched shirt and stiff trousers, they appeared to be of western make. He hesitated for a long, painful moment, which made Duja think he had never interacted with royalty before, then stumbled to his knees. When he lowered his head, he let out a garbled sound that might have been an attempt at obsequiousness. Duja couldn't be sure.

A frown tugged at the corners of her lips. "Do you not understand Maynaran?" she asked the alchemist as she appraised him. "I'm afraid I didn't think about that."

The alchemist looked up in surprise. "N-no, I understand. If you speak slowly, at least, Your . . . Your Majesty." He answered her not in Maynaran, but in a sister tongue. His accent had a foreign twang, and his mouth stretched strangely around certain vowels, but otherwise she could understand his speech.

Duja's eyes lit up in realization. She took in the alchemist's language and his western clothes. Suddenly, everything made sense. "You're Orfelian," she gasped, unable to contain her shock.

Orfelia was one of their closest neighbors, lying about a week's sail from Maynara. Like countless other islands in the Untulu Sea, they fell centuries before to foreign invaders with faster ships and paler skin. Maynara was the sole kingdom in that corner of the world to have survived conquest. For generations, mighty Gatdula kings and queens had kept the invaders at bay. None of Duja's ancestors had wished to entangle themselves in the troubles of their fallen neighbors, and for good reason. The western masters were a selfish breed. They'd had their greedy eyes on Maynara's wealth since their ships first cut through their waters. If the Gatdulas had learned anything from their neighbors, it was that conflict with the west would prove costly. Fortunately, Maynara had steered clear of it thus far.

As for the alchemist, Pangil must have discovered him in Orfelia, that sad little island across the sea. That wasn't the island's true name, of course. The conquerors rechristened it in honor of their foreign king, then scorched any trace of its original name from history. From what Duja understood, Orfelia was a land of forgotten names and stolen riches. Its plundered, impoverished villages had nothing to offer the likes of an exiled prince. Duja wondered what on earth had brought her brother *there*.

"Yes, Your Majesty, I am from Orfelia," the alchemist said. Behind his spectacles, a shade of sadness flickered in his expression. "I came here because I needed to escape. That man—Pangil. He said he could help me."

Duja stiffened. How strange it was to hear her brother's name uttered from a foreigner's lips—although she suspected her brother must have befriended a great number of foreigners during his many years in exile. Twenty-two years earlier, she'd watched her men drag him onto the first ship out of Maynara. The ship had disappeared into a blanket of fog on the horizon, and her brother along with it. In the beginning, she had her people track his whereabouts. They followed Pangil north to Wakon, then west to Xitai. Last she heard, he had ingratiated himself with the sultan of Mandoo, who'd financed his trip to the Sunset States. Before discovering his letter in the king's stack of books, Duja had never expected to hear from Pangil again.

And now, the alchemist rose to his feet before Duja—a common Orfelian and a strange choice for a messenger. How he had wandered into Pangil's path, Duja didn't know. If she hadn't been afraid her brother had sent him to waste her time, she would have almost felt sorry for him. He looked haggard, confused, and out of his depth.

"What did Pangil promise you? Safe harbor in Maynara?" Duja asked. "I don't know what he told you, Orfelian, but I am the only one who can grant you that." She raised her chin to give the alchemist the impression that she was looking down at him. Her mother did not teach her this; despite the blood of Mulayri that had run in her veins, the old queen had been softer than wool.

No, Duja had learned the move from Imeria—another memory that came with the bitter sting of regret.

The alchemist's mouth flattened into a line. His body language shifted. He slid his spectacles up the bridge of his nose, which made him look taller. Duja observed him, fascinated. This was a man who was accustomed to conducting negotiations.

"You are correct, Your Majesty. I do seek safety in Maynara. And I understand I am in no position to make demands of a queen. However . . ." He trailed off. His eyes flitted to General Ojas, who was standing behind Duja's shoulder, no doubt with one hand on the hilt of his sword. The alchemist swallowed hard and met Duja's gaze. "I would not have come if I did not have something to offer in exchange."

Duja's heartbeat quickened. She remembered the promise Pangil made in his letter. *"The key to abiding glory,"* she echoed.

The alchemist let out a surprised chuckle. "Yes," he said, nodding slowly. "Or something to that effect."

Hope fluttered without warning in her chest. She shoved it down. The alchemist looked harmless, but Duja knew nothing about him—what he offered, why he needed to leave Orfelia. For all she knew, he came to Duja on her brother's orders to lay some elaborate trap. She studied him closely. "If we're going to strike a deal, I can't go on calling you Orfelian," she said. "Tell me, young man. What is your name?"

The alchemist opened his mouth just as a violent tremor shot through Duja's hand. She fisted the silk of her sash and spun around.

"Your Majesty!" Ojas gasped.

Duja shook her head to hold him back. The vibrations rocked up her arm to the stiff muscles at the base of her neck. She bit back a hiss of pain, cradling her hand until the shaking dissipated.

"You—yes. *Of course.*" The alchemist's voice rang out across the room's vaulted ceiling, awestruck.

Duja looked up. Her hand fell limply to her side. "What on earth are you talking about?"

"The tremors. I've seen them before. Do you see now? This is why he sent me." The alchemist's eyes lit up in excitement. He spoke in rapid Orfelian. With his accent, Duja found him hard to understand.

"Are you talking about Pangil?" she asked incredulously.

"Yes, Pangil. He had these tremors. I helped him. I can help you too—" The alchemist's mouth snapped shut. His cheeks flushed red in embarrassment when he remembered who Duja was. "Your Majesty," he added, lowering his head in deference.

Questions flooded Duja's mind as she stared at the alchemist. She detected no trace of treachery in his eyes. Maybe her brother had been telling the truth after all.

"Pangil," she said again. A shiver of apprehension ran through her body. "How did you help him, exactly?"

The alchemist's eyes trailed down to Duja's fingers, which quivered like dying leaves at her side. Something clicked in his gaze. For a brief moment, he didn't appear lost at all. In fact, he appeared to understand more than Duja gave him credit for.

Duja stared as he leaned closer. Judging by the nervous glint in his eyes, she half expected him to start babbling in Orfelian again. Instead, the alchemist took a tentative step toward her. In a hushed voice, he asked, "What do you know about precioso, Your Majesty?"

Eight

IMERIA

The rice wine soured on Imeria's lips as she gazed up at the soaring ceilings of the great hall. Resplendent patterns of orchids and kingfishers swirled along the arched doorways, gilded walls, and marble pillars. Fragrant bowls of rose mallow lay at the center of each table lining the hall. Servants wove in between them, offering the noble guests platters topped with food and drink.

At the end of the hall loomed Hara Duja's throne. It sat upon the back of a crocodile, which served as a dais and was carved from black volcanic stone. The crocodile's neck curved toward the supplicants below, its jaws frozen midsnap. Imeria remembered counting its teeth while she knelt at the base of the throne as a young girl. She and her mother had been summoned before the old queen to plead for their lives. The old queen was kinder than the Gatdulas before her, and she harbored inside her enormous bosom a soft heart and strong ideals.

I see a great deal of my daughter in yours, the queen had said to the late Lady Kulaw. She thought Imeria an immaculate, harmless thing whose father had been at war for most of her life. The rebellion kept him far from home, unable to taint her with his treasonous misdeeds.

Ironic that Imeria's guilelessness had saved them.

She must have played her role well, because the old queen invited her to live at the palace not as a prisoner, but as a promise of peace. *Let us put these years of bloodshed behind us,* she'd said, *and live as one people, as we were always meant to be.*

Imeria didn't like to be reminded of the years she had spent there, of the happiness they'd brought her and the grief. Standing in the great hall, the memories came flooding back. Music chimed from the back of the room. In the ring of gongs and bamboo zithers, she heard the soft, shy laughter of the former princess, calling her to hide with her behind the billowing batik curtains. She saw, creeping across the tiled floor, the dark, slender shadow of the former crown prince.

A lifetime before, Dayang Duja once pulled her into this very room, pressed her forehead to hers, and whispered, *You are my heart, as I am yours. Promise you will never forget.*

Imeria's fingers tightened around the stem of her wine goblet. She didn't want to remember.

She devoted her attention instead to the room before her, cataloging every change the Gatdulas had made since she'd last visited Mariit. She took stock of the new reinforced locks on the windows, their brass dowels gleaming in the afternoon light. She counted the guards posted along the walls, finding that their ranks had nearly doubled over the past two seasons. She studied the palace foundation for the slightest hint of a fault line. But not once did she catch a glimpse of the Maynaran queen.

Imeria hadn't seen Hara Duja since the end of the procession, which struck her as odd. This was one of the few occasions when the nobles could address her openly. The queen owed them her presence. Imeria knew better than anyone that Duja was infuriatingly stoic. She had never been the type of sovereign to renege on her duties.

"Datu Kulaw," a man's voice called. Imeria turned. It was Datu Tanglaw, head of one of the six highborn families and fellow council member. He was a distant cousin of the king and had more daughters than one could consider useful. Bato, his eldest child and sole son, was two years Luntok's senior. From what Imeria could gather, they were not friends.

"Datu Tanglaw. Been some time, hasn't it?" Imeria said.

He nodded stiffly. "It has."

It had been an entire year, in fact, since she'd seen most members of the Maynaran court. The last time Imeria had come to Mariit had been during the feast days the previous year. She had been expected during the Day of the Weeping Goddess, and again during the Fire Moon. Her failure to accept the queen's invitation had been interpreted as an insult, and the other families had shunned her for her disobedience.

"Will your son be competing in the tournament?" Imeria asked out of courtesy. Datu Tanglaw and his ilk were soulless lackeys who groveled at the Gatdulas' feet. She couldn't care less what they did.

"Yes," Datu Tanglaw said. "And yours?"

She nodded, taking another sip of her drink. Her eyes fell to the center of the room, where, unsurprisingly, Dayang Laya had stolen the court's attention. She was radiant in her dress, which fell from her shoulders in a luminous cascade of lapis that rivaled the Untulu Sea. Suitors flocked to her like greedy pigeons. Among them Imeria counted Bato Tanglaw, with his unremarkable face the shape of an upside-down arrowhead. She watched as the princess shifted her gaze between suitors, never lingering too long on any man. Bato leaned in to make a joke, which made her chuckle. The princess angled her body toward him as she sent him a coy smile. The other suitors knew her attention to

Bato was fleeting, and they had yet to grow discouraged. When Laya opened her mouth, her eyes sparkled with spellbinding confidence. It was no wonder they hung on to every word.

"The princess seems very taken with Bato," Imeria remarked.

A rare smile spread across Datu Tanglaw's face. "She certainly does."

Imeria knew what he was thinking. That his son was a worthy suitor of high birth, and Hara Duja would be happy to marry off one of her precious daughters to a boy like him. But Datu Tanglaw knew nothing about Laya, of her appetites and her wiles, nor the fact that another suitor had already caught her attention.

A new presence ruffled Laya's flock. It was Luntok, dazzling in court attire of scarlet silk. Rather than greet the others, he planted himself at Laya's side. They didn't dare protest the intrusion, but rather parted like waves to make room for him—as if they knew in some unspoken way that he belonged there.

Imeria smirked and glanced at Datu Tanglaw over the rim of her goblet. "Well," she said vaguely, "it seems she's very taken with my son too."

Datu Tanglaw harrumphed and looked away. He was no longer smiling.

The weight of another's gaze pulled Imeria from their conversation. She glanced to her left to find a serving girl waiting with a wine pitcher in hand. She looked Imeria in the eye, bolder than any girl of her rank should have dared.

"Care for more refreshment, my lady?" she asked. Her High Maynaran was convincing, but Imeria could detect the choppy lilt of the southern provinces.

She held out her goblet. "Yes, thank you."

The girl met her gaze again as she poured the wine, and once more over her shoulder when she turned to leave—a clear signal.

Imeria straightened. She waited a tactical moment, exchanging a few more pleasantries with Datu Tanglaw, then excused herself to follow the serving girl to the ladies' sitting room.

Two women of medium rank had gathered in front of the mirror. Both wore skeletal stacks of gold on their wrists and patterned skirts the shade of seaweed—a modest imitation of the Gatdulas' incandescent green. They quieted as she approached. She ignored them and made as though she were straightening her raptor-shaped headpiece, shifting it so the weight of its golden wings lay evenly on either side of her forehead.

"Datu Kulaw," the woman closest to her said, bowing her head in respect. Imeria recognized her as the wife of an undistinguished nobleman from the north, likely affiliated with the Luma family.

"Yes, that would be my name," she said, eyeing them coldly. Her message registered as both women gathered their skirts and left the sitting room without question.

Once they left, the serving girl emerged from the shadows in the back of the sitting room. "We're alone," she said in a low voice. "I've already checked."

Imeria met her gaze in the glass. The girl might have been lovely if not for her sallow cheeks and sickly pale skin. She was a well-reared girl from the south, but not much to look at—this was exactly the kind of person Imeria liked to collect. "So, Yari," she said, "you have information for me."

Yari nodded, a flush of excitement spreading over her thin cheeks. "It happened only this morning, right after the procession. I saw the general herding a man toward the eastern wing," she whispered hurriedly. "His guards waited until the other servants were upstairs with the guests. Then they snuck him in through the kitchens. I hid when I heard them coming. They didn't look like they wanted to be seen."

Her information made Imeria take pause. The queen was particular about her private affairs, but this reeked of suspicion. What man would Hara Duja try to sneak within the walls of the palace? And why did she want to conceal him?

"This man. What did he look like?" she demanded.

Yari bit her lip. "I'm afraid I didn't see his face, my lady. He was dressed very strangely."

"Oh?" Imeria raised her eyebrows. "How was he dressed exactly?"

"In a stiff white shirt and heavy trousers. Almost like a westerner," she said. "You don't think he's actually from the west, do you?"

Imeria diverted her gaze, unable to give Yari an answer. Instead, she reached for the tiny purse in the pocket of her skirt and counted its contents in the palm of her hand. "For your services," she said, tossing Yari a gold coin. "If you learn more, you know how to contact me."

Yari bowed once again. "Anything for you, my lady," she said, eyeing the coin greedily.

Imeria glanced again at her reflection in the sitting-room mirror. She looked tired, and not as young as she had once been. "Thank you again," she said to Yari, before returning to the clamor of the dawn feast.

Servants had appeared with more trays of food: glass noodles, steamed mussels, and salted duck eggs, followed by pickled cabbage and tender oxtail and dipping sauces of every color. The smells assaulted Imeria's senses, and the music soared even louder than before. She couldn't hear herself think.

According to Yari's observation, Hara Duja could be harboring a foreigner behind these walls. He must have posed a threat if she was so determined to keep him a secret. Imeria needed better information, and for that she needed a keener set of eyes—eyes that could penetrate deeper into the palace's inner workings. A lowly serving girl would be of little help to her there. Perhaps Luntok's tryst would prove useful, after all. In a single gulp, Imeria finished her wine and threw her goblet onto a passing tray. Her gaze, alert now, swept over the crowded hall of the receiving room. She needed to find her son.

Nine

LAYA

Laya collapsed against Luntok's chest, pink cheeked in pleasure. "Oh, darling," she whispered breathily, "tell me you are never leaving Mariit."

Luntok sighed into her hair, his breath tickling her earlobe. They'd snuck away after the feast, stumbling and sloshing wine across the wax-glazed floorboards, and were now lying naked beneath Laya's sheets. The sun, once high and bloated on the horizon, had long since dipped beneath the golden crocodile jaws that dotted the palace roofs. Pale shadows streaked through the window screens, painting lines across Luntok's flushed face. Laya hadn't thought she could want him more until just minutes before, when he had been pressing their hips together and moaning her name. She loved that it was her name on his lips, no one else's. She'd wear his name like a brand. She'd let him carve it with his nails, sharp as razor blades, into her unmarked skin.

"I'd stay in bed with you forever," Luntok said as he ran his fingers along her back, leaving a trail of goose bumps down her spine.

Then stay. Laya swallowed the words. The bustle and alcohol of the feast had made her giddy, but she had yet to completely lose her head. Instead, she allowed herself to giggle—and Laya never giggled. She raised her head to peck him on the lips, her mouth curling and wet and ravenous.

"You must never leave. I forbid it," she said.

"Would you take me as your prisoner, Dayang?" Luntok asked, grinning.

"Oh, yes." She clambered on top of him. The feast wine had given her a playful spark of energy, along with a set of thumbs. She grappled for his wrists, pinning them clumsily to the sheets. When she sat up, the room spun around her. Laya braced her weight against Luntok's shoulders to steady herself. Maybe she was more inebriated than she'd thought.

Nestled between the pillows, Luntok feigned confusion. "And what crime have I committed, Dayang?"

She leaned over him, close enough that she could smell the tang of rice wine on his breath. "You, my lord, are much too handsome. The other ladies have started to take notice."

His grin darkened. He flipped her onto the bed and crawled on top of her. "Jealous, Laya?" he murmured against the hollow of her throat.

"No," Laya said. She threaded her fingers through his hair and pulled back hard enough to make him wince. The corners of her lips turned up into a smug smile. She lowered her voice an octave. "Not as long as you're imprisoned with me."

Luntok swallowed, the lump bobbing in his throat. For a moment, the fire in his gaze dampened. "I just want to be with you. I don't care about anything else," he said, tightening his grip on her waist. She heard a hitch in his tone, a kind of desperation that stretched deeper than lust.

Of all the women in Maynara, Luntok wanted *her*. Be it the wine or the bustle or the desire surging in her veins, Laya wanted him more than anything else on earth. This was not a war she could win, but she wouldn't surrender him without a fight.

Laya gazed up at him with a challenge in her lidded eyes. Rather than push him away, she yanked his lips down to meet hers. Luntok kissed her back hungrily, as if he were a dying man devouring his final feast, as if they hadn't made love mere moments before. He dragged his mouth down her jawline, along the delicate skin of her neck, then lower, lower still.

Her toes curled in delight, and she reached for him beneath the sheets. Luntok tore himself from her touch with a strangled groan.

"Laya, wait."

Laya fell back against the mattress, relenting. "It's OK if you can't keep up, you know," she told him.

Luntok scowled. "You know I can keep up just fine."

"I'm only saying," she said with a shrug. "We can always do *other* things while we wait." Laya looked down, pretending to examine her fingernails. Out of the corner of her eye, she saw a smirk spread across Luntok's face.

"We can do whatever you like, Laya," he said, hovering over her. "Tell me something first."

"Oh? What would you like to know?" Laya's eyes fluttered shut as Luntok leaned forward, skimming his lips along her throat once more.

"I've heard rumors."

"Rumors?" She let out a dry laugh. "I'm afraid you'll have to elaborate."

He kissed down to her shoulder, and she sighed in contentment. "There have been stories—of strange men smuggled inside the palace," he said, his breath dancing across her collarbone. "I don't suppose you've heard anything to do with that."

His question struck her as oddly specific. Had she been of sounder mind, she might have thought to question him. But Laya's need for him burned stronger than any ember of suspicion she might have harbored.

"Are you suggesting I smuggle all kinds of strange men into my bed?" Laya asked airily. With a long finger, she traced the column of tattoos on his back. The muscles in his shoulders tensed as he suppressed a shiver.

"Are you suggesting there are other men?" He parted her thighs and stroked between them. She gasped in spite of herself. His smirk widened.

"Oh, Luntok." She sighed once more as waves of pleasure rippled through every inch of her body. "You know there are no other men for me."

Luntok fell silent. Laya closed her eyes, horrified. Damn the wine—she wished the bed would swallow her whole after this rare display of vulnerability.

Luntok withdrew his hand. She whined in protest, but he kissed her, swallowing her complaint. "I truly have heard things," he whispered against her lips. "Foreigners hidden within the palace walls."

"Mindless gossip," Laya said, shaking her head. She curled her legs around his hips and rocked against him. A noise like a desperate snarl rose in the back of Luntok's throat. She reached for him, helped him slip back inside. That effectively put an end to the subject.

"I want you," he said, breathing raggedly as they settled into their usual rhythm.

Laya wrapped her arms around his neck. Silent promises didn't count for much, but they were the best she could give him. *You have me, Luntok,* she vowed in her head. *Tonight, you have me.*

She awoke with an incessant pounding in her skull and the flutter of someone else's breath against the side of her neck. Slowly, Laya opened her eyes. Across the room, yellow light streamed in through the open window. Outside the hall, she heard the dim chatter of servants on their way to their posts. She yawned. The inside of her mouth was dryer than volcanic ash. As she reached for the pitcher of water at her bedside table, Luntok's arm wrapped around her middle, pulling her back to the mattress.

"Morning," he mumbled against the pillows.

"Good morn—" Laya began to say when she caught herself.

It was morning. Luntok slept the night at the palace. *Luntok shouldn't be here.*

Panic surged through Laya when she realized their error. Why did they have to drink so much at the feast? She bolted out of bed and shrugged on her dressing robe. "You need to leave before someone sees you," she told him as she fished around the sheets for his clothes.

Luntok sat up and rubbed his eyes. "At least give me a moment to wake up first."

"No time." Any second now, a maid would knock at her door, summoning her for breakfast. Laya plucked Luntok's trousers from the foot of the bed and threw them at him. They hit him squarely across the face.

"For Mulayri's sake, Laya," Luntok said, annoyed. He grabbed his trousers and yanked them on over his legs.

Before he turned toward the balcony, Laya saw the disappointment flash in his expression. Gone was the softness of the previous night. The girl who stood before him, impatient to push him out the window, was the version of Laya who paraded about the court, haughty and unmoved.

Good. Laya brushed aside the guilt. The more she disappointed him, the faster he would leave.

She watched him, impatient, as Luntok finished dressing. He avoided looking at her as he headed to the balcony. In the terse silence, his words from the night before returned to her. They rang out, clear as a gong, piercing through her drunken haze—*foreigners hidden within the palace.* Laya frowned. She thought back to her mother's brisk walk through the courtyard, of the nervous glances she'd cast over her shoulder as she hurried to the eastern wing.

Hara Duja *had* met with someone in secret during the dawn feast. Someone in the palace must have told Luntok about it—but who?

Laya hung back to study the back of his head. His dark hair was mussed from sleep. The faint scratches she'd etched into his shoulder blades glowed dully in the morning sun. As she watched him, her stomach turned. Luntok *loved* her. He had never lied to her before.

He didn't look at her as he swung one leg over the balustrade. She grabbed the collar of his vest to stop him. "Luntok, wait."

"What is it?" He looked up at her.

Laya tried to ignore the glimmer of hope in his gaze and forced her face into a neutral expression. "What was it you said last night?" she asked. "About those strange men smuggled inside the palace?"

The shades swung shut over Luntok's eyes, which, mere hours earlier, burned with nothing but love for her. "Oh, that," Luntok said. He stared back at her stonily—a challenge if Laya ever saw one. "It was just something I overheard."

Lies, she wanted to scream. Questions fought their way to her mouth, but pride kept Laya from asking any of them. Most days, she relished the competitive undercurrent that pulsed between them, making every interaction feel like a dangerous game. That was what drew her to him when they were younger. Unlike the other noble children, who groveled in response to Laya's taunts and cruelty, Luntok was willing to match her.

At fifteen, when Laya decided she wanted to have sex, Luntok was the only boy she respected well enough to invite into her bed. By then, she already saw him not as the traitor's grandson, but as the forbidden treat she'd never have to share with anyone else. They were older now, and they sought more from each other than passing thrills. For once, Laya was ready to admit that things between them had changed. Luntok's challenges were starting to feel less like a game and more like an actual danger.

But that morning, she didn't have time to press him. She stood, still as a statue, as Luntok hopped down from the balustrade. He landed with a quiet thud in the bushes below her window. By some miracle, no guards were passing through. He disappeared into the gardens undetected.

Laya slammed the window to the balcony shut. She sagged against the cool glass pane as a wave of nausea crashed over her. First, her mother. Then, Luntok. Who else was keeping secrets from her?

She turned to her wardrobe and started to get dressed. The unsettled feeling hung over her like a cloud as she washed her face in the water basin and brushed the knots out of her long, crow-black tresses. The queen's furtiveness was nothing new. Hara Duja would place all her faith in that string of crusty, old advisers before she even thought about trusting Laya. But this was Luntok, the man who loved her unabashedly, who would give up his sword arm for a chance to be with her. Laya had thought she could read him as easily as she could read any of her cow-eyed worshippers. What if she had been wrong?

Laya tried to push her doubts aside as she made her way to the terrace. Her father was waiting, a pipe sticking out of the corner of his mouth as he sliced a sweet bun in half. Eti sat across from him, legs swinging underneath the table. She didn't look up as Laya sat down, her eyes glued to the gold pellet floating above her palm. Eti's goal for the next year was to pull from that pellet a metal filament no thicker than a strand of hair—an act, Laya knew, that required intense concentration.

"If it isn't my Buaya-Laya," her father greeted. "What would you like for breakfast? A tall glass of water, perhaps?" His eyes twinkled, and he smiled at her knowingly.

Unlike her sisters, Laya had inherited his sharp, clever chin. She regretted that she didn't inherit his smile as well. Her father had such a broad smile, which captivated everyone to whom it was directed. It was the smile of an inveigler, not a king.

"Water. Yes, we can start with that," she said as a servant set a glass and place setting in front of her.

"You disappeared early last night." He watched as she finished the water in a single gulp.

"Too much wine," she said, holding out her cup for the servant to refill.

"I suppose none of the boys you had fawning over you had anything to do with it."

"*Father*," she chided, the questions that had been plaguing her momentarily forgotten.

He chuckled, sending a cloud of pipe smoke over his shoulder. "You were always destined to break hearts, Laya. I pray to the gods you will spare mine."

She smiled into her lap. Her father was the only member of her family who didn't find her horrible.

"And what of your admirers, then?" she teased.

During the feast days, all the noblewomen flocked to the king, young and old, married and unmarried alike. Like Laya, they adored his colorful stories and booming laugh. It amazed her that her mother never got jealous. Maybe she was proud that the king could command such rapt attention. Laya surely was.

"You're very kind to think so highly of your father, but I'm afraid I'm too old for admirers." When he smiled at her, a burst of warmth spread inside her chest.

"Oh, Father," she said, "I could never think lowly of you."

The king and queen were nothing alike. At times, she wondered how they came to fall in love. They were born under different moons—her father, who laughed at the worst jokes if only to make the teller feel at ease; and her mother, who offered her thin, tight-lipped smiles only sparingly. As Laya grew older, she came to understand. Her mother was the firm, solid ground in which her father planted his roots. And for her mother, he was the tree that stretched high into the heavens. His branches swayed in the wind but didn't break.

Hara Duja needed someone who could enrapture and enchant, who bent to the court and its many demands—at least, on the surface. With his winning smile and his cleverness, her father could do all these things. Once, her mother remarked that he was more powerful than the rest of their family combined. Laya laughed then, but as she grew older, she realized it had never been a joke.

The king opened his mouth, surely to wave aside Laya's compliments, when something beyond her head caught his attention. "Ah, there you are, Dr. Sauros. Come, join us."

Laya turned. Her jaw dropped open. A man unlike anyone Laya had ever seen hung back at the entrance of the terrace. He wore ill-fitting Maynaran clothes—a shirt buttoned all the way to the throat and trousers that tapered off laughably above his knees—but he was not Maynaran. She could tell by the way he held himself, a stiff posture unknown to this island, and his western-style spectacles, which pinched his abnormally high-bridged nose.

When he opened his mouth, a peculiar nasal accent came out. If Laya had not been so stunned by the foreigner's presence, she might have laughed aloud. "Thank you, uh, Your Majesty," the man said.

He took a few tentative steps toward the table where Laya and her family were seated. Behind his spectacles, his eyes darted from side to side, overwhelmed by the sight of the Gatdulas. But when his gaze fell on Laya, his expression steadied. The spectacles magnified his eyes, which were round and bright and full of questions. Up close, he appeared curious, not overwhelmed. She scowled in return. He continued to stare brazenly at Laya, not as though she were a gift from the gods, but like she was some stubborn equation. If the king had not invited him over, she would have had the guards escort him out. Who did he think he was if not some common foreigner?

Laya didn't know this man, but she decided in that moment that she hated him.

"It's probably time for you to meet my daughters," Hari Aki said jovially. He gestured to them. "This here is Dayang Laya. And fiddling over there with her metals is my youngest, Dayang Eti."

Eti jerked to attention at the sound of her name. Her eyes settled on the stranger, blinking as if she had just noticed his presence. "Father, who is this?" she piped up.

Laya frowned at the king. "Yes, Father. Who *is* this?"

The king chortled, unperturbed by their questions. "Don't you see, darlings? I thought I'd surprise you." He rose and clapped the strange man on both shoulders. "This here is Dr. Ariel Sauros. He's one of the finest scholars on this side of the Untulu Sea. I've invited him to stay with us a while at the palace as our honored guest."

"I don't see what that has to do with us," Laya said.

To the king's right, the man named Ariel cleared his throat. Her gaze snapped to his. She could have sworn she heard him bite back a chuckle.

"I was about to get to that, my dear." Hari Aki looked pointedly at Laya, a silent warning sign she had seen over a thousand times before—*Be nice*. He drew another puff from his pipe, then guided Ariel to his side of the table. "Dr. Sauros is a skilled linguist, philosopher, and writer, among other things. He's traveled all the way from Orfelia, so I suspect we have a great deal to learn from each other."

"Orfelia?" Laya echoed, incredulous. "That pathetic little colony to the east?"

"They speak a wide variety of tongues in Orfelia, including Salmantican, which I hear is rather useful in the Sunset States," the king said, brushing off Laya's concerns with a wave of his hand. "I invited Dr. Sauros here to teach you some of them as your language tutor. Notwithstanding, he arrived much earlier than anticipated. We plan to announce his visit after the feast days, when we shall throw Dr. Sauros the celebration he deserves."

"So, the Orfelian is to remain a secret. At least, until the feast days are over." Eti, who couldn't resist a bit of intrigue, perked up in interest.

Hari Aki beamed at her. "Precisely, my dear. And until then, your mother and I are relying on your discretion."

Laya's eyes narrowed. "But—"

"Dr. Sauros may be our secret for now. But in the meantime, I hope you will treat him with the respect he deserves," her father said calmly. He looked back at her with his inveigling smile, and the last protest died on her lips.

Another lie. Laya knew from the thin crease in the king's forehead—the same crease that appeared each time he brushed off the myriad sycophants prowling about court. She gave the Orfelian a cold stare. He was busy pulling at his sleeves, visibly uncomfortable in his borrowed clothes. Her father was too clever. He wouldn't reveal his hand, no matter how hard she pressed. Neither would Mother, nor Luntok. As for the foreigner—Laya's gaze hardened the longer she observed him.

The Orfelian was hiding something. However, it was not the time to pressure him for answers. Laya returned the king's smile with one of her own. "Yes, Father," she said, nodding. "I understand."

Primly, Laya reached for a sweet bun from the center of the table. The Orfelian took a seat across from her. Hari Aki engaged him in cordial conversation, and she let the subject fall for the time being. Out of the corner of the eye, she watched the man. He was more than some bumbling fool, as she had assumed when he'd first appeared on the terrace. Several times over the course of their breakfast, she caught him staring back. He had an inquisitive, nonthreatening gaze, but it was constant enough to make Laya clench her teeth.

A servant swept over with a fresh pot of tea. Laya glanced at the Orfelian over the gold-encrusted rim of her cup. Notes of citrus and honey wafted from the liquid's surface, tickling her nostrils. The Orfelian's foreign features blurred in the hot steam—with time, she might make sense of them.

She frowned into her tea. Her mother and father, and now this Orfelian—they were playing a game of bluffs, the lot of them. They could lie to her as much as they liked. Laya knew how to play this game too. She did not possess her father's smile, but she liked to think she had inherited his cleverness. And, unlike the others, she knew who would be the first to crack.

Two

LETTERS FROM THE EAST

Dear Nelo,

My comrade, my dream, my love—

For the hundredth time, I find myself thinking about how much easier it would be if I, like you, were dead.

I sound like an ungrateful, sorry sap—which we both know I am. Allow me to start again.

I write to you from Maynara, the land of gods and spirits; the same Maynara in the tales they told us when we were boys. I never believed in those myths. I was wrong, as I have been wrong about so many things.

All of Maynara vibrates with a magic too ancient to name. It whispers in the wind that rustles through the nipa palms. It hums through the cracks in the stone walls that line the palace. The queen can erect islands with a jerk of her fingers. She granted me protection in exchange for my services. And I will serve her willingly, as I've served so many masters before her.

I sold my soul to buy more time on this unforgiving slab of earth—a gift, my love, I wish I could offer you.

Has it truly been a year since the rebellion fell? I whisper your names every night as a kind of penance: Nelo, Israh, Elazar, Rufina. No incantation will bring you back from the killing fields. They told me what happened in Orfelia after I fled. How the Salmanticans hunted you down and shoved you in front of King Orfelio's firing squads. How, unlike me, you stayed true to your word and kept fighting until your last breath.

I was a coward, Nelo. I could not watch you perish, and now I am haunted by your death. When I close my eyes, I hear your rousing war songs and raucous laughter. When I dream, I see you, muzzled like a dog, knee deep in mud before a row of bayonets.

One year since you died, and I have not stopped running since. I have survived thus far by sheer luck and an aptitude for chemical synthesis—what too many fools have dubbed alchemy *and what you used to call my* remunerative gift. *Precioso is more a curse than anything. Without the money it gave me, I would not have thrust weapons into your hands and dreams inside your head. Precioso is the reason you are dead.*

A necessary evil, you once said. But you, who have seen my mind and body bare, you understood my guilt more than anyone. We watched how the precioso stripped even the frailest laborers of their natural weaknesses and turned them into fine-tuned machines. Round the clock, they would toil until their impossible strength faded to mind-numbing addiction. Before our eyes, they transformed into emaciated skeletons while their masters grew fat on blood-won riches.

These masters—I thought I could drain their wealth and funnel it toward your rebellion. You were my dream, Nelo, the one person who could bring about their demise. But not even precioso could turn the game in our favor. Look at what it has cost us. When I left Orfelia, I vowed never to touch the infernal drug again.

But I lie to myself, as I lie to all those around me. You know this.

Six months ago, I met a man who defies all I know of mankind and divinity. He introduced himself as the queen's brother, Maynara's exiled prince. I thought him a swindler, but like Hara Duja, he bears godlike gifts. He suffered from tremors that seized his entire body and caused excruciating muscle stiffness. My precioso is the sole substance that alleviates the pain, and he had been searching for it for decades. He knows it is not a cure, but a costly reprieve from human weakness.

The prince and I have struck a deal. I will produce precioso for him and his sister. In exchange, I have been granted asylum in Maynara, free from the Salmanticans, free from the bounty on my head. I have done nothing to deserve this fortunate end.

My nobler friends have perished, and I live in their stead. I choose a haunted life with you as my ghost. I write to you, Nelo, even though you are gone. Even though you cannot reproach me for my mistakes. Even though you cannot grant me forgiveness.

I abandoned my heart to save my head. Now you know this. Would you still love me if you lived?

—Ariel

Ten

DUJA

Duja heard her husband's laughter all the way from the entrance hall of the eastern wing. It echoed across the gilded nooks in the coffered ceiling. She took a right down the narrow servants' passageway and followed it to the open door at the end. The king brightened when she stepped inside. The Orfelian, garbed in what Duja recognized as the king's old clothes, dropped to a nervous bow beside him.

"There you are, my love," Hari Aki said, holding out his hand to her. "Come see what we've done with the place."

Duja scanned the room. Pineapple silk drapes did not cascade from the ceilings. Gilded ornaments did not adorn the paneled wood. The walls were plain even for the eastern wing, which stood barren most of the year. The air inside was stale. Light shone dully through the opaque panels of the window shades. All were sealed shut, and Duja wondered how long it had been since they were last opened. Before the eastern wing collapsed, the room had once served as a break area for the servants of their guests' private households. Hara Duja had not dared house anyone there after the second accident. Part of her agreed with the rumors: the eastern wing was cursed.

When it came to the Orfelian, however, she didn't have a choice. During the feast days, nobles with keen ears and prying eyes crawled like fire ants across the palace grounds. The Orfelian, with his peculiar features and foreign accent, was sure to provoke questions. If one of Duja's subjects caught sight of him, vicious rumors would spread across the island like her brother's wildfire. How long before they found out who he was and about his precioso? No, Duja needed to keep him out of sight until Mariit quieted. The eastern wing was her only option—no one would search for trouble there.

Duja turned to the Orfelian. "I hope your new workshop is to your liking."

"Yes, Your Majesty," he said, nodding enthusiastically. "I think this workshop will suit my needs perfectly."

A long, narrow table of unfinished rosewood stood at the center of the room. Duja ran a finger over its rough, dusty surface. The table had been there for years. As for the cupboards at the back of the room opposite the paneled windows—that morning, the Orfelian and Aki had hauled them down from the upper floors. Duja balked at the idea of her husband doing this sort of labor, but he had insisted. The fewer servants milling about the eastern wing, the better.

Through the cupboards' glass doors, Duja spied several canisters of varying sizes, some as stout as teakettles and others as slender as bamboo flutes. Many were unlabeled, but the Orfelian had given her the names of the ingredients he needed. Duja didn't recognize most of them—chemicals with strange, multi-syllabic names—but she had passed this list on to General Ojas, who'd sent one of his most trusted guards to the city proper to acquire them.

"I see you've already received the materials," Duja said with a small, approving grin. "Unfortunately, my people were not able to find the quantities you requested, but we've put in an order—"

"Oh, no, these will be more than enough for a sample batch," the Orfelian said, then turned pink in the cheeks when he realized he had interrupted her. He bowed his head and added a brief *Your Majesty* in one breath.

Hari Aki's eyes twinkled when he glanced between Duja and the Orfelian. Unlike Duja, he was amused by the young man's occasional breaches of formality. "If you'll allow us, Duja," the king said, "I was just about to give Dr. Sauros here the lay of the land."

That was his name—Dr. Ariel Sauros. The Orfelian had told Duja this when they'd spoken during the dawn feast, but she still had trouble thinking of him as anything more than an outsider.

"Allow me to accompany you," she said, leading the way out of the workshop. Her muscles screamed in protest when she reached the staircase. Ariel's precioso couldn't come soon enough. Even when the tremors did not plague her, their effects lingered—an ache that seeped deeper into her bones with each passing day. Precioso would slow the tremors' progression, but the Orfelian had told her how it had poisoned the people in his homeland. The sickest ones craved the drug with a feverish desperation, consuming it before water, before food, until their bodies wasted away.

Even her husband had shared the warnings from his research; precioso addiction would creep in slowly, then all at once. However, there were ways to mitigate the risks. Once Ariel started producing it for her, she'd have to limit herself to small, sparing doses. Duja prayed that the Orfelian's guidance—and the discipline she'd built over the past twenty-two years of her reign—would save her from such a fate.

On their way upstairs, Aki remarked over his shoulder, "As

happy as we are that you've come to stay with us, Ariel, we do hope you understand the delicacy of your presence here."

Duja bit her lip to conceal her smile. Her husband was not a man for straight talk. Every other sentence hid a riddle of a sort. In a number of words, the king had made one thing clear. No one was to know about how Ariel Sauros truly came to Maynara, nor the fact that the queen commissioned him to produce precioso.

She glanced at the Orfelian. Behind his thin wire-framed spectacles, understanding flickered in his eyes. "Yes, Your Majesty," he said, this time in a careful, obsequious tone. "I understand."

The king would never outright threaten him, but Duja could not deny the guilt simmering in her stomach. They had asked people to lie for them before, but the Orfelian was a different case. The previous day, Ariel had briefly spoken of the horrors awaiting him back home. The westerners slaughtered his friends and robbed him of everything he had. She sensed the sadness in Ariel because the same sadness lived at the core of Duja's being.

An unbearable hollowness swelled in her chest as she ascended to the upper apartments of the eastern wing. When Duja's mother was alive, she would flood these halls with heady banana-flower perfume. If Duja closed her eyes, she could still smell it, and her heart lurched at the memory. Her kind, unsuspecting mother. Duja wanted to lean over Ariel's shoulder and whisper: *I, too, know what it's like to lose.*

They stopped on the second story. The king had assigned Ariel a set of apartments in a dark corner of the eastern wing. They stood in front of the modest sitting room adjoining Ariel's bedchamber. The sitting room offered a small writing desk, an antique divan with a lattice cane back, and, if they rolled back the window screens, an unobstructed view of the central courtyard.

"As we discussed earlier, you'll have one servant to attend to your chambers. Otherwise, you will not be disturbed," the king said.

Ariel shook his head and tried to protest. "That's kind of you, but a servant really won't be necessary."

"Nonsense," Hari Aki said. "I don't think you realize how valuable your services are, Dr. Sauros. One servant is the least we can offer in return."

The other man remained silent. Duja saw from his conflicted expression that Ariel was not accustomed to such luxuries. How different he was from the horde of highborns who'd bombarded Duja during the dawn feast. She knew not to be too critical of her own subjects, but they were the reason she dreaded the feast days year after year. The constant cavorting, the endless stream of requests—it was Duja's duty as queen to entertain them, but to her, the feast days felt more like a military campaign than a celebration. Compared to that spectacle, Ariel's humble presence, despite the risk it posed in Mariit, was a welcome relief.

Beyond the window screens, angry shouts rang out from the courtyard below. Duja's ears perked up—her daughters' voices. She sighed and turned to her husband.

"I'll see to it," Hari Aki murmured as he backed out of the sitting room.

Ariel watched the king head downstairs, confused. "Is something the matter?"

"Nothing out of the ordinary," Duja said with a shake of her head. "It seems Laya and Bulan are fighting again."

Duja had long struggled to mitigate the tensions between her eldest daughters. If not for their shared Gatdula traits—murky, green-flecked eyes and deep-brown skin—one would never guess they'd come from the same womb. Their weekly clashes, though trivial and short-lived, reflected a deep-seated fracture between the sisters, which Duja often blamed herself for.

She crossed the sitting room and struggled to pry open the window screen. Her fingers had gone rigid, a warning of coming tremors. Ariel rushed to her side and helped her slide the screen open a few inches. Duja offered him a small smile of thanks, then glanced through the window. She half expected to find her daughters at each other's throats. What she saw was even more surprising. Laya and Bulan weren't fighting, nor were they in the courtyard alone. Eti was scampering across the tiles to stand between them.

"Are you ready?" Eti's voice, small and childlike, floated up to Ariel's sitting room. The girl raised her right palm. A pellet of pure gold rose about a foot above her head, its rounded surface glinting in the sunlight.

Duja let out a delighted laugh. "I don't believe it. They're playing a game," she said, amazed, and waved Ariel over to watch. He stood behind her shoulder, the window screen concealing most of his profile.

Down in the courtyard, Eti made the first move. Her eyes darted between her sisters, deciding upon her target. After a few seconds' deliberation, she drew her hand back and hurled the pellet at Bulan. The pellet zoomed across the courtyard in a yellow streak. Bulan was ready. She lunged to the side, catching the pellet with the flat edge of her sword. It soared back to Eti, who jumped to catch it with a satisfied cheer.

"Your turn, Laya!" she cried, casting the pellet in her other sister's direction.

But neither Bulan nor Eti could match Laya's winds, which cut through the air like a dagger. Laya needed only to thrust out her hands, and a blast erupted across the courtyard, rattling the windows in their metal frames. The blast whisked the pellet high above the girls' heads. It sailed over fifty feet away to the opposite end of the courtyard, before crashing to a stop a few inches in front of the entrance to the palace gardens.

"Whoa," Ariel whispered, astonished.

In the courtyard, Bulan groaned. "Laya! We agreed to keep it within bounds," she yelled.

Eti crossed her arms and pouted. "I don't care what you said. I'm not fetching it."

"Well, I'm not fetching it," Laya yelled back.

"What's going on here?" the king called. Duja caught sight of the top of his head as he stepped out of the eastern wing. He joined his daughters in the courtyard, his hands clasped behind his back.

Eti pointed at Laya. "She's cheating."

Duja could see Laya roll her eyes all the way from the sitting room. "Please. There are no winners or losers in this game," Laya said.

"So?" Bulan asked.

Laya shrugged. "If you can't win, you can't cheat. Everyone knows that."

"Oh, I don't know if that's true," Aki said in a good-natured tone.

"Of course it's true," Laya said. Eti stuck her tongue out at her, and Laya stuck out her tongue back.

With Laya's attention on her younger sister, Aki barreled toward her, catching her off guard. He hauled Laya over his shoulder like a sack of rice. "Does this count as cheating, my dear?" he asked.

Laya pounded his back while her sisters howled. "Let me down, Father! That's not fair!" she cried. But Laya could never be angry with her father. Even as she protested, tears of laughter streamed down her cheeks.

"I thought you couldn't cheat!" Aki teased.

"I'll save you, Laya!" Eti ran for them, tackling their father at the knees. With a dramatic cry, he tumbled to the ground and Laya with him. Before they could get up, Bulan threw herself atop the pile. All four of them collapsed on the tiled ground, their shoulders shaking as they laughed.

Warmth burst inside Duja's chest as she watched the scene unfold. She leaned against the glass, her joy numbing the stabs of pain shooting down her fingertips. "They're happy," she said, more to herself than to Ariel.

He gave her a shy smile. "A happy family indeed."

Duja looked back at her children. It was so rare to see them like this, especially Laya. A broad, unguarded grin stretched across Laya's face. She looked as young as Eti when she smiled like that. Duja saw bits of herself and Aki in Laya's face; but, with her sharp gaze and delicate features, Laya looked most like her uncle.

Oh, Pangil. Lately, she saw her brother everywhere. Duja still pictured Pangil as a young man, lithe and handsome with skin the shade of narra wood. She remembered when they played in the courtyard as children. As she watched her daughters, another rare and tender memory struck her, of another sunny day, the day Imeria Kulaw challenged Duja to a race.

"First to the garden gate wins the loser's yam cakes," Imeria had said. She was smaller than Duja, and she ran on much shorter legs. That did not deter the Kulaw girl. She set her jaw as she tucked her hair into a neat plait that wound over Imeria's shoulder like an eel. Imeria had thick, straight hair the shade of ink. For weeks, Duja had itched to touch those strands. Surely, they weren't as silky as they looked.

Duja's cheeks had heated at the mere thought. She tightened the straps of her sandals to distract herself from Imeria's troublesome beauty. When Duja reached down, a shadow stretched across the tiles at her feet. She looked up.

Pangil stood before them, coconut flakes dusting the corners of his lips. He had been raiding the palace kitchen for sweets again. It was the first time in days she saw no contempt in his expression. He stared down at her and placed his hands on his hips.

"A race, you say?" Pangil said.

To Duja's right, Imeria gave him a challenging grin.

In the end, Ojas gave the signal. He was a junior guard then, with a young man's gait and a trim, dark beard. Though he always wore the same stoic expression, he doted on Duja and would do whatever she asked.

"Ready . . . Set . . . Go!" Ojas called, his voice booming across the courtyard like thunder.

But Pangil had taken off a split second before Ojas had given the go-ahead.

"No fair!" Imeria cried out. As Duja opened her mouth to protest, Imeria took off after Pangil. She dashed across the courtyard, her plait shooting from the back of her head like a dart. Though she was a full head shorter than Pangil, she caught up close enough to lunge at his knees. Pangil toppled to the ground under the younger girl's weight.

"Hey!" he cried.

"Pangil, wait!" Duja sprinted for them, fear rising in her throat. She had seen the little tyrant her brother became when angered.

But Pangil didn't strike Imeria. He didn't even yell at her. Instead, he threw his head back and laughed. To Duja's shock, Imeria joined him. They laughed until their bellies ached and they ran out of breath.

So rarely had they been that happy, the three of them. That moment was a small, lonely island. If it didn't glow so brightly amidst Duja's ocean of memories, she'd have been convinced it was nothing but some faraway dream.

Duja thought of that moment as she stared at her family. At Laya, who kept her softest angles hidden, even though she was lovelier for them. Laya, whose dark eyes burned with unharnessed potential. Fearless, passionate Laya, who might one day build things far greater than the walls her younger self tore down.

"So much like Pangil," Duja murmured. For the first time, the thought didn't fill her with dread.

"Pangil," Ariel echoed, jolting Duja from her thoughts.

"Yes?" she said, embarrassed. She didn't realize she had uttered her brother's name out loud.

"Will he also come to the palace?" Ariel asked, hesitant.

Duja faltered. Would she allow Pangil to return to Maynara? The same question had been plaguing Duja since the previous evening. She and the king had agreed to wait until the end of the feast days before they entertained the possibility. Given the facts, Pangil had told the truth. Ariel was a worthy messenger, and so far, Duja's intuition told her to trust him. He testified as to precioso's efficacy on her brother, and it was thanks to Pangil that Duja had access to the drug. Maybe Pangil deserved Duja's pardon, but the feast days were no time to grant it. The last thing Duja needed was a scandal to erupt concerning Maynara's exiled prince. No—Pangil needed to be dealt with quietly. She could not risk seeing him until the nobles left Mariit.

In the meantime, Ariel promised to concoct a small quantity of precioso for her to sample. Duja didn't need her brother's word when she could test the drug herself.

The queen saw no need to tell the Orfelian any of this. She shook her head and diverted her gaze. "The matter is still being debated," she said curtly.

Unlike the nobles, Ariel did not pry. He closed his mouth, and they turned back to the courtyard below. Bulan pulled her father and sisters to their feet. Hari Aki dusted his clothes off, still chuckling to himself. He reached for his three daughters, bundling them into a bodily embrace.

Duja's heart swelled once more. "The king is a good man," she told Ariel, turning away from the window.

"He is, Your Majesty." He nodded in agreement and grabbed hold of the window screen. Duja shook her head, gesturing for him to stand aside.

The tremors hadn't withered her body to dust. Not yet. From closing a window to combing her own hair, the tasks were small victories for Duja but victories all the same. Precioso would make them easier. Until then—

The queen reached past Ariel for the window screen. This time, with steady fingers, she slid it shut behind him.

Eleven

IMERIA

Imeria fanned herself with one hand as her gaze swept across the tournament ring. Her thick golden bangles glared in the light as they slid down her wrist. The crowd's raucous cheers pierced the air. They shouted the names of their prized warriors, an endless list of nobles that shuffled year after year. Each spectator had their favorites, but only one contender would win.

"I've brought a present for you," Datu Gulod said by way of greeting. He sat beside her under the parasol shielding her from the afternoon sun.

Imeria wrinkled her nose at the intrusion. "Are you always fishing for scandal?" she said dryly. It was bold to address a widow like her with such familiarity, and Gulod was fully aware of this.

His grin widened. "I'd risk anything to remain in the presence of such an enchanting woman."

She rolled her eyes. The entire court knew that Gulod had no interest in women, enchanting or otherwise. He was several years her junior and much younger than the other datus. Court gossip informed her that he doted on the page boy who warmed his bed at night. For his bloodline to continue, however, he would need to take a wife. Imeria doubted Gulod had ever considered her for this role. The lesser nobility boasted no shortage of beautiful, unmarried women, fertile of womb and free of baggage, all of whom were eager to marry up the ranks.

"Find another woman to shower with your affection," she said, dismissing him with a wave of her hand. "I'm here to watch my son."

They were seated in the stands high above the tournament platform. Several levels below, crowds gathered, eager to watch Maynara's highborn sons battle each other for a sliver of glory. She spied Luntok on the left side of the platform. He was warming up with Vikal. Imeria smiled as she watched Vikal correct Luntok's posture, nodding in encouragement each time Luntok followed his instructions. Vikal had long before proved that he was not the Kulaws' groveling lackey, and Imeria owed him a great deal.

He had done more than train Luntok over the years. He had cared for him, raised him. He'd taught him strength when Imeria, weak as she'd been after her husband died, was unable. Imeria yearned to make up for those sad, painful years, during which Vikal proved himself a better parent than she could ever hope to be.

This was the first year Vikal deemed Luntok ready to compete in the tournament. *The best I've ever trained,* Vikal assured her before they left the capital. *I think you'll be pleased, my lady.*

I am already pleased, Vikal, she'd said. And as Imeria watched how Luntok moved in the pit below—his sword arm strong, his hands and feet gliding in perfect symmetry—a savage pride burst inside her chest. *My son.* Luntok was a man, and a worthy heir of the Kulaw legacy.

Gulod followed Imeria's gaze. "Ah, yes, Luntok. I've hardly seen him since the start of the feast days. Where have you been keeping him?"

"Where do you think?" she said testily. Gulod knew about Luntok's infatuation with Dayang Laya, same as the rest of the court, much to the queen's chagrin.

He chuckled, twirling the stack of rings on his pointer finger. "I mean no offense to your son, but that girl could eat a grown man alive. Shall I warn him for you?"

"Worry about yourself, my lord." She looked at him out of the corner of her eye. Imeria was more than some lovesick girl, and she'd been playing these games far longer than Datu Gulod realized. Whatever he came here for, if he gave her one reason not to trust him, she'd eat him alive too.

He leaned back, hearing the warning in her tone, and cleared his throat. "I'll leave you soon to enjoy the tournament. But first, I'd be honored if you could open my gift." From the inner pocket of his vest, Datu Gulod retrieved a small box of smooth, unfinished mahogany. He pressed it into her hands.

Curious, Imeria lifted the lid. Inside, on a thin bed of velvet, lay a golden hair comb inlaid with drops of pearl and jade. "How beautiful," she said, almost in the form of a question. The comb *was* beautiful. Why he had given it to her, Imeria couldn't begin to guess.

Gulod stared at her. She caught a knowing gleam in his eyes. "Go on then," he said in a slow, careful whisper. "Take a closer look."

She reached into the box to pick up the comb. When she touched it, the velvet underneath shifted to reveal something hard and thin. Imeria glanced up at Gulod, who nodded almost imperceptibly. With featherlight fingers, she lifted the velvet and found a tiny trio of vials, each containing white crystals as fine as sand. Imeria's heartbeat quickened, and she pulled the velvet back up before anyone could see.

Gulod lifted the comb from the box. "May I?"

Wordlessly, Imeria nodded and turned to the side. He ran his fingers through her hair, pushing it back—far too intimate a gesture for a place like this. Heads turned toward them as the nobles, seated in the stands to their right, took notice. Imeria willed herself not to scowl at the rising chorus of titters.

Gulod leaned forward, easing the comb through her silky strands, his breath hot against her ear. "Precioso from the west. A pain in the ass to procure, but I thought a lot about what you said," he whispered.

Ah. A smirk tugged at the corner of her lips. She'd mentioned precioso when Gulod had visited her in the south last season. From what she understood, it was a fickle substance; few souls on earth knew how to produce a mediocre sample, much less at the quality she desired. Precioso was illegal in Maynara, but that was just as well. Gulod was a clever man, and smuggling was his singular talent. He was known to accept delicate requests, and he didn't even ask what she needed it for. The promise of payment was good enough for him.

Imeria snapped the box shut and slid it into the pocket of her skirt for safe keeping. "Come dine with me later tonight, perhaps after the tournament," she said. "I must thank you properly for your generous gift."

"The pleasure is all mine, Datu Kulaw." He stood and took her hand, brushing it against his lips.

She watched him return to his own seat as the whispers in the stands grew louder. Let them talk. Imeria cared little for their idle gossip. Her fingers curled against the thin fabric of her skirt, itching for the vials nestled beneath it. Knowing they were within reach rendered her breathless, giddy.

Later. From the platform below, drums sounded. Imeria sat

up straight as a hush washed over the crowd. She found Luntok in the pit once again. He was waiting beneath the platform with Vikal and the rest of the warriors. Her chest filled with a premature spark of triumph. She would have the rest of the night to deal with the precioso. The tournament was about to begin.

This was the one feast-day event Imeria enjoyed, perhaps because the royal family rarely attended. With the exception of Bulan, sword fighting did not interest the Gatdulas. What use did they have for weapons when the power of Mulayri shot through their fingertips? But for ordinary Maynarans, this was their prized sport. Imeria used to sneak past her maids to watch the Kulaw warriors train on the grounds below their estate. Her father had been the strongest of them all. He'd stood tall as a pillar amidst the browning haycock hills, his rousing orders carrying in the salt-sprayed wind. That was one of Imeria's few memories of him.

Before her father went to war, he represented the Kulaws in the tournament alongside the fiercest warriors in the kingdom. The tournament was ceremonial, intended to unite the ruling families around their shared sword-fighting tradition. Over the centuries, it grew into Maynara's fiercest competition. It was a frequent source of shame for the losers—like the Gulods, who cared more about their ledger books than they did for the martial arts. But for the families with war in their veins—notably the Kulaws, Lumas, and Tanglaws—the tournament was their one chance at glory. Vikal had represented the Kulaws since Luntok was a child. Now it was Luntok's turn.

Below the stands, crowds swarmed the tournament platform, held up on rickety stilts. Imeria counted hundreds of spectators, stuffing their mouths with fried fish balls, chanting battle songs, and drinking. Judging by the rumble, the crowd was growing rowdier by the minute. The beating drums announced the first fight of the tournament, the beast-like Utu Luma versus a scrawnier Sandata upstart who was in over his head. The crowd cheered as Utu Luma charged across the platform. The air filled with the sounds of clashing metal as the Sandata boy matched him blow for blow.

Imeria did not pay their fight any heed. She stared at her son as the noise swelled to a ferocious pitch. This was a far cry from the Kulaws' secluded training grounds. Luntok had never battled in such conditions before. She worried he would lose his head amidst the surrounding chaos.

But rather than decenter him, Luntok seemed to draw energy from the crowd. Imeria recognized his stance—the squaring of his shoulders, the firm tilt of his head—Luntok was deep in concentration by the time the tournament judges announced his name.

She held her breath as he mounted the platform, the wooden boards already smeared with the rust-brown traces of bloodstains. People rarely died in the tournament. After all, it was a friendly affair. Victory came in two ways, by knocking one's opponent off the platform or by pushing them to surrender. Participants might not fight to the death, but they could still draw blood. It was a well-known fact that the tournament judges were biased worms who turned a blind eye when their favorites played dirty.

The Tanglaws, expectedly, were among the judges' favorites. Across the platform waited Datu Tanglaw's son, Bato. Imeria frowned. She had heard after the dawn feast of their plot to secure Bato's betrothal to Laya by the end of the week. No doubt Luntok was aware of this. He unsheathed his sword and stalked toward Bato with a face of pure venom.

In the stands, Imeria's hands balled into fists. *Don't you dare lose your calm,* she wanted to scream. Luntok was stronger and more skilled than the Tanglaw boy, but Imeria knew his weakness: if Bato taunted him about Laya, Luntok wouldn't just retaliate. Luntok would implode.

Bato drew out his sword, half turning to face the watching crowd. His taunt echoed up to the stands so the highborn spectators could hear. "First fight, Kulaw? Don't worry, I'll go easy on you."

Luntok barked out a laugh as the two young men began to circle each other on the platform. "Give me your worst, Tanglaw. Wouldn't want to lie to Hara Duja about your valor when they're done scraping you off the floor," he called.

At Luntok's remark, titters rippled through the crowd. Bato stiffened and raised his sword. Luntok followed suit. They stared at each other, any attempt at banter screeching to an abrupt halt.

"On my mark . . . Begin," a deep voice boomed from somewhere in the pit, cutting across the rising cheers.

Bato made the first move. He lunged for Luntok, who dodged his sword easily, making the Tanglaw lose his balance.

Bato righted himself and attacked Luntok again. Luntok parried and made a swipe at Bato's face. Bato leaped out of the way, but not before the tip of Luntok's blade scraped his left cheek. Droplets of blood dripped down the side of his neck. The cut wasn't deep, but it was all he needed to distract Bato.

Wiping the blood with the back of his hand, Bato raised his sword to attack from above. Stupid choice. Luntok knocked the blade to the side, using the opportunity to close in on him, then drove the hilt of his sword into his stomach.

The surrounding crowd roared as Bato doubled over, heaving. Luntok backed off and let Bato pull himself together. Up in the stands, Imeria allowed herself a smug smile. The court could spite the Kulaws as much as they liked. Luntok had honor in him after all, and the fight was only beginning.

Though Imeria was no warrior, she could not help but marvel at the fight. Her son was stronger and more muscular than Bato, yes, but Bato had a different fighting style. Where Luntok relied on overwhelming his opponents with animalistic ferocity and brute force, Bato practiced an evasive, serpentlike technique. Imeria had watched Bato compete in the tournament the previous year. He had made it to the later rounds because he'd tired his opponents out, managing to slip away from their attacks with surprising finesse; only when their arms were quaking from exhaustion, too weak to swing their swords, did he fight back with full force and knock them out of their misery.

But when Bato came at her son once more, Luntok made him abandon his usual tactics. Bato was forced to attack again and again until he was the one gasping for breath like a dying fish. Luntok fended off his advances with ease. It was when the fight in Bato's eyes began to dull that Luntok moved to the offensive.

He went in, first with a steep angle strike that Bato used all his remaining strength to deflect. The plea for surrender was there on the tip of Bato's tongue. Luntok had to coax it out of him. Farther and farther, Luntok advanced. He didn't stop until he had Bato cornered at the edge of the platform.

Bato's sword hand shook. A hush swept over the crowd. Imeria straightened in her seat.

"Do you yield?" Luntok asked. From up in the stands, Imeria could make out his cocky grin.

Bato glowered. A beat passed. Then his posture shifted. "You're too late, you know," he said.

"Late for what?" Luntok demanded.

"Dayang Laya," Bato said, loud enough for the spectators to hear.

Luntok froze. Imeria's stomach sank. She resisted the urge to run down from the stands and shake him. *Next to you, Bato Tanglaw is an ugly, humorless asp. Don't listen to him.*

But Luntok had already taken the bait. "What about her?" he growled.

Bato leaned forward and lowered his voice. As she watched their conversation unfold, Imeria chewed her lip. She couldn't hear Bato's next words, but she saw fury spread across Luntok's handsome features. He raised his sword and took a swing. He could hardly control his aim, and Bato was able to slip away. Imeria's fingers clawed into the edge of her seat. She wanted to scream in outrage. He had allowed himself to get distracted. And he lost his biggest advantage.

Bato didn't hold back. He moved in so fast, Luntok could barely react. Bato's blade sliced through the air, sharp steel glinting in the sun. He feinted, tricking Luntok into a deep lunge. Then Bato swung his sword at Luntok's exposed right arm.

Imeria gasped. Out of the corner of her eye, she could see a dozen heads turn toward her. She ignored them and stared at her son. Blood dripped down Luntok's bicep, pooling at the hilt of his sword. From a distance, the wound didn't look fatal, but it was deeper than any injury Luntok had yet endured.

"Had enough, Kulaw?" Bato jeered.

Luntok threw himself at the other man with a snarl. This time, he attacked with every ounce of his strength. Bato couldn't fend off Luntok for long—not when her son was like this. Imeria stared at Luntok in awe. She had never seen him fight this way before. He moved in a trance, delivering blow after decisive blow. Bato's arms shook from the sheer force of it.

Around the platform, the crowd grew louder and louder. Their energy invigorated Luntok. They were calling for blood, and he planned to give it to them.

Bato tried to recover from his shock, but Luntok ended the fight before he could. A final cut from below ripped Bato's sword from his hands. It clattered to the rust-stained platform at their feet. As Bato scrambled to retrieve it, Luntok pressed his blade against Bato's throat. The tip grazed the skin below his chin, close enough to draw blood.

Bato stared at him, dumbfounded. "Yield," he whispered hoarsely. "I yield."

No one dared move. Luntok kept his blade to Bato's throat, chest heaving. Stunned silence filled the air. Not until Vikal jumped onto the platform and held Luntok's arm in the air did he realize that he'd won the fight. From all four sides of the platform, the crowd exploded into cheers.

Imeria leaped to her feet, almost knocking the servant holding the parasol above her head to the ground. Her heart sang as she shrieked in triumph. She beamed at Luntok. She couldn't tear her gaze from him. *My son, my son, my son.*

Nobles flooded to Imeria in the stands to congratulate her on Luntok's win. She did not spare any of them a glance. She kept her eyes glued to Luntok, down on the platform. Vikal was still holding him up. Luntok blinked, wide-eyed, stunned speechless by his own victory.

The cheers grew louder, drowning out the beating drums. Imeria's gaze swept over the crowd. The awe and admiration on their faces—she couldn't be imagining that.

The warriors clambered onto the platform. They swarmed Luntok, clapping him on the back, mussing his hair as they congratulated him on his first win. Pride swelled in Imeria's chest as she watched him. Finally, they saw what Imeria saw. Finally, they saw Luntok the way he was supposed to be seen. They gazed at him the same way Luntok gazed at his precious Laya—as if he were the key to their salvation. As if he were greater than the cosmos itself. As if he were a deity.

After the fight, Imeria saw Luntok for no longer than a minute. Vikal whisked him away with a handful of the other Kulaw warriors to celebrate. She smiled as she watched them drag Luntok deep into the alleyways of Mariit. Luntok deserved to relish this victory. She planned to congratulate him when he came home—hopefully in one piece and not too inebriated. Imeria had more important matters to address that evening.

Datu Gulod arrived at the Kulaws' town house early. One of the servants showed him to the small receiving room at the front of the house, where Imeria was reading. He swooped over and offered her the bouquet in his hands.

"You really have no sense of subtlety, do you?" she asked. She set her book down and accepted the flowers. They were lovely—like everything that passed through Gulod's greedy fingers—lush, bloodred lilies the size of dinner plates. Imeria handed them to her maid, who was waiting at her side. "Give them some water, please. We wouldn't want their beauty to fade."

"Your beauty hasn't faded, has it, Imeria?" Without waiting for an invitation, Gulod took a seat across from her on the divan and studied her openly. "You look exactly as you did when I was a boy."

"I'm not *that* much older than you," she said, annoyed. "And since when are we on a first name basis?"

"You may call me Namok, if you wish," Gulod said, grinning.

"I like to be familiar with the women I'm courting."

Imeria rolled her eyes. "Please. We aren't courting."

"What else would you call this little dance?" Gulod leaned back on the divan and crossed one leg over the opposite knee. He had changed into more extravagant clothes since she saw him at the tournament and was dressed in fine silks the shade of Xitai pears.

"A farce," she said curtly.

He chuckled. "It's a courtship of a sort. Call it whatever you like."

"I didn't think you were interested in wives, Namok." Imeria gave him a wry smile, although his choice of words caught her by surprise.

"No wives," he said, shaking his head. "But I would like to present myself as a partner for whatever endeavor it is you're planning."

Gulod's frankness made Imeria take pause. "And what makes you think I'm planning something?" she asked in a level tone.

Before he could answer, Imeria's maid returned to the receiving room with a bottle of palm wine. She poured them each a glass and asked, "Will you be requiring anything else, my lady?"

"That will be all." Imeria took a sip of the wine, staring at Gulod over the rim of her glass. They sat in tactful silence until the maid retreated into the kitchens.

"Precioso," he said, "is a peculiar drug. Did you know the industrialists out west force their workers to take it? I've heard that some of those slaves stay at the assembly line for five days straight without sleep."

"Horrible, isn't it?" she replied tonelessly. Imeria knew all about precioso and its horrifying uses. She'd heard how barons in the west used it to bring their subjects to heel. They pumped their colonies full of it until the people living there fell victim to precioso's addictive effects. It was an ingenious way to hollow out a native population, swifter and more lucrative than the plagues of yore. The westerners would simply count the days until the natives were too weak, too dependent on precioso, to fight back. And then, they'd shove the drug further down their throats.

Precioso not only enriched the westerners who trafficked it through every far-flung port. It also numbed fatigue so their victims could work long, arduous hours without once stopping to rest. Around the world, precioso kept thousands of workers chained to their overlords' factories, mines, and farmlands. It was a dreadful practice—enslavement by any other name. But that's not why she had asked Gulod to procure it for her.

"I've also heard rumors of a certain . . . resurgence. The return of a power long vanquished from the earth," he said. His eyes shot up to meet hers. "The Kulaws were once wielders of mind and flesh—the only enemies the Gatdulas truly feared."

"Once," she said in a soft voice. "Before Thu-ki fell and my ancestors bent the knee."

For her entire life, Imeria dreamed of Thu-ki, her family's fallen kingdom once carved into the southern tip of Maynara, and their magnificent powers now lost to history. She filled her son's head with these dreams, convinced him that one day, soon, his birthright would be within reach.

Gulod clicked his tongue. "Ah, but your father seemed to think that the power hadn't disappeared. That the Kulaws would rise again."

"Yes, well, the power would have been useful to them then." Imeria forced herself not to cower beneath Gulod's unwavering gaze.

These days, few people dared speak of her father's foolish

rebellion against the Gatdulas. Without their ancestral power in his veins, the late Datu Kulaw hadn't stood a chance. Imeria was told her father had been killed in a decisive battle that soiled the family legacy. She was a child of ten back then, but she hadn't forgotten what the rebellion had meant.

Neither had Datu Gulod. He took a long sip of his wine as he appraised her. "That brings me back to precioso. I've been wondering, What interest could a highborn lady possibly have in a dirty western drug? Forgive me if I'm wrong, Imeria, but I have my theories."

"You wouldn't have come all the way here unless you planned to share them."

Gulod was no half-wit. The theories he was hinting at danced dangerously close to the truth. If he guessed correctly, how could she know whether she could trust him?

"I've heard rumors concerning you," he said. "They say you're more than some sour-faced noblewoman. Why else would Hara Duja cast you out of the palace—you, her once-treasured companion? There had to be a reason she came to hate you so. She's afraid."

Her gut clenched at Gulod's words. She forced herself not to look away.

The wood of the divan creaked as he perched forward. The truth fell from his lips. "I believe the Kulaw power has risen once again. I believe you possess the spark that rose from the embers. And I believe precioso is the tinder you need to stoke the flame."

Imeria's breath hitched in her throat. She held his gaze. "Drugs that can enhance abilities the world hasn't seen in centuries. How on earth did you come up with that?" she said coolly. She thought herself a gifted liar, but Gulod saw straight through her.

"Do you find me fanciful?" he asked, quirking an eyebrow.

Her lips tightened. "I think you're a fool."

"Ah, but I'm not a fool, Imeria. And neither are you." He glanced over his shoulder to make sure none of the servants were within earshot, then lowered his voice. "I have resources, Datu Kulaw. And if you're planning what I think you're planning, you can't rely on precioso alone. You're going to need powerful friends."

Her fingers tingled with anticipation. She tried to calm herself by smoothing out her skirt. "Careful, Datu Gulod," she warned. "It sounds like you're offering far more than friendship."

Gulod set down his wineglass, the teasing gone from his tone. "I'm offering you my assistance, Imeria. You'll need it, I think."

"And what makes you think I can't manage on my own?"

"Because you are one woman, and the most abhorred datu at that," he told her candidly. "Power, gods blessed or not, means nothing without allies—and I can procure anything you need."

She frowned. His offer was tempting, but she didn't understand it. "Why would you help me at all, Namok? You're not known for your generosity."

Gulod's grin widened. "Allyship is a two-way street. I expect you'll find some way to repay the favor when you are queen."

She understood now. The Gatdulas had never held the Gulods in the highest regard. Their kadatuan sat too far to the south: their trade routes, their people, all in uncomfortably close proximity to the Kulaws. Long before the rebellion, the Gatdulas ignored the Gulods' pleas for newer roads and stronger defenses—all out of fear the Kulaws would co-opt those resources for their own gain. The money went instead to the Tanglaws, to the Lumas, families with already-thriving kadatuans and no need for the capital's generosity. Over the years, the Gatdulas had driven the

Gulods away with their blatant biases and casual neglect. Datu Gulod was wise to seek a kinder ally on the throne—one who would shower his kinsfolk with favors and line his coffers with gold. But he was wrong in assuming it would be Imeria.

A chill spread through her body. "It was never my intention to install myself as sovereign," she said. Never before had she dared utter her own treasonous thoughts aloud. In truth, Imeria could not place herself on the throne, even if she genuinely wanted to.

None could refute the fact that she had been exiled along with Duja's brother, the forgotten prince. Although Duja hadn't ordered Imeria to leave the realm, the queen's decision to banish them both from the capital had undeniable significance. It meant that Imeria Kulaw could not be trusted. That she was no different from her traitorous father—no different from Pangil, whose name few Maynarans dared utter, even after all this time. Already, she'd wasted countless years in an effort to shake off the accursed association. So she knew better than to try.

Surprise flickered over Gulod's face. "Then, pray tell, what was your intention?"

"Luntok," she murmured. "That honor should go to him."

"Your boy?" Gulod leaned back in his seat, unconvinced. "He's awfully young."

"Young, but beloved. You saw how they looked at him after the tournament today." Pride swelled in Imeria's chest once more when she remembered how the crowd had worshipped him.

Gulod's brow furrowed in confusion. "If all you want is to put Luntok on the throne, why not have him marry Laya? They seem to like each other enough."

Her expression hardened. "Hara Duja would never allow that to happen."

"Are you certain? Because marriage is much easier to negotiate than a coup."

Imeria shook her head. Although the rebellion was long over, it was futile to try to negotiate the terms her family had agreed to after they'd surrendered. Twenty-two years earlier, Hara Duja made it painfully clear that the Gatdulas would have no affiliation with the Kulaws and their ungodly bloodright. It didn't matter if Imeria threw herself at her feet and begged Duja to let her stay. Imeria's own naive words came back to her. *Turn me out and push me away. I am your heart, Duja, always.*

"If we want the throne, we must force Hara Duja out ourselves," she said in a hollow voice. "It is the only way."

"And what of Dayang Laya? Do you plan to expel her as well?" Gulod stroked his chin.

Imeria glowered. She would exterminate the entire Gatdula bloodline from the earth if she could, but Laya—Laya was a brash, empty-headed girl, but she was not her mother.

"Let me deal with her when the time comes," she told him. Imeria would restore her son's title and birthright. If everything went to plan, she would be able to grant Luntok his princess too.

Twelve
LAYA

Once the others had eaten breakfast and gone off on their own agendas, Laya followed Bulan to the upper terrace, where she stood looking over the palace gates and the long, narrow canal that flowed down to the giant balete tree at the heart of the city. She was fuming in silence, her shoulders hiked up to her ears.

"There's something odd about that Orfelian, don't you agree?" she said.

"Oh, drop it, won't you?" Bulan snapped from behind her.

Laya sniffed and folded over the balustrade. Sunlight slid like butter down the sides of the twisting spires dotting the skyline. Mariit melted beneath the midday heat, which had climbed to unbearable heights rarely seen in the city during the dry season. Laya thought about summoning a few clouds for shade, but she settled on a gentle breeze instead. She held her hand out above the latticed railing. The air rushed to meet her fingers in swirling currents that tickled her skin.

She sighed in relief and squinted up at her sister. Bulan crouched barefoot on the palace roof, balancing in the break between the two highest tiers. Her profile was silhouetted against the sun, its rays glaring off the laminated steel of her blade.

"I'll drop it when you get down from there," Laya said. She

had witnessed Bulan dart across the roofs with impressive speed over a dozen times before. Her sister took too much care to fall, but the sight of her standing so high above made Laya jitter.

"It helps to practice balance," Bulan explained. She tucked her sword back into its sheath and slid down the slope on the lower tier. Laya watched as her sister swung over the side and landed on the terrace with a graceful thump.

After breakfast, Laya had tried to discuss her theories regarding Ariel Sauros's sudden appearance at the palace, but Bulan refused to entertain any of them.

Have you considered that maybe Father truly invited him to be our language tutor? Bulan had said in the same exasperated tone she used when playing the role of Laya's handler.

At this, Laya seethed. She knew she was right to suspect the Orfelian. One doesn't sneak off to meet a language tutor in the midst of an opening feast. One doesn't hide a language tutor in a dusty corner of the palace where he wouldn't be seen.

Her sister had witnessed the same thing Laya had, but she could not be convinced. Bulan turned from the balustrade and made her way back inside the palace. "If you want to make it to the tournament, we need to leave soon."

"The tournament?" Laya scoffed. "Why on earth would I attend that?"

Bulan stared at her, half in shock, half in wonder. The corners of her lips turned up in a faint smile. "You truly didn't lie. He means nothing to you," she said with a chuckle.

Laya frowned. "What do you mean?"

She raised an eyebrow at her. "I thought you would want to watch the tournament, because Luntok will be competing for the first time this year. He's in love with you, after all. I thought he would have invited you."

"Oh. I—well." Laya stuck out her chin before Bulan could see her falter. "The tournament's a bore. Luntok may have invited me, but he knows I'd never agree to watch something like that."

Bulan shrugged and continued on her way. "Suit yourself."

A deep flush spread across Laya's cheeks as she watched Bulan's retreating back. Luntok *had* told her about the tournament—several times, in fact. Guilt churned in her stomach when she imagined how his eyes would have lit up at the sight of Laya in the stands. She told herself she was the one making a sacrifice by not attending. It was better this way—for Bulan to think Laya did not care for Luntok. But she *did* care for him. She loved Luntok from the deepest pits of her soul, and yet she'd completely forgotten his invitation to watch him compete.

Laya banished all questions of love from her mind as she swept across the terrace. She skipped down the stairs two steps at a time—Eti, thankfully, was not there to trip over—then barreled toward the eastern wing. For a long time, she had avoided looking in that direction, given the shame it brought her. Laya hadn't meant to destroy it, and she promised her mother she would do better. Still, the queen would never let her forget that accursed day. It was shortly after Laya had shown Luntok the entrance to the tunnel. Bulan had confronted her, swearing she caught a glimpse of Luntok lurking about the gardens. Their argument exploded into a whirlwind of insults and accusations. The blood of Mulayri surged in Laya's veins, clouding every last scrap of sense. In the throes of anger, the threads spun from Laya's grip, and the wind roared in her ears like a wrathful god. It was her power, not Laya, who'd won that battle. Her fingers still itched from the desperate desire to wrangle back control.

The accident had been years earlier. Since then, the eastern wing had stood empty—until now. Curiosity prompted her to march up to the doors of the eastern wing, where one of Ojas's men stood guard. "I request an audience with our guest," she said curtly.

Surprise flickered on the guard's face, but he did not deny her. "Shall I bring him to the main building, Dayang?" he asked.

"No," she said, shaking her head. "If you let me in, I shall call upon him myself."

Wordlessly, the guard moved. Laya was pleased, for it meant the guard hadn't received orders to forbid them from visiting the Orfelian. She swept past him and mounted the steps to the sparse apartments on the upper floor, taking note as she did so of the dusty shadows striping the floors. The eastern wing was darker inside than a tomb. Someone should have thought to open a few of the windows, given the sweltering heat. But the window screens lining the entry hall stayed stubbornly shut, as if the eastern wing were devoid of occupants. Laya's face brightened with the spark of triumph. She was right; the king and queen did not want to call attention to their Orfelian guest.

She made her way to the study at the far end of the hall. To her delight, the Orfelian was nowhere to be seen. *Perfect.* Laya's gaze fell on the writing desk at the center of the study. Its surface was littered with empty inkwells and handwritten notes. She leaned over the desk to read them, when footsteps echoed from one of the adjoining rooms. No time—Laya snatched the first sheet from the pile that looked like correspondence rather than formulae and stuffed it into the pocket of her skirt. The door beside the writing desk opened a second later.

"Oh!" Ariel's lanky form burst from the adjoining bedroom. He blinked in surprise when his gaze landed on her. "Laya. What are you doing here? I mean—to what do I owe the pleasure?"

"I came to see if you were being treated well," Laya lied. How strange to hear her name uttered in that awful accent. It rang out through the airless study like some discordant note—but that wasn't the only thing Ariel had said wrong. She gazed at him sharply and added, *"Dayang."*

"I'm sorry?"

"If you wish to speak to a princess, you will address her as *dayang.*" She could have sworn she heard Ariel suck in a breath as she inched closer. Her eyes narrowed. "To be frank, Orfelian, your familiarity offends me. You've never been in the company of royalty, have you?"

Ariel stiffened. "No, Dayang," he admitted.

Laya smirked to herself in triumph. It was hard to believe her father would have invited to the palace a common tutor who didn't have the slightest clue how to comport himself around royalty. She continued in the same lofty tone, "To tutor a daughter of Mulayri is one of the highest honors a sovereign can bestow. I wonder what compelled my father to bestow such an honor upon you."

In his fright, his curious spectacles slid down the abnormally high bridge of his nose. He pushed them back up, his eyes darting around the room. Was he looking for a treat to offer her, or a means of escape?

"I . . ." Ariel faltered, struggling to find the words. "I shall strive to make myself worthy of this post, Dayang."

She cocked her head to the side. "Is that your best attempt at groveling, Orfelian?"

Ariel stared back at her. "Do you wish me to grovel, Dayang?" he asked, a discernible bite in his tone.

Laya glanced at him, amusement flickering in her eyes. "I know you've been told to lie to me, and I would hate for you to fall back on your word," she said mildly. "But I will find out your true business here. Try to stay out of trouble until I do."

"But—"

"In the meantime," she went on as if she hadn't heard him, "you can keep me company this afternoon."

Ariel blinked in surprise. "Yes, of course, Dayang. Um, would you like to sit down?" He gestured to the divan near the study window, the paneled shades rolled back since no one else was around.

Laya ignored him and leaned back over the writing desk. Openly this time, she scanned the papers littered across its surface. Plucking one sheet from the pile, she held it to the light. At closer glance, she saw that every inch was filled with the same spiky western script she had never learned to read. She thought back to the history texts she'd once memorized in the course of her studies. The same story echoed across time in other corners of the world. Centuries before, the islands in the Untulu Sea fell to a set of vile conquerors, all of whom were eager to carve a bounty for themselves in the east. Orfelia fell to a western power by the name of Salmantica. They stole the Orfelian natives' wealth and imposed their ugly language and even uglier script.

"Is this what Salmantican is supposed to look like?" she asked with a grimace.

"Yes," he said, approaching her with caution, as if she might attack him. "I often write in Salmantican."

"Not Orfelian?"

Ariel shook his head. "Sometimes it's more natural for me to write in Salmantican. It was the language of my studies."

"You feel more at ease in the language of your masters?" Laya sneered as she handed the paper back to him. "Forgive me if I find that rich."

"Salmantican has its uses, you know," he said. "For me, it

opened the door to some of the best universities in the world. Some of the greatest literature, as well."

"Does Orfelia have no great literature of its own?"

"I'm afraid much of our literature was lost centuries ago in the conquest, Dayang." Bitterness crossed his eyes, and she took note of it.

Idly, she made her way to the open window. In the courtyard below, servants were sweeping dried leaves and withered petals from the ground ahead of the guests' arrival. "I bet you haven't seen much of the palace, let alone the rest of Maynara," she remarked. "Although I expect my father will lengthen your leash after the feast days, once all the visitors leave."

His cheeks reddened as he shuffled his feet. "I'm afraid I don't understand your meaning."

"Liar," she said, keeping her voice light. "As I said, Ariel, I will pretend that you are my Salmantican tutor for now. But one day, I'll find out why you're truly here."

"I *am* your Salmantican tutor, Dayang," he said, stone-faced.

Good. That was the sort of challenge Laya liked.

"Suit yourself, then." She drew a second chair to the desk and had a seat. "If you have nothing better to do, I'd like to request an advance lesson."

Ariel raised an eyebrow at her. "I would be delighted to teach you. But—really?"

"Really." Laya nodded and reached for the pen. The paper she'd stolen rustled faintly in her pocket. It would be written in the same script as the rest of Ariel's damn notes—how else would she learn to read it?

They began with the alphabet, which she hated. She found it lifeless and ugly, and at first, she didn't understand how it worked. Ariel was so patient in his explanations Laya began to question whether he was brought there to be her tutor after all.

"You mustn't think of it in terms of the Maynaran script, where each symbol represents a syllable. Because in the Salmantican alphabet, each letter represents a distinct sound. See, this is your name here." He etched out her name on the paper. In Maynaran, she could spell *Laya* with two symbols, but the Salmantican alphabet required four arrow-like shapes that didn't appear to represent her name at all.

Ariel wrote out all the letters for her on a fresh sheet, leaving space for her to copy them beneath. Laya felt like a child again as she clumsily retraced his scrawl. It was a humiliating exercise, and she wanted to give up after less than an hour.

"How tiresome," she said, throwing down the pen. "Perhaps I ought to teach you the Maynaran alphabet instead."

Laya had intended it as a joke, but Ariel nodded. "I would like to learn. I can only recognize a few symbols."

"You come to Maynara, and you cannot even read the language?" she asked, shocked.

"I never had to learn, as spoken Orfelian shares many similarities with Maynaran. It's the writing system that's different."

"Uncultivated fiend," Laya chided him. She reached for another sheet of paper. "Here, I will teach you, lest you wander my country looking like a fool."

They spent the next hour going through the Maynaran syllabary. Ariel, admittedly, was a better student than Laya could ever hope to be. He mimicked the swoop of her script with surprising precision and laughed in delight upon writing his name in Maynaran for the first time.

To her shock, Laya found herself warming to him, which didn't sit well with her. She tossed him a thinly veiled insult to make things right. "For an ignoramus," she said, "you certainly are a fast learner."

Ariel chuckled. He didn't appear to take offense. "You chide me, Dayang, for knowing so little about your country, but how much do you know about the rest of the world?"

Her smile faltered. He was right. She had never left Maynaran soil and never cared to. This was her home, her kingdom—the only country that had ever mattered to her. But she wouldn't let the Orfelian make her feel like an ignoramus herself.

She turned up her nose and said, "I've heard how people like us are treated in other parts of the world, Ariel. Those places do not interest me."

"If I grew up in a place as magnificent as this, perhaps I would think the same way you do. Unfortunately, I did not have that luxury." His expression sobered, and he caught himself. "I apologize, Dayang. Perhaps I have been too forthright with you."

"You don't need to apologize. I'd rather you be forthright. I prefer when people are honest with me," she said, looking at him intently.

The pen fell from Ariel's fingers with a clatter. Around them, the air in the study stilled.

"Dayang . . . ," Ariel began, his voice strained.

"Yes?" She leaned forward, wondering if, for once, he decided he liked her enough to tell her the truth.

His eyes snapped to hers. He didn't say anything, merely stared at her as if she were a puzzle to be solved.

A spark wound through her body then, something wild and stinging that had nothing to do with curiosity. Under the scalding heat of his gaze, a flush crept up the sides of her neck. She stood abruptly, the legs of her chair scraping against the floor.

Through the window, the light outside had begun to dim.

Was it dusk already? Laya realized with a start that she had spent half the afternoon with the foreigner.

"It's getting late. There's somewhere I have to be," she said.

"Yes," he agreed. "And I ought to disappear."

Laya strode to the exit, pausing for a moment as she leaned against the doorframe. "Thank you, by the way, for the lesson," she said without turning around.

"I should be thanking you as well," he called from behind her, softly, as if not to frighten her.

But he *had* frightened her, and Laya did not understand how that could be.

Her exchange with Ariel still haunted her an hour later as she stood with her sisters on the deck of a riverboat. The motor chugged beneath the water, an incessant warbling that did nothing to alleviate her headache. Her thoughts were swimming and her stomach was in knots, yet her skin tingled with the euphoria of connection—as if Ariel had seen her in ways others could not.

"What's the matter with you?" Eti piped up beside her.

"Nothing," Laya said, shaking her head. She had enough to worry about without losing her head over a common Orfelian.

Bulan gave her an inquisitive look but said nothing.

Laya leaned against the metal railing at the bow as the riverboat chugged along the main canal. Months had passed since their last trip to the spirit houses, and with half of Maynara in the city for the feast days, they needed to put on their best face. In past years, the king and queen would have gone with them. Hara Duja always said they didn't visit enough. Their father, frankly, couldn't be bothered. He often liked to say that Mother, Bulan, Laya, and Eti were the only goddesses he would ever need. Then he would add in a theatrical whisper, *I joke more than I should, but this one, I truly mean.*

He told them before they left on the riverboat, *I believe you're all old enough to handle this engagement on your own.* But Laya wondered if Hara Duja's furtive behavior at the dawn feast had anything to do with her absence.

There had once been a time when Laya had delighted in their rituals. They made her feel connected to something ancient and unspeakable. These days, however, they felt like showmanship—a hollow display more than anything else. As her power grew, the less pious she became. That was because she knew if the gods ever deigned to punish them, she could return their wrath tenfold. Laya was as much at the gods' mercy as they were at hers.

In spite of this, she humbled as the balete tree came into view. It was centuries older than Maynara and nearly half the size of the palace. During one of Laya's lessons, High Shaman Maiza had sworn the tree was as old as the island itself. People claimed that the first humans emerged from its twisting, snake-like branches. They said the fools who dared climb it got swept inside, doomed to wander the realm of the spirits forever.

For all of Laya's blaspheming, even she could sense that the gods had touched the tree. Its branches whispered in a chorus of a thousand hushed voices; whether they bore blessings or warnings, she could never be sure.

Beyond the platform at the end of the canal, dozens of spirit houses circled the balete tree. They weren't uniform and were built of different types of wood. Some were smaller than birdhouses, others large enough to hold three men Ojas's size. When the boat steered to a stop, Laya followed her sisters onto the platform facing the balete tree. They climbed up to the spirit house reserved for the royal family—the one with the smooth, sloping roof with finials in the shape of crocodile jaws and the highest dais. One of Ojas's men stood guard outside while Laya, Bulan, and Eti knelt on the floorboards.

The past few times they'd come, Laya had remained silent while her sisters prayed. The gods couldn't grant her what she wanted. That evening, however, she found herself speaking to them. She didn't beg for her mother's favor or Luntok's love. Instead, she prayed for answers.

They sat there in silence for a long moment. She scoffed when the gods didn't whisper their reply.

Eti was the first to rise and climb out of the spirit house. "I think the gods listened to me this time, don't you?" she asked as Laya and Bulan followed her.

Laya didn't think the gods cared for humans a single mite. She opened her mouth to tell Eti this, when the distant sound of drumming caught her attention. The beating grew closer, shaking the stilts upon which the spirit houses stood, and rattling Laya's bones.

Eti's face brightened. "That must be the parade. Oh, we have to go and see."

The guard looked uneasily between them. He looked to be around Bulan's age—young and, until then, untested by the Gatdula sisters. "I'm not sure that's such a good idea," he said.

"Why not?" Laya asked, crossing her arms.

She had always wanted to watch the parade, but rarely did the royal family take part. Yesterday's dawn ceremony was for the nobles, but this celebration was for the rest. Laya loved how the city transformed in a matter of hours. During the parade, joyful shouting and colorful masks flooded the streets. Warriors showed off for the swooning crowd in the central square, and every merchant decorated their storefront with towering chandeliers made of crispy cassava wafers. At sundown, star-shaped lanterns lined the canals and Mariit burst into song, with music and dancing everywhere.

"Spirits will be high tonight," the guard warned. "It could get dangerous."

It was not Laya who spoke this time, but Bulan. She placed a hand on the hilt of her sword. "With all due respect, I think we're more than capable of protecting ourselves."

"I don't doubt that, Dayang." Still, he spared a wary glance at Eti, the smallest and gentlest out of all of them. Laya stifled a laugh. She forgot how Ojas's men admired her. They saw Eti as an ethereal, absent-minded goddess. Mostly, they feared the other Gatdula sisters.

"I suppose there's no harm in a bit of extra protection," Laya said, to put his mind at ease.

Eti let out a squeal of excitement and dragged her sisters along. They followed the swell of laughter and music. A crowd had already formed in one of the nearby squares. They bore baskets of fruit and bamboo torches. Their bodies were covered with feathers and beads and vivid paint. Laya and her sisters were among the few who weren't in costume. The crowd cried out in joy at the sight of them and swooped over and around them to the beat of the drums. The Gatdulas became an island, them and their guard, surrounded by a sea of birds.

"We should leave," the guard shouted over the noise.

Eti gave him a serene smile and grabbed his hand. "Dance with me," she said, as if she hadn't heard him.

To their surprise, the guard complied. He looked mesmerized

by the princess's close proximity. Laya rolled her eyes—and people called her the wily one.

She turned to Bulan, only to find that her elder sister had been swept into the arms of one of the women in the crowd. To Laya's shock, Bulan didn't look like she was about to murder her. For once, she was beaming.

Laya's mind swam in the swirl of color and voices. She stumbled back, searching for a partner, when a strong arm wrapped around her waist.

"You're out late," the man said, face hidden by a warrior mask. The painted eyes bulged, and the carved mouth opened to reveal fangs long enough to frighten any predator. His vest was unfastened at the collar, revealing the web of tattoos on his chest. She recognized him instantly.

Laya gasped. "Luntok! How did you find me?"

He ran his finger over one of her necklaces. "With all that gold, you're hard to miss."

Her heart rate quickened. She pulled him closer, unable to deny the glee that burst in her chest at the sight of him. "How was the tournament?" she asked.

"Oh." Luntok drew back in surprise. "I thought you had forgotten."

Laya bit back the guilt. She *had* forgotten, but Luntok didn't have to know that. "Something came up at the palace. I'm sorry I wasn't there," she said sincerely. "How did you do?"

"I beat Bato, and it wasn't even close. You should have seen him, Laya. He was pathetic." He chuckled nastily.

Laya found herself laughing too—she didn't care for Bato Tanglaw and would have enjoyed watching Luntok destroy him. "I really am sorry," she said quietly in his ear. "I know you wanted me to be there."

"You must come to the next fight, then," he said. "I'm meant to fight Utu Luma."

"Utu Luma?" she echoed, incredulous. Laya was no fighter, but she knew Utu Luma was a brutish warrior nearly twice Luntok's size, as well as the winner of several past tournaments.

"You look worried."

"I'm not worried," she lied. Laya remembered how Utu Luma would grunt through dinners at the palace, scoffing whenever the king made any mention of music or poetry. Manhood, in Utu's mind, was a singular endeavor in which Hari Aki fell short. As far as Laya was concerned, Luntok could gut him.

He cocked his head to the side, the mask concealing his expression. "You are . . . a bit."

"Not at all," she said, more lightly this time. "But after the fight, you must tell me how you defeated him."

Luntok chuckled against her cheek. "Minx. You know I would never betray the warriors' secrets."

Laya couldn't help herself. She leaned even closer, making her voice deep and husky. "Warrior, I will break your iron will yet. I know just the thing to entice you."

His grip tightened around her waist. They grew reckless, dancing closer than any strangers should. His hands wandered, and his need fed hers. During a pause in the music, she grabbed his hand. They broke away from the crowd.

"Wait! Where are you going?" the guard shouted after them.

"Oh, let her go," she heard Eti say. "Laya knows what she's doing."

From the balete tree, they ran, pulling each other through the narrow streets until the cacophony of the parade faded into a distant echo. Then they collapsed, laughing, over a faraway canal on an empty footbridge. The tournament, the bespectacled

Orfelian, and all the troubles of the day disappeared. Outside the palace, Laya allowed herself to be freer with Luntok than she had ever been.

They laughed for what felt like hours before falling into silence, as their breathing steadied.

"If you won't share the warriors' secrets, tell me a story," she finally said.

"What story?" he asked, reaching over. His fingers tickled her spine through her blouse, making her shiver.

She looked around for inspiration. Someone had strung up lanterns along the bridge just across from them. The candles inside glowed purple and red from the translucent, colored paper. Below the bridge, moonlight skated across the black water.

"Tell me about the serpent who swallowed the moon."

"You already know that story."

"Tell me another story, then. Any. I'm not particular."

"Come on, Laya. We all know that's not true."

He leaned against the railing with his hands on either side of her ribs. Laya turned to face him, trapped between his arms. They were both sweating from the excitement of the parade, the run through the city, and their shared body heat. She reached up and removed his mask to find that Luntok was smiling.

"At least I know what I want," she said.

His smile broadened. "Tell me what you want, then."

She brushed her thumb across Luntok's cheek, smooth as glass. The truth would shatter him. If she could lie to him, she would. She could lie so easily to anyone—anyone else. Instead, she told him, "I want us to stay as we are."

"Like this?" he breathed, cupping her face in his hands.

Yes. She willed herself not to melt. "Exactly like this."

Laya's eyes fluttered shut as she leaned into their kiss. She never wanted to stop kissing him. She would flood the entire land if it meant they were the only humans left. When she was with him, there was no need for solid ground.

Oh, Luntok. She sighed against his lips.

Loving him was like flying. When she was with him, she soared.

Thirteen

LUNTOK

Luntok drifted alongside Mariit's canals as if on a cloud. He hummed as he walked and smiled vacantly at passing strangers. He almost forgot to stop and spit on the ground as he traversed the foreign district, which still stood, withering, in the shadows of the palace walls—such was the effect Dayang Laya had on him.

The princess had left him in front of the row of deserted consulates, with their cracked windows and crumbling facades. It was foolish to let Luntok escort her back to the palace. That was as close as Laya dared bring him. They'd been careful to stay off the main roads, stealing kisses in the privacy of shaded alleyways, to avoid being seen.

When, at last, he'd kissed her goodbye, every inch of his body whined in protest. Laya pulled away from his embrace, a sad smile tugging at her lips. She looked so lovely, the moonlight softening the sharp angles of her chin. Luntok's grip tightened around her fingers. He released her only when he saw her wince.

"Brutish warrior. You must take better care," she'd told him wryly. "I am nothing without these hands. Half the kingdom seems to think it." Melancholy flickered in her gaze then. Through Laya's hands, the wrath of Mulayri flowed. Her hands allowed her to wield her power—the same way his hands allowed him to wield a sword—but they were only a small part of her. Perhaps a few irrelevant, pea-brained Maynarans thought of Laya as nothing but a broken vessel. Judging by the slight quiver in her lower lip, she almost seemed to believe it herself.

Luntok responded with a vehement shake of his head. "You are so much more than your hands," he told her, raising her fingertips to his lips.

"What else do I have to offer, then?" Her eyebrows quirked up, the same way they always did when she was wheedling for compliments. And, as usual, he indulged her.

What *did* Laya have to offer? His breath hitched in his throat as he studied her features. A pretty face, although an accurate observation, was not what she wanted to hear. So he told her, "A sharp mind. A quick tongue. I've watched you outwit nobles twice your age. Their admiration for you grows year after year."

Laya blinked. His choice of words surprised her. "Noticed all of that, did you?" she asked, her voice uncharacteristically tight.

"I notice everything that happens at court," he replied.

Everything about you.

They stood there for a long, pregnant moment. Laya gazed at him, not with lust, but with what appeared to be genuine gratitude. "Dear Luntok. If I kiss you now, I fear I may never make it back to my chambers," she murmured as she stepped into the shadows. "But know that it brings me great comfort, having you around."

Not once did she mention the word *love*, but Luntok could taste it in the muggy night air that hung between them. A lump rose in the back of his throat as he watched her go. In another life, he'd follow her up to her bedroom, make love to her, and then fall asleep at her side. According to some, Luntok had no right to that future. All because ancient rules governed their lives and forced him to relinquish Laya. It tore him in half every time.

Not for long. Luntok spat again at the foreign district for good measure. Maynara was changing, becoming a place where even ancient rules could be snapped in half like brittle reeds. Luntok and Laya were proof of this. Fortune would favor them if they were brave enough to carve their own path. And they belonged together. Anyone with eyes could see it. Why shouldn't they have the future they both desperately craved?

Often, when Luntok worked himself up with feverish fantasies, his mother's voice burst through his bluster to soothe him: *Soon, my boy, soon.* This once, Luntok leaned into the imagined comfort. He knew he needed only bide his time and Laya would be his, as she always should have been. Never again would he watch her spin out beyond his reach.

He squinted up at the nearest consulate, a miserable, gray block of a building. Once, it had housed the delegation of some western power—Luntok had never learned much about the Sunset States, that faraway continent, their countries a messy patchwork of strange tongues and stupid names. Those consulates had no place in Maynara; they were a scar upon the Gatdula legacy. Hara Duja's mother, the late queen, should have demolished them when she'd expelled their emissaries several decades before.

High above the street, shadows moved behind the consulates' cracked windows. Squatters, no doubt, siphoning what they could from the westerners' meager refuse. Through a hole in the dirty glass, a baby wailed. Luntok stuffed his fists into the pockets of his trousers and quickened his pace. He despised the foreign district. Although the westerners were long gone, their houses still stank of failure, of waste.

The noise grew louder as he worked his way back toward the heart of Mariit. Judging by the swell of music and laughter, the parade was in full swing. The other warriors didn't tell Luntok where to find them, but he knew well enough to guess. They were waiting for him at the inn that straddled the canal separating the merchant quarter, a smattering of newer dwellings and ancient guildhalls, from the noble town houses of the central district. The family who owned the inn had moved to Mariit from the Kulaws' kadatuan. In recent years, it had become a popular meeting place for Kulaw-affiliated visitors and any capital dweller with southern roots.

When Luntok stepped through the front door, the innkeeper, a lanky man around his mother's age, greeted him in the old dialect people only spoke back home. On the wall behind him hung a gigantic wooden carving of a raptor bird—the Kulaw family's symbol. He gestured to the staircase next to the entryway, which led to the lower dining room reserved for the inn's most prestigious guests. "Right this way, my lord."

Over a dozen warriors burst into raucous cheers when Luntok came downstairs. In the fleeting hour he'd stolen with Laya, the group had already drunk themselves merry and red-faced. They'd left their weapons stacked against all four walls of the dining room. Smoky, yellow light winked off the flat edges of their blades. In the spirit of the feast days, they would spend the rest of the evening clustered around the inn's round mahogany tables, snacking on parade leftovers, and playing dice games.

Luntok grinned as he wove between the warriors, clapping them across their shoulders in greeting. At the opposite end of the room, Vikal leaped to his feet and thrust his glass into the air. "All hail Luntok, the Swift-striker, favored by the old gods of Thu-ki," he proclaimed.

Around the room, the warriors echoed Vikal's praise—*to Luntok, the Swift-striker*—and raised their glasses in turn. Luntok's grin broadened as he looked Vikal in the eye. His great-great-grandfather, Luntok the First, the last of the Kulaw monarchs, had been given several titles throughout his lifetime: *Swift-striker* by the warriors who revered him, *Beast-maker* by the Gatdulas who despised him, and *Haribon* by his most loyal followers—that was Luntok the Second's favorite title, meaning *Bird King*.

Haribon Luntok wielded the one power the Gatdulas had ever feared. He had not merely transformed men into magnificent creatures but could also manipulate his own flesh. According to southern legend, he could morph into a giant raptor with a bone-crushing beak and a wingspan the length of four men laid out from head to toe. When Luntok was younger, his mother used to rock him to sleep with tales of the Haribon's gory victories. Then she'd brush his hair back behind his ears and whisper, *You, my son, are destined for wondrous things.*

Luntok did not possess the ancient powers of his family, but he, too, was destined to be king. Imeria knew it. Vikal and the rest of the warriors did too. In Mariit, this was among the few places they could think it, in the concealed back room of an inn, safe in the company of southerners.

"Care for some wine, my lord?" A serving girl appeared before him, a pitcher in one hand and a seductive lilt in her voice. When Luntok nodded, she poured him a glass. She didn't give it to him right away. Instead, she leaned in to whisper, "Let me know if there's anything more you desire, my lord. It would be my *sincerest* pleasure to serve."

She leaned into his side, the warm swell of her breasts brushing against his forearm with alarming forcefulness. Instinctively,

Luntok snatched the cup from her, the corners of his mouth curling in distaste. "That will be all," he quipped. Then he waved her off without so much as a thank-you.

The serving girl shrank back with a wounded look. She swept back upstairs as Vikal and the others guffawed.

"By the gods, Luntok, you don't need to bite the poor girl's head off," Vikal said, chuckling heartily. "She has a pretty-enough head, as it is."

"Not as pretty as Dayang Laya's, though. Isn't that right, my lord?" Jit teased. He was among the freshest warriors in the Kulaws' ranks, only a few years Luntok's senior.

The moment Jit uttered Laya's name, a chorus of disgruntled sighs rang out across the inn's lower dining room. Not every Kulaw warrior held the princess in such high esteem. Like half the kingdom, they prayed Laya would grow into a more diluted version of herself, sweeter on the tongue and easier to subdue. Hara Duja was the worst of them. If the queen had her way, she'd keep Laya from knowing her full power. Then she'd deny Laya the only person she had ever loved.

From across the room, Vikal gave Luntok a pointed look—a warning of a sort, but Luntok ignored it. He took a long sip of his wine to wash down the bitterness, his fingers tightening around the stem of the glass. He could scarcely hear the warriors' grumblings over the memory of Laya's mocking laughter, forever ringing in his ears. The princess liked to be challenged, and Luntok was not one to back down. *Marry me,* he burned to ask her. *I'll never force you to be anything you are not.*

For Laya Gatdula was many things—a vessel of divine power, a woman of frightening wit, and, most of all, their future queen. Many Maynarans, northerners and southerners alike, did not hide their misgivings. They knew that some Gatdulas burned steadily like Hara Duja, guiding the kingdom like a dying candle, easy pickings for their enemies to snuff out. But most Gatdulas blazed brighter than the sun, as likely to burn the island to cinders as they were to bathe it in their glory. Laya was the latter fire. Her power would propel her to become the greatest queen Maynara had ever seen—or a fearsome tyrant. After her destruction of the eastern wing three years before, more and more Maynarans questioned whether she was worth the gamble.

But Laya *was* worth it. Luntok understood this, the same way he understood that peace would only come to Maynara if Laya chose a Kulaw for her king. And Luntok would be exactly the kind of king Laya needed. He'd show her where to direct her strength, but he'd never tame her bluster. If she were the ship captain, he'd be her barrelman, always with his eyes on the horizon, telling her how to angle her sails. Their reign would unite the island from north to south. They'd rule side by side. A Gatdula and a Kulaw, coming together as equals.

According to his mother, Luntok would take the throne through battle, not through love. Luntok disagreed. He was convinced his path to the throne—and to Hara Duja's heir—lay somewhere in between.

In the downstairs room, the Kulaw warriors were staring at him, waiting to see how Luntok might react to Jit's teasing. When it came to Laya, it was too early to say what was on his mind. The night was young, with hours of games and drinking ahead. No one was in the mood to quarrel over the Gatdulas. Luntok would have to profess his undying devotion to the princess another evening.

"Maynara boasts no shortage of pretty girls, but only one will be my queen," he said, choosing his words with care. It was a half promise, half joke. Around him, the warriors broke out into triumphant roars. Although the inn was far from the Gatdulas' lackeys, and they were safe there among kin, none dared utter the truth. Luntok was born to take the Maynaran throne and honor his family's legacy. To become the king the southerners hungered for—that became his fate the moment Imeria Kulaw granted him his great-great-grandfather's name.

But to utter the truth was to commit the highest treason, and the feast days had scarcely begun. The warriors toasted to their future king in silence. He was Luntok the Second, a young man swept up on the wings of his own destiny.

The sole Kulaw a Gatdula could trust and love.

When Luntok returned home that night, his mother was not sipping wine on the veranda as he'd expected. He slid open the capiz-shell screen. A second later, their maid, Huna, swept past, bearing a tray stacked with dirty dinner plates. On a table in the entryway stood a fresh bouquet of scarlet lilies. Their petals spilled over the edge of the vase, which had been empty when Luntok left for the tournament earlier that afternoon. The signs were telling. Imeria had just received a visitor.

"I wasn't aware we were entertaining guests this evening," he remarked.

Huna froze in her tracks when he addressed her. She'd started working for the Kulaws the previous season. Luntok forgot how skittish she was. Her previous employer had been a vicious old nobleman from the north. He was notoriously cruel to all his servants, but he reserved his most creative abuses for those of southern origin. On countless occasions, the nobleman ridiculed the maid's accent and subjected her to the most demeaning tasks—from plucking a sackful of rice off the kitchen floor grain by grain, to polishing the banisters wearing nothing but her underthings. Desperate, the young girl had pleaded her case to Datu Kulaw, begging for a position in her household. And, just this once, Imeria gave in.

Offer favors sparingly, she'd warned Luntok once. *Your benevolence won't always be rewarded.*

Huna had gotten lucky—to work in the Kulaw household was no small favor. Unfortunately, Imeria couldn't extend the same favor to every southerner struggling to find dignified work in the capital. There were hundreds of Hunas in Mariit, not all of them equipped with the discretion required for the post. The Kulaws thus selected their servants with painstaking care. The same held true for each guest they invited into their home.

"Datu Kulaw received Datu Gulod this evening, my lord," the maid informed him. "He couldn't stay long, but he sends his regards."

"Datu Gulod? Very well." Luntok struggled to contain his surprise as he dismissed Huna with a flick of his hand. Datu Gulod was known across Maynara to be a smart, crafty fellow, but he was not Imeria Kulaw's typical houseguest. Luntok wondered what he had done to earn an invitation.

At the top of the stairs, his mother's door stood ajar. Dark shadows flitted in and out of the narrow opening. Imeria was pacing, as she often did when sleep evaded her. Usually, Luntok left her to her warring thoughts. But this night, curiosity caught the better of him. He raised his hand to the doorframe and gave it a gentle knock.

"Enter." Imeria's voice cut through the stillness, sharper than the edge of his blade. When he stepped into the room, she looked up from the stacks of paper strewn across her bed. Luntok recognized the brushstrokes, cross-sections, and carefully stenciled lines. These were the maps of the palace they'd collected over the years—some stolen by hired thieves from the royal architect's private chambers, others drawn by Imeria's own hand.

"I hope you weren't waiting up for me," Luntok said as he shut the door behind him.

His mother's expression softened. "My darling, clever boy. Come—I've yet to congratulate you on your victory." She opened her arms. Part of Luntok was ashamed of how eager he was to fall into them.

"Did the fight please you?" he asked, his voice cracking involuntarily.

"I've never been prouder to call you my son," she said warmly.

Luntok closed his eyes, his nose filling with the scent of her jasmine perfume. A smell he still associated with safety, even after all these years. Now that he was home, the weight of the day's trials—from the aching muscles in his sword arm to the goblets of wine he'd consumed back at the inn—dropped on top of him like a heavy stone.

"Could we speak more in the morning?" he asked, stifling a yawn. "I really ought to turn in."

Imeria drew back, an unfamiliar spark in her gaze. "Of course, you must be exhausted. Let me show you something first." From the pocket of her skirt, she withdrew a thin glass vial. Its contents gleamed in the moonlight filtering in through the open window. In her palm, the crystal substance looked like crushed starlight. Knowing his mother, it was anything but.

An uneasy feeling slithered down Luntok's spine. "What in Mulayri's name is *that*?"

His mother explained what he had already guessed. The finely ground substance was no ordinary crystal. It was a drug called precioso. Dread built deep inside Luntok's gut as she told him how it could enhance her dangerous abilities—and how the drug had landed in her possession.

"Datu Gulod," Luntok echoed, incredulous. "Are you sure you can trust him?"

"Even before rising in the ranks, Namok Gulod has been straining at the Gatdulas' lead. His loyalties have long been up for question. However, I needed him to approach me." Imeria cut him a sharp look. "Do you understand now, Luntok? Our efforts may have just begun to bear fruit, but I've spent my entire life planting the seeds."

At her small rebuke, he tried not to grimace. He may have learned swordsmanship from Vikal, but his mother had taught him how to navigate the battlefield that was the Maynaran court. She showed him how to sniff out dissatisfaction in a room full of sycophants. To keep his lips tight and his eyes peeled. To till the ground in preparation of a future of which no one dared speak. Imeria Kulaw had learned this from her father, whose failed rebellion nonetheless rattled the Gatdulas to the core. And she was passing her knowledge down to him.

"With this *precioso*," Luntok began, the foreign word rolling awkwardly off the tip of his tongue. "Could you overpower— anyone?" He didn't dare say Hara Duja's name.

"An ordinary guard? Easily. As for a Gatdula . . ." Imeria cast her gaze toward the window, a somber line creasing her brow. "My father used to tell me stories passed down from his own father—and his father before that. Few could resist the Kulaw's power to wield mind and flesh. Not the fiercest warrior. Not even the mightiest datu."

"None but the Gatdulas," Luntok said as the dread formed a pit beneath his ribs.

"None but the Gatdulas." His mother turned back to him, a cryptic smile creeping across her face. "The blood of Mulayri runs strong, shielding them generation after generation. From afar, I cannot overpower them. However, no Gatdula is impenetrable. If I could only close the distance—" She broke off, her hand rising to hover over Luntok's cheek.

Imeria was his mother. She would never hurt him. And yet, he forced himself not to flinch.

"A simple touch," she whispered, "and the queen would bow to my will."

Luntok had never heard his mother speak of her schemes so boldly. His eyes dropped once again to the vial of precioso between her fingers. Something told him that the drug had broken the delicate balance between his family and Laya's in a way that was irreparable.

"Is that what Datu Gulod believes?" he asked, his voice hoarse.

Imeria barked out a laugh as her hand dropped to her side. "Datu Gulod? His aptitude for deduction stretches only so far—and I wouldn't have come all this way based on theory alone."

Luntok's eyebrows shot halfway up his forehead when he realized the meaning lurking beneath her words. "You've already tried it." He shook his head in disbelief.

In the moonlight, his mother's gaze hardened to steel. "One touch is all it takes," she repeated, without a single trace of doubt. "A tempest is brewing on the horizon, Luntok. We must bide our time until it comes."

He frowned. "All because of the precioso?"

A harsh breeze rattled the window screens in their panes.

Imeria gave an incriminating nod, her next words nearly lost to the wind. "Precioso, Vikal, Gulod—they will give me the rest of Maynara. But when the storm comes to pass, I can overpower the Gatdulas on my own."

Fourteen

DUJA

Each time Duja felt herself dozing off, she cast her gaze toward the window. In the streets beyond the palace, the uproar of the previous evening's parade had faded to a distant buzz. Guests had begun to arrive and were trickling in through the courtyard to the royal gardens. Hari Aki remained downstairs to receive them. For the hundredth time that morning, she wished to be by his side instead of trapped inside the palace. She was convinced that one does not know boredom until one has listened to Datu Tanglaw drone on about matters in the north, his dull voice echoing across the domed ceiling of the council room.

"Relations with the Skyland tribes remain amicable. I have zero conflicts to report since last season. The situation in the foothills along the northern road, however, remains tenuous—if I may, Hara Duja, propose a few suggestions?" Datu Tanglaw, at last, broke off his speech to address the queen.

She nodded to encourage him—at any rate, Datu Tanglaw could not expatiate forever. The feast days ran on a tight schedule, and this council meeting was expected to conclude within the next half hour.

Duja did not hate these meetings with the Council of Datus, as many of her entourage assumed. In fact, she preferred the intimate, closed-door affairs to the bustling feasts, where she found herself accosted by hundreds of nobles from all sides, each of them vying for her attention. It was easier to focus on the six nobles who joined her at the council table. To her right sat Datu Luma, Datu Tanglaw, and Datu Sandata; and to her left, Datu Patid, Datu Gulod, and Datu Kulaw. Across from Duja might have sat Laya, her heir.

Next year, Duja thought, which was what she told herself the year before. Next year, she would prepare Laya thoroughly. The council had never criticized Laya outright, at least not in the queen's presence. Three years had passed since the accident in the eastern wing—not long enough for the council members to forget what it had cost them. They'd accept Laya as their queen, but unless Duja proved Laya was ready for the role, they wouldn't make her daughter's reign easy. It didn't help that the heir to the throne had a habit of speaking out of turn, brusquely, and in utter defiance of Duja's warnings. Laya was showing signs of maturity, tempering her tongue before the rest of the court, albeit more slowly than Duja would have liked. But soon they would have to address the datus together. These were the heads of the highest-born families in Maynara. Once sovereigns in their own right, each family first knelt to the Gatdulas after conquest, then in search of protection. Their own ancient magic might have dried out eons before, but they wielded more political power than Laya could fathom. Bound they may be to the Gatdulas, but they required a gentler hand.

The Council of Datus was a curious invention, formed by Duja's ancestors to consolidate their hold on the island. Before the council, Maynara was less a kingdom than a loose network of warring clans. That changed generations earlier when invaders from the west barreled into the Untulu Sea. They gobbled up the gold and enslaved the natives. They worshipped one false god who whispered in their ears. The god convinced them that the world's wealth was theirs for the taking. With the blood of Mulayri in their veins, the Gatdulas were the only sovereigns powerful enough to keep the invaders at bay. Hatred of the foreigners, with their pale skin and ardent greed, united Maynara. The datus pledged their loyalty to the Gatdula family in blood. They named the Gatdula heirs the paramount kings and queens of Maynara, whom they served willingly, reverently—all the datus, except one.

"Before we move on to the Skylanders, I was wondering, Hara Duja, if we might take this opportunity to speak of the gold tax on foreign traders," Imeria Kulaw said, jolting Duja from her thoughts. The men around the table stilled. Imeria needn't raise her voice to send a pang of dread through Duja's body. The faintest echo already promised a challenge.

Duja cleared her throat. The king had tried to teach her how to handle Imeria. If allowed to speak, Imeria enjoyed spinning tales of the Gatdulas' drama and negligence—tales that rarely portrayed the queen in a favorable light. Duja knew after two decades on the throne that Imeria's disrespect was a contagion. To grant her the floor was to give her power—and Duja couldn't allow that to happen. "The gold tax was not on the agenda for this meeting," she said flatly.

Imeria refused to drop the subject. Unrelenting, she held Duja's gaze. "I'm arguing that it was wrong to omit it."

It was Datu Luma, this time, who defended her. He was an old man with white hair and serious, sunken eyes. He had sat at this table since Duja was a child. "The sovereign dictates the agenda, Datu Kulaw," he said in a stern voice. "You are out of bounds."

Imeria's gaze hardened. Duja wished she could forget, but there were times when she looked at Imeria—at the curve of her eyebrow and the spite in her smile—and saw with painful familiarity the beautiful, fearless young girl she had once been. Years had passed since they'd lived alongside each other in the palace, and Imeria had only grown more beautiful, more fearless. When their eyes locked across the council table, a trace of the old longing shivered across the queen's skin. Even after so much time, Duja found herself drawn to Imeria's flame.

"I merely have Maynara's interests at heart," Imeria replied. "Your office has proposed to lower the tax on foreign gold. I fear this sets a dangerous precedent for our trade policy. It will bring economic ruin far more disastrous than any of your advisers have foreseen."

Ah yes, Duja was familiar with this tactic. Imeria had a flair for the dramatic, and that had been the fun of her when they were children. Duja no longer indulged her as she had back then. "I apologize, Datu Kulaw," she said before Imeria stirred further anxiety around the table, "but we don't have time to entertain your unfounded beliefs."

The bangles on Imeria's wrists clapped against the wood when she pressed her palms against the table. A faint flush crept across Duja's cheeks as she gazed at the other woman. Imeria was lovely in her fine jewels and scarlet silks, and her anger made her lovelier. "Ah, Hara Duja, but they aren't unfounded. Our recent history has taught us never to allow foreigners to enter Maynara in any fashion, no matter how innocent they appear. They come as merchants and missionaries one day, and the next, they start calling themselves our masters."

A murmur of dread spread among the Council of Datus, who exchanged dark glances across the table. The truth alone would not reassure them. Duja wished she possessed her husband's warm voice and easy grin, a balm against Imeria's bluster. Guilt wound through the queen when she thought of a time when words of love, not venom, dripped from the Kulaw woman's sweet, tender lips.

Duja shifted her thoughts back to the other council members. "The policy change would apply to foreign imports, not individuals," she said. "The world has changed so much in the past few decades. We cannot remain friendless. In isolation, our people will suffer. Our wealth will dwindle."

Across the table, a few datus nodded in agreement. But Imeria had a brutal vision of the world, and she had since she was a child; she could not be convinced. "And what of our friends across the Untulu Sea?" she demanded. "The Orfelians thought themselves clever when they gave Salmantica the key to their kingdom, and now they are slaves in their own land. I am urging you, Your Majesty, not to fall prey to the same trap."

"Of course not, Datu Kulaw. Do you think me a fool?" Duja asked more harshly than she ought to have dared. The other council members interpreted her bitterness as strength. They nodded somberly.

"No one thinks you are a fool, Your Majesty," Datu Tanglaw said, bowing his head in deference.

"Thank you, Datu Tanglaw, but I was speaking to her." The rest of the table quieted as Duja fixed her sights on Imeria.

"I am merely worried," Imeria said in a tempered voice, "that these foreigners will mistake your goodwill for weakness." Her demeanor changed. She appeared more resigned than she had a moment earlier. Briefly, Duja thought she had her tamed.

"We must make concessions," she said, "but that does not make us weak."

Imeria's eyes flitted up to hers once again. "Like your grandfather made concessions?"

Knots formed in Duja's stomach. Briskly, she shook her head. "No. This is not the same."

"The old king once opened his arms to these foreign invaders. He invited them within the walls of Mariit, built them grand embassies in the heart of the city. They, too, preached goodwill and comity as they plotted to depose him and plant a puppet in his place," she said scathingly, as if to hold Hara Duja accountable for her grandfather's mistakes.

Oh, but she was wrong to speak to Duja this way—so very wrong.

"Imeria." Her first name slipped out of Duja's mouth, sharp as a bone shard and achingly familiar.

The other datus looked up, surprised at the rare hint of informality between the two women, but Imeria went on as if she hadn't heard her. "I admire your idealism, Hara Duja, but we have no friends in this changing world. First you concede on gold, next it will be the throne. This is how it begins."

Her words echoed in the vast hall of the council room. Duja could never admit it, but Imeria had always been the cleverer of the two. She remembered the tales the noblewoman had once spun of her people's gods and their fallen kingdom. In those moments, Imeria had sounded like her father, who had died in a futile attempt to restore the Kulaws to their former glory.

Oh, Duja, to be a god like you, Imeria once mused. But Duja never wanted to be a god. As a child, she had wanted nothing more than to run her fingers through the Kulaw girl's long, inky hair. To match Imeria's whip-sharp tongue and troublesome beauty. That was before she saw Imeria for what she was—before she realized what she was capable of.

"You didn't regret it then," Duja said softly, "when my mother conceded and spared your life."

Imeria's mouth snapped shut. Her cheeks reddened as if she had been slapped.

Duja should have felt relief when Imeria finally fell silent, but all she wanted was to shake her. *Spite me and slander me all you like, Imeria, but you will not win. You are the danger. You are the source of ruin. You—*

Her hands began to tremble. She clutched at the edge of the table, but the tremors radiated from her palms and up the length of her arms. Beneath their feet, the ground shook. The glass windows rattled in the frames. On its clawed mahogany legs, the council table lurched.

"Your Majesty!" the datus gasped.

For the past couple of years, Duja had fought to control the tremors. But as she met Imeria's gaze across the table, a spark of defiance shot through her body. Duja squared her jaw and leaned into the vibrations. The threads of energy braided themselves firmly through her fingertips.

She sucked in a breath and pulled the threads taut. Below her feet, the earthquake intensified.

A shadow of fear flickered in Imeria's expression. Finally, she bowed her head. "My apologies, Your Majesty," she muttered, her voice barely audible above the rumbling earth.

Once, Duja remembered, Imeria had looked at her as if she were the pillar that held up the universe.

The queen tore her gaze away. She straightened her shawl, collecting herself, then planted her palms flat against the armrests of her chair. The threads pulled free of her grip. A moment later, the shaking subsided. Her hands remained motionless, free of tremors. Duja had taken a monumental risk wielding her powers like that. She sighed in relief and prayed to the gods her hands wouldn't tremble again.

Duja stole a glance at Imeria, who did not look up from her lap. The queen hadn't forgotten. Long before Imeria had pointed fingers at Duja from across the council table, she had traced lullabies into her skin.

The other woman's tearful words echoed back to her from another lifetime, the last words she'd said to Duja the day the eastern wing had burned down: *You're cruel to me. It's not fair.* Was it cruel of the queen to threaten her subjects so? To threaten Imeria, whose slender fingers once entwined so perfectly with hers, whose passion once set Duja's soul ablaze?

Duja shook off the guilt when she remembered that the Kulaws required special treatment. If Imeria stayed quiet for the rest of the meeting, Duja's stunt with the earthquake would have been worth it.

"Now," she said after a long silence, her voice surprisingly calm as she turned her attention to the other council members, shock etched across their graying faces. "Does anyone else take issue with the gold tax?"

Fifteen

LAYA

Laya, lost in thought, was pretending to marvel at the spotted orchids at the garden entrance when the earth beneath the courtyard shifted. Earthquakes were a common occurrence in Maynara—some by natural causes, others by her mother's will. They rarely lasted longer than a few minutes, but never did they hit the capital with such fervor. As the vibrations intensified, Laya lost her footing. She pitched forward, grabbing on to the person nearest her for balance.

"Are you all right, Dayang?" It was Waran Sandata who helped her gather her bearings. He was Bulan's age, two years her senior, and the youngest of Datu Sandata's many sons. Although he possessed no spectacular talent and an unremarkable face, he had a kind smile and a genuine sense of humor, which was rare among highborn children, who often took themselves too seriously for their own good.

"I'm fine, thank you." Laya looked around. Several nobles in the courtyard had also lost their balance. Many had stumbled onto the tiled ground and were dusting off their fine silks.

"The gods must be displeased," one man joked as he passed Laya on his way into the gardens. She looked up at the palace, where Hara Duja was hosting a council meeting.

"Not the gods," she mused aloud. She could feel the threads of power in the earth beneath her feet, even if she couldn't wield it. She could sense someone on the other end, struggling to tug back control. If the queen had allowed her heir into the council room as she had promised, Laya would know for herself what was going on. She thought of her mother's worsening tremors. Occasional lapses in control were to be expected in a Gatdula of Hara Duja's age, but there was something about this earthquake—a wild, defiant energy weaving its way through the threads—that caught Laya's attention. She glanced at the eastern wing, where Ariel Sauros lurked out of sight of the nobles behind the closed window screens. What else was her mother not telling her?

"Sorry, Dayang?" Waran eyed her, confused.

Laya glanced back down and realized she hadn't let go of his arm. She gestured to the gardens with her free hand. "Care to escort me inside?"

He grinned broadly and inclined his head. "It would be my honor, Dayang."

They started down the main path, where began the tour. The palace opened its gardens once a year, and Hari Aki did not spare any expense. For weeks, he had been enlisting horticulturists and architects to revive the parts of the garden he deemed dull or uninspired. Laya wished she had half her father's vision. Mere steps into the gardens, and she was dumbstruck. For as far as she could see, flowers bloomed in patterns too complex for her mind to decipher. Marigold and carmine and cerulean, and other shades too lovely to be named, swirled together in a visual feast. Her nose flooded with the flowers' scents, sweet and nectarous, as yellow sunlight streamed through the swaying palms above.

None of that would last—none of it. But for a moment, Laya,

delighted by the gardens' ephemeral beauty, forgot the secrets plaguing her.

"You are awfully quiet today, Dayang. Have I said something to upset you?" Waran asked as they reached the fountain at the end of the main path. Jets spouted from the open jaws of the golden crocodile perched at the heart of the white-jade basin.

"Not at all, Waran. I have a lot on my mind." Laya leaned against the mouth of the basin and dipped her hand into the water. The liquid was cool against her fingers. She cupped the water in her hands and let it fall back into the basin, watching rings ripple across its clear surface.

Waran leaned on the edge of the fountain beside her. "Forgive my boldness, Dayang, but please know I am here if ever you're in search of a confidant."

Laya looked up to find Waran eyeing her hopefully as he inched too close for her liking. *Not him too.* "You're very kind, Waran," she said, feigning a smile.

The presence of one suitor summoned the others. Bato Tanglaw strolled over to the fountain, a bandage pressed to the side of his face. He'd been wounded at Luntok's hand, which made Laya brighten in glee.

"Is he bothering you, Dayang?" Bato asked, eyeing the other boy with disdain.

Waran's kind face contorted into a frown. Laya spoke for him. "No, Bato. No one is bothering me."

Long before the tournament, Bato saw himself as Luntok's rival. Whenever Bato appeared, Luntok was never far behind. As expected, the Kulaw boy appeared then in a bolt of scarlet, the hornbill hilt of his sword peeking over his belt. Laya met his gaze as he, too, sauntered over to the fountain. "La—Dayang," he called, catching himself before he lapsed into familiarity.

"Luntok," she said breezily, "how wonderful of you to join us."

He planted himself at Laya's other side on the edge of the fountain, his shoulder brushing against hers. Boldly, he reached over, a honey-colored narra bud between his fingers. "May I?"

Demurely, Laya nodded and leaned in so he could tuck the flower behind her ear. She held her breath, giddy at their sudden closeness. For a brief moment, his fingers trailed from her ear, grazing the underside of her chin. The touch was featherlight, nothing like the kiss they'd stolen after the parade the previous night. Her skin grew hot when she thought about it.

With a sharp breath, she drew back against the fountain, lest the others see the fool Luntok made of her.

"Kulaw," Bato barked, displeased with the onslaught of competition. "Don't you have somewhere to be?"

Luntok glanced at Laya, smirking, before turning to Bato. "The tournament doesn't resume until sundown—ah, but you were eliminated in the previous round, weren't you?"

"Come now, you mustn't gloat," Laya said, but her reprimand was without teeth. Luntok smiled over at her, shoulders shaking with a suppressed chuckle.

Bato scowled. "You may have defeated me, but I don't envy you. Utu Luma will slice you to ribbons."

"I have nothing to fear from Utu Luma," he said, his chest puffing up with all the confidence he had yet to earn.

Bato opened his mouth to retort when Bulan rushed over. His posture shifted, and he greeted the other princess warmly. "Good afternoon, Dayang!"

Laya resisted the urge to roll her eyes. Bato had his sights set on Hara Duja's heir, but he couldn't resist courting her eldest daughter as well.

"How lovely to see you," he added, and Laya heard an echo of his father's groveling in his tone. She wasn't surprised to find him pursuing her sister. Bulan did not possess the power of Mulayri, but perhaps Bato thought her Gatdula blood might revive the Tanglaws' ancient ability to sketch out omens in molten candle-wax or divine the future from runny egg yolks—or whatever it was his family believed.

"Yes, hello." Bulan all but ignored him—flattery, like most games of courtship, slid over her head like butter. She swept past Bato to join her sister, her brow knitted in worry. "You felt it, didn't you?"

"What do you mean?" Laya asked.

"The earthquake."

"Oh, that was but a minor tremor," Waran said with a wave of his hand. "Hardly lasted more than a few seconds. I made sure Dayang Laya was unhurt."

Bulan met Laya's gaze. In an unspoken way, they both knew what that earthquake meant. Something strange was happening with their mother.

"I'm sure it was nothing," Laya said, but she gave a subtle nod to the flock of overly attentive suitors surrounding them. *We'll speak of it more later.*

Bulan nodded in understanding and made to turn away, but Bato called her back with polite conversation. "We were just discussing the tournament, Dayang," he said. "Will you be attending the final round tonight?"

"I should think so," Bulan said, her shoulders relaxing. This was her uncontested domain. Laya did not take any particular joy from sword fighting and weaponry, but Bulan could discuss it for hours on end. She glanced between Luntok and Bato. "I caught a glimpse of your fight the other day," she told them. "I didn't make it up to the stands, so you might not have seen me."

Luntok looked up in surprise, his attention momentarily pulled away from Laya. "What did you think of it?"

She stared at him. "You fought marvelously for a beginner. I was impressed," she said, and Luntok's smirk grew wider. When she turned to Bato, however, she frowned. "You surprised me, Bato. In previous years, you were more consistent."

Red splotches spread over his wounded cheeks. He was embarrassed. "I suppose I wasn't destined to win this year," he said flatly.

Anyone with sense would have let the subject drop, but not Bulan. "I don't know if destiny has anything to do with it," she remarked, oblivious, and went on to describe every mistake he made in frightful detail. "Toward the end, you had the upper strike of an untrained infant. And you have to admit, when you're tired, your footwork gets sloppy. Not to mention your stamina—"

Laya was cruel, but she knew not to be insulting. "Bulan," she said tentatively.

"What is it?"

"To fight in the tournament at all is an achievement, is it not?" she asked, hoping Bulan would catch the warning in her tone.

"Yes," Bato agreed, a bit too enthusiastically for Laya's liking. "With all due respect, Dayang Bulan, you have never competed in the tournament yourself."

"Oh." Bulan's expression hardened. "I suppose that means I know nothing, then."

Bato hesitated then, sensing he had edged into hazardous territory. "I only mean to say, Dayang, that it's not the same when you're up there on that platform. It's nothing like training. You fight differently. Every reaction is heightened somehow. I don't know how else to explain."

Laya knew nothing about fighting, but she knew when her sister was being talked down to. "I'm sure you don't have to tell Bulan that," she said harshly. "She's the finest swordsman in all of Maynara."

Bulan's eyes snapped to hers, shocked at the ferocity with which Laya defended her.

"Of course. I never meant to imply she wasn't." Bato's skepticism might not have been intentional, but it seeped out anyway.

Laya frowned. She might have cut him down where he stood had Luntok not butted in.

"Bato's right," he said abruptly. "I didn't realize it until yesterday. When you're up there and the crowd is jeering . . . It's nothing Vikal could have ever prepared me for."

Laya rolled her eyes. "Yes, well, Vikal is no Ojas."

"No, that wouldn't be fair, would it?" Luntok shot back sarcastically.

"What's that supposed to mean?" Laya tensed. The gentle breeze ground to a halt around them. Beyond the palm leaves, the sun ducked behind a passing cloud, casting shadows across the white-jade basin. Any shred of lightheartedness between the lovers faded.

"Laya," he groaned, reaching for her arm with brazen intimacy. This time, she recoiled from his touch with a terse shake of her head—another warning.

It was Bulan who spoke first, breaking the tension between them. "You don't believe I can win, do you?"

Bato's eyes widened. "No, Dayang, that's not at all—"

"It's OK, I know what you meant . . . Anyway, like Luntok said, it wouldn't be fair," Bulan said in a tight voice, more to herself than to anyone else. Distracted, she turned away, her fists caught in her skirts.

Laya frowned. "Where are you going?" she demanded.

But Bulan barreled through the gardens as if she hadn't heard her, leaving Laya to ward off her suitors alone.

Her sister was still missing long after the royal gardens' visiting hours ended. The sun began to set on the horizon, and the nobles departed through the palace gates in a steady stream. Laya joined them. Feeling guilty from missing the beginning of the tournament, she agreed to watch Luntok's final fight. She tried her best not to worry about him as she made her way to the tournament platform, oddly with Eti in tow. Laya tried to tell Eti that fighting was ugly and dull, but Eti had insisted on coming. Why, Laya knew better than to guess, but she was grateful not to have to watch Luntok's fight alone.

The entire capital had gathered around the platform to watch the tournament conclude. Laya could hear the crowd all the way from the palace gates. Drums echoed over the shouts, their harsh, hollow beats rolling off the goatskin membranes like thunder. The pounding built, growing louder and louder as she and Eti hurried along the edge of the canal.

Long bamboo torches stood at each corner of the tournament platform, basking it in an orange glow. Luntok Kulaw and Utu Luma had already climbed up to the top and were standing on opposite sides of the ring. Laya stopped at the edge of the platform to admire Luntok. He was not as brawny as Utu Luma, but his sturdy silhouette stretched just as tall across the platform. The hazy light emphasized the toned muscles of his abdomen. And the glow of the flames danced across his smooth, handsome face.

"Let's go up to the stands," Eti said, tugging Laya along. She held back. "No," she said with a shake of her head. "We'll see the fight better from down here."

Both Laya and Eti stood out amidst the throng of commoners with their gleaming jewelry and fine clothes. Over her shoulder, curious whispers broke out. A few of the commoners would have jumped at the chance to speak with them had the fight not been about to begin.

A small smile spread across Laya's face as she gazed up at Luntok. He held the love of the crowd tonight, that was certain. Maynara may have hated his mother, but they adored him. How could they not, with his easy smile and chiseled features? Desire flared in the pit of her stomach as she watched Luntok draw his sword from its sheath.

Gods help her, she loved him.

Utu Luma's bulky form towered over the opposite edge of the platform. He wore nothing but a handloomed loincloth and a boar-tusk necklace, whose curved ends jutted from Utu's chest like gnashing teeth. He brandished a single-edged sword with a thick blade and a buffalo-horn hilt. He gazed coldly at his opponent, face melded into a mask of steel.

Above, the sun dipped lower on the horizon. Clouds stretched, painting pink and purple streaks across the sky. Day faded into dusk as the crowd in the pit grew restless. Laya's hands clenched into fists as the two men started to circle each other on the platform. The drums came to a halt. Around her, the crowd held its breath.

On the other side of the platform, a deep voice rang out, cutting through the silence. "Begin."

Utu charged at Luntok first. The air cracked with the sound of clashing metal as Luntok fended off his attack. The sheer force made Luntok's arms quake, but he managed to parry each and every blow.

The fight had barely commenced and already, Laya saw the sweat gleaming off Luntok's face and chest. If he was scared, he didn't show it. He matched Utu move for move. But Utu was the one setting the pace. He forced Luntok to keep up his defense, never once giving him a moment of rest. Luntok had the nimbleness of youth, but he lacked the stamina that came with experience. Laya was no expert in swordsmanship, but she knew that much. How long would he be able to keep it up?

The crowd jeered as Utu made a swipe at Luntok's neck, missing the skin by a mere fraction of an inch. A cutthroat act for a friendly tournament, and it wouldn't be the last. Fire raged in the dark pools of Utu's eyes. Had Luntok done something before the match to anger him? Utu looked ready to kill.

Utu Luma didn't relent. Each slash of his sword pushed Luntok back farther and farther until his right heel slipped off the platform's edge. The air left Laya's lungs as he swung his arms forward, regaining his balance.

"Luntok!" Her shriek pierced the air. Hundreds of heads turned toward her. Laya didn't glance at a single one of them. She didn't care who heard.

Luntok looked up, meeting Laya's eyes. She gave him a nod of encouragement. *Win*, she urged him, clasping her hand over her chest. *If not for you, then for me.*

He stood far away atop the tournament platform. But to reach Luntok, Laya didn't need words. Her burning gaze told him everything he needed to hear. Moments after she called out Luntok's name, something in his demeanor shifted. He held himself taller. The crowd could sense the shift as well. They spurred him on with deafening cheers.

Utu's thick eyebrows were furrowed in concentration. He raised his sword, beckoning to him. Luntok didn't hesitate. He attacked.

Finally, Laya understood why the nobles had begun to whisper after watching Luntok's first fight in the tournament. Why the men in the crowd gasped in awe, calling Luntok a god. He moved with inhuman speed, like a bird midflight. In some maneuvers, his feet barely touched the ground. His relentless strokes took Utu by surprise. Not even a seasoned warrior like him could anticipate Luntok's next move.

What use were the tusks of a boar against the swift wings of an eagle? Before long, Luntok gained the upper hand. He was the one forcing Utu to retreat across the platform. He was the one setting the pace. Utu could charge all he wanted, but none of his attacks landed. Luntok slipped out of every trap Utu laid for him and succeeded in setting up a few of his own.

"Argh!"

Utu cried out. Luntok had slashed him across the outside of his thigh. When he drew back his blade, blood splattered over the stained surface of the platform. The wound glowed red—deep and, judging by the anguished expression on Utu's face, debilitating. Around Laya, the crowd grew rowdier. Never had Utu been wounded in a tournament like this before.

Bravely, Utu lunged for Luntok, but he couldn't place much weight on his leg without crying out in pain. Luntok made the end brisk, bringing his weight down on Utu's sword with two decisive strokes that brought him to his knees. He cracked the hilt of his sword into the side of Utu's head for good measure. With a cry, Utu crumpled to the ground in a bloodied heap.

Luntok raised the hilt again. The flash of steel in the torchlight brought terror to Utu's eyes.

"Yield," he gasped, raising his palm to defend himself. "I yield."

Luntok lowered his sword, relenting at last. On all sides of the platform, the spectators burst into worshipful applause. Laya threw her arms around Eti and hooted in delight. The fight was over, but Luntok did not take a moment to relish his victory. He stalked over to Utu like a tiger. Before Utu could react, he raised his sword and cut the boar-tusk necklace clean off his neck. Luntok met Laya's gaze as he sauntered in her direction. When he knelt over the edge of the platform, she reached for him instinctively. He poured the necklace into her open hand.

"A token for you, Dayang," Luntok announced and brought her free hand to his lips. Cocky bastard that he was, he didn't kiss her knuckles like a gentleman. He turned her hand over and ran his lips over the tender flesh of her palm—a ridiculous, sensual gesture that sent a naughty ripple through the watching crowd.

Laya forgot herself completely. Her brown cheeks flushed pink. She swayed on her feet, gazing up at him in rapture. She could not help herself; love turned her into an idiot. A helpless, moon-eyed idiot.

"Fool," she whispered, so only he could hear.

"A fool for you," Luntok murmured and released her hand.

By the time he rose, Vikal had fought through the tittering spectators. He crossed the platform and raised Luntok's arm high in the air. "Ladies and gentlemen," he roared, "I present to you the greatest warrior in all of Maynara!"

Laya laughed as she watched Luntok drink in the glory. He raised his bloody sword to the heavens, inviting more applause. The drums resumed their thunder. Joyous shouting swelled above the music like a wave. How she yearned to join Luntok on the platform and kiss him for the entire city to see. So giddy was she, she might have done this, when a new figure broke away from the crowd.

"This tournament isn't over," Bulan declared as she climbed up to the platform.

Eti gasped in Laya's ear. "What on earth is she doing?" she cried.

Laya didn't answer. Her heart sank as Bulan stalked closer to Luntok at the center of the platform. She remembered the broken look on Bulan's face when the men insulted her earlier that afternoon in the gardens. Oh, Laya had a good idea what her sister was doing; she prayed to the gods she was wrong.

At the sight of the princess in the center of the fighting ring, the sea of spectators fell silent. Luntok dropped his arms. He and Vikal looked at Bulan in shock.

"Dayang Bulan!" Vikal said. "What are you—"

Bulan ignored him and faced the crowd. She cleared her throat. "I, Bulan Gatdula, challenge the greatest warrior in Maynara." Then she turned to Luntok with a hardened expression. "That is, if he's brave enough to accept."

Fury surged in Laya's veins. "Luntok's already won. Don't be ridiculous!" she called out, only to be ignored.

"I accept the princess's challenge." Anger flashed on Luntok's face. He took a threatening step toward her.

Bulan gave him a cold nod. She drew her sword and threw the sheath over the edge of the platform. "I knew you would."

Vikal pulled Luntok to the side and whispered in his ear, trying to reason with him. Laya lunged forward. She wanted to grab Bulan and shake some sense into her, but Eti grabbed her wrist.

"Laya, no," Eti pleaded, yanking her back. "Not here."

At the tears threatening to spill from her little sister's eyes, Laya relented. Maybe Eti was right. For Laya to clash with Bulan within the privacy of the palace walls was one thing, but to air their grievances before all of Mariit? Their mother might never forgive them.

Laya bit back a groan as she glanced back at the tournament ring. Healers had mounted the platform. They dressed Utu Luma's wounds and carted him away for further treatment. Servants came with buckets and rags, mopping up Utu's blood the best they could. Laya's stomach turned at the rusty smell.

This was how the tournament would end—her sister versus her lover. Laya wanted to strangle both of them. Instead, she stood helpless in the pit. What else could she do?

Vikal whispered one last thing in Luntok's ear. He patted him on the back and descended from the platform, casting a grave glance at Bulan before he left. Vikal was afraid, either for Luntok or for Bulan. Laya's eyes darted between the two warriors, terrified for both.

The drums picked back up as Bulan and Luntok began to circle each other on the platform. The sun had set fully now. In the glow of the torches, Luntok's blade gleamed red, his face half basked in shadow. Laya didn't need to see him to know what he was thinking. That this was his victory. That Bulan couldn't rip this away from him. He wouldn't let her.

And Bulan—Laya wanted to scream at her sister. Couldn't she have chosen another moment to prove her worth?

Bulan attacked first from the upper right. Luntok blocked with a flick of his sword. Unlike in his previous fight, he shifted immediately into offensive mode and attempted a low strike to her knees. Bulan parried and maneuvered out of his range.

With frightening speed, they continued to exchange blows. The crowd roared as they watched them dart back and forth across the platform in a perverse imitation of a dance. Luntok had speed and strength on his side, but Laya had watched her sister train her entire life. He couldn't match Bulan's eye for weakness. Bulan pursued every opening he gave her, no matter how fleeting. She forced him to defend and counterattack again and again, refusing to let him catch his breath.

Luntok's chest heaved, slick with sweat, as he came at her with an outward strike. She deflected and returned his attack, aiming at his ribs. This time, Bulan didn't need to exert quite as much effort to push him back. He was slowing down, tired. Any physical advantage he lorded over her was useless. Bulan broke free from the breakneck rhythm they'd fallen into and thrust forward, aiming straight for his groin.

Below the platform, Laya fumed. *No, Bulan, don't you dare.*

Luntok parried in time but lost his balance. He regained his footing and stared at Bulan with wild determination in his eyes. Bulan met his gaze with equal fervor. Laya's heart raced. She knew what was next to come.

Bulan whirled her sword and advanced on Luntok in relentless, fanlike patterns. He tried to gain the upper hand, tried to fly above her. Each time, Bulan dragged him back to the ground, breaking his graceful footwork. His frustration built. He grew sloppy. Bulan feinted, tricking him into a forward lunge. Then she spun around him and swiped at the tattooed plane of his back.

Luntok cried out, and Laya gasped. The cut was angry and long and red, but it wasn't deep. The true damage Bulan had inflicted was to his pride.

He whipped around, snarling. "You'd wound a man with his back turned?"

"Don't be a baby," she shot back. "That was a fair blow."

In the shadows, his jaw tightened. "What are you trying to prove?" he asked in a low voice.

"I've got nothing to prove to you."

The corners of his mouth curled into an unkind grin. "You're a decent warrior, Bulan, but you'd have made a terrible queen," he said, loud enough for the watching crowd to hear.

Bulan froze. A look of alarm passed over her face for a brief moment, but Laya caught it. Luntok had noticed it too.

Laya's eyes narrowed as she gazed at Luntok. Bulan may have challenged him to an unfair fight, but he had no right to speak that way to a princess. To Laya's *sister*.

Bulan swallowed hard. In the torchlight, Laya could see the glint of tears threatening to spill from the corners of her eyes. But Bulan didn't crumble at Luntok's taunts. She squared her shoulders. Raised her sword above her head.

Bulan refused to let him win.

After the tournament, no soul in Maynara would dare underestimate Bulan again. Laya watched, horrified, as she descended on Luntok like a charging bull. No clever strike could hold her back. Any restraint she might have afforded him vanished. She aimed for his heart, his throat. Her blade threatened to maim, to disembowel. Laya recognized the power radiating from Bulan's body with every movement—that immeasurable, godlike rage.

One mistake, and Luntok tripped over himself trying to match her. He dived for her in a center thrust. She sidestepped him and grabbed his arm. Without hesitation, she switched the angle of her weapon and jabbed the hilt straight into his gut. Luntok doubled over. She raised her sword again and drove the hilt straight into the side of his skull.

Laya gasped as the force knocked Luntok to his knees. Bulan kicked the sore spot. The jeering grew louder. Bulan didn't care if they cried foul. She drove the hilt onto his wrist. He cried out, and his blade clattered to the platform. Bulan couldn't stop, didn't want to stop. Once more, she raised her sword and brought it straight down on his head.

And Laya—Laya could no longer bear to watch.

"Stop!" she screamed, thrusting out both palms.

Before Bulan's hilt could make contact, the air above the platform split. A violent blast of wind nearly sent Bulan hurtling from the platform's edge. She skidded backward, away from Luntok, her sword swept from her grip.

Laya clambered into the ring and threw herself at Luntok's side. She cradled his swollen face in her hands, not caring who saw.

"Laya," he groaned, leaning into her palm.

She smoothed back the hair from his bloodied brow and hushed him. Her heart sank as she inspected the damage. An angry, purple splotch had already spread across his cheekbone. After witnessing the force with which Bulan had struck his head, Laya knew it was a miracle Luntok was still conscious.

"Bulan, you absolute maniac," Laya breathed. Her shoulders shook with anger. She couldn't bring herself to look at her.

"Don't be so dramatic," Bulan said. But her confidence from the start of the fight had long since faded, and doubt crept into her tone.

"Dramatic?" Laya let out a spiteful laugh. "You could have killed him."

She waited for another retort, but her sister said nothing. After a long, painful moment, Bulan walked away. Her footsteps echoed as she stalked across the platform. The crowd had no cheers for her, no applause. Only stunned silence.

Laya didn't watch her sister leave. She could not tear her gaze away from Luntok. He stirred feebly in her arms. Fear bubbled up in the back of her throat as she wrapped her arms around him. She bit back tears as she wiped the blood from his swollen lips.

"I'm here," she whispered. "I'm not going anywhere."
My love. My only love.
Luntok stirred again but did not try to speak. Laya held him until the crowd emptied from the stands and the pit. She held him until the beating drums and thunderous cheers faded to deafening silence. She would have held him for hours longer, but then the curtain of night fell over Mariit. With the moon came a unit of healers with their potions and dressings. They waved her off, impatient, as they hoisted Luntok onto a stretcher. Laya's throat constricted as she wavered, alone on the platform. She had no choice but to watch him go.

Sixteen

IMERIA

"I have failed you, Mother," Luntok slurred as she helped him into bed. He was under the influence of the sleeping draft the healers gave him to ease the pain. They had stitched him up the best they could with their prayers and petty sorcery, but Imeria could do better.

He groaned as she eased him onto his side and, as lightly as she could, undid the bandages on his back. The cut that awful Gatdula girl gave him was shallow, but it would scar if Imeria didn't act quickly. Her hand hovered over the wounded flesh. She closed her eyes as she reached deep into the blood, deep into herself, grasping for the power she had long been forced to hide.

The power greeted her like an old friend. It wove itself into the space between her fingers and Luntok's wound. The skin on the edges, cut cleanly by Bulan's blade, glowed. At her coaxing, it sealed itself shut.

"Tickles," Luntok murmured into the pillow.

"Hush." She needed all her concentration if she wanted to finish healing him.

Her forebears would not have blinked twice at such an injury. They once wielded power far greater than the Gatdulas could have imagined. That power was lost generations before; it died alongside the Kulaws' shamans and their sacred texts. And the Gatdulas, who thought themselves their saviors, rejoiced as they marched all the way south to Thu-ki and watched everything the Kulaws built burn.

The power to wield mind and flesh was believed to have disappeared generations before Imeria was born. But it lived, a flame born of the brutality and righteous anger that surged in her blood. It was a mere scrap of what she might have possessed had she received the proper training as a child, but maybe it wasn't too late. Her free hand wandered to the pocket of her skirt, where she kept the vials of precioso hidden.

Soon, she thought to herself. With haunting certainty, she remembered how Hara Duja threatened her with the earthquake earlier that morning. Perhaps it would all come to a head sooner than she realized.

When the last bit of skin was mended, Imeria released her hold on the power. The slightest use drained her. She sat down heavily on the edge of the bed. Her bones ached.

Luntok groaned as he rolled onto his back. He looked at her, bleary eyed. "You didn't have to do that."

When he'd been old enough to keep a secret, Imeria decided to show him what she was. He didn't understand it completely. The Kulaws' power did not dwell within him.

"Of course I did." Softening, she ran her fingers through his hair, as she had when he was a little boy. "You fought bravely today, Son."

"I lost," he said, stiffening when she kissed him on his forehead.

"You didn't lose. She stole your victory from you," Imeria said spitefully. She harbored more than enough rage for the two of them.

"I'd already won." A moan escaped from him, pitiful and childlike. He wrapped his arms around his middle as if to shield himself from the humiliation.

Imeria continued to stroke his hair. The last of her strength she used to prod at the warring energy she sensed within his skull. She couldn't read his thoughts, but she could feel the shame and anger and vindictiveness, emotions that crashed into one another like waves.

I know, Son. I know.

She laid her palm flush against his temple. It warmed as she calmed his thoughts into flat, bloodless plains. As her power worked through his mind, he began to relax into the mattress. His eyelids drifted shut.

"Thank you," he whispered as he slipped out of consciousness.

"Sleep now, darling. I will fix this." Slowly, gently, she withdrew her hand from his temple and rose from the bed. His head lolled to the side. By the time she reached the doorway, his breathing had steadied. He was fast asleep.

Imeria headed down to the veranda. For the dry season, the night air was abnormally thick with the metallic taste of rain. As she sprawled out on the divan, fanning herself, a servant arrived with a pitcher of rice wine.

"Leave it here," she said, and served herself.

If Imeria could have wielded her own mind, she would have rid herself of her spite long before. It festered in her blood like venom. Each time she found herself in Mariit, the gilded prison of her childhood, she could think of little else.

She finished her glass in a single gulp and served herself another. The Gatdulas relished humiliating them—first Imeria, now her son. In her own mother's eyes, that was the price of mercy. And Imeria had paid dearly.

The servant returned, hovering over her on the veranda. "My lady, a messenger stopped by from the palace." He presented her with a letter bearing the ancient seal of the Gatdulas.

Curious, Imeria opened the letter and held it to the light. "Oh my," she murmured. "Have the carriage ready in ten minutes," she told the servant, sweeping past him on her way back inside. Her fingers tingled with the last traces of the Kulaw power. A power that could do far more than heal shallow wounds.

Tonight. The word echoed in her head, louder than her own heartbeat.

Tonight, she had a meeting with the queen.

Hara Duja didn't turn around when Imeria was announced. She stood in the center of the great hall. The sconces burning from the tops of the walls illuminated her profile. The queen cast a long shadow, which stretched across the cavernous space.

"Leave us," the queen said to the guard who had escorted Imeria in. He nodded and left the room. The weighty giltwood doors groaned shut behind him.

They stood in silence for a long moment. Hara Duja was unable to look at her. Imeria fought the urge to fidget. She had never liked this room at night, how the shadows danced across the vaulted ceilings like vengeful spirits. The sandstone tiles, freshly scrubbed, gleamed between them like a desert sea. She cleared her throat, and even so, Duja said nothing.

The room was far too big for the pair of them.

Imeria remembered the last time they'd been alone together in this very room, though she wished she didn't. She had lost all sense of pride when she'd thrown herself at Duja's feet. *I am loyal. All I've ever wanted was to serve you. Please, Duja, don't send me away.*

And Duja had stood there, stone-faced, the same way she was looking at her now.

"Imeria. I'm sorry for what happened today," she said in a quiet voice. "It was dishonorable. I've spoken to Bulan. She will reach out to your son with a formal apology."

"An apology would be the least you can offer," Imeria said stiffly as she plucked at the stack of bracelets on her wrists. She did her best to ignore her heart racing. The queen had chosen to be alone with her, knowing full well the danger. However, Imeria couldn't move too fast, lest she ruin the opportunity. Her best bet was to draw out the conversation. For years, she had dreamed of what she would say when she had a chance to speak to Duja frankly like this. But the decades-old hurt had frozen her tongue. She found herself staring like a fool, struck dumb by the queen's presence.

"I wish I could offer you more." Duja looked at her then—truly looked—and Imeria saw genuine pain in her eyes.

"Duja . . ." She hated how her voice suddenly shook. She tore her gaze away, angry tears spilling down her face.

"Please," the queen said weakly, "I didn't wish for you to cry."

"If not my pain, what did you wish for?" she bit back. She felt like a child again, sobbing against the tiled floor.

"I'd hoped—" Duja's voice hitched. She cleared her throat. "I'd hoped we might put the grief between our families behind us."

Imeria let out a watery laugh. "And who are you to offer me peace? I've respected your desires and kept my distance. It's *your* daughters who have subjected *my* son to humiliation time and time again."

The queen didn't try to argue. "I know, Imeria, and that is my failure." Guilt clouded her features. In a quieter voice, she added, "One of my many failures as a mother."

Imeria swallowed. In Duja's words, she heard echoes of her own shame. She understood, intimately, the struggles of parenting a child with a frightening will of their own. Despite her rage, the tension in her shoulders slackened. "No, Duja," she murmured. "You know that's not what I meant."

Their eyes met. Years of unsaid questions flooded the air, filling the space beneath the vaulted ceiling. For the first time in two decades, the queen stood within arm's reach. One touch, and Duja's mind would be hers to wield. And yet, Imeria, who had come to the palace with a head full of schemes, found herself wavering where she stood.

The queen's gaze swept across the empty throne room. "The last time we were both here, we were scarcely more than children. We gave little thought to the years ahead. And motherhood was but a distant dream."

A wave of nostalgia coursed through Imeria's unwilling body. "Those days are long over. I try not to dwell on them," she lied.

The queen was not one to think rosily about the past. Yet to Imeria's surprise, Duja closed the distance between them. Her next words dripped with such bald-faced sincerity Imeria willed herself not to pull away. "I owe you more than one apology, I think."

She set her jaw. "If you're talking about that accursed day, I'm afraid you're twenty-two years too late."

But Duja didn't shrink back. She stared back at Imeria, pity flickering in her expression. "I never wanted to hurt you, Imeria. I was merely afraid."

They spoke not of the tournament, but of another battle. A battle that took place twenty-two years before. A battle that refused to end.

At long last, the accusation tore from her lips. "How could you fear me?" Imeria asked. "I protected you. I am the reason you defeated him. Without me, he might have—"

Imeria broke off midsentence. She knew Duja feared her powers. Feared the threat they might pose to her own. She remembered the heat of the fires that shot out of the crown prince's fingers, the cruel echo of his laughter, the way his eyes glowed red. The eastern wing crumbled to ash before him, yet he did not stop. Would not stop. He turned to Duja. He would have hurt her too if Imeria hadn't reached for her power, clawed deep into the rotten crevices of his mind, and stole his will from him.

She did this, knowing it would unveil her as the monster she was. But she took the risk and wielded her power anyway. Back then, Duja was the air in Imeria's lungs, the sun in her sky. Imeria would have risked everything to help Duja. To save her.

"I know," Duja said hoarsely. "I shouldn't have been so harsh with you. But you have to understand—I had lost so much so quickly. I was afraid."

Imeria had watched Duja mourn her mother from afar and was not without sympathy. But as she grew older, she realized Duja acted with a cold rationale that was rooted beyond fear. "If you had asked me to leave the capital, I might have understood," Imeria whispered. "But you didn't just send me away. You made me marry *him*."

Anguish flashed in Duja's eyes before she tore her gaze away. "You forget how the memory of the rebellion was so fresh in those days. Few would have married the traitor's daughter if not at my bidding," she said breathlessly. "I didn't want to cast you off on your own, Imeria. I wanted you to marry a good man."

Imeria didn't want to think of her late husband, who *had* been a good man. For a time, he almost made her feel whole again after Duja had ripped her from her life. He was kind and just and sweet, but not sweet enough to make Imeria swallow her bitterness. "That's not why you wanted me to marry him," she spat. "You thought he was barren."

Her late husband, Luntok's father, had had two wives before he married Imeria and no children of his own. Duja could present as many arguments as she liked, but Imeria knew the truth. Duja feared the resurgence of the Kulaws' power. She did not want Imeria to pass it on to her own kin.

Duja's lips flattened into a line. She did not deny it. "I thought it would be better this way," she said simply.

Imeria's mouth hung open in disbelief. *Better?* She wanted to rip the hair from Duja's head. Slash the gold from her collar.

Run her fingers over the tender skin where her shoulder met her neck.

It didn't have to be this way.

"I married him because I wanted to please you," she said as she wept. "I'd have done whatever you asked. I . . ."

She had been in love with her, but gods be blessed, Duja didn't let her say it.

"I know. I never should have doubted your devotion. I truly am sorry." A shade of sorrow passed over Duja's face—something akin to regret.

Something Imeria could use.

"If you truly regret what happened, Duja, perhaps you might consider this," she said, wiping her cheeks on her sleeve. Her tears stained the silk, but she didn't care.

"What is it?" Duja asked.

In one wild moment, Imeria forgot her treasonous plans. She reached for the queen's wrist and felt the rapid pulse beneath. *Push me away,* she willed her, but Duja didn't. Her fingers tightened around her wrist, just in case. She could have dug her claws into the queen's mind. Could have seized the opportunity dangling above her very nose. Instead, she lowered her voice to a desperate whisper. "Please, Duja. Let them have what we could not."

Duja's hand twitched in hers. Her eyes snapped open, watery and bleak. Imeria had bared her heart to Duja the same way twenty-two years before, the last time they'd been alone in the throne room. Was Duja also thinking about the life she might have had, had she opened her heart in return?

"I cannot," she said in a cracked voice. "You know why I cannot."

Imeria had not come here to beg, but she begged anyway. "Please. Luntok is no threat to you. He loves your daughter. I can see it. As do you."

Duja gave her a small, sympathetic smile. "Our children are young and foolish. Calf love does not a marriage make." Despite the queen's dismissal, Imeria detected the slightest hitch of desire in her words. A desire that mirrored her own.

"We were once young and foolish, Duja. Don't you remember?"

Duja swallowed hard. Imeria inched toward her, but the queen stopped her with a jerk of her head. "Imeria, *don't*," she whispered.

Imeria froze but didn't let her go. The fantasies she had shoved down for years flew from her lips. "The answer is so simple. How can you not see it? Despite the odds, despite your wishes, I bore a *son*. The same year you bore Laya. My son and your heir, our families united as they were always meant to be—this is how the gods willed it."

You and I, together once more, Imeria thought. That fantasy, she did not dare speak.

When Duja stayed silent, Imeria reached for her, brushing her thumb across her jawline. The queen reached up to cup Imeria's hand to her cheek. Her arm trembled with the onset of a minor tremor. She didn't pull away.

"Imeria," Duja sighed, and the sound of her name sent a cascade of want down Imeria's spine.

"Say yes," Imeria pleaded. "Think of how wonderful, how easy it would be."

Imeria no longer spoke on Luntok's behalf. She knew what she was asking. Her heart pounded in her ears. *Don't push me back. Don't say it's too late.*

The queen quivered on her feet. For one agonizing second, she leaned toward Imeria—close enough that Imeria could see the skinny tail of the burn scar peeking out from the collar of Duja's dress. But instead of edging closer, Duja drew back and closed her eyes as if the sight of her had become too painful. "Oh, my heart. If only my world was as easy as it appears to you."

Her answer was no, then.

Imeria felt as if a thread had broken inside of her. She wrenched her hand back, fresh tears threatening to spill over her eyelids. "You make it complicated," she all but hissed.

"Please understand. Laya is my heir. Like me, she cannot marry her first love. How I wish I could afford her this indulgence." She contemplated Imeria longingly, mournfully, as if she were a ship that had left her behind. Moments before, Imeria mistook her remorse as an opportunity to twist Duja's heart for her own gain. But now, to gaze upon her this way was like falling on her own knife.

"Oh, I understand, Duja. I understand that, however little I ask, you will never indulge me," she said, jerking back. The girlish yearning soured once more as rage boiled in her veins.

From high up on her obsidian throne, the queen liked to pretend she was a pillar of duty and sacrifice. But Imeria knew that beneath the steady veneer, Duja was calculating and selfish and cruel. She had preyed upon Imeria's devotion in the past when she'd cast her out of the palace. Scathingly, Imeria wondered if she'd summoned her to the throne room to humiliate her one last time.

Duja frowned. "That isn't fair. What you ask, Imeria, is no small thing. If we can speak rationally for once, perhaps we can—"

"No, Duja. You've said your piece."

The queen called out her name, but Imeria had already turned her back on her. She could no longer listen to Duja's reasons. No longer play this game. No longer pretend that, in the hollow stone of Duja's heart, Imeria had ever carved out a place.

Three

LOST ELEGIES

Dear Luntok,

    I have no words, my darling, other than to tell you how my heart aches on your behalf. Bulan is no sister of mine. Know that I will hate her forever after what she did today.

    The healers assured you a speedy recovery, but I need to see you to be sure. The moment you feel well enough, you must come to me. Dash the guards. Come through the palace gates if you must. I long, more than ever, to be with you.

    Since the tournament, I have asked myself over a hundred times how you could ever love a woman like me—a woman who is selfish and cruel, and who has never treated you with the kindness you deserve.

    Do you still love me, Luntok? I pray to the gods that this sentiment has not changed, given how awfully my family has treated you.

    I have not been fair to you in the past. So generous you've been with your promises and poems, while I've kept mine strapped inside my chest, hidden from view. Would you come if I asked?

    These are the words you have long yearned for, Luntok. I'm finally ready for you to hear them.

    All my love,
    Laya

Seventeen

DUJA

Duja's hands trembled as she steadied herself on the mahogany railing that wound around the main staircase. Her body shook from more than the tremors. Imeria's shadow followed her from the main halls. Haunting her, after all these years.

She continued, one careful step at a time, until she reached the upper floor. Night had fallen over Mariit. Moonlight slanted over the gleaming floorboards in riverlike streams. Most of the staff had retired for the evening. To Duja's relief, a stillness had settled over the palace. The upstairs corridor leading to the royal family's private chambers was empty, save for a serving girl, who bowed as Duja passed.

"Your Majesty," she said. In her arms, she bore a gown of delicate indigo silk. Laya had been wearing it in the gardens earlier that day.

"How is Dayang Laya?" Duja asked. After the tournament, Laya and Bulan had had a devastating fight. Their hateful words echoed across the courtyard. Everyone in the entire palace complex heard them. Duja had tried to calm Laya down earlier that evening, but her daughter was beyond consoling.

"One of the lady's maids saw to Dayang Laya's bath. I assisted her," the serving girl said. She was a scrawny thing with wan cheeks and a slight provincial accent. She must have been a recent recruit, because Duja had never seen her around the palace before.

"And?"

"The princess has been in there for hours, and she refuses to open the door." The girl diverted her eyes to the ground, hesitating. "Pardon my frankness, Your Majesty, but we fear she might be trying to drown herself."

Duja sighed and waved the girl off. "Go on. I'll see to her myself."

"As you please, Your Majesty." She bowed again, then scurried off to the laundress.

Duja continued to the end of the corridor. Dim, yellow light shone through the slit beneath Laya's door. Duja pressed her ear to the thick mahogany panels. On the other side, she could hear the faint sound of sniffling.

She knocked softly. "Laya, it's Mother."

The sniffling silenced. Then a pattern of angry footsteps echoed across the floorboards as Laya approached the door.

"What do you want?" Laya snapped, her voice muffled through the layers of wood.

"I want to speak to you," she said. "Please let me in."

A reluctant sigh, then Laya relented. The door creaked open. She leaned against the frame, her arms crossed. "You have my attention," she said in the lofty tone Duja hated.

Laya could be as awful to her as she liked, but no haughty expression could hide the red splotches around her irises or the puffy bags under her eyes. The poor girl had been crying for hours. Her hair, damp from her bath, hung limply around her shoulders. She looked less like the steel-faced tyrant she pretended to be and more like a drowned rat.

"I was worried about you," Duja said.

Laya stared back. Her bottom lip trembled. The haughty mask fell from her face like cracked stone. "Oh, Mother," she said, crumpling as she barreled into Duja's arms.

Duja froze, surprised. She had not seen Laya cry since she was a child. Back then, she would always run to her father for comfort—never Duja. *She still needs me,* Duja realized. She softened as Laya sobbed into her chest, her tears seeping through the fine silk of her blouse.

"Hush, darling." Duja wrapped her arms around Laya and led her into the bedroom. They sat together on the edge of the bed, and Laya sobbed in earnest.

"Mother, I don't know what to do. I cannot bear it." She leaned against Duja as if she no longer had the strength to hold herself up. Her body shook so violently, Duja stared at her in alarm.

"Come now. Everything will be all right." Duja brushed the tangled waves from Laya's face. As much as she hated to see her daughter in pain, she could not deny the warmth that spread through her chest as she held her. How long had it been since they'd embraced each other like this?

"Everything is ruined," Laya said between ragged sobs. "Everything is ruined, and I can do nothing about it."

Duja pursed her lips. "Is this about Luntok?"

At the sound of his name, Laya let out a pitiful wail. "He refused to speak to me after the tournament. I know I shouldn't, but I sent for him. And because of what Bulan did, he hates me. He will never come again."

The tension in Duja's shoulders receded. She was relieved to hear that Luntok was keeping his distance, but she didn't dare tell Laya so. "He could never hate you," she said, which was the truth. Imeria hadn't lied earlier in the throne room. Luntok was obsessed with Laya, and Laya returned his infatuation. But Duja ought to have warned her that to tangle oneself with a Kulaw was dangerous.

Laya drew back and gazed at Duja, her eyes wide in watery hope. "If there was a way for us to be together—truly together this time..."

Duja's heart lurched. "Oh, Laya."

She couldn't indulge her. She couldn't go down this road again.

Laya heard the resignation in her tone and grasped her hands, begging, "Please, Mother. I know you hate Imeria, but Luntok is different. He would never harm me... or anyone else. If you would allow him—"

"No, Laya, I cannot allow that," Duja said, more harshly than she intended.

"Mother, please." Fresh tears spilled out of the corners of Laya's eyes. Duja knew her daughter and her wily tricks. Knew how skillfully she could feign heartbreak, just to cajole others into doing her bidding. But these were true tears. And this was raw pain—Duja knew because she had felt it once herself.

She wanted to comfort Laya the way she'd wished to be comforted. Instead, she gave her shoulders a firm shake. "You have no idea the danger these people pose to our family."

Laya's brow furrowed. "What sort of danger?" she asked. "I can marry Luntok without reviving any sort of ancestral bloodright. Don't tell me you actually believe in those stupid myths."

Except they weren't mere myths. Magic *did* lie dormant in the noble bloodlines. And the Gatdulas were no longer the only ones with divine powers. Fear pierced her body at the reminder. *Imeria Kulaw, wielder of mind and flesh.*

The memories flooded Duja's mind with a vengeance. Her

brother's laughter. Imeria's screams. Her nose stinging with the caustic scent of ash. Angry, black clouds billowing above the eastern wing, where Pangil's fires continued to rage. Ear-piercing screams ringing out from inside the building, but all Duja could focus on was Pangil's face.

His head lolled back into Imeria's soot-streaked hands. He stared up at the smoke-filled sky, unseeing. Inky pools seeped out from his irises, blotting out the whites of his eyes.

Duja could barely bring herself to speak. "Imeria—*by the gods*," she had whispered.

"Duja. I can explain," Imeria said, releasing Pangil as if his skin burned. She reached for her, but Duja recoiled from her touch.

"It can't be," she said in a strangled voice as she stared back at Imeria. Her gut knotted in dread. She squeezed her eyes shut, blinding herself to the horror. She wanted to scream. *Not you, my heart. My dearest heart.*

Duja blinked away the memories of ash and smoke. Imeria's shadow disappeared. Laya was still sitting beside her on the bed. She clutched Duja's hand, impatient for her reply.

"You wish to know what danger?" Duja's voice cracked. The inside of her throat had gone dry. She shook her head once more as she pulled away from her daughter. "Let Luntok go. If you don't, I fear you may not survive the consequences," she said. The words came out harsher than she intended.

Laya's eyes widened. "I don't understand."

"Let him go, Laya," Duja repeated. "I don't want to hear of this again."

"*No*," she said, her voice rising with the threat of oncoming sobs. "Mother, please—"

"Enough of this." With a heavy heart, Duja swept away from

the bed. Laya's sniffling followed her on her way out. Duja hadn't told her what she wanted to hear. She could not bear to reveal the truth about Imeria's powers, but how else could she make Laya understand? She paused, leaning against the doorway. "I promise you, Laya. You will find a better man—a man worthy of your affection. Luntok is not him," she added without turning around.

This time, Laya did not answer, but Duja could sense the storm inside her. Duja could say nothing to console her.

Swallowing the lump in her throat, she eased the door shut behind her. It was too late to summon Maiza, even though every inch of Duja's body protested at the slightest movement. Each step she took away from Laya was harder than the last. Her joints groaned as she made her way to her own chambers, where Hari Aki was in bed, reading. He set his book aside and looked at her with a somber expression.

"Well?" he asked.

"Laya is distraught." Duja kicked off her sandals and stretched out beside him on the bed. Her fingers shook as she reached up to trace the fine black stubble on his chin.

He took her trembling hand and planted a gentle kiss atop her knuckles. "Give her a few days to mend her heart. She will understand in time."

"I don't know about that," Duja said with a weary sigh. She knew that this kind of pain had a way of braiding itself into the fleshy tendons of your soul. Time did not heal this kind of heartbreak; rather, it allowed it to fester. Duja had not realized the extent to which such pain could endure until she spoke with Imeria in the throne room.

Earlier that evening, Imeria had wept just as she had the first time Duja sent her away. Imeria saw it as a punishment, but Duja truly had wanted to protect her. Marrying Imeria was out of the question—and not simply because they were both women. If they had been born into different families, Duja might have continued to love Imeria all her life, taking a husband for the sole purpose of producing Gatdula heirs. The royal court was no stranger to such arrangements. But in their eyes, loving a Kulaw was not only dangerous. It was unforgivable.

In the years after the Kulaw rebellion, the scars remained fresh. Few of the datus loyal to the Gatdulas would have taken news of their power's resurgence lightly if they had known. They might have demanded Imeria's removal, or worse—her death. And if Duja had allied with Imeria against their wishes, the other royal families might have banded together against them. The ensuing war would have brought an end to Maynara as they knew it.

As much as Duja feared Imeria, she couldn't let that happen.

After twenty-two years, she hadn't told a single soul about Imeria's infernal abilities. Not the rest of the council. Not Maiza. Not even her husband, with whom she kept no secrets. None, except this.

"I'll speak to Laya again in the morning. You mustn't worry so." Aki kissed her on the forehead. Her devoted husband. When it came to Duja's true history with Imeria, he had his guesses. Even after all their years of marriage, she had yet to muster the courage to tell him.

Duja chewed the inside of her lip. "I suppose you're right."

She changed into her night things and crawled under the sheets. They turned the lights down and rolled back the window screens. Silvery light streamed through the capiz-shell panels. A light breeze rolled in from the Untulu Sea, and the panels quivered in their rosewood frames. Aki drifted to sleep minutes later. Duja listened to his soft, steady breathing as she stared into the darkness.

Despite Aki's words, she could not calm the thoughts warring in her mind. After the tournament fiasco, Duja's worries grew to terrifying heights.

Twenty-two years earlier, Imeria had accepted Duja's rejection. She left the palace and married her husband on Duja's orders, albeit with spite and bitterness. Given the love they once had for each other, Imeria obeyed. That love was gone now, burned to a crisp. Duja could count on Imeria's devotion no longer.

What good was love in the face of power? Would she steal Duja's will from her if she had the chance?

No. Duja couldn't trust love, couldn't trust any Kulaw with a scrap of strength. Imeria had no place in the capital—much less in the queen's bedchamber. Duja had no choice but to cast her aside.

As for their children—she thought back to the tournament with a sinking feeling. If Luntok was anything like his mother, he would not live down this heartbreak easily. How would Luntok react when Laya, at last, turned him away?

The king was right. She needed to conserve her strength for the rest of the feast days, until the end of the week. This was a worry for another evening.

With a last sigh, Duja pushed the question from her mind. The wind outside the window quieted to a distant murmur. Her thoughts stilled as fatigue beat down her worries. Finally, she closed her eyes, surrendering to the haunting shadows and smoke-filled dreams.

Eighteen

LAYA

The muted rapping on Laya's door announced that a new day had once again broken over Mariit.

Laya rolled onto her side with a groan. The other half of the mattress was cold. She dreamed Luntok had come to see her, but when she opened her eyes, she was alone.

A maid's voice chimed from the other side. "Dayang, could I help you—"

"Go away," Laya snapped, and spent the rest of the morning watching patches of sunlight creep sluggishly up the whorled wall panels across from her bed.

No one was waiting for her on the terrace when, after several hours of deliberation, she summoned the strength to leave her chambers. A wave of sadness washed over her as her gaze fell on the empty breakfast table. It was foolish to think she would find anyone there. With the feast days ending the next evening, the king and queen had an endless list of engagements. The king, she knew, had gone to Mariit's lower wards to hear the commoners' grievances, while Hara Duja was trapped inside one of the palace's receiving rooms with members of minor nobility. It was just as well, for Laya did not wish to speak with her mother after their conversation the previous evening.

Let Luntok go, she'd said. Maybe Laya did have to let him go. It was better to forget him now. If he returned her letter with hateful words, Laya did not know if her heart could bear it.

For company, Laya had no one else to turn to but her sisters. Eti, as was typical, was nowhere to be found. And Bulan—Laya seethed at the thought of running into her that morning. After the tournament, they'd exchanged violent words. Laya had been furious enough to summon a monsoon, but she'd kept her head on her shoulders. She didn't want to give Bulan the benefit of confirming that she was the more levelheaded, more rational one. Laya, despite her frustration, refused to prove her sister right.

Laya knew life hadn't been kind to Bulan, whom the gods cursed at birth. Compared to Laya, she had so little. Without the power of Mulayri, what gifts could Bulan claim? Sword fighting was the sole domain in which she excelled. The day before in the gardens, the boys had wounded her pride when they implied her claim to excellence was empty, like most things about her. Laya might have pitied her had Bulan chosen to inflict her vengeance on anyone else but Luntok.

Later that night, in the heat of anger, Bulan screamed at her, tears streaming down her face, "You would choose Luntok, the traitor's heir, over your own blood." The words continued to rattle in Laya's mind, denying her peace. Bulan was wrong. Laya loved Luntok, but she was a Gatdula above all else. Yet she knew Luntok's heart as if it were her own—a Kulaw he may be, but he was no traitor.

But Laya did not want to agonize over Luntok any more than she wished to think about her sister. He had not answered her letter the previous evening, which worried Laya more than she cared to admit. Did he truly hate her, or had Bulan wounded him so badly he could not hold a pen?

Laya didn't know what she was thinking when she left the terrace and made her way downstairs to the central courtyard. She marched up to the guard stationed before the eastern wing and demanded entrance.

"If you please, Dayang," the guard said, opening the door to let her in.

Muffled voices carried down to the shadowed entrance hall. Laya's ears perked up. She looked at the staircase leading to the upper floor, confused. Ariel wasn't alone.

Laya crept upstairs. She kicked up small clouds of dust as her sandals padded across the tiled corridor. A faint vinegary scent hung in the air, mingling with the dust. She wrinkled her nose. The Orfelian was a commoner, but he was still a guest. Surely, her mother would have sent someone to clean his living quarters.

At the end of the corridor, the door to the Orfelian's study hung open. She peered inside. Ariel was once again hunched over his writing desk. Laya blinked, shocked to find Eti sitting across from him. Their heads were bent over a book. Eti jabbed her finger at one of the pages, chatting animatedly. Ariel nodded, his spectacles sliding down the bridge of his nose as he followed her finger. Unlike so many members of the court, who merely humored Eti when she spoke, Ariel seemed genuinely interested in what the younger girl had to say.

The corners of Laya's lips quirked up in a tiny smile. She stepped into the room, clearing her throat. Both of them looked up from the book.

Eti brightened. "Laya, look! I've saved Ariel from eternal boredom. Come see."

Laya raised an eyebrow before settling into the chair beside her. "Oh?" she said. "How can that be?"

"Dayang Eti was kind enough to bring me some reading

materials from the royal library," Ariel clarified, meeting Laya's gaze.

Laya's cheeks warmed at the sight of his grin. She remembered the spark that wound through her the last time she and Ariel were alone together. A trick of the mind, she was convinced. That spark wouldn't strike her again.

She turned her attention to the book laid out before them. "What sort of books did you bring him?" she asked.

Eti hauled a few heavy tomes from the floor and deposited them at the edge of the desk. They landed on the lacquered mahogany surface with a loud thump.

"Mostly historical accounts," she chirped. "I asked Father to bring me the most comprehensive volumes. Ariel's got nothing to do at the moment, so I thought these would keep him busy."

Eti was a kindhearted child, and she never failed to impress Laya with her thoughtfulness. Although if Eti wished to keep the Orfelian entertained during his stay at the palace, she ought to have chosen something a touch more entertaining than Maynara's densest historical texts.

Laya scanned the titles of the books beside her, biting back a chuckle. "Everything you've chosen is in Maynaran," she remarked.

"That won't be a problem," Ariel said. "I know how to read Maynaran now, after all." He gave Laya a pointed look.

"In that case, these books ought to keep you enthralled," she said dryly.

Ariel's grin broadened. For Eti's sake, he did not say anything to the contrary. "You will find, however, that my vocabulary is lacking," he told Laya.

"I should think, then, that another lesson is in order," she said, her eyes twinkling with the promise of a challenge.

Surprise flickered in Ariel's expression. "If that is what you are offering, Dayang, I would be grateful," he said, bowing his head.

She stared at him. He had yet to lose his nasal Orfelian accent, which grated Laya's ears to no end, but something had changed in his inflection—the rolling dips within words, the slight upturns at the ends of his phrases. In the few days since Ariel had arrived, he had begun to adopt Maynaran's songlike speech patterns.

Fascinating. Laya smiled to herself. The Orfelian was definitely not a fool.

"Ariel can speak over a dozen languages. He's traveled around the world," Eti piped up between them. "Laya, did he tell you that?"

"No, he did not." Well, that explained how fast Ariel had picked up Maynaran. Once more, she met his gaze. "I suppose we have a great deal to learn from each other."

"Yes, Dayang. I suppose we do."

Ariel stared back at her with the same brazen openness, which Laya might have mistaken for insolence in other circumstances. This time, she didn't mind. She understood the intent she saw behind those spectacles. Ariel wished to read her, the same way he wished to read the book splayed out on the desk between them. The same way Laya wished to read him.

She had not forgotten the vow she'd made to Ariel before their first language lesson. She would discover his true business in Maynara. In the meantime—

Laya reached for a sheet of paper on the other side of the desk. "Another lesson," she said without preamble.

Ariel chuckled and reached for his pen. "Certainly, Dayang. Whatever pleases you."

They went over the Salmantican alphabet once more. He taught her how to link the letters together to form words. Laya found the alphabet easier to understand than she had the first lesson, but perhaps that was because she poured every ounce of her concentration into mastering it. The paper she had stolen from Ariel's desk earlier that week was still hidden beneath the floorboards in Laya's bedroom, and she had pored over it the previous night to distract herself from her sorrows. She quickly discovered it was a letter, addressed to someone named Nelo and written in Orfelian. Her first lesson with Ariel had not taught her much, but she was able to cobble together a baffling string of words and transcribe them into Maynaran: *comrade*, *prince*, and most cryptic of all, *precioso*. Laya would learn to read the rest of it, no matter how painful.

With the letter in mind, she watched Ariel's gestures and mimicked them, committing each stroke to memory. The awful, ugly script kept her hands occupied—and her thoughts oceans away from Luntok and Bulan.

When Ariel complimented Laya's progress, her stomach betrayed her and fluttered in excitement. "Now that you know this writing system, you'll be able to read most western languages as well as Orfelian," he explained.

"I'm not sure what good it will do me, but that's satisfying to hear," Laya said with a shrug.

In the seat beside her, Eti yawned. She had been following the lesson until then. But she'd become bored. "If this is what you plan on doing all day, then I'm going to practice my wielding," she said.

Laya tousled her hair. "Go on, then," she said, dismissing her. She turned back to Ariel, a renewed hardness in her tone. "I don't believe our lesson is over quite yet."

"Suit yourselves." Eti set her pen down and swept from the room, no doubt to spend the rest of the afternoon crafting a bangle or two.

Ariel held Laya's gaze, this time with a frown. "You truly don't believe learning to communicate in these languages will be useful to you?"

"To communicate with foreign dignitaries, you mean?" she asked.

"To communicate with anyone who isn't Maynaran."

"When I am queen, I shall require any foreign dignitaries to study my language before I deign to speak with them. As for non-Maynarans..." Laya trailed off with a laugh. "I hardly think I will encounter them enough in my lifetime to make learning their languages a worthwhile endeavor. You, of course, are the exception."

Ariel's frown deepened. "With all due respect, Dayang, Maynara is but one small island in a vast world. I understand your people's policy of isolation, but even isolation has its limits. There are dozens of countries out there with whom you might form a beneficial alliance. As a future sovereign, you must be at least a bit interested in this."

Laya matched his frown with one of her own. "By the gods. You sound like you've been spending too much time with my mother," she said, annoyed. She was willing to tolerate Ariel's insolence, but she was not going to allow this foreigner to presume he knew what was best for Maynara's future, more than she did.

"Hara Duja is being realistic," Ariel said, frustration rising in his tone. "Maynara must open the door to the rest of the world in some way, be it through trade agreements or diplomacy. Openness does not always end in conquest."

"Oh, but it does. We need only look at your homeland to know this," Laya retorted. She slouched back in her seat, crossing her arms in front of her chest. "No matter what you believe, Ariel, Maynara does not need the rest of the world. We've survived hundreds of years for a reason. If closing our doors protects our people, so be it."

"Maynara may not need the rest of the world, but the rest of the world needs Maynara. Did you once consider that?" Ariel shoved his spectacles back up the bridge of his nose and leaned in. "I watched you in the courtyard the other day, Dayang. Had I an ounce of your power, I—"

Laya cut him off with a harsh laugh. "Go on, then, Orfelian. You would not know the first thing about Mulayri's power. All this talk of the rest of the world, you speak like an enslaved man."

Ariel's gaze snapped to hers. "You dare speak to me of enslavement?" he asked in a low, gravelly voice.

"What else are we to speak of? It's all your people know," Laya said, raising her chin. She was accustomed to hurling cruel words at anyone who dared challenge her. Less often did they throw their own cruel words back.

Ariel threw his pen down, splattering ink trails across the sheets of paper. Behind his spectacles, his eyes bulged with anger.

"And what do you know of Orfelia, sitting up here in your palace?" Ariel said, his cheeks reddening with each sentence. "For centuries, my people have fought for freedom. We penned pamphlets. We rallied the resistance. And my friends—these uncultured imbeciles, as you regard them—they could not carve out islands from the ocean floor. They could not summon the wrath of the skies at their fingertips. Their power was but a *dream*, and they *died* for it." Fury flashed in his sharp, scholarly eyes. He jumped to his feet, the legs of his chair scraping across the floorboards. "Tell me, Dayang, what kind of mindless slave would risk their life for that?"

His words rang out across the room, which suddenly felt too small for the pair of them. Ariel fell silent, bracing his weight against the edge of the desk. His shallow breaths filled the study. Laya didn't dare speak. She stared up at him in astonishment, her mind reeling from his impassioned words. Of all the information she had hoped to wheedle from the Orfelian, this was not what she'd expected him to confess.

Ariel flushed as he caught his breath. He sat back down, horrified. "I—I apologize, Dayang," he said quietly, shifting his eyes to his lap. "I should not have lost my temper. You meant no disrespect."

She blinked as she gazed back at him in awe, momentarily struck speechless. His candidness caught her off guard. Laya's cheeks heated, not in rage, but in shame. She cleared her throat. "No, Ariel, I am the one who should apologize. I meant every disrespect. And that was wrong of me."

Ariel's outburst hung heavy in the air; in comparison, her words came out thin, feeble. Inadequate. Rarely did she admit fault, and miraculously, the Orfelian had startled an apology out of her.

His eyes flitted back to hers in shock. "You aren't angry?"

Laya shook her head. No, she wasn't angry. Her skin prickled as the damned spark burst through her once again.

She stared at him and, this time, truly drank in his features. In the muted light of the sitting room, Ariel appeared to be in his midtwenties—younger than Laya had initially thought him to be. But she could sense a weariness in him that belonged to a man twice his age. The Orfelian was lying about what had brought him to Maynara. He was not who he said he was. But something he said struck a chord with Laya. Maybe Hari Aki was right. They did have much to learn from each other after all.

Laya did not know what overcame her when she reached across the desk and cupped her hand over his. The slight touch alarmed them both, but Ariel did not pull away. "I am sorry, Ariel—about your friends," she murmured. "They were brave to fight. And what happened to them was awful."

Her words did not encapsulate half of what Laya wished to say, but to make amends, they were enough.

Ariel swallowed. "Thank you, Dayang . . . It was awful," he said, his voice tight.

He was still in pain, she realized. She did not want to press him any further. Instead, Laya leaned back and reached for her pen. Something told her that would please him.

"If you don't mind, Ariel," she said gently, "I suggest we continue with our lesson."

Ariel continued to plague Laya's thoughts until she retreated to her chambers after supper. The evening's festivity had been an intimate affair involving the Gatdulas, cousins from Hari Aki's bloodline, High Shaman Maiza, and a handful of the queen's closest, crustiest advisers. Her father had invited Maynara's most exclusive troop of dancers and musicians to perform for them while a singer narrated their ancient myths. Normally, this was the feast-day event that excited Laya the most.

But throughout their performance, Laya did not pay attention to the gongs and flourishes, nor to the story of Mulayri, who'd sent his birds down to earth and pecked mankind into creation. Her mind wandered to the Orfelian's fallen rebel friends. She imagined them to be as young as Ariel, wide-eyed fools who dived headfirst into a battle they knew they could not win. A vision of Ariel charging alongside them, a saber in his scholar's hands, his wire-framed spectacles splattered with blood and soot, broke her heart, but she couldn't stop thinking about it.

Was it Maynara's responsibility to balance the odds in those unwinnable fights? To bolster the scrappy rebels scattered about the world? That was what Ariel had implied. His words echoed in her mind as she shut the door to her bedroom behind her. So absorbed was she in their conversation earlier in the eastern wing, she did not realize she was not alone.

"Laya."

Luntok's voice, softer than rustling palm leaves, jolted Laya back to reality. She looked up with a gasp. He was standing on the balcony, his profile silhouetted against the full moon. When he stepped out of the shadows, he gazed at her, his smooth face fixed in a somber expression.

"Luntok," Laya cried. She forgot about the world beyond her bedroom when she ran to him. Every inch of her body sang in delight. Luntok had come to the palace. He hadn't abandoned her.

"I'm here," he whispered, gathering her in his arms. The blood and swelling were gone, flushed away by the healer's touch. Luntok stood before her, as strong as he'd been before his fight against Bulan the previous evening.

Laya pulled back to cup his face, her brow knitted in concern. "When you didn't answer, I thought you were deathly hurt. Or perhaps . . ." She trailed off, swallowing hard. "Perhaps you didn't want to see me again."

Luntok caught her hand and held it to his cheek. "I would die if I couldn't see you. I'd throw myself off the summit of Mount

Matabuaya. I'd pitch myself into the Untulu Sea," he said, and pressed his lips into the tender flesh of her palm.

"A poet's words." Her tone was playful, but her eyes were not. Luntok was there. She threaded her long, slender fingers between his. She thought back to her mother's warning, and her heart grew heavy. No, Laya wouldn't let Luntok go—not yet.

"I meant them," Luntok said. His gaze scalded her skin, a flame that blazed hotter the longer he looked at her. Laya remembered what she had written in her last letter; that was what she'd promised him.

Without hesitation, she wrapped her arms around his neck, reeling him closer. "You must be careful with your words, poet," she whispered in his ear. "My heart cannot bear the beauty of them, and I have already fallen so deeply in love."

"Love," he repeated, his voice strained, as if the word were fragile porcelain that would fracture the moment he uttered it.

Laya nodded. "I love you, Luntok," she said as her heart pounded in her chest.

With trembling hands, he drew her closer by the waist. Laya tilted her mouth up to meet his and melted into their kiss. Her heart soared. Her heart ached. She ran her hands up the tattooed skin on his arms, tugging him toward her, desperate to eliminate every last inch of space between them.

As she deepened the kiss, her fingers trailed down the front of his vest, tracing the soft, scarlet threads. Farther they traveled, down his torso and abdomen, before coming to rest atop the hardening tent at the inseam of his trousers.

Luntok jerked back. "Don't say this is love, Laya," he said, shaking his head. "Not unless you truly mean it."

Laya's eyes widened in alarm. She cupped his face once more in her hands, but he refused to meet her gaze, his jaw tautening beneath her fingers. "Of course I mean it," she said, breathless. "I love you, Luntok. I have always loved you—you and no one else."

"*Then marry me.*" The proposal tore through Luntok's lips like a snarl. He grasped the nape of her neck and pressed his forehead to hers. "Marry me, and I'll love you the way no other man can love you. Marry me, and I'll make you happy until the end of our days."

Laya laid a hand on his chest. She didn't shove him back right away. "For Mulayri's sake, Luntok," she told him weakly. "What do you expect me to say?"

"Say *yes*. Damn the kingdom. Damn your family. We belong together, Laya. And we'll silence anyone who dares tell us otherwise," he said, and gave her a sudden shake. Laya stared up at him in shock. He didn't hurt her—he wouldn't dare hurt her—but she'd never heard him speak with such raw panic before. For the first time, Luntok scared her.

When she didn't answer right away, he blustered on. "In your heart, you know who I am—and what kind of king I could be. I understand the south, same as I understand the rest of Maynara. Unlike Bato or Waran or the other imbeciles clamoring for your hand, I'm the only one who could rule justly by your side. I wouldn't whisper mindless drivel in your ears, nor would I grovel at your feet. *You* would be the hands that steer this land in the right direction. And I—" He drew in a deep breath, tenderness momentarily dampening the madness in his expression. "I would be your eyes."

Laya's face fell. She could see how ardently Luntok believed he was the sole man in the realm worthy of being her king. Part of her wanted to believe it as well. It was true; no one understood her better than he did. Their utter acceptance of one another drew them together all those years before—a mutual appreciation that stretched deeper than lust.

But Luntok did not understand Maynara as well as Laya. Although the rebellion was long over, contempt for Thu-ki permeated deep into the core of the island. Her people could never stomach a Kulaw on the throne. To marry Luntok would be to lose their favor. To risk her right to the throne. And no love—not even one as fierce and unwavering as Luntok's—was worth such a gamble.

Carefully, she disentangled herself from him and took a step back. "I love you, Luntok. Believe me. I *want* to be with you," she said. Her voice cracked, along with the walls she'd built up to protect herself. The lie couldn't go on—it wouldn't be fair to either of them. She swallowed the grief rising in her throat and, more firmly, added, "But I cannot go against the will of my family."

Luntok stared at her, unfazed. "Why not?" he demanded.

"Why not?" she echoed. *"Why not?"* She wanted to scream at him for his stupidity. Instead, she sputtered out a sardonic laugh. "Because I am Hara Duja's heir, not some minor noblewoman you can pluck from the masses. Because soon I will be queen of Maynara."

"All the more reason we should marry. As queen, you will be able to do as you please," he insisted. "Just like generations of Gatdulas before you. Just like the rest of your family."

Laya felt the blood drain from her face. "What do you mean? That Gatdulas simply *do as we please*?" she asked, stiffening.

"Oh, I don't know. Just look to your great-grandfather," Luntok said, and threw up his arms in disgust. "The old king ignored every datu on his council when he opened Mariit to foreigners. The datus warned him, and still, he didn't spare a single thought about the harm they might inflict upon the city. Or look no further than your sister. She forced her way into the tournament after it had already ended. Although she's not a true Gatdula, is she?"

Enough. Luntok went too far. The moment he insulted Bulan, Laya clenched her hands into fists. She took a threatening step toward him. "My sister is as much a Gatdula as you are a Kulaw," she said, lowering her voice to an icy pitch. "And it doesn't matter how much we love each other. We cannot change who we are. *That*, Luntok, is why we can never marry."

The truth swung between them, swifter than an executioner's blade. Luntok flinched as if she had struck him. For a long moment, he stood in front of her, unable to speak. Laya watched the emotions warring in his expression. Shock crashed into outrage, which erupted into despair. He crumpled at Laya's feet and buried his face in her skirt. Without thinking, Laya reached out to comfort him. His shoulders shook with silent sobs.

"Oh, darling," she sighed, relenting as tears slid down her cheeks. She cradled his head in her hands as he sobbed into her knees. They stayed like that for a long while. When Luntok quieted, he looked up at her with glassy, red-rimmed eyes.

"I cannot lose you," he said, in a voice of sober resignation. "I can't, Laya. I refuse."

Sensing the panic of denial rising inside him, Laya pulled him to his feet. She leaned in and kissed him, long and deep, so he knew she meant it. The last fraying thread inside her broke when she pulled back to whisper, "Lie with me tonight, Luntok. Be with me, as if it were the last time."

Luntok's breath hitched in his chest. He didn't lunge to make love to her as he would have in the past. That was when they'd thought their love might be spared from the harsh rules that governed their world. When they believed their tragedy would be different. Gently, he caressed her face, tracing a line with his knuckle from the ridge of her cheekbone to the curve of her bottom lip.

"I cannot lose you, Laya," Luntok said again. This time, her name rolled off his lips like an ardent prayer. He looked down at her, his eyes darkening with a zealous need. Then he gave her another shake, this one more restrained than the first. "How can I make you understand?" he asked. "I would do anything for you. I love you. Gods help me, I love you."

Luntok's urgent pleas didn't scare her anymore. Hearing the desire in his voice, Laya's blood surged. She drew him to the bed. "Come, then," she murmured, pulling him on top of her. "Show me how much."

They did not tear off each other's clothes. Rather, they shed each layer with care, as if unwrapping a delicate gift. For once, they made love slowly, as if they were the only creatures on earth, as if time had yet to begin. Laya shivered when he dragged his lips down her throat and past her stomach, lower and lower, until he reached the juncture between her legs at last.

"Luntok!" she choked out, tangling her fingers in his hair.

This, too, they took time with. Luntok teased out her pleasure nimbly, patiently, as she arched into his tongue.

The rattan bed frame creaked afterward, when Luntok joined her on the mattress. Laya moaned against the pillows as he eased inside her, her legs still quivering from her climax. Laya did not recognize the foreign rhythm. Tonight, Luntok rocked against her with a different kind of desperation—that of a dying man, craving a last, gentle touch.

The rhythm built gradually to a crescendo. That, Laya recognized. It crested over her body, rippling up from her core, shooting past her toes and fingertips. She drew him closer to her by his shoulders, feeling the strong muscles rippling beneath his skin. In her arms, Luntok became an eagle, arching his mighty wings. Deeper and deeper, he drove into her. Then his hands curled around her hip bones, and he finished with a strangled cry.

"By the gods," he sighed, breathing heavily as he collapsed beside her on the pillows. He wrapped his arms around her, pressing a kiss to her forehead.

Laya curled into his chest. "I love you," she said again to make sure he heard.

Luntok didn't answer right away, nor did he speak of the argument they'd had mere moments before. After they made love, a new peace seemed to dawn over him. He retreated to some faraway place as he traced small, featherlight circles on her shoulder. Laya listened to his heartbeat. It thudded in her ear, strong and steady, like soldiers marching through the rolling foothills. For once, she didn't ask him to leave—didn't want him to. Their bodies molded together so easily. How warm she felt in his arms.

The fatigue washed over her, pressing her into the gentle night. Laya didn't fight it. She nestled deeper into Luntok's embrace. Her eyes fluttered shut. She was half-asleep when he finally stirred. He leaned over to kiss her once more, his breath hot against her cheek.

"I love you, Laya. Whatever happens, I pray you won't forget this." But the darkness swallowed his whisper. So soft and strange it sounded, like rain rapping against shattered glass, Laya was convinced she must have dreamed it.

Nineteen

IMERIA

Imeria watched as Datu Gulod filled the bowl of his pipe for the fifth time that evening. Vikal struck a match against the side of the tea table and held it to Gulod's pipe.

"Where's your boy, Imeria? Isn't he the reason you called this meeting?" Gulod asked. He drew in a deep puff before sighing impatiently, flooding the veranda with the scent of burning cloves.

Through the thick cloud of pipe smoke, Imeria scowled at the two men sitting before her. She might have found the physical differences between Vikal and Gulod comical in other, less traitorous circumstances. Vikal was not only taller than most men, but he also had a broad chest and arms strong enough to swing the heaviest sword. Beside him sat Gulod, who was hardly taller than Imeria, was slight, and had thin swindler's fingers. Gulod was a pest, but a useful pest. Imeria had done well, cementing such alliances. With their combined strength and the vials of precioso, they might stand a chance to achieve Imeria's perilous schemes.

They gathered at the Kulaws' town house late that evening to discuss how they might proceed. After what had happened at the tournament, Mariit was beginning to grumble, condemning the Gatdulas for their brutality and negligence. It was not the first time one of Hara Duja's daughters had nearly brought their family's regime to its knees. Three years earlier, Laya had horrified half the kingdom when she'd destroyed the eastern wing. The previous night, the entire capital had watched Bulan steal Luntok's victory. Maynarans, low and highborn alike, squabbled over gold and land and influence, but dishonor was the one thing none of them could stomach.

Imeria wondered to what extent she could spin their outrage in the Kulaws' favor. She had invited Vikal and Gulod that evening to hear their thoughts about the matter. Luntok was supposed to attend the meeting, but she had sent him to the palace first. Imeria knew he would take his time with Laya, but it was nearing midnight. He should have returned hours earlier.

The front gate swung open. Luntok's long, lonely shadow appeared, splitting the yellow lantern light that illuminated the veranda. He slammed the gate behind him and trudged inside, his uneven footsteps echoing across the cobbled pathway. His shoulders were hitched up to his ears, his hands balled into fists at his sides. He dragged his feet as if he were drunk, but Imeria knew he was not. She saw from the pain in his eyes and the tight muscles in his jawline that Luntok was tormented.

Imeria waved him over. "Come, darling. Join us."

He obeyed, barely acknowledging the other men at the table when he slouched into his seat. "So, have you decided?" he asked in a flat voice.

She frowned. "Decided what?"

"How you're going to destroy them." Luntok's gaze snapped to hers. Beneath his stone-faced calm, he was furious—but Imeria could not tell at whom the anger was directed.

Luntok had barely spoken to Imeria since his loss during

the tournament. She'd distanced herself to give him the space to lick his wounds, the ones inside, which Imeria couldn't heal. The one time they had spoken, he'd asked how she planned to take down the Gatdulas, which surprised Imeria. Sneaking in and out of the palace was one thing, but Luntok had never played an active role in Imeria's schemes. He loved Laya too much, and the rift between their families confused him. For a long time, Imeria had kept him in the dark, thinking it would spare him the guilt.

But now, Luntok stared at her with an expression of stony resolve. This was not the same version of her son who'd gaped moon-eyed after Laya, the princess he thought would one day fall within his reach.

"You're contentious tonight," Imeria said. "Is there a reason for this change?"

Luntok exhaled sharply through his nostrils. "I've learned something, Mother. The Gatdulas will grant us neither love nor victory, even when it's earned. If we want anything in this swamp of a city, we'll have to steal it on our own." He met her gaze and, in a low voice, added, "I think this is what you've been trying to tell me all along."

Imeria glanced at Vikal, who was staring at Luntok intently. After years spent ignoring her warnings, her son finally understood.

"You asked how we will destroy them," she said. She held his gaze, a smile tugging at the corners of her lips. "I suppose that depends on what you've brought me."

Luntok reached into the pocket of his trousers and retrieved a letter. "Here's the information that serving girl—Yari or whatever her name is—promised. She slipped it beneath Laya's door earlier tonight. Said she found it in Hara Duja's laundry."

Imeria snatched up the letter, her eyes widening as she scanned its contents. *To His Royal Highness, Hari Aki.* Her stomach plummeted when she reached the name at the bottom of the letter.

Pangil Gatdula. Maynara's exiled prince. He used to threaten Imeria with fireballs to the face when they were children. At some point in the twenty-two years since he was banished, he'd found a way to contact the king—but that was not Imeria's most shocking realization.

"Well," Gulod snapped from across the table. "What does it say?"

A cool wave of dread washed over Imeria. She set the letter down on the table with shaking hands. Pangil's words were bafflingly cryptic. *Alchemist. Abiding glory.* But Imeria was no halfwit. Her fingers flew up to the vials of precioso, which she now wore on a chain around her neck.

"It seems the queen has found a way to hold on to her powers. A cure for the passage of time—or something along those means," Imeria said. She reached for her wine and took a sip. The inside of her throat had gone dry.

Gulod's eyes narrowed in confusion. "What are you insinuating? Do you believe Hara Duja has also gotten her hands on precioso?"

Luntok answered for her. "I don't know about the precioso, but Yari heard something about a man living in the eastern wing. Hardly any of the servants have seen him. According to Yari, the guards stocked his chambers with chemicals and potions and a strange number of things."

"He's an alchemist, surely," Imeria said as she pondered Pangil's letter. If that man was the alchemist of which Pangil spoke, then he had been brought to the palace for a reason—to produce precioso, or a similar substance, was the only theory that made sense.

Vikal rubbed his temple and let out a low whistle. "Forgive me, my lady. I don't know much about alchemy, but if I understand what you're saying, the queen will be very hard to defeat."

"Not if we act quickly," she said, her thoughts racing. According to Yari, the alchemist had only arrived in Mariit when the feast days began earlier that week. Imeria remembered the tremors that overcame Duja the other day in the council room. Precioso promised more control over her powers, which meant Duja did not yet have access to the drug. If that was the case, Imeria could still overpower her. She chewed her lip as she weighed her options—it was a very big *if*.

"Imeria, are you truly considering this?" Gulod asked. Imeria ignored him, staring at the swirling patterns etched across the table's surface. When she didn't answer, he threw up his hands in exasperation. "For Mulayri's sake. This is madness."

"Is it?" she asked. "With Vikal's sword-trained servant boys, we have nearly enough men to stage an attack. After all, we brought them to Mariit for this very purpose. And what of those mercenaries you told me about, Namok? Have you contacted them?"

For conducting unsavory business deals such as these, Datu Gulod did not lack contacts. He knew about a ring of hired swords that operated out of Mariit. If Imeria could pay for another dozen of them, their odds would improve immensely.

At the mention of the mercenaries, Gulod nodded, but he did not appear convinced. "They've agreed to your conditions. They only ask for an advance on their services," he said.

She waved her hand, distracted, as a plan began to form inside her head. "Tell them I will arrange it."

Vikal turned to Gulod, lowering his voice. "Money isn't the issue, my lord. Neither is the number of men. The main problem I see lies in infiltrating the palace, and then holding it." He glanced at Imeria, a shadow of uncertainty crossing his expression. Vikal was not Gulod. He would die for her if she asked. But for their plan to succeed, she needed to find a way to quash both their doubts.

"We will be able to hold the palace—and the entire capital, for that matter. The Royal Maynaran Guard will fall to our command. I know it," Imeria said as she stroked the vials of precioso on her neck.

She had sampled the drug the previous evening. A small dose was all she'd needed to coax her power into a fire that roared through her veins. Never had Imeria known power so strong. At high quantities, she could overcome an entire army with a wave of her hand. She did not need to wield her power over all of them. For the guardsmen's loyalty did not exceed their fear; they would fall to their knees the moment they saw what she was capable of. As for those who refused to surrender—Imeria remembered how she felled Pangil in the courtyard the day he burned down the eastern wing. With precioso's power in her blood, she would make them bow. Every last one of them.

"As for getting into the palace . . ." Vikal paused, stroking his chin. "We can mount the attack during the feast tomorrow night. You three have been invited to the palace, after all."

"What of the rest of your men, Vikal?" Gulod demanded. "I don't suppose Hara Duja's sent an invitation to all thirty of them?"

"Datu Kulaw can slip away to the servants' entrance," Vikal suggested. "I can lead them in through there."

Imeria hesitated. "I suppose that could work."

"No. It won't." Luntok's voice rang out with surprising force, reverberating across the hollow walls of the veranda.

"And why not?" Gulod asked, watching Luntok with beady eyes. He stared at the younger man, for once intrigued by what he had to say.

"The servants' entrance is too far from the great hall," Luntok explained, exasperated. "There will be dozens of people flooding in and out. Unless, of course, we have the numbers to subdue them all—otherwise, we'll be caught in seconds."

After Luntok's interjection, they sat in silence for a brief moment. A quiet breeze broke the thick night air, rustling through the canopy of palms that shielded them from view.

Imeria cast him a curious glance. Something burned behind the dark film over his eyes, a thirst she had never seen in him before. "What would you suggest, then?" she asked.

"We ought to maintain the element of surprise as long as possible. It is our biggest advantage." Luntok leaned over the table, the muscles in his cheeks pulled taut. He *knew* something—something they could use to their advantage—but why wasn't he sharing it?

"Datu Kulaw could take out the guards posted on the outer wall. Then we could climb the gates," Vikal said tentatively, even though they all knew it was a terrible idea.

"*No.* We absolutely are not doing that." Roughly, Luntok brushed his hair away from his face. He reached for Imeria's wineglass and swallowed its contents in a single gulp. Then he turned toward his mother, his brow furrowed in turmoil.

Ah. She understood now; this was about Laya.

Luntok knew that if he betrayed Laya's family, he risked losing her love forever. Imeria had made her choice long before. As for her son—maybe he'd convinced himself there was a path to

Laya that didn't begin with treachery. Luntok may have coveted the throne—and the right to kingship of which the Gatdulas had robbed him—but Laya was the only prize he'd ever wanted.

Imeria yearned to reach out and calm the warring thoughts in his head. Instead, she prodded him. "Tell us, Son. What do you mean?"

"No one is climbing the walls." Luntok kept his lips tight, as if to seal himself from the storm waging inside him. Imeria's heart rate quickened as she watched the thoughts settle in his eyes. Finally, Luntok understood. Fate had only ever given him one path. Now was his chance to carve it straight to the throne, to justice for the south, to the princess who belonged to him. Laya had been his tipping point, the sole force strong enough to blow him over the razor's edge. Having her was the one battle he couldn't bear to lose.

Luntok centered himself, laying his palms flat against the table. He sat in jaw-clenching silence as he made peace with his decision. He did not speak until he let out a last, shaky breath.

"The way is under, not over," he said, meeting Imeria's gaze with damning certainty. "And I can get us in."

Twenty

DUJA

The door to Ariel's workshop was half-open when Duja strode into the eastern wing. As she walked down the corridor, her nostrils filled with the sharp, acidic smell of vinegar. She stopped before the wainscoted wall lining the hall, where she glimpsed herself in the mirror. Duja wore her finest skirt, a voluminous balloon of viridian silk that billowed with every step. Her headpiece weighed heavily atop her hair, a magnificent crown of gold plates shooting out from her temples like sunrays. A handmaid had added some charcoal to her eyelids and a touch of rouge to her lips. She looked majestic; she felt like a fraud.

High Shaman Maiza had arrived early for the midnight feast and headed straight to Duja's chambers for a healing session. The sorcery had worked; her muscles felt loose, and her fingers were free of tremors. Duja hoped the enchantments would last until the end of the ceremony. She couldn't allow herself to appear weak before the Council of Datus, and especially not this night.

Maiza's enchantments were effective, but unpredictable and weak. Duja needed a solution more potent than such petty sorcery allowed. For the first time in years, the solution lay within reach.

With a deep breath, Duja pushed the door open. Ariel was

sitting at the table in the center of the workshop, a magnifying glass in hand. He held the glass to the tray before him, muttering to himself in Orfelian, his eyes glued to its contents. He did not notice Duja standing over his shoulder until she cleared her throat.

"Good evening, Dr. Sauros."

Ariel jumped to his feet and whipped around. His eyes widened in awe when he caught sight of Duja in full ceremonial dress. "Oh my—I mean, good evening, Your Majesty."

The corners of Duja's mouth curled up into a shy smile. "Don't worry, Ariel. I suspect we'll have you fitted for your own court attire soon," she said, peering into the tray before him. "Would that be the precioso?"

Ariel nodded and gestured for her to come closer. "I'm monitoring it for now, but it looks like the precioso will be fully set in a few hours. Would you like to see?"

A jolt of excitement wound through Duja. She swept over to the edge of the table and leaned over the tray. The precioso lay in a dozen crystal bars of varying lengths, the smallest no bigger than her thumb and the largest measuring from the tip of her pointer finger to her wrist. The bars were as clear as glass. Duja marveled at how the light changed as it skated across their smooth edges and jagged tips.

"I didn't know a drug could be this beautiful," she said, resisting the urge to run her fingers over the bars' surfaces.

"Precioso doesn't always look like this. It's rare for one to produce a sample of such pure quality," Ariel said. Duja thought she heard a faint note of pride in his voice.

"Well, then. I shall consider myself lucky to have one of the best precioso makers under my employ," Duja said as she appraised the Orfelian. Her brother was blessed to have found him.

Ariel must have spent a great deal of time with Pangil. It made her curious. "You've been in my brother's company. Is he well? Truly?" she asked.

Is my brother a better man? Duja yearned to know, but she didn't dare ask Ariel that.

"The precioso has aided him. He lives without pain, healthier than many men his age. His tremors don't trouble him as they used to. He can wield his powers without endangering himself and those around him. But I have warned him regarding overuse, as I've warned you, Your Majesty," Ariel said. He never gave a dishonest answer. Duja liked that about him.

"I know, and I promise to heed your warnings," Duja said, nodding. At least once a day, her husband continued to caution her about precioso, citing grim anecdotes from his research. Both he and Ariel made it abundantly clear that precioso was not the answer to all her prayers. Duja wasn't looking for one. If she could control her powers for a few more years, she'd have enough time—time to prepare Laya for her duties. Time to iron out any misgivings the court held about her daughter's rule.

She glanced at the clock hanging on the wall above the cupboards. Two hours until midnight—she needed to make her way to the great hall soon.

He followed her gaze. "Ah, yes. They are probably expecting you at the midnight feast."

"Correct," Duja said. She straightened, smoothing out the creases in her skirt. "I suppose Hari Aki has already informed you about the guests we will be receiving tonight."

"I'm well aware, Your Majesty, and rest assured that no one will know I'm here. And it was, um, Dayang Laya who warned me," he added as he braced his weight against the side of the table.

"Laya? Really?" Duja raised an eyebrow at him, incredulous.

"She requested an early Salmantican lesson. We've actually had a few lessons this week," Ariel said. He took off his spectacles, diverting his gaze as he polished the lenses on the embroidered hem of his shirt.

Duja's brow furrowed in suspicion. Laya was far from the studious type, and her distaste for foreign languages was no secret. The king had introduced Ariel to the girls, and they knew he was living in the palace. As for the Orfelian's true purpose there—Duja's stomach churned when she took in Ariel's shifting gaze and nervous fidgeting. Laya had a way with the opposite sex, a gift she no doubt inherited from her father. Duja could see she had already cast a spell over the Orfelian, even if he did not seem to be aware of it yet himself. The realization brought a frown to Duja's face. Ariel was not a bad-looking man, with his soft eyes and high-boned features, but he possessed none of the danger Laya sought in her suitors. Duja knew her daughter; Laya would not have wasted her time with Ariel if she did not have something to gain from him.

The queen stiffened. Her daughter was too clever for her own good. When it came to Ariel's presence in Maynara, Laya could sense something was amiss. If she did not yet know about the precioso, she would soon. Duja prayed she would have a better explanation for her interest in the drug by then. For Laya was as clever as she was impatient. She would not understand Duja's hesitancy to pass down the title. She would assume Duja didn't trust her to hold that much power, and the discovery would render her furious.

But that conversation, like most of the queen's worries, would have to wait until another evening. Duja was almost late for the midnight feast.

"Thank you again for your efforts, Dr. Sauros," she said as she brushed past Ariel on her way out of the workshop. "I will visit you again in the morning to see how the precioso has progressed."

Ariel dropped his head into a respectful bow. "Of course, Your Majesty. I hope the feast goes well."

Duja gave him a curt nod before shutting the workshop door behind her. She hurried downstairs and across the courtyard. She entered the great hall to find it empty save for the long table spanning the full length of the room. Despite her detour to Ariel's workshop, she was the first to arrive, but the datus were expected at the palace within the next few minutes. This was no ordinary meeting. The midnight feast marked the end of the past week's celebrations, and only the six ruling families were invited. It was a peculiar, closed-door spectacle that felt to Duja as old as the gods themselves. Once she had been crowned queen, Duja dreaded the midnight feast, because it required her to play a role she despised.

"Are you ready, darling?" Hari Aki asked as he strode through the open doors of the hall. Their daughters trailed in after him, and for a brief moment, the sight of them rendered Duja breathless. Not long before, they were little round-faced girls wreaking havoc in the palace. Those little girls were slipping away fast. They were growing into beautiful women, each with awe-inspiring powers of her own.

"As ready as I'll ever be." Duja leaned in as he kissed her on the cheek. They took their seats—Aki, the king, at the opposite end of the table and Laya, her heir, to her right. Since they had spoken earlier that week, Laya was noticeably more churlish with her. Duja sighed, resolving to make amends the following morning. She did not possess the patience to mitigate another clash with Laya at the moment.

Through the doors strode Datu Luma, Datu Patid, and their respective families. They bowed their heads respectfully to Duja as they entered. She straightened her back and greeted them with the distant regard of a sovereign. She needed to fully commit to her role with the arrival of the first guests.

Duja wished they had music, like at the opening ceremony. The midnight feast's atmosphere was somber, almost funerary, the only noise coming from the faint murmur of conversation as the datus and their families filed in.

Before long, servants arrived with platters stacked high with food: pork buns and pan-fried milk fish and sweet sausages on steaming beds of rice. Absently, she served herself. As she ate, servants kept her wine goblet full without her asking. She swallowed its contents, too lost in her thoughts to taste anything.

"Mother," Laya whispered. It was the first word she had spoken to Duja since the start of the evening.

Duja looked up. "What is it, Laya?"

Once again, Duja was struck by how much her heir had grown. Not even the flickering shadows of the great hall could hide Laya's beauty. A cunning spark pierced through the murky-brown depths of her eyes. From behind her head, sconces lit her temples in crowning rays. *Regal*, Duja thought. *Without even trying.*

Duja was queen by blood, but not queen by nature—not the way a Gatdula was meant to be queen. If her older brother's crimes had been pardonable, she never would have sat upon the throne. In a way, it was a blessing. To grow up her mother's heir would have been a heavy burden. Laya had borne it for years. That night, when Duja met her daughter's gaze, she saw the queen she would become—swift-fingered in the way she shifted her pawns about the court. Godlike in her justice, as in her cruelty. The kind of Gatdula their subjects would come to respect and, one day, adore.

Born a queen, in all the ways Duja could never hope to be.

"Look." Laya nodded toward Aki's end of the table, where two seats remained empty. "The Kulaws have yet to arrive."

"It isn't like them to be tardy." Duja kept her voice calm, but her gut twisted with an uneasy feeling.

Her last meeting with Imeria had resurrected painful memories. Duja knew Imeria resented her, but she had not known that buried deep beneath her bitterness dwelled a tiny spark of hope. It was the last surviving speck of the love they had felt for each other as girls. Imeria had clung to it, unwilling to let go. By granting Laya and Luntok the future they could never have, Imeria wanted to see the sentiment echoed in their children. If she were crueler, Duja might have played on her love, teased a gentleness out of Imeria, and cajoled her to join her side for once. Instead, she crushed Imeria's hope. She had thought she was being merciful. Suddenly, she feared she had misjudged her.

She waited as the feast continued. Servants emerged once again with dessert: pillow-light sponge cakes, sticky-rice balls drenched in coconut sauce, and glutinous rolls wrapped in pandan leaves. Her goblet was filled and refilled, and time ticked on, and still, the Kulaws did not appear. As midnight grew closer, Duja's gut flipped in apprehension. Imeria's absence had not gone unnoticed by the other datus. They could not conduct the closing ceremony without her.

Once the servants came to clear the plates, Maiza appeared at Duja's shoulder. "The ceremony must start soon, Your Majesty," she said in a low voice.

She nodded and met Aki's eyes at the other end of the table, where the two seats remained empty. The king's brow was knitted in confusion. This was unlike Imeria. Although she had insulted the Gatdulas with a string of absences in the past, not once had she forgone the closing ceremony. After all, Imeria was not an idiot. She knew the evening was too vital for her position on the council, and for the functioning of the Maynaran government, to miss.

The queen thought hard about their last conversation for any hints she might have forgotten. She would have heard if Imeria had left Mariit, but Imeria would never have dared return to the south before the end of the feast days. Any other absence could have been forgiven. This was the one night she needed to be in the palace.

Duja scanned the hall, her gaze landing on General Ojas, stationed at the wall across from her, flanked by two of his men. He met her gaze and swept across the room when she gestured him over.

He stood beside Maiza, leaning over Duja's other shoulder. "Yes, Your Majesty?"

Duja glanced at the guests seated nearest her. Datu Luma and his wife were sitting within earshot. Although they were close friends of the crown, she didn't want them to know the extent of her troubles with Imeria.

She lowered her voice to a whisper. "Could you sweep the perimeter? See if perhaps Datu Kulaw and her party have gotten lost somewhere in the palace grounds."

Recognition flickered in Ojas's eyes. "Right away, Your Majesty." He straightened and strode out of the room, a pair of junior guardsmen marching at his heels.

Duja watched him leave, unable to shake the anxious feeling that she had forgotten some dreadfully important detail. High above the doors, the clock ticked. Around the table, the datus began to grumble. Duja kept her gaze trained on the entrance to the great hall, expecting Imeria to appear any moment in a flutter of scarlet and gold. But the clock hands edged closer to midnight, and the Kulaws remained conspicuously absent.

"Mother," Laya whispered again.

"Yes, darling, I know," she said, distracted.

Questions swirled in the queen's mind, along with the sensation that, by sending Imeria away in the throne room the other night, Duja had done something horribly wrong.

Twenty-One

IMERIA

The walls of the tunnel were cool and smooth—too smooth for Imeria to find a handhold as she stumbled through to the other side. Her eyes struggled to adjust to the darkness.

"Hold on to me," Luntok whispered as he reached for her other arm.

Behind them crouched the first wave of attackers: Vikal and five of the men chosen for this mission—a mix of Kulaw warriors and Gulod's mercenaries. Imeria couldn't hear their breathing over the sound of her own. No one spoke, and the tunnel filled with the muted sound of swords rattling in their sheaths. In the dark, they couldn't see how afraid she was, but Luntok felt how her hands shook. He threaded his fingers between hers, his own breathing steady as he led them beneath the eastern walls of the palace.

Imeria had never seen Luntok so calm. Hours earlier on the veranda, he went over the plan with Vikal and Gulod a final time. They and the other men on the mission fed off his stone-faced confidence. They followed him into the tunnel without question. With a burst of pride, she recognized how they looked at him. It was the same blind faith so many Maynarans placed in their beloved Gatdulas.

Water dripped in fat drops from the roof of the tunnel onto Imeria's forehead. She let go of the wall to flick it away, her fingers catching on the left wing of her raptor-shaped headpiece. For the midnight feast, she had come dressed in armor of her own: scarlet silks that blazed like phoenix fire and her gaudiest jewelry. Hidden beneath her blouse lay the heaviest piece, a single vial of precioso she had attached to a thin chain around her neck. The other vials she'd hidden away for safekeeping; one would suffice for this night if they were lucky. She groped for the one at her neck, sighing in relief when she felt the hard glass slide beneath her fingertips.

"We've reached the gardens," Luntok announced in a low voice. He squeezed Imeria's hand. "Mother, are you ready?"

No. Imeria wasn't ready. She had prayed to the old gods of Thu-ki, her ancestors' fallen kingdom, to clear her mind and harden her heart and make her the monster she needed to be. The gods never answered her, but that was expected. She wasn't one to wait for divine intervention. Imeria was fully capable of becoming a monster on her own.

"Yes," she said, and heard Luntok rustle in his pockets for the pipe. Beside him, Vikal struck a match on the cave wall. In the flame, their faces glowed orange. The other men hung back, shuffling in trepidation.

They watched solemnly as she reached for the vial around her neck and unscrewed the cap. Carefully, she poured its contents into the bowl of the pipe and held it to her mouth. Vikal lowered the flame to the bowl. Imeria felt the heat on her face as she inhaled deeply. When she breathed out, her eyes watered from the smoke. She leaned against Luntok, fighting the urge to cough. The drug had flooded like poison into her veins, but she felt nothing.

A jolt of panic wound through her—*no*. It wasn't possible. They had come so far. She'd waited too long. The precioso *had* to work.

Imeria steeled herself and took in another breath, letting the smoke fill her lungs slowly. This time, as she exhaled, her skin tingled. The cold sensation began at the crown of her head. It oozed down her spine and arms and, finally, through her fingertips. She felt detached from her body, yet she could not ignore the power that pulsed in her veins.

"Mother?" Luntok called.

She felt his gaze, even though Vikal had long let the match go out. He was staring at her, eyes wide in concern. Beneath his calm, she could feel his fear like turbulent waves pressing up beneath the icy surface. Imeria reached for his face, and the threads of his mind wrapped around her fingers. She need only tug, and his mind would be hers to wield.

I could make him sleep, could make him slit his own throat if I wanted to. I could—

Imeria wrenched back her hand, startled by her own thoughts. "Careful. The drug is potent," she said, and thrust Vikal the pipe to pass around.

Around her, the drain tunnel filled with smoke. It smelled chalky and medicinal, and it burned the inside of Imeria's nose. In mere moments, the precioso would take root in each of the men. A single puff would make monsters of them. Not even the palace guard, the finest trained in Maynara, would stand a chance against their superior speed and strength.

The pipe passed to Luntok last. Imeria struck another match and relit the bowl for him. His chest expanded like paraw sails as he inhaled, and his gaze snapped to hers in the second before the flame went out. She saw the spark of power reflected in his eyes.

"Very potent," Luntok muttered. He clenched his hands into fists. Imeria heard his knuckles crack in the dark.

Vikal laid a hand on Imeria's shoulder. "We are ready, my lady."

Imeria closed her eyes. Took a deep breath. At this quantity, she didn't know how long the precioso's effects would last. She could only feel how its power pooled through every pore of her body. The drug possessed her with the vehemence of a wrathful god.

Again, she reached for Luntok's arm. "Lead us in, Son," she said.

He parted the vines and hauled himself up into the palace gardens before reaching down to help her climb. When they breached the surface, a calm breeze broke the night air, which was thick with humidity. Silvery light streamed through the canopy of palms. The nectarous scent of flowers drowned out the last remnants of smoke.

"Full moon tonight," Vikal murmured. "They might see us coming."

"They won't," Luntok said. "I'm sure of it."

For the first time that night, she shared his confidence. So what if they did catch them?

With the precioso in her veins, Imeria was the master. And she was going to make every last one of them bow.

Twenty-Two

LAYA

Laya gazed at the opposite end of the table. The sight of Luntok's empty seat filled her with the same hollow feeling that struck her that very morning, when she'd seen the faint dent in the pillow where Luntok had rested his head.

The previous night, Laya had told him she loved him. And when she'd woken, he was gone.

Luntok must have slipped out before dawn, and he hadn't wanted to disturb her. She ought to have been pleased with his tactfulness. Instead, she felt abandoned, as if a vital part of herself had been ripped away.

She wondered what was keeping him. The midnight feast was the most important ceremony that week. None of the datus, not even Luntok's dreadful mother, would dare miss it. Not unless—

"Could you pass me that yam cake over there?" Eti whispered, jolting Laya from her thoughts.

Laya turned to her little sister, who was sitting on her right. Sugar flakes and coconut sauce coated her fingers. A precarious pile of desserts teetered atop the napkin in her lap.

"What in Mulayri's name are you doing?" Laya asked.

"Ariel. He must want to try some of this," Eti said. When

Laya didn't budge, she reached across her and snatched a purple yam cake from one of the platters at the center of the table.

"You're going to take dessert to him? Right now?" she said, incredulous.

Eti nodded. She tossed the yam cake in with the rest of her desserts. Carefully, she folded the napkin around the pile, tucking in the corners so none of the desserts would fall out.

Laya glanced at the back of the hall. Her mother was standing by the throne with her father and Maiza. They were whispering among themselves, likely discussing how to deal with Imeria's absence, while the rest of the datus started to leave the table and make their way to the throne. In a few minutes, the ceremony was supposed to begin. Laya doubted it would start on time, as Imeria had yet to arrive.

"Fine," Laya told Eti, nudging her toward the door. "But you have to hurry."

"I will," Eti promised. She grabbed the bundle of desserts and scampered out of the great hall. With her light tread and small stature, hardly anyone noticed her leave. The way Eti moved, she would make a formidable assassin, Laya mused, as she watched her disappear into the long shadows striping the room.

Long dinners made Eti restless, yes, but the true reason Laya let her go was because she thought Ariel was in desperate need of company. It pained her to think of all the hours the Orfelian had spent shut away in the sad, dusty eastern wing. She could no longer deny her growing fondness for him.

That afternoon, before getting ready for the midnight feast, Laya had sought him out. The pattern was becoming too comfortable, slipping into the eastern wing, her entire body hollowed out with loneliness. Initially, she went to Ariel to distract herself from Luntok's abandonment. She should have known the Orfelian would surprise her.

When she showed up in his study, he greeted her with a hesitant smile. She insisted on another writing lesson, to which Ariel agreed. He had little choice in the matter, but Laya had caught a glint of eagerness behind his spectacles when he saw her standing in his doorway. Perhaps he was growing fond of her as well.

The lesson carried on with surprising ease, until Laya spilled ink across the table. They both reached for the same crumpled piece of paper to mop up the mess. Their fingers touched. Foolishly, Laya met his gaze instead of pulling her hand away. She was used to people staring, but Ariel was different. Even behind those stupid spectacles, his eyes sent the familiar spark buzzing beneath her skin.

To stop the spark from spreading, she demanded, "Tell me the truth, Ariel. Why did my father invite you here? Or, better yet, what is your business with the queen?"

If Ariel was taken aback by Laya's candor, he didn't show it. He merely shrugged and said, "My business is with you and your sisters, Dayang. If the queen wished for me to serve as anything other than a language tutor, I'm sure she would have told you. You are her heir, after all."

Laya sputtered out a laugh. "I may be Hara Duja's heir, but she hasn't spared me a word. Sometimes, I don't think she even wants me to be queen."

"Do *you* want to be queen?" Ariel asked.

She frowned at him. "What kind of question is that? Of course I want to be queen."

"I suppose 'What kind of queen do you want to be?' is the better question." Ariel leaned back in his seat, rubbing his chin as he pondered the question himself.

"I want to be the best queen Maynara has ever seen," Laya replied. It was the only honest answer she could give, but not even she could deny how childish it sounded coming out of her own mouth.

"Ah, but what does the best queen look like to you?" Ariel asked, eyeing her with curiosity.

Laya kept her mouth shut. She didn't know what the best queen looked like or the legacy she wanted to leave. Maybe it was petty and shallow. But Laya wanted it more than anything in the world—to be a greater queen than her mother. Greater than any Gatdula before her.

When she didn't answer right away, Ariel went on. "Perhaps Hara Duja sees this as a lack of intention, and that is why she might be so reticent," he said, shocking Laya once again with his perceptiveness. "But I imagine you'll figure that out with time, Dayang. You are so young."

He stared deeply at Laya's face. What he saw there seemed to distract him, because he kept staring, as if any rational counsel he wished to give her had disappeared from his head. Laya stared back. She couldn't help herself. The Orfelian brought up a good point. Hours later, she couldn't stop thinking about it. No one had ever challenged her like that before, questioning the kind of queen she wanted to be instead of telling her how to be one. Ariel was the first to ask and the first to listen. Not once did he presume to know her answers before she uttered them. He showed her ways of contemplating Maynara—and the rest of the world—that Laya had never considered before. Their conversations enthralled her. Just thinking about their last writing lesson rattled her more than she wanted to admit.

For the first time, she didn't care what had brought Ariel Sauros to Maynara. Whatever his business, she hoped it would keep him in the palace a while longer. *Friendship* was not the right word to describe the bond she sensed budding between them. All she knew was that she liked him. After the feast days ended and the capital quieted once more, she looked forward to having him around.

In the middle of the great hall, Laya continued to mull over Ariel's question as she poured herself another glass of wine. The alcohol would do little to cool the heat rising in her cheeks, but she needed something to do with her hands. As she took a sip, her older sister leaned over her shoulder.

"What are you doing?" Bulan asked. "We should join Mother. The ceremony is about to begin."

She glared at her. "I doubt that. We're one datu short, in case you haven't noticed."

Bulan let out a sharp sigh. They had yet to make amends after the tournament. Although Laya was not yet ready to forgive her for what she'd done to Luntok, a day of distance had allowed her anger to ebb into dull annoyance.

"That woman truly has no shame," Bulan said. "I don't suppose Luntok mentioned anything to you about being late."

Laya scowled. "I haven't seen Luntok since you slashed open his back," she lied. Images flashed of the previous night. His lips on her collarbone, her neck. She had run her fingers over his skin, which was warm against hers and smooth as glass—

Smooth. His back had been smooth, no broken skin or scar tissue, as if Bulan's blade hadn't touched him at all. She had been too swept away by his romantic pleas to notice. Healers attended to his wounds after the tournament, but Laya had seen how much of his blood had splattered the platform. Their ointments and enchantments would not have been potent enough to stitch him up overnight.

Bulan noticed the shift in her expression. "Are you all right, Laya?" she asked. "You look ill."

Laya faltered. "I've just remembered something," she said.

The doors of the great hall swung open. All heads turned to watch Imeria stride through the entrance in a billow of scarlet silk. Luntok was close behind her. He met Laya's gaze for a brief second. Her heart leaped, singing louder than the whisper of suspicion.

Someone very powerful had healed him after the tournament, but who?

"You're late, Datu Kulaw," Hara Duja called from the opposite end of the room. She did not sound pleased.

"Apologies for missing the feast, Your Majesty." She glanced over her shoulder at the clock above the arched doorframe. With a faint click, the hands struck midnight. "As you can see, I've arrived in time for the ceremony."

The queen pursed her lips. She didn't seem to have the energy to berate Imeria any further. "Very well," she said and raised her arms, inviting the datus to join her around the throne.

Laya took that as her cue to stand beside her father on the dais. Bulan followed her. Their mother remained with Maiza in front of the throne. A small table lay before them, atop which rested a golden wine goblet and a ceremonial dagger, its hilt made of an enameled buffalo horn. The blade glinted dully in the faint sconce light of the throne room. Some believed the blood of generations of datus past to be absorbed into the steel. Laya didn't place much stock in blood magic, but she appreciated the symbolism of the closing ceremony same as anyone else.

"Where's your sister?" the king whispered as she climbed the dais to stand at his side.

"She must have been overwhelmed," Laya said. It was

odd—Eti should have been back by now. But everyone knew she hated feasts, always calling them *stuffy* and *pretentious*. Most likely she was hiding in some staircase after bringing the desserts to Ariel, tinkering with her precious metals.

The king frowned, which was rare of him. "Look for her when this is over" was all he said.

The receiving room quieted as Maiza began to chant in Old Maynaran. It was a haunting language, the whisper of gods. As she chanted, the lights dimmed, bending themselves to her magic. Only Hara Duja stood fully illuminated. The rest of the room was basked in darkness.

The six datus formed a semicircle around her. Like them, Laya watched in awe as her mother transformed. Hara Duja cast an imperious gaze down at her subjects from where she perched on her obsidian throne. She raised her chin, and shadows danced across the hollows of her cheeks. Her eyes hardened to steel. When her mother carried herself like this, she became the most magnificent creature Laya had ever seen.

And when she spoke, Hara Duja's voice resounded over Maiza's chants. Laya had committed her speech to memory long before, because she knew she would give it one day as well: "My friends, I address you, not as your sovereign but as Duja Gatdula, daughter of Mulayri and defender of the Maynaran throne. Like the thousands of ancestors who sat on the throne before me, I have been granted the sacred role of steward. With my power and might, I have sworn to protect Maynara against those who might harm Her.

"As Maynara's most loyal servants, you have pledged to act on my behalf and protect our people in the farthest reaches of the realm. To mark the closing of this year's feast days, I have summoned you before me to renew your vows. All who accept my protection may humbly serve. And all who serve must kneel."

Maiza stopped chanting to gather the goblet and dagger in her leathery hands. Head bowed, she offered them to Hara Duja. "Your Majesty," she murmured.

The queen accepted the objects in preparation for the final act of the ceremony. Her voice dropped to a bone-chilling whisper. "Who among you is loyal? Who among you will serve?"

Datu Luma, the oldest and most faithful of the datus, stepped forward without hesitation. "I will serve." He took the dagger from Hara Duja and drew a thin, horizontal line across his wrist. The blood beaded at the surface of his skin, and he let it drip into the empty goblet.

Datu Tanglaw stepped forward. "I will serve," he proclaimed, a touch too eagerly for Laya's liking. She had heard about his conspiracy to match her with Bato. If he thought groveling would be enough to convince Hara Duja to agree to that marriage, he had a lot to learn. With an added flourish, he whipped the knife over his wrist before spilling his blood into the goblet with Datu Luma's.

Datu Gulod followed, his waxy face uncharacteristically sober as he made his own offering. Then came Sandata. And after Patid. The only datu left was Kulaw.

Imeria didn't waver when the goblet and dagger passed to her. She stared at the objects for a long moment before casting her gaze at Hara Duja. There was something different about her eyes—a savage resolve that warned of danger. Imeria did not bow her head in deference. She did not pull back her pagoda sleeve to drag the dagger across the delicate skin of her wrist. She merely stared, motionless, as the throne room fell into agitated silence.

"I said," Hara Duja repeated, her voice cold and unbending, "who will serve?"

Imeria looked down at the goblet in her hands, then back at the queen. Slowly, the corners of her lips twisted into a cruel grin. "I'm sorry for this, Duja," she said, and let the goblet slip from her hands. It fell to the floor with a loud clatter. The rest of the guests gasped and scuttled back as noble blood spread across the pale tiles.

The ground began to shake. The rivulets of blood trembled as they branched out across the tiles in spidery veins. Hara Duja was livid. *"Imeria,"* she barked, and took a threatening step toward her.

Imeria didn't flinch. Before anyone could move, the doors burst open. Footsteps thundered over the tiles as over two dozen warriors stormed into the great hall. They did not wear the golden armor of the royal guard. Over their breastplate, they wore sashes of scarlet silk. *Kulaw warriors.*

Laya's mouth fell open. *It can't be.*

"No." Next to the throne, Hara Duja gasped. The ground beneath them lurched as she flung out her hands. Laya stumbled, grasping Bulan's arm for balance. The tremors halted as quickly as they began. When she looked up, Imeria had her hands pressed to the queen's face. Hara Duja stood frozen, her mouth open in a silent scream.

"Duja!" the king yelled. He ran for her, halting midlunge. An invisible force froze him in his tracks.

Panic jolted through Laya's body. She threw out her hand. The air above the throne split into a powerful blast that threw Imeria from the queen.

"Mother!" Laya cried. But Hara Duja didn't budge. She remained rooted where she stood, staring blankly at the ceiling.

Laya's gut lurched when she noticed the whites of her eyes had disappeared, replaced by twin pools of black. "She's cursed," she whispered in disbelief.

"Guards! Attack Imeria's men!" Bulan bellowed over Laya's shoulder.

Laya whipped around. General Ojas had yet to return to the great hall. A handful of his men were posted along the sides of the room. They gazed blankly as the scene unfolded, unable to move. They, too, were cursed. She watched their still bodies, fear rising at the back of her throat. No one was coming to rescue them. Laya would have to fend off the intruders alone.

Her heart raced when she glanced back at the horde of warriors advancing into the hall, their scarlet sashes glittering like rubies in the sconce light. The noble guests cried out in indignation, in horror, as they shrank away from the warriors' menacing blades.

"Shame on you. Shame on all of you," Datu Luma roared over the chaos. Laya caught sight of his white hair in the throng. He, along with several of the other noblemen, snatched the swords from the hands of the cursed guards. They pushed their way in front of the panicked guests to meet the Kulaw forces. The steel in their borrowed weapons gleamed orange beneath the great hall's muted light. Their ragged breaths broke the tense silence that swept across the room. None of the cursed guardsmen ran to the nobles' aid. The Kulaw men outnumbered them, and they were closing in fast.

A towering figure emerged before the scarlet-sashed warriors. Laya recognized his broad shoulders and boxy face from the tournament ring. It was Vikal. "I beg you, Datu Luma, not to act in haste," he said, his deep voice reverberating across the room. He slid his sword back into its sheath and held out his hand, as if calming a skittish buffalo. "You need only listen. If everyone cooperates, there will be no bloodshed today."

Laya's blood ran cold. She understood with a sickening pang what Imeria had brought these men there to do. The rage surged through her veins, sharpening her focus. Whatever power Imeria and her warriors wielded, Laya refused to hand the throne over to her.

"Get back," she hissed at Bulan.

Bulan blinked, her cheeks gray in shock. "I don't understand," she whispered.

Laya didn't wait for her sister to regain her bearings. She grabbed Bulan's wrist and shoved her behind herself. Without warning, she thrust her palms to the sky. The air in the great hall grew frigid, freezing in Laya's hold. The threads of energy wound between her fingers. With a desperate cry, she drew her hand downward in a clean slice. The blast ripped from her grip, whistling over the terrified crowd and crashing through the windowpanes.

Screams echoed under the great hall's soaring ceiling as glass shards rained on their heads. Laya's blast had knocked down most of the Kulaw warriors, as well as the midnight-feast guests. They tumbled to the glass-strewn tiles, groaning.

Laya's gaze shifted to the exit. Her blast had cleared a path straight through the Kulaw warriors. If they hurried, they could flee the palace. To stay was suicide; they couldn't fend off Imeria alone. Out there, they'd find Ojas, or maybe rally their allies in the city.

She reached back and shook Bulan. "Grab Mother and Father. We need to run."

"No, Laya. You're not going anywhere," a cold voice cried. Imeria planted herself in their path. She stared at Laya, her jaw clenched in determination. Laya's previous blast had knocked her raptor headpiece askew. A thin line of blood streamed down her cheek from where a glass shard had nicked her.

"You," Laya hissed. Her heart hammered in her chest when she met Imeria's gaze. She didn't hesitate. She raised her arm once more above her head, where the threads of energy swirled in wild, raging currents. They shot down to her hands, wrapping around her fingers like knotted rope. If she concentrated, she could summon a tornado that would fling Imeria Kulaw to some faraway ditch, where she and her infernal powers belonged.

Laya sucked in a breath, hatred sharpening her vision. But as she started tugging at the threads, someone yanked her arm back. Her concentration broke, along with her grasp on the air above.

"Get off!" she screamed, then fell silent when she saw who had grabbed her.

Pain contorted Luntok's face, his smooth, handsome face, which, less than a day before, had shone with nothing but love for her. The Luntok that stood before her was a stranger. She felt no tenderness in his embrace. The hands restraining her were rough. His eyes were glassy with unshed tears. A sour chill oozed down her spine when she realized what those tears meant. That Laya had been a fool. She'd believed him. She'd given her heart to him. And now—

Luntok had betrayed her.

"It's over," he said, his voice hard.

"Let me go." She thrashed in his grip, but he held fast.

"Laya, it's over." He was stronger than she knew him to be—inhumanly strong. Even with the blood of Mulayri that ran through her veins, she could not fight him.

"*No.*" Furious tears ran down her cheeks. Pangs of pain and helplessness wracked her body. She raged and spat, tried to claw at his cheeks. "How could you," she sobbed. "I hate you. I hate you. I—"

"Luntok, let me," Imeria said.

Laya jerked back, but she was too slow. Imeria flattened her hand against Laya's forehead. Laya met Luntok's gaze a final time. He was crying. He was remorseful. She didn't care. *I'll kill you*, she thought. *I'll blast you over the edge of the terrace. I'll—*

She blinked. Someone had cast a veil over her eyes. The chaos of the throne room disappeared in an instant. Ahead, she saw a black, starless sky that stretched for an eternity. The shouting in the background dimmed. She could hear nothing but her own ragged breathing before that, too, faded to silence.

Calm, said a gentle, honey-coated voice that did not belong to her.

Laya refused to be calm. But the blackness in front of her eyes called to her, as tiredness settled into her bones. She did not want to be calm, but she did not want to fight either.

Come, cooed the voice, as the blackness opened its arms. The velvety fibers of a worn blanket. The warm embrace of an old friend.

Yes, Laya thought. She wanted to sleep. To rest. *I will come.*

Her eyes fluttered shut. Her knees buckled. Her muscles sighed in relief.

At last, Laya pitched herself forward into the void. Deep, deep into the night she sank. Her fall was welcome and sweet, and the void lovingly claimed her.

Four

WHEN SKY MEETS SWORD

BY ORDER OF GENERAL OJAS, ON BEHALF OF HER MAJESTY HARA DUJA

Dispatch all province-based units to the capital immediately.

The Gatdulas have fallen. Imeria Kulaw has wrested control of the palace.

Hara Duja lives. The royal family and their closest allies have been taken hostage. We must liberate them. We must not yield to Kulaw reign.

War is upon us, my friends. May the gods look kindly upon us all.

Twenty-Three

IMERIA

Dawn fell on Mariit beneath a blanket of haze. From high up in the palace, Imeria felt trapped inside a puff of smoke. Gray clouds blotted out the sun above, and thick fog veiled the city below. The terrace should have promised unobstructed vistas of Mariit's town houses and twisting spires, of the green-topped balete tree at the heart of the capital and the jagged face of Mount Matabuaya on the horizon. Instead, nature had blinded her. Imeria wondered if the Gatdulas' gods had robbed her of sight as punishment for the crimes her family had committed.

A memory returned to her, piercing through the haze. Imeria's mother had come to visit her at the palace. By then, Imeria had been living there for over three years. The old queen had granted them a private lunch on this terrace. Imeria's mother could not stop staring at her from across the table, her frown deepening as they ate.

"By the gods," the late Lady Kulaw had said in a hushed voice. "You've changed."

"You sound displeased," Imeria said as she fiddled with her sleeve. She had outgrown most of the clothes her servants had packed for her when she'd first arrived in Mariit. Before she could ask for money to replace them, Duja had gifted her a new wardrobe of Gatdula green.

"Not at all, darling. You left home a child. Now look at the woman you've become." Her mother's gaze lingered on her new silks. Imeria could hear a quiver of sadness in her voice when she added, "I suppose I must thank the queen for that."

"The queen has shown me nothing but hospitality. Dayang Duja, as well," she said, and gestured one of the servants over to refill her drink.

Her mother was silent for several moments. She fiddled with the brooch pinned above her shoulder. It was in the shape of a great raptor bird—the Kulaw family's symbol. When she opened her mouth, she spoke in a careful tone. "You are very much missed in the south, Imeria. As well as they treat you here, I hope you will not forget us."

Imeria wrangled her mouth into a neutral line. "You are my family. How could I forget?" she said—unknowingly making a promise that would seal her fate.

Over two decades had passed since, and she had not forgotten. Imeria had once been forced into Gatdula silks, but she'd never betrayed the Kulaw blood that ran in her veins. Starting this morning, the palace belonged to them.

She glanced at Luntok, who stood beside her on the terrace. He no longer had to crawl beneath the gap in the garden wall. If he desired, he could come and go through the great gates at will. He could stroll through the arcaded walkways in broad daylight. He could visit Laya in her chambers without repercussions, except she was in no state to speak to him. When they saw her last, she was still submerged in Imeria's enchantments, her murky eyes black and unseeing.

But the precioso's potency was waning fast. Of the wildfire

that had surged through Imeria's veins at midnight, a mere ember remained. Imeria could feel its absence like a nagging itch. She'd been warned that precioso cravings often crept in slowly, only to later spiral out of control. To avoid falling prey to addiction, she resolved to consume it as seldom as she could manage. Thankfully, she had not needed the precioso's aid since she had gotten Laya under control. But as the drug wore off, Imeria's powers were also weakening. Her hold on the Gatdulas wouldn't last much longer. Thankfully, Imeria had come prepared with a solution.

"My lady. Luntok." Datu Gulod approached them on the terrace. He had gotten caught in the scuffle in the great hall, and his fine clothes were worse for wear. Blood mottled the pale-green silk of his trousers, and the embroidered hem of his right sleeve was badly torn.

"How are the prisoners?" Imeria asked. At the mention of the word, Luntok flinched.

"The prisoners are appeased," Gulod said, his waxy features fixed in a somber expression. Imeria knew that meant her men had forced sleeping drafts down their throats. None of them posed a threat any longer—not the other ruling families, not even the mighty Gatdulas. All of Maynara was at their mercy.

Triumph flared beneath Imeria's ribs. She had won the palace for Luntok. After years of scheming, the throne was finally his.

"What about Vikal?" she asked.

"He and the men have finished securing the rest of the palace. After General Ojas surrendered, his men turned to Vikal's command—just as you said they would, my lady," Gulod said with a wry grin.

"Loyalty is a fickle thing," Imeria remarked, leaning against the railing. A cramp shot up her legs. She had been standing on her feet for so long. As the precioso seeped from her blood, the battle's exhaustion had begun to wear on her.

Gulod joined her at the balustrade. The fog had cleared, and they gazed down at the streets below. They were empty. It was early, and the city had barely begun to stir. "Mariit sleeps for now, but it seems many of the servants have fled. They'll talk, Imeria. There may be anger in the streets, but we are prepared."

She nodded. Soon, word would spread across Maynara that the Kulaws had taken the capital. Vikal had warned Imeria of riots and complots. Her son was a Kulaw, not a Gatdula. Not all Maynarans would bow to him of their own accord—but Luntok wouldn't ascend to the throne alone.

"What about Laya?" Luntok asked hoarsely. He hadn't said a word to Imeria since they'd left the throne room. That was the first question he had asked in hours.

Dropping the deferent tone, Gulod chuckled. "You're awfully devoted for a conspirator, aren't you?" he asked. When Luntok scowled, Gulod waved his hand dismissively. "Rest assured, she's sleeping. We've placed her in her own room, as you asked. It's heavily guarded."

"Good," Luntok said, his shoulders relaxing. Imeria sighed. She would have thrown Laya into the prison hold along with the others, but Luntok would hear none of it.

"If you wish to see her, I would go now while she's placated," Gulod said blandly. "I daresay she will be less pleased to see you the longer you wait—*my lord.*"

Luntok bristled. "If you don't hold your tongue, Datu Gulod, I'll cut it off myself," he growled, taking a threatening step toward him.

Imeria laid a hand on his shoulder to calm him. "Namok

meant no harm, darling," she said. "Allow us to finish here. You ought to rest."

In truth, Luntok was beginning to worry her. Since they'd stormed the great hall, he appeared to relish the Kulaws' victory, running wild through the palace's gilded rooms, chanting southern battle cries along with their men. But Imeria watched him when he thought no one was looking. During rare moments of quiet, he wandered the palace with a dazed expression. His triumph dulled in those moments, and he looked just as forlorn as the Gatdula prisoners down in the hold.

Luntok tensed beneath her hand. "I knew going into this, Mother. I knew the cost we would have to pay. I was *ready*. Then we got to the throne room, and the way Laya looked at me . . ." He faltered for a lingering second, then squared his shoulders. "There was no other way. One day, she'll understand. Don't you think so, Mother?" he asked in a level tone. Imeria could still sense his distress. With uncertainty still creasing his brow, he looked exactly as he had as a little boy, tiptoeing into Imeria's bedroom after a nightmare.

Gulod barked out a laugh. "Great Mulayri. The throne is in your hands now, and *that* is what you're worried about?"

This time, Luntok ignored him. He shook his head to himself as he stared at the sleeping city below. His expression hardened into one of grim acceptance.

Imeria knew his heartbreak intimately. She wished to comfort him but didn't dare say a word in front of Datu Gulod. "Don't trouble yourself with that now, Luntok," she said softly. "You are going to be king of Maynara, my darling. Soon, you will have everything you have ever dreamed of."

"The crown. The throne. Maynara and Thu-ki, united at

last," Luntok listed, as if reminding himself what the entire coup was for.

She nodded to encourage him. "You will herald the realm into a new age, my boy. You and your lovely queen."

In an ideal world, Imeria would have slaughtered Laya without a second thought. But the Gatdulas were far too beloved, and their murder would have provoked a wasteful, drawn-out war. Coercing them into a marriage alliance was the cleanest way for the Kulaws to take the throne. It would bind their families together by blood. And nothing in Maynara was held more sacred than a blood vow. No one—not even the datus—could protest their union after that.

For Imeria's plans to work, she needed to maintain the pretense of Gatdula rule. Southerners were still received with suspicion in the capital, but the royal family's fiercest worshippers craved continuity above all else. They might decry the marriage at first, but dissent was tiresome, and their anger would wane with time. She was certain she could tame the court, as well as any unrest that would soon sweep through the city. Even if it meant keeping Laya Gatdula, and the rest of her family, alive.

At the mention of Laya, Luntok's expression brightened the slightest shade. Imeria regretted choosing those words to comfort him. She could say with complete confidence that the princess would never live down their treachery. But Laya's love, like her forgiveness, couldn't matter less. The girl would rule at Luntok's side whether she wanted to or not. Luntok would one day learn to accept it. Vaguely, Imeria wondered how her son would manage disappointment with the weight of a crown upon his head. Doubt twisted in her gut, but Gulod was watching them too closely—she refused to let him see it.

With a sigh, Imeria reached for Luntok once more. In a firmer voice, she told him, "You've had a trying few days, Son. The fatigue has gone to your head. Promise me you'll rest."

To her surprise, Luntok didn't protest. "You're right, Mother," he said with a resigned nod. "You should rest too."

A bittersweet warmth burst in Imeria's chest. He leaned into her palm as she brushed a thumb over his cheek. *Do you see now, my son?* she thought, casting her gaze back to the skyline of Mariit. *All of this belongs to you.*

As Imeria drew Luntok into an embrace, Vikal burst onto the terrace. He bowed before Imeria, breathless. "Datu Kulaw."

"What is it?" she asked, perplexed. Rarely did she see Vikal so flustered.

"We thought we'd find her hiding in a cupboard or in the gardens somewhere," Vikal said, "but we've combed through every inch of the grounds. She's gone."

"Who's gone? What are you talking about?" Imeria demanded.

Vikal met her gaze with tired eyes. "Dayang Eti. It seems she's fled the palace."

"The little one? She can barely wield," Gulod scoffed. "If Laya were to escape, now that would be a greater concern."

"Eti is a Gatdula all the same. She can't get away," Vikal said, lowering his head. "I'm sorry, my lady. I don't know how we allowed this to happen."

Imeria pursed her lips. It was dangerous to let one of the Gatdulas escape, but Gulod was right. Eti was a child, and she didn't possess half the power of her mother or sister. Alone, she was no threat to them, but she was a loose end; one of their enemies need only find her and tug, and their fragile hold on the city would unravel.

"Rally the Royal Maynaran Guard, the ones we're sure we can trust. We must secure the perimeter. No one will be allowed to leave the palace." Imeria glanced back down at the labyrinth of streets below. Mariit was enormous, with plenty of nooks and shadows for a child like Eti to hide in. But, like her sisters, Eti had grown up sheltered in the palace; she would flounder without its protection.

"There was one more thing, my lady," Vikal said in a grave voice.

Imeria's stomach dropped. "What is it?"

"One of my men found this lying in the courtyard." Vikal reached into the pocket of his trousers and retrieved what looked like a block of pure glass no bigger than an inch square. The pale morning sun glinted off its smooth surface. He dropped it into her hand.

Gulod leaned over Imeria's shoulder. "Precioso," he said with a gasp. "Imeria, you were right about that."

Imeria's fingers curled around the item. Her heart raced in excitement. "That means the alchemist was here after all," she said, remembering Pangil's letter. "Please tell me you found him."

Vikal shook his head. "I'm afraid not, my lady. We swept the eastern wing several times. Someone had been living there recently, but there was no sign of the man. No trace of any more precioso either."

She cursed under her breath. Precioso was too precious a resource to lose, and they couldn't let the alchemist get away. "Find him," she told Vikal. "The little girl too."

Give them a few days, Imeria thought as she tucked the precioso into the folds of her skirt. She glanced over her shoulder at the horizon. Neither Eti nor this mysterious alchemist could have gotten far in Mariit's winding streets. They could find a hole somewhere and burrow down there for as long as they liked. But the royal guard belonged to Imeria, and they would catch up with them soon.

Dear Nelo,

How fast the mighty fall. You told me how anger sweeps through a nation. How it builds and crests, until it tears down fortresses and topples regimes. You told me this while we were lying together in the caretaker's shed behind the rector's office, the strawberry trees shielding us from the inventor's merciless eye.

I have taken refuge in a ramshackle warehouse on the edge of a canal. Once again hiding, once again lost. Despite the danger that awaits me beyond these walls, my mind wanders to those stolen moments with you in that shed.

I'm not alone. Hara Duja's youngest daughter was with me when the intruders overtook the palace. She's a small, clever thing—so unlike her sisters. One moment, she was in my workshop offering me sweets. Next, the queen's general came barging in, blood pouring down the side of his leg.

"Grab the precioso and run," he said. "Take the princess with you."

So Eti and I ran. We found this warehouse, and she used her powers to snap open the brass padlock on the door. She spent the better half of the night crying. She asked me what would become of her family. I didn't lie to her, but I could not bear to tell her the truth.

Hara Duja has been deposed. My soul aches

when I think of her tight-lipped smile. When I think of Laya, and her enigmatic, green-flecked eyes. I know what happens when governments fall. Anarchy will consume the island in a matter of days. I know what you are thinking. But I cannot stay.

I have a way out, as I always do. With the precioso in my pocket, I can bribe my way onto the first westbound ship. Your voice, low and vicious, echoes in my head: Would you abandon a child, Ariel? The people who granted you protection?

Damn you, Nelo. The will to save the royal family has come to me in nagging whispers. I know it's because of you.

You ask so much of me, my love, even though you know my answer.

This time, I won't cower. This time, I will stay and fight.

I will not abandon Eti like I abandoned you.
—Ariel

Twenty-Four

ETI

Stabbing pain rocked up from the soles of Eti's feet to her knobby knees. She had never walked so many steps in her life. The panic that flooded her veins as they'd fled the previous night had dimmed to a soft but constant pitch. Eti was anxious, exhausted, and, once she allowed herself a moment to let it all sink in, absolutely miserable. The crowds didn't help. She was trailing behind Ariel as they walked alongside the market canal. The shirt he'd found for her was scratchy and hastily stitched together, but she needed to blend in.

Although the morning was young, the sun still pale and low on the horizon, it appeared as though half of Mariit had clustered around the canal. Their chatter rang in Eti's ears. Their elbows rammed into her sides as they brushed past. The bustling market was a far cry from the peace of the palace courtyard. Eti kept her eyes to the ground and tried to shut the rest of the world out.

Part of her longed to return to the warehouse where she and Ariel had spent the night. It wasn't much, but it felt safe enough, dusty stacks of inventory shielding them from view, a wall between them and the rest of Mariit. But they couldn't stay there. The warehouse belonged to someone, Ariel warned—and that someone would not be happy to discover that Eti had broken their padlock.

Eti had broken a great deal of locks lately: the padlock on the warehouse door and, before that, the lock on the servants' entrance through which she and Ariel had escaped. Perhaps all she was good at was breaking things.

"Come along, Eti," Ariel murmured, casting a concerned look at her over his shoulder. "Just a bit farther now."

He'd offered her the same words of comfort as they'd fled the palace, when Eti couldn't breathe through the panic rising in her throat. Any fear the Orfelian harbored he'd transformed into gentle protection. Eti hadn't realized how much she needed that until the midnight feast, when the walls shielding her from hardship came crashing down.

The tears came before Eti could stop them. She froze where she stood, wrapping her arms tightly around her middle. "I can't, Ariel. Everything that's happened—it's all too much," she whispered. If she rolled herself into a tiny ball, maybe she could slip between the cracks in the cobblestones and hide there until this all blew over.

"Hush, now. We'll find a way out of this." Ariel wrapped her in a brief hug. Outside the palace walls, he was the only ally Eti could count on. The Gatdula family had fallen, and it was just the pair of them against Imeria Kulaw. Who knew what other horrors awaited them at the palace? As the initial shock of the midnight feast began to fade, Eti's new reality struck her with alarming force.

"What are we to do?" she asked, despondent. "My family's in trouble, and I can do nothing to save them. I'm not like my sisters. I'm useless."

Eti had grown up knowing she'd never be able to blast

through her enemies like Laya or strike them down with a flash of steel like Bulan. She'd guessed what people whispered about her—that she was a daft child, worthless apart from tinkering with her precious metals. She told herself she didn't care. But suddenly her family needed her, and she had no choice but to abandon them.

The word continued to rattle in her mind. *Useless, useless, useless.*

"Listen. We're going to save your family. But first, we must come up with a plan." Ariel reached over to brush aside Eti's hair, which hung limp and knotted from their late-night run through the city. "By the way, you're not useless," he added, and gave her a small, encouraging smile that was so like her father's, Eti's heart flooded with a tender ache.

They ended up walking the full length of the market canal. Along the way, they bartered one of Eti's golden bangles in exchange for sweet rolls to quench their hunger and two sturdy pairs of shoes. During their venture, they eavesdropped as customers gossiped with the vendors floating along in their boats.

According to the gossip, dozens of servants had fled the midnight feast with tales of bloodshed and Imeria Kulaw's infernal powers. By midday, news of the coup had swept through the city like wildfire. Fear hung in the air, mingling with the copper-pipe scent that wafted up from the canals. From frenzied arguments Ariel and Eti had overheard, bloody fights had broken out across the city. If anyone had died, it was too soon to say. Eti assumed the clashes were between the cowardly guardsmen, who'd capitulated to the Kulaws without hesitation, and the loyal people of Mariit, who would die for the Gatdulas if justice demanded. The violence, Eti was convinced, was the start of a cresting tide that would steer Maynara back to the light.

"More will rise, and together, they outnumber the Kulaws. Imeria won't be able to hold the palace for long. Isn't that right?" she muttered to Ariel in a short-lived spark of triumph.

But Ariel merely pressed his lips into a thin line and said, "We shall see, Eti." He explained that more violence would likely follow. He wanted to make sure that Eti didn't get caught up in the thick of it.

A small, naive part of Eti believed the coup had been nothing more than a minor fluke and that she'd be back in her mother's arms by sundown. But another night would soon fall over Mariit, and Imeria Kulaw was still in charge of the palace. Eti knew she couldn't fight for her family on her own, but surely their people would flock to their aid. Why, then, did the entire capital not rebel?

For this, Ariel offered no simple explanation. "People will always seek to save their own skin. What good is loyalty when your survival is at stake?" he said, his gaze clouding with a dark, unspoken thought. Eti wondered where he crawled to in his mind during those rare but worrying moments when his expression became guarded. Distant. By then, the feeling of dread hovering over the canal had escalated to disquieting heights. He told Eti they needed to leave the market as soon as possible. The farther they got, the better.

They walked as far as the dockside districts on the outskirts of Mariit, where they knocked on half a dozen doors before finding a boardinghouse with an available room. The boardinghouse keeper, an old woman with gray hair and kind eyes, ushered them inside without question. She didn't recognize Eti as a Gatdula princess, but she'd seen the ashen look on her face and took pity on them. The old woman must have been accustomed to unusual guests, because she barely raised an eyebrow at Ariel's accent when he paid for their meal and a week's rent. She merely pocketed the coins and insisted on feeding them.

They exchanged few words as they ate. The boardinghouse keeper served them fresh steamed rice and a hearty tamarind stew. The hot homecooked meal warmed Eti from the inside and momentarily made her forget the anxiety gnawing a hole through her stomach.

Out of politeness, the old woman asked Ariel what he did for a living. The moment Ariel froze up in hesitation, she waved off the question and diverted her gaze. "Never mind my prying. A man's business is a man's business" was all she said.

Once Eti finished eating, she sat back and yawned. It wasn't yet dusk, but her body needed rest. In the warehouse, she'd only managed to get a couple of hours of fitful sleep. The boardinghouse keeper stood and started clearing the plates. "This child is in need of a nap, I think," she said.

Ariel and Eti complied, and the boardinghouse keeper took them upstairs to their room. It was simple, with two cots pressed up against the walls and paint chipping off the ceiling. The previous tenant had moved out in a hurry. He'd left behind a number of items, including a row of liquor bottles lined up in front of a mottled window. When Eti lay down on one of the cots, she noticed the sheets were clean, at least. Eti kicked off her shoes, her feet still aching from all the walking, and closed her eyes.

For over half an hour, sleep evaded her. In the quiet, worries clouded her head. She thought of her family, and the panic rose inside her chest again and again. With a sigh of frustration, Eti rolled onto her back. If she couldn't sleep, she might as well pray for the gods to keep everyone safe. She clasped her hands over her belly and whispered her prayers.

The gods didn't answer her, but the prayers calmed her mind.

Eti stilled in her cot as the afternoon air trickled in through the open window, filling the room with the scent of sea salt. Whenever the wind was thick like this, Eti imagined it was the Weeping Goddess sighing, her breath coating Mariit in a blanket of warmth. That afternoon, Eti could hear a whisper of sadness in her breath. The goddess's pity: *Oh, my children, look at what you have become.*

What *was* Eti to become? Her life had changed so quickly in the span of a single day. Not long before, she'd been wielding gold pellets in the privacy of a palace stairwell. Then suddenly she was on the run, and not even the Royal Maynaran Guard was coming to rescue her. The boardinghouse did not offer the same protection as the palace. As long as Eti was a Gatdula, she wouldn't be safe there—not forever.

"There's some sweet rolls left over from this morning if you want them," Ariel called without turning around. He was staring pensively out the window, the half-empty bottle of palm liquor the previous tenant left behind dangling from his fingertips.

Eti rose from her bed and joined him at the window. Their room, which stood at the top of the boardinghouse's run-down staircase, overlooked the shadow-cloaked alleyway below. No one passed through there, save for stray cats and hungry orphans.

"You ought to lie down. You barely slept last night," Eti said in the same kind tone Ariel had used with her since the day her father introduced them. The Orfelian was so unlike the king's past palace guests, the brightest subjects in Maynara. Loyal and talented they might have been, but Laya had warned Eti they sought only to improve their station. According to her sister, they saw Eti as a pea-brained little girl, easy to cajole with sugary treats and empty promises. Ariel, on the other hand, never asked a single favor of Eti.

From where Eti stood, she could make out the sharp edges of precioso lining Ariel's pockets. He'd smuggled it out of the palace the night they'd escaped. Eti understood little about the drug apart from the fact that it was the true reason Ariel was in Maynara—and, should the precioso fall into the wrong hands, it would doom the entire kingdom to a ghastly fate.

She noticed then that Ariel was holding one of the crystal pieces in his fist. Sunlight winked off the glassy tip, which stuck out over his knuckles. He'd told her that precioso had cursed the people back in Orfelia, burrowing itself deep inside their minds, enslaving them. As curious as she was about the precioso, she didn't ask to see it. There was something about the drug's spotless, manufactured beauty that didn't sit well with Eti—a magic not even the mightiest Gatdula could wield. She reached instead for the liquor bottle's narrow stem. That jolted Ariel out of the fog that had settled over him. He batted Eti's hands away with a frown.

"Hey," he said, chiding her for the first time. "You may be a princess, but you're not of drinking age."

Eti raised her eyebrows in surprise. "Do you have to be a certain age to drink, where you're from?"

"Yes. In most places, actually." Ariel raised the bottle and took another sip. Eti waited patiently for him to offer her one, but he never did. When her surprise morphed into mild annoyance, the corners of his mouth quirked up into an amused grin. "You look so much like your sister when I offend you."

Eti had two sisters, but Ariel could only be referring to one of them.

"Why? Do you often offend Laya?" Eti asked, and a faint flush crept across Ariel's cheeks. Clearly, the sound of Laya's name fazed him. Eti took the opportunity to pluck the liquor bottle from his grip. "I turn thirteen in a few weeks," she said as he opened his mouth to protest. "That is old enough to drink in Maynara."

"Only a sip," he cautioned. "One of us must keep their wits about them."

"One sip." Eti brought the bottle to her lips. It was much stronger than the wine they served at the palace feast. She swallowed the liquor and handed the bottle back to him, fighting the urge to gag. "I've changed my mind. I don't like the taste."

Ariel chuckled. "Few people drink for the taste, Eti." He'd stopped calling her *dayang* for fear of being overheard. As long as the Kulaws controlled the city, no one could know who they were. She liked that he didn't use her title. It made her think that, maybe, he considered her a friend. Eti didn't have many of those. And she needed friendship more than ever.

"Oh, no. I've heard how people try to drink away the sadness . . . Although you didn't strike me as one of those morose types." Eti smiled at him, openly, trustingly. She half expected Ariel to smile back in that shy, reassuring way of his. But the alcohol had loosened Ariel's features. His expression fell into one of abject helplessness.

"But I am," he murmured. "I am morose and pitiful. Unlike you, I truly am useless. How am I to get you out of this mess alive?" Panicked questions seemed to rise in the back of Ariel's throat before he coughed, choking his worries back down. "Forgive me, Eti. I promised I was going to help you. I just need to find out how." His brow was creased with worry, but this time, he spoke with shaky reserve.

Ariel was afraid, but he'd never leave Eti on her own. He was as determined to save the Gatdulas as she was. Gratitude swept through her, a force so strong she couldn't put it to words. She threw her arms around his neck. Ariel returned her embrace, leaning down to rest his chin atop her head. Warmth filled Eti's chest as she thought once more of her family. She'd see them again soon.

Finally, her mind cleared from the shock of the midnight feast. Her entire body began to vibrate with a fierce determination Eti had never felt before. What did it matter if she couldn't wield a sword or summon typhoons? Eti was a Gatdula. The blood of Mulayri flowed through her veins. She could break through locks and whittle down iron bars with a twist of her fingers. She wasn't strong, but she was small and fast. If she could fade into the city undetected, she could slip past an entire army if she needed to.

And, above all else, Eti wasn't alone. The mere reminder gave her strength. She squeezed Ariel's shoulders, breathing in sharply through her nose. "We'll find out how to rescue them," she vowed into the rough fabric of his shirt. "Together."

"Together," Ariel echoed.

He didn't budge when Eti stepped back and tucked herself under the cot's threadbare sheets. Although he set the bottle down, he stayed at the window for a long moment. Eti didn't bother him. She was too alert to sleep. In her mind, she stalked the halls of the palace. She sifted through hazy memories, lessons in cleverness passed down from her father. She searched for a solution, anything that could help free her family from the Kulaws' clutches.

The queen, the king, Bulan, Laya—Eti knew she could help them better than anyone. But how?

Twenty-five

LAYA

Her tongue awoke before the rest of her body. She felt it, thick and rubbery, against the roof of her mouth. The grassy taste of herbs clung to it like medicine, and Laya wondered if she had caught a fever. The last time she woke up swimming in sweat-soaked sheets, she had been ten years old. Hours later, when the fever had broken, Maiza was leaning over her, the back of her hand pressed to her forehead. Her father was curled up next to her on the bed. Maiza had said he didn't want to leave her in case sickness-induced nightmares jolted her awake.

But Laya was alone this time. She was in her room. Someone had drawn the panels of her window open to the sun. The light blinded her the moment she opened her eyes. She lifted her hand to shield her face, only to find that her wrists had been bound together in front of her chest. She shot upright. She couldn't wrench her hands free. And without her hands, she was powerless.

Panic coursed through her as memories of the midnight feast flashed in her mind. She remembered the explosion of glass above her head. The blood-slick tiles. Her mother's blank-eyed stare as she froze in the middle of the throne room, caught in Imeria's grip.

She scrambled to get out of bed. Her vision swirled. She

struggled to plant one foot in front of the other. Whatever Imeria had done to her, the effects lingered. Laya's limbs betrayed her. She fell to the ground with a thud.

Voices echoed on the other side of the door, and it slammed open. Laya blinked at the sight of sandaled feet as they hurried over to her.

"Dayang, you're awake," a woman said—a servant. Gently, she pulled Laya by the arms into a sitting position.

"Mother," she said in a feeble voice, her throat dry as sand.

"You must be parched." The servant reached for the water jug that was sitting on one of Laya's bedside tables. She poured some of its contents into a cup and knelt by her side, bringing the cup to her lips.

Laya gulped down the water and nodded. "More."

The servant obliged, holding back her hair as she drank. Sleepiness made Laya clumsy. Some of the water leaked down her chin and onto her clothes. No one had thought to remove the soiled dress she had worn during the closing ceremony. She felt filthy and ill all over. Her wrists chafed against the shackles, fastened tight against her skin.

"They told me to let them know when you woke up," the servant said quietly. She set the cup down on the floor and made to stand, but Laya snatched her by the elbow.

"Wait," she croaked. "Don't tell them yet. A moment longer—please."

The servant hesitated but, at Laya's pleading eyes, gave in. "One moment, not more," she said, and refilled the cup.

Laya tried to drink slowly this time. Less dehydrated now, her mind cleared. Her gaze settled on the servant before her. She was young, around Laya's age, pleasant looking but unremarkable. She had to be someone Imeria trusted, enough to allow her to be alone with her. "What is your name?" Laya asked, lowering the cup.

The servant stared, surprised, then bowed her head. "My name is Yari, Dayang."

A southern accent, maybe from the Kulaws' kadatuan. Clipped speech marked her as lowborn. The palace must have employed her as a scullery maid, too common to serve the royal family this intimately. Laya wondered what she had done to win Imeria's trust.

The girl was not loyal to her, but she had to know something about Imeria's plans for the Gatdulas. The chains rattled when Laya took her hand and whispered, "My family, Yari. What has become of them?"

Yari hesitated. Fear creased the corners of her eyes. "They are alive and well, Dayang," she told her, bowing her head lower. "Datu Kulaw has been merciful."

Anger flared beneath her ribs. "Merciful," she echoed, releasing her hand. "Does this look like mercy to you?"

Sensing her wrath, Yari scrambled for the door. "You're awake, now. They'll want to know."

"Wait!" Laya cried, but it was too late. She had spoken too brashly, and the servant girl disappeared. The door locked shut behind her.

Cursing loudly, Laya tossed her cup to the side. Her thoughts raced as she searched her room for options. Yari would be of no help to her. She had to act while she was alone, because she wouldn't be for long.

Her gaze landed on the open window. She struggled to her feet and rushed toward it. Laya glanced over her shoulder. The door remained closed, and she couldn't hear any footsteps from the outside. Cautiously, she headed onto the balcony. The chains on her wrists clanked against the balustrade. When she leaned over the railing and saw the drop to the ground below, she felt like vomiting. Luntok may have survived that fall dozens of times before, but he had use of both his hands.

Sweat beaded across Laya's back. She could try to climb down. If she watched her step, she could make it. The sun was too bright, and the flower bushes below taunted her. She squeezed her eyes shut. She couldn't keep thinking about falling, or she would lose her nerve. She thought instead of her family, trapped somewhere within Imeria's clutches. Laya needed to escape—for them.

With a deep breath, she braced her bound wrists against the edge of the balcony and swung her right leg over the balustrade. As she slipped over to the other side, guards burst through her door.

"Stop right there!"

Now. Jump now, you coward.

Laya's wrists slid against the balustrade. She panicked and lost her balance. The second she righted herself, a guard grabbed her by both arms and wrenched her back onto the floor of her bedroom. She balked when she heard the window screen slam shut. What if that had been her only chance to flee?

"I wouldn't try that again if I were you," a deep, hearty voice called. She looked up, half expecting to see Ojas crouched before her. Instead, it was a towering man with rows of tattoos that wound their way up the thick muscles of his arms. Laya recognized him.

"You're Vikal," she said. "Luntok's told me about you."

"He's told me about you too, Dayang." Vikal helped her to stand.

"I won't see him. You can't make me." Laya hated how small and spiteful her voice sounded. She had stood beside a great deal of warriors, and never had they made her feel so weak before. With her hands bound, the blood of Mulayri would be of no use to her. For the first time, she wished she had at least a kernel of Bulan's training. If she knew how to wield a dagger, how to sink it between a man's ribs, maybe she could overpower him.

Vikal sighed. He addressed her as if she were a petulant child. "Come, now. They only wish to speak to you."

She tilted her chin up at him. "Tell them they have no right to make demands of me."

"Dayang, listen. You are in no position to refuse." He reached for her arm, but she shrank away, shaking her head violently.

"I won't speak to him. I won't."

"Dayang, please—"

"*No.*"

She screamed when Vikal reached for her again. Exasperated, he called one of the other guards to help him. Laya lost all sense of reason as she struggled to break free from their hands.

"*Let me go!*"

Like a wild animal, she thrashed and kicked and dug her nails into whatever skin she could reach. She threatened their lives and the lives of their families. She cursed them and called them traitors. Nothing she said fazed them. They half dragged, half carried her downstairs to the great hall.

"My lord," Vikal said as he deposited Laya gracelessly on the floor.

"I told you to be *gentle* with her."

"Fetch her yourself next time, then."

"Laya?" Luntok's voice cracked so sincerely, her gaze snapped to his. He was kneeling beside her, his brow furrowed in concern.

"You wished to see me," she said between labored breaths.

Luntok brushed the sweaty strands away from her face. She

knew his touch too well to flinch. "There's something we would like to discuss with you," he said as he helped her to her feet.

She didn't understand it—the shade of hope she heard in his voice. Her gaze shifted over his shoulder to the crowd gathered toward the back of the hall. The guests of the midnight feast were still there—the Council of Datus and their closest kin—all surrounded by armed guards who wore sashes of scarlet silk. She saw Datu Luma, a shock of blood crusting over his white hair. Datu Tanglaw, ashen-faced, with Bato seated silently beside him. Their eyes were downcast. They didn't dare look up when Laya arrived. They, too, were prisoners.

"What is this?" she asked in a low voice.

"Laya, pet, come closer. We've called this meeting expressly for you." Before the throne stood Imeria Kulaw, with beady-eyed Datu Gulod at her side. Laya's gut twisted. The traitor. Had he been working with her the entire time?

"The queen," Laya demanded as the blood turned to ice in her veins. "What have you done to her?"

"Your mother is fine. If you cooperate, you may see her. Now come, child." Imeria beckoned to her once more.

"Don't toy with me." Laya's voice shook and her hands balled into fists. "Where are they, Imeria? What have you done with the rest of my family?"

"Laya, please," Luntok begged. He placed a hand on her back, nudging her forward. The heat of his palm radiated through the thin silk of her dress. She recoiled. He would never touch her again—she vowed it.

"Get off." Laya swung her bound wrists over her shoulder as if she were wielding a bamboo rod. The brass shackles crashed into the side of his face with a loud crack.

Luntok stumbled back with a gasp, rubbing his cheek. *"Laya,"* he hissed. She hadn't struck hard enough to break any bones, but one of the notches on her shackles had caught his mouth. A thin trail of blood trickled from the corner of his lips to his chin.

By the throne, someone coughed. Laya glanced over. Datu Gulod's beady eyes glimmered. He was biting back a chuckle.

"Stop this. Now." Imeria had lost her patience. She cast Laya a withering glare. "Do I have to ask again, or are you ready to talk civilly?"

"*You.*" Laya rushed toward her in a rage. "You have attacked my family. Imprisoned me in my own home. Betrayed the crown. How dare you lecture me on civility?"

But Imeria didn't shrink back. She answered her calmly. "I understand this must all be a shock to you. Before you tire yourself out, can I ask you a question?"

"You already have."

Imeria's eyes flitted to hers. She cocked her head to the side. "Aren't you ready to be queen?"

Laya faltered. She sought answers in Imeria's face, but her expression betrayed nothing. "I don't understand."

Imeria gazed upon her with pity. "Laya, child, don't tell me your mother kept it a secret from you?"

She stiffened. "I don't know what you mean."

A wry grin spread across Imeria's face. She reached into the pocket of her skirt and retrieved something small and clear, no bigger than Laya's thumb. "Precioso," Imeria explained, holding it out for Laya to see. "It's worth more than gold, this substance—the key to immeasurable power. Hara Duja wanted it to keep the tremors at bay. According to my sources, she sought out an alchemist to produce it for her—one of the finest makers of precioso in the world, by the looks of it."

Laya stared at Imeria. Her thoughts raced as she began to

piece the information together. Images flashed through her mind. The furtive glances her mother gave over her shoulder as she snuck away from the dawn feast. Ariel's sudden appearance in the eastern wing. The peculiar smell of vinegar wafting from his borrowed clothes. He hadn't come to Maynara to be Laya's Salmantican tutor at all. No, he—

"You truly don't know anything about it," Imeria said, amused by the shock etched across Laya's face.

"No," she said hoarsely. "I truly don't."

A humiliated flush crept up Laya's neck when she realized what the precioso meant. Her mother had wanted the drug for a reason. She hadn't wanted to step down from the throne as her predecessors had when their tremors grew out of their control. She hadn't trusted Laya. She had been terrified of her, just as Laya feared.

Imeria understood this. Soon, the rest of the court would too. She took a measured step toward Laya. "Hara Duja was a coward. It's time for a new sovereign to take her place." She met Laya's gaze and added in a conspiratorial whisper, "She didn't think you were ready, but I do."

Laya frowned. "Me?"

If Imeria's plan was for Laya to become queen anyway, why would she have gone through the trouble of staging a coup? Unless...

"I have one condition, though. I believe it will please you." Imeria's smile broadened, and she held out her hand. Luntok brushed past Laya to join her. "You will become the queen Maynara needs, Laya. And your betrothed will join you on the throne," she declared for the entire room to hear.

Laya's gaze snapped to Luntok, who nodded in encouragement. "You mean—"

"We will marry," he told her. "Isn't that what we always wanted?"

Her heart hammered in her chest. Her gaze trailed down to Luntok's hands—the hands that had traced prayers across the length of her spine. The same hands that had held her down in the great hall the previous night.

"I *wanted* to marry you," she said weakly. That had been before—before Luntok had joined the attack on her family. Before he'd allowed his mother to string her up in chains.

"Hara Duja never would have allowed it, for the same reason she'd never have stepped down from the throne. She's stubborn, unaware of her own shortcomings," Imeria said. "Don't you see? She gave me no choice but to intervene."

Laya shook her head. She knew what Imeria was doing. She was trying to poison her mind, same as she poisoned the minds of Luntok and Datu Gulod and all the others with whom she conspired. She thought Laya was as weak-willed as them, that she could be swayed by flattery and empty promises.

"I cannot marry Luntok," she said, and stared him straight in the eye. "I refuse to marry a traitor." The words echoed beneath the vaulted ceiling of the throne room, loud and damningly clear.

Imeria's jaw tightened. "What a change in tune from a few days ago," she said, "when you let my son play you like a lute."

Laya's cheeks burned, but she refused to let Imeria humiliate her. "I am not the one who was played." Defiantly, she met Luntok's gaze. This time, however, he looked away.

"Oh, child." Imeria clicked her tongue in pity. "Who do you think engineered the attack on the palace? Who do you think snuck our men through the gap beneath the garden wall?"

A clammy feeling spread across her skin.

"Luntok couldn't have broken into the palace on his own," Imeria said. "How generous of you, Laya, to show him the way."

Laya's throat constricted. A weight dropped on top of her chest. Years earlier, she'd been the one who'd taught Luntok how to sneak past the palace guard through the tunnel under the wall—the tunnel that belonged to no one but the pair of them. She had been so sure that he loved her. That he was devoted to no one else. Had he fought to win her heart, knowing he could twist its strings for his own gain? Had he always planned to betray her?

Tears splashed down her front unchecked. Imeria sighed when she noticed. "Remember, no marriage is without flaws. You'll find a way to forgive him, in time."

"No," Laya croaked out. She shook her head, aghast. "You cannot expect me to marry him. Not after this." She glanced at Luntok with bruised eyes. She had loved him, and he'd betrayed her. How could she be his wife when she couldn't bear to look at him?

"A Gatdula must sit upon the throne. That is how the gods willed it," Imeria said with a grim smile. "Believe me, Laya, if I could have chosen any daft highborn girl for a daughter-in-law, I wouldn't have wasted my energy with you."

"No. You cannot make me." Out of instinct, she groped for her powers. Her hands strained against the shackles. It was no use.

Desperate, she whipped around and beseeched the council members, who were watching Laya's horror unfold before them in silence. "My lords, how do you tolerate this farce?" she cried. "You, who have sworn your loyalty to my family. You, who bowed before my mother, Maynara's chosen steward. How can you sit there, meek as sheep? How can you fall to your knees before a traitor whom you all hate?"

When no one budged, panic gripped at the base of Laya's throat. She tried to shame them. "What noble datus you claim to be," she spat. "You tremble in the face of the enemy. You renege on your blood vows at the first sign of threat. Stay silent if you must. I will fight these traitors on my own, and when I win, I will not forget who betrayed me. I will not forget your groveling or your cowardice. I will—"

"Enough." Imeria grabbed her by the chin.

Pain unlike anything Laya had ever endured radiated from her skull. Her own brain had erupted, sending rivers of lava down her spine. She shrieked in agony, as scorching heat flooded her entire body. The taste of rust stung the inside of her mouth. She couldn't speak. Couldn't beg for mercy. Her vision melted into a white-hot blur. The sound of her wails rang in her ears. Death couldn't come soon enough. Laya welcomed it. Let her die on her back, screaming. At least she wouldn't die the wife of a traitor.

The pain lifted for the briefest moment. In the quiet, she sucked in a ragged breath. Darkness circled her like a swarm of vultures. With all her strength, she pushed up against the night. It hammered against her skin, the relentless beating of a thousand wings.

Submit, a monster murmured, its voice a soothing balm against Laya's torment. *Submit, and mercy will be yours.*

Never. The defiant thought shot through Laya's mind without hesitancy. The monster roared and plunged Laya back into the searing flames. As she fought back, the renewed pain pierced deeper. An imagined knife sliced through her flesh, tearing it from the bone in slow, harrowing strips. The monster wanted her to beg. Laya refused. She would last until the monster grew tired of its torture—maybe then Imeria would kill her.

Between wave after wave of agony, she heard Luntok pleading. He sounded a thousand miles away. *"Leave her. Mother, please."*

An eternity later, Imeria complied. The pain finally ebbed to a dull ache. Laya opened her eyes to find herself plastered across the floor of the throne room. Fresh blood trickled from her mouth and splattered against the tiled floor. She must have bitten her tongue, helpless against the pain that wracked her body. Salty tears ran down her cheeks. Sweat soaked through her dress. When she tried to push herself off the ground, her arms shuddered beneath her weight.

With tremendous effort, she lifted her head. Several of the palace guests were on their feet. They stared at Laya in worry and terror. Not even Luntok dared rush to her side. They were too afraid—of *her*.

Imeria laid a hand against her cheek. Laya blanched, but no pain came. "You know, when Luntok told me a Gatdula girl had caught his eye, I prayed to the gods he didn't mean you," she said in a quiet voice. "Couldn't he have gone after the little one? She's just as pretty and twice as weak. But no, Laya. He had to have *you*."

A faint spark of pride swelled within her heart—the one place the pain didn't reach. Steadily, she met Imeria's gaze. "You would not crown me if I were weak."

"No, I wouldn't." Something twinkled in Imeria's eyes—something akin to respect. Her mouth hardened. "You *will* marry Luntok," she told her. "Or whatever pain I inflict on you, Bulan and Eti will receive tenfold."

Laya's eyes widened with the threat to her sisters. "No, Imeria, please. Leave them out of it."

"So complicated, just like your mother," Imeria said. "I'm giving you what you've always desired, Laya. I merely ask for your cooperation in return."

How dare she act as if she were doing Laya any favors. Fury slashed lines of red down either side of her face, clouding her vision. With her last ounce of strength, Laya lunged for Imeria. But Imeria was too fast. She sidestepped the attack easily. Instead of digging her fingers into Laya's mind, she struck her hard across the cheek.

Shocked gasps ripped through the room. Too drained to right herself, Laya plunged to the ground. Her ribs collided against the cold tiles. No one rushed to her defense. She howled in pain, helpless. She wanted to charge at Imeria Kulaw again. Wanted to claw the eyeballs from her sockets and tear her limb from limb. But Laya's fall had jolted the fight out of her; she needed all the energy she had left to keep from bursting into sobs.

Imeria clicked her tongue at her. "Oh, Laya. I could beat you within an inch of your life, and still, you'd refuse to surrender. Your resistance is admirable. I wonder, Are your sisters cut from the same cloth?"

Her heart threatened to pound out of her chest. She imagined Bulan's tortured screams in place of her own. She pictured Eti writhing on the floor, her hair streaked with blood. They were not strong the way Laya was strong. Whatever pain Imeria inflicted on them, they would not endure. Laya herself could barely survive it.

The truth came as a crushing blow. Fighting the Kulaws would only put her family in further danger. No one was coming to save them. For the first time in her life, Laya found herself cornered from all sides.

"Please, Imeria. Don't hurt them," she said, lowering her head in defeat. "I promise, I will cooperate."

Imeria stared down at her. She raised her hand, and Laya flinched. Instead of striking her again, Imeria offered her hand to Laya and helped her to her feet. "Wise girl," she said with a cold grin. "I hope you won't give me a reason to regret making you a part of my family."

Twenty-Six

LAYA

Laya's mind was still reeling when the Kulaws' guards deposited her back in her chambers. She was unable to overcome the dual sting of betrayal. First, Luntok. Then, her mother. Ariel had come to Maynara to produce a power-enhancing substance for the queen, and Laya had learned about it from Imeria, of all people. How could Hara Duja keep such a secret from her?

The pain from the discovery was almost strong enough to make Laya forget her new fate. She was to be Luntok's wife. If Imeria had told her that days earlier, Laya's heart would have sung in happiness. But once Laya knew the truth, the prospect of marrying Luntok filled her mouth with the taste of bile.

She had been standing at the balcony, wondering whether she ought to throw herself off the ledge, when someone knocked at the door. She ignored it. She knew who was waiting on the other side.

When she didn't reply, the door creaked open.

"Laya," Luntok murmured.

She didn't turn around to greet him. He felt more like an intruder standing in her doorway than he ever had climbing over the balustrade.

"Why have you come, Luntok?" she asked in a broken voice. "Did you wish to humiliate me further?"

"I came to see how you were doing," he said.

"I have been imprisoned. Tortured in my own home. And a few hours ago, I learned that to spare my family from Imeria Kulaw's wrath, I must marry the man who engineered our destruction." Laya let out a bitter, high-pitched laugh. When she opened her mouth again, her voice shook, on the verge of tears. "I truly did fall in love with you, you know. You played your part admirably. Your mother must be very proud."

Luntok joined her on the balcony. "But I do love you, Laya. I never lied about that," he said hoarsely. He reached for her arm out of instinct. The moment he touched her, she shrank back. He could not hurt her the way his mother had hurt her, but his touch burned.

"You've locked me up in chains, Luntok. Is that what love is to you? By the gods." Laya sagged against the balustrade. Her shoulders shook, and she finally broke down in sobs. She could fight them no longer. This time, when he reached for her, she folded into his embrace. "I should despise you after everything you did. I should want to claw your eyes out and curse your name," she gasped between shuddering cries. "I loved you once, Luntok, gods help me. But you betrayed me. Betrayed my family. How can I ever forgive you?"

His arms tightened around her. He held her until her breathing calmed. When her sobs quieted at last, he drew back and pressed his forehead against hers. "I can't take back the pain I've caused, Laya, but I can promise to keep your family safe. To keep her from hurting you ever again."

Laya met his gaze. Her muscles still quivered in the aftermath of Imeria's torture. "Even if you wanted to protect me, how would you stop her?" she asked. "No one can match Imeria's power."

"I swear no one will touch you," he said, an impassioned growl creeping into his voice. "Not when you are my queen."

His queen. A faint blush spread over Laya's cheeks. "Don't tell me this was all part of some ruse you concocted simply to marry me."

"Of course not, Laya. It's more complicated than that. You wouldn't understand," Luntok said, turning away.

"Then help me to," she said firmly. "I want to know what would push a man like you to do such a terrible thing."

Luntok's face tightened. He leaned against the balustrade, gesturing at the royal gardens with a wide sweep of his arm. "How could you understand, Laya, when you grew up with this your entire life?" he said. "My people were once the mightiest and most revered sovereigns in the land before your ancestors decimated them. The Gatdulas slaughtered our shamans. Burned down our palace. They did this, and once the westerners began laying claim to the Untulu Sea, they claimed to be our protectors."

"Please," Laya said with a scoff. "Your people would never have stood a chance against the westerners. You *needed* us."

Luntok shook his head. "The Gatdulas didn't care about protecting us. They merely wanted uncontested power. So they made sure to destroy us before bringing us to heel. Not once did they consider the alternative."

"And what was that?" she asked, incredulous.

"How much stronger we could have been—together." He looked at her, hope burning in his gaze.

Together.

The word cleaved Laya's heart in two. She swallowed hard. A balmy wind swept over the palace roofs, carrying with it the sting of nectar and rotting fruit. He reached for her again, tangling his fingers in her limp, grime-ridden hair.

Her eyes fluttered shut, and she sighed. "Maybe you were right, Luntok."

"Right about what?" he asked, his breath warm against her cheek.

"We should have run away."

Had it only been two weeks since Luntok had asked her to run away with him? He hadn't meant it. Part of Laya wished he had.

When she didn't pull away from him, he cupped her face in his palms, wiping the tears from her cheeks. "Now we don't have to."

Pain erupted in Laya's chest. His gentle touch reminded her of what they once had, and she couldn't bear it. She launched forward, beating Luntok's arms and torso with her shackled wrists.

"Luntok, you damned *fool*. Some glorious union. Is this how you always dreamed it?"

Laya spat and kicked, but not once did Luntok strike her back. He stood still as a statue, collecting her wild blows as if they were loving caresses. "Coward," she said as a sob tore through her lips. "You damned *coward*."

With a desperate snarl, Laya grabbed the collar of his vest. She yanked him close. She wanted to blacken his sorrowful eyes. To bruise his smooth jawline, squared in anguish.

Instead, she curled into his arms and wept into the hollow of his neck.

How many times had she sought refuge in Luntok's embrace? He was supposed to hold her the way no one else could hold her. He was supposed to love her in ways the rest of Maynara could not.

"Try to understand that I did this for us. Your family would have held you back. Forced you to marry someone you didn't love. I refused to let that happen. I couldn't bear to lose you," Luntok murmured, his shoulders relaxing as he wrapped his arms around her. The damned traitor. He was relieved, Laya realized—because she could no longer push him away.

Disgusted, Laya recoiled. "I'm tired," she said in a flat voice. "If you don't mind, I think I will sleep."

He followed her back into the bedroom. "Don't you want to bathe first?"

Laya looked down. She had yet to discard the clothes she had worn during the midnight feast, wrinkled and bloodstained at the hem. It was once a lovely dress made of amethyst silk with canary-yellow trim. The serving girl Yari had offered to help Laya out of it, but she'd sent her away.

"I can't undress myself in these shackles. And I will die before I allow that little tart to touch me." Laya shook her head vehemently. She hadn't lost her pride, despite the grime that coated her clothes and the chains attached to her wrists.

Luntok nodded in understanding. He called for the guard posted outside the door to come in.

"What is it, my lord?" the guard asked, bowing his head.

"Remove the shackles," he said without preamble.

The guard hesitated. "My lord?"

Laya's eyes narrowed. "Is this another trap?"

"While the princess bathes, no longer." He clarified his order and gave her a somber look. "I wish for us to trust each other again, Laya. But if you hurt me or try anything stupid—"

"*I know.*" She exhaled sharply and held out her hands. "You have my family hostage. I'm not a fool."

Luntok studied her for a long moment. Laya stared back, fighting to maintain a neutral expression. She hadn't lied about the fatigue, the aches that lingered after Imeria's torture. The events of the day had drained her. She couldn't hurt Luntok, even though she ardently wanted to.

He nodded to the guard, who reached into his belt for the keys. The shackles opened with a click. Laya sighed in relief, massaging her wrists. Her gaze snapped to his, and instinctively, Luntok tensed. But she did not raise her palms to summon a blast of wind. She merely clutched her hands to her chest.

"Thank you," he said to the guard as he led Laya along by the elbow. "I'll manage from here."

The suspicion never left the guard's gaze, but he gave Luntok a curt nod and exited Laya's chambers. Alone once more, they headed into the water closet adjoining her bedroom. In the center lay a circular tub carved out of rich rosewood. Yari had already pumped it full of warm water. Steam wafted up from the surface, leaving the air in the room thick with humidity.

Laya reached for the buttons at the collar of her dress. Luntok's gaze followed her as she crossed the water closet. He wanted her as much as Laya once wanted him. That desire had been her undoing. But beneath the curdling heat of Luntok's gaze, Laya straightened.

Desire was a weakness—something she could use.

She paused, glancing at him from beneath her eyelashes. "Are you going to stand there and ogle me?"

"No, but I won't leave you unattended," he said as a bead of sweat dripped down the side of his temple.

Laya wondered whether the water in the tub was hot enough to scald her skin. She felt trapped inside a bathhouse sauna.

"Instead of standing there, perhaps you would like to join me."

Laya didn't have the strength to destroy him. That wouldn't always be the case. But Luntok would be weak as long as he wanted her.

She revealed nothing as she stared back at him. Her body language shifted as she finished unbuttoning her dress. He watched, transfixed, as it slipped from her shoulders. Laya let it pool on the tiles and stared at him, garbed in a gauzy white camisole and petticoat. She tilted her head. Parted her lips. How many times had Laya given him that look, knowing it would make his blood sear?

He swallowed hard. "Laya, I . . ."

I don't trust you.

Laya could read his thoughts, because they mirrored her own.

Her gaze softened. She held out her hand. "Please," she said gently. "Let's pretend things are as they were before."

Luntok was too vulnerable to refuse her, and she knew this. He shrugged off his clothes, watching her out of the corner of his eye while she stepped out of her underthings. Laya did the same. She thought back to how they'd danced together at the parade—wildly, recklessly—how she'd yanked him close, pulling his skin flush against hers. This was not the same kind of dance. In the water closet, they circled each other in a cautious orbit. The hard lines of his body wavered in the hot steam. Although they had stood naked in front of one another a hundred times before, the version of Luntok that appeared before her was unrecognizable.

She sank into the bath first. Luntok settled in the opposite end of the tub. The heat coaxed the tension from her muscles, held taut for so long. She stretched out her legs under the water, her feet bumping against his knees. Then she dipped beneath the surface long enough to wet her hair. Luntok watched her run her fingers through her dark, matted strands. She thought he might reach for her again. He grabbed the bar of soap lying on the edge of the tub instead.

"Come here," he said in a low voice, gesturing her closer with a wave of his hand.

To his surprise, Laya obliged him. *Let him want. Let him hanker.* She turned around and leaned against his torso. His shallow breaths reverberated in her ear, and she could practically hear his heart hammering in his chest.

Laya didn't need to call upon Mulayri's power. One day, she would strangle Luntok with her bare hands.

Despite the water's scalding temperature, she shivered when he lathered the soap over her shoulder blades and down the side of her neck. The trials of the past day had made her entire body stiffer than a bamboo rod. He rubbed slow circles into the knotted muscles in her upper back. His thumb dug into a sore spot, and rather than recline against him, she hissed.

Her hand jerked above the surface. Water sloshed over the edge of the tub. In his panic, Luntok snatched her by the wrist.

Laya's gaze snapped over her shoulder. "I . . . I wasn't . . ."

The brass of the shackles had dug into her skin mere moments before, only to be replaced by his bruising grip.

"Oh. I'm sorry." Luntok released her, and she winced. He turned away, flushing with shame as she rubbed her wrist. But Laya could tell from the hard gleam in his eyes—Luntok wasn't sorry. He'd gotten what he wanted: Laya for his wife, and the throne his family had coveted for centuries.

"This is how it's going to be from now on, isn't it?" she asked bitterly as she inched away.

"Wait." Gently this time, Luntok pulled her back by the waist and rested his chin against her shoulder. She waited for him to say something, but he had no words of comfort for her. Laya didn't care. Luntok could feed her all the pretty words he liked. Never again would she believe him.

Water dripped from the pump in light staccato. The strength flushed out of Laya all at once; she could no longer play the coquette. She cried again, a plaintive wail that filled the water closet. Her sobs this time were quieter, more restrained.

Luntok stayed silent. He comforted her until her tears subsided. Several minutes later, she calmed herself long enough to gaze at him with red-rimmed eyes.

"Great Mulayri. I wish I could forgive you," she said, in a thick voice of resignation.

Luntok's face twisted as if slapped. "I pray that one day, you will," he said stiffly.

Fool. Rage surged in Laya's blood, but she could no longer argue with him. Sniffling, she drew her knees up to her chest. The steam in the air cooled as they sat in the bathtub in silence.

Twenty-Seven

ETI

Mariit was even larger than Eti had realized. Parts of the capital she knew as well as the inside of the palace: the goldsmiths' guildhall, where Eti would sometimes study the young, deft-fingered apprentices for inspiration; the towering stone town houses of the central district, where noble Maynaran families held tiny courts of their own; and the ring of spirit houses encircling the giant balete tree at the heart of the city. Still, Mariit sprawled across dozens of neighborhoods where the royal family never deigned to venture. The boardinghouse where Eti and Ariel sought refuge was in one of the dockside districts on the outer fringes of Mariit. General Ojas's men would never have allowed Eti to go there, but Ariel reasoned it was their safest bet. The Royal Maynaran Guard started patrolling the palace and the busy center of Mariit—the deepest pockets of unrest. They would be too thinly spread to keep a watchful eye all the way out there.

From what little of the dockside neighborhood Eti had seen, it wasn't dangerous. No one bothered them the few times she and Ariel dared go outside in their new unsuspicious clothes. During normal circumstances, the people there mainly kept to themselves, toiling for hours on the docks beneath the hot Maynaran sun before trudging home to their families at dusk. But the

Kulaws' coup had shaken the outlying districts. Fear hung heavy in the air, pungent as the scent of sea salt and fresh-caught fish. Eti saw it stark on each face she passed. Since the coup, the bustling docks had ground to a halt. For two days, ships had waited in the harbor to be unloaded. No one was working; they were waiting for the fate of Maynara to be decided.

The brothel owner next door, a well-coiffed woman with a daggerlike gaze and painted lips, came over during breakfast to trade gossip with the boardinghouse keeper. In the middle of the night, a client had shown up to the brothel with a bloodied nose and news that a riot had broken out in front of the palace gates. Scores of the Gatdulas' loyal subjects tried to overtake the guards. They might have succeeded had Imeria Kulaw not felled them with her abilities. According to the brothel's client, Imeria merely raised her hand, and the rioters froze, black-eyed, where they stood. The guardsmen rounded them up and threw them in the prison hold. The riot died in minutes.

The news made Eti's stomach churn in apprehension. "Imeria Kulaw could reach into the minds of that many people?" she asked in quiet terror.

Ariel gave a glum nod, but he said something that made a small bubble of hope rise in Eti's gut. "Perhaps she can. But how many people can she stuff inside your family's prison cells?"

That same morning, Ariel and Eti spoke briefly with the two boarders who were renting the room across the hall. The boarders were a young married couple, both around Ariel's age. The husband was a tall, broad-shouldered man who spent most of his time heaving crates and barrels off cargo ships. His wife was small in stature, a mere inch taller than Eti, with a round, pregnant belly. Ariel introduced himself to them as Eti's brother, a fact neither of the boarders questioned despite the obvious lack of resemblance. Unlike the nobles prowling about court, the people here respected secrecy. They rarely questioned anything in these parts, Eti learned.

During their brief conversation, the husband pried once out of concern. He leaned in and clasped Ariel by the shoulder. "Listen, brother. Do you have family outside Mariit? I'm only asking because I have a friend who's sailing out of the city tonight. There's room on the boat if you wish to join us." He cast a worried glance at Eti and added, "The tides here will turn fast. And we both have children to think about."

"You can come stay with us," his wife said when she saw Ariel hesitate. "My grandmother lives in the south. She'll take you in should this matter up in the palace sour. And, knowing the Gatdulas, they will."

"The Gatdulas?" Eti echoed. She had never heard her family's name uttered that way—like some common, dirty word.

The wife nodded grimly. "Of course, you're too young to know about the rebellion, aren't you? My grandfather fought for the Kulaws before he surrendered. Nevertheless, the Gatdulas killed him. Burned him alive as he begged. Why, they even—" She broke off with a shudder. Her round eyes were glassy when she met Eti's gaze. "Forgive me, child, you don't want to hear this. But believe me when I say that if they survive, the Gatdulas will show no mercy. Best go to a place where we know we are safe."

An unpleasant tingle trickled down Eti's spine. She was half listening as Ariel politely declined the boarders' invitation. Whatever excuse he gave, they seemed to believe him.

"May the gods look kindly upon you, brother," the husband said. "We're leaving here at dusk, in case you change your mind." He gave Ariel a last pointed look. Gently, he slung his arm around his wife's waist and helped her back upstairs to their room.

For a long moment after they left, Eti didn't budge. She didn't realize she was trembling until Ariel laid a hand on her shoulder. "Come along," he whispered. "Let's see if we can find more of those sweet rolls."

She nodded, keeping her mouth shut as Ariel led her outside. The sun was too bright. The main street around the corner from the boardinghouse was too chaotic. People were rushing back and forth, toting carts piled high with jugs of oil and sacks of rice—reserves should supplies run low. Fearful chatter from every corner, everyone whispering of the Kulaws, of civil war. Eti tried to stamp out the noise, but the voices echoed louder in her head. No matter how much she blinked, she couldn't force her vision to focus. Instinctively, she grappled at her wrist for one of her bangles. Then Eti remembered they'd peddled most of them, which had given them more than enough money to survive over the next couple of weeks. The rest of her jewelry they'd stashed beneath the floorboards in the boardinghouse alongside Ariel's precioso. Her fingers itched for a tiny scrap of gold to wield, but she couldn't risk it. The city was on high alert. The slightest wielding would reveal Eti for the Gatdula she was.

Without her wielding to center her, panic swelled inside Eti's chest. Crowds overwhelmed her often—during her mother's dinner parties and royal ceremonies and, of course, the feasts. In the palace, she knew where to hide. Behind the mahogany bookshelves in her father's library. Inside the half-forgotten stairwells where not even scullery maids bothered to go. Eti couldn't escape to her favorite shelters. Not as long as she was stuck here.

She let out a whimper of frustration. A second later, Ariel thrust something soft and toasty into her hands. "Eat," he said. "It will help you feel better."

Eti looked down. Sure enough, Ariel had found her a sweet

roll. Shakily, she took a bite. The bread was light and airy on her tongue. She discovered with delight that Ariel had found one with sticky coconut filling.

"You were right, Ariel," she said, licking the coconut flakes off her fingers. Food didn't quite curb the panic cresting up and up inside her, but it helped.

They were standing next to the long, narrow canal that cut through the outlying districts. Her gaze traced the water down to where the canal began, at the massive stone walls shielding the city. She often looked down at those walls from the palace terraces. How mighty they loomed from afar! But up close, Eti could spy cracks branching up from the walls' foundations. They cut so deep into the stone in some parts that it wouldn't take more than one of Laya's half-hearted gusts to knock them down.

Doubt swirled in Eti's stomach. The palace walls couldn't keep the Kulaws from invading the palace. Nor would the city walls keep any foreign invaders at bay. Her family was their biggest protection, but some Maynarans didn't see it that way. Perhaps it was true what so many members of the court assumed of her: Eti was nothing more than a daft, useless child who allowed the world to fill her head with lies.

"You read the books on Maynaran history I gave you," she said. "Do you think it's true? What that woman said at the boardinghouse?"

"You mean about your family?" Ariel asked.

Eti chewed her bottom lip and nodded. Never had she thought of her forebears as anything more than ancestral spirits. Born to be respected. To be revered. Eti had heard no reverence in the woman's voice as she told them what the Gatdulas had done to her grandfather. Even if it wasn't true, Eti had heard a tremor of fear in the woman's voice. A hatred that ran old and deep. Those convictions did not manifest the moment Imeria Kulaw stormed the palace. They had been born in a dark place where no Gatdula went.

Ariel gave her a long, weighty look before opening his mouth to reply. "I am not Maynaran, so I can't say much about your history," he said. "As for legacies, they're not a footprint you press into the face of the world. Rather, they are layered, like tangled webs—as complex as the creatures who weave them."

He clasped her shoulder, a brotherly gesture that chased away Eti's fears for a fleeting moment. They followed the canal back to the boardinghouse. The panic thrumming through the air dulled as midmorning faded to noon. Not as many people were rushing through the streets, their arms laden with whatever supplies they could scavenge. Smells wafted down from the rows of open windows overlooking the water: garlic crisping in the pan, meat simmering in thick, salty stew. People were pausing their frenzied preparations to eat lunch with their families. The ritual was familiar to Eti, and it made her shoulders relax to see it.

Some things were sacred even on the brink of ruin.

Peace after the quelled riot lasted less than a day. Eti and Ariel had spent those scarce, fragile hours trying to cobble together a plan. They were sitting on the floor of their room, their heads pressed close together so they could hear each other's whispered ideas. The walls of the boardinghouse were thin, so they had to keep their voices low.

"If we could only get inside the palace, I could free them from the prison hold," Eti lamented for the hundredth time. Based on the information they'd overheard in the streets, the royal guard had doubled down on their patrols after the riots. They intended to hold the palace at all costs, as if it were a prized fortress.

"The Kulaws got into the palace somehow. They took advantage of the feast that night. Now, with violence spreading across the city, their defenses are weakening. If we bide our time, they'll give us an opening—a distraction," Ariel said, his spectacles sliding down his nose. He wore them only in private these days. With their western design, they were too distinguishable.

Eti pulled her legs up to her chest. She rested her chin between her knees as she pondered a reply. Ariel traced the patterns on the warped floorboards between them, humming to himself as he thought. They had just fallen into a comfortable silence when three sharp raps at their door jolted them alert. Ariel jumped up to open it, tearing off his spectacles. The boardinghouse keeper was standing on the threshold, a basket in her arms piled high with mangoes and leafy vegetables from her trip to the market canal. Her eyes were wide and fearful as she stepped into their room without invitation. Swiftly, she shut the door behind her.

"You both need to leave," she said in an urgent whisper. "Now."

Ariel tried to feign confusion. "I don't understand. Is there an issue with our rent?"

The old woman shook her head curtly. Wisps of gray hair tumbled over her face. "I passed guardsmen, dozens of them, on my way back. They're coming down the main street, combing through every building. They were looking for a man—an alchemist, they said, or some kind of foreigner. And a young girl—small with long, black hair—just like you, my dear."

A chill ran down Eti's spine. The boardinghouse keeper's warning spurred her to action. "We need to go," she agreed, meeting Ariel's gaze. He gave her a terse nod, and they rushed to pack their things.

The boardinghouse keeper didn't say a word as Ariel lifted the floorboards next to his bed. He scooped out the precioso and what remained of Eti's jewelry. A shadow of recognition flickered in the woman's expression. Her eyes shifted back to Eti as if she were seeing her in a new light. Once Ariel had gathered the few precious belongings they had in a small sack, he slung it over his shoulder. No time to waste—they piled out into the hall.

"Keep to the alleys. They'll find you too easily in these parts. Your best bet is to hide in plain sight," the boardinghouse keeper said as she rushed them down the stairs. She took them to the back door near her kitchen, where the guardsmen wouldn't see them leave.

"Thank you," Eti said, breathless, her voice ringing out, tinny and insignificant. Those two words were too small to contain her gratitude.

"It is my duty." The boardinghouse keeper's expression changed as she took Eti's hand. Instead of shaking it, she bowed low and pressed it to her forehead, a sign of respect for a much older woman. "I pray for your family, Dayang. May the gods keep you safe," she said in a hushed voice. Then she opened the door and hurried them into the alleyway. "I can hear them coming. You must go."

They fled from the outlying districts. The streets in this part of Mariit were no longer strange to her. The renewed sense of urgency sharpened her senses. She kept pace with Ariel the best she could, the sandals she'd bought at the market slapping against the uneven cobblestones. They rushed past shaded alleys and winding canals. They didn't let up until they reached the heart of the city. Eti realized she recognized the quiet street they were walking down. They were edging dangerously close to the places in Mariit she knew well. If they crossed the nearest canal and continued a few paces north, they'd find themselves in front of the goldsmiths' guildhall, where she'd spent many an afternoon.

They ought to take extra heed there. Eti opened her mouth to whisper a warning to Ariel when he grabbed her arm and whisked her behind an unattended set of crates. They were stacked up into a teetering pile across the street from what looked like a respectable inn. It was one of the better-maintained buildings in Mariit, with clean windows and an ornate giltwood door swinging on its hinges.

As they stalled outside, Ariel fumbled in his pockets for matches and a pipe, another trinket the previous boarder had left behind. He needed an excuse for stopping so suddenly. Eti understood the moment she heard heavy boots marching down the street. She kept her head down as Ariel struck a match against the sole of his shoe. With trembling fingers, he lowered the flame to the cracked pipe bowl. Eti watched in silence, her blood pounding a desperate rhythm in her ears. They'd miscalculated the Kulaws' resources. Imeria had sent her guardsmen after Eti, and no district was safe; the Kulaws wouldn't leave a single stone in Mariit unturned.

Eti didn't budge as the guardsmen swept into the inn. She barely glimpsed them from where she stood, hunched behind the crates, which concealed her from their view. Judging by their footsteps, there were no more than three of them. Eti tried to picture what they looked like, young men as broad as Ojas, with red traitors' silk draped over the brass clasps of their armor, their blades glinting menacingly beneath the afternoon sun.

At her side, Ariel took a nervous drag from his pipe. The burning scent of cloves made Eti think with another longing pang of her father. The memory of the king's gentle, knowing voice calmed her enough to hold still for several agonizing minutes. Then the guardsmen emerged from the inn, grumbling over their unending lack of success. They didn't stop to question Ariel. From their vantage point, they couldn't see Eti. The gods must have blessed her, because the guards hurried on.

Their footsteps grew quieter as they charged farther down the street, venturing deeper into the merchant district. When they at last disappeared from view, Eti let out a sigh of relief. Ariel wiped the sweat from his brow and pulled the pipe stem from his lips. They debated where to go next. Eti was half-tempted to go inside the inn the guards had just deserted—anything to get off the street. Then she noticed the scrap of scarlet fabric nailed above the entryway like a banner. Eti swallowed hard when she recognized the inn, a favorite meeting point for southerners who kept to their own even after they moved to Mariit. Bulan had pointed it out to her months earlier in passing, a place where the fiercest Kulaw warriors exchanged battle tactics and drank themselves stupid. Whether or not there were Kulaw warriors lurking inside, Eti knew they wouldn't be safe there. Somberly, she nodded toward the banner. Ariel grimaced in response. In silence, they agreed to move forward.

They kept walking in the guardsmen's wake until they reached another inn a few streets away. Above its gilt-edged window, the owner had pinned a long strip of green. Once Eti started looking for signs of loyalty, she could find them everywhere—dozens of little green banners waving in silent allegiance to Eti's family. In that neighborhood, at least, they outnumbered the few scarlet banners they'd passed. It was the closest thing to refuge Eti had seen in days.

When they rushed inside the green-bannered building, the

innkeeper raised an eyebrow at Ariel's accent and Eti's disheveled appearance. If he guessed their true identities, he said nothing. Eti prayed the innkeeper's loyalties were sure, and that he'd keep his silence for one more day. Ariel warned they shouldn't stay in one place too long. They'd be gone the next morning without a trace.

Ariel got them a room for the night; it was twice the size of the room in the boardinghouse and at least three times the price. Above the bed hung a relief carving of a crocodile, a date etched beneath its curved, spiny tail. Eti recognized it as the day of her mother's coronation. She allowed herself a relaxed sigh. If such an artwork hung in every room, it meant the innkeeper revered the Gatdulas the same he would any deity. They'd be safe there for the time being. It wasn't home, but the sheets were clean, and the pillows were almost as soft as the ones that lined Eti's bed at the palace. If she stretched out across the mattress, she might sleep for a week. But she knew better than to get comfortable.

"We can't go on like this much longer," Ariel said as he sat down at the foot of his bed, sighing.

Eti nodded. He was right. Soon, they'd run out of places to hide. She thought about what the boardinghouse keeper told them. Her eyes fell on the sack of gold and precioso lying at Ariel's right. "Do you have a knife in there? Or anything sharp?" she asked.

Ariel gave her a quizzical look. "No. Why?"

She chewed her lip as silly tears sprung to the corners of her eyes. She knew it was frivolous and vain, and that the price she was about to pay counted little in terms of personal sacrifice. "For my hair," she croaked out and met Ariel's gaze. "The Kulaws won't find us. Not as long as they're looking for a little girl."

Recognition dawned on Ariel's face. He stood and rummaged

about the room for something to cut with. Chopping off her hair wouldn't conceal Eti's identity forever, but it would buy them some time. The Kulaws were still looking for the youngest Gatdula princess—a guileless, airheaded girl, unaccustomed to life without luxury. If she disguised herself as a boy, she could heed the boardinghouse keeper's advice and hide in plain sight.

A small writing desk stood in the corner by the window. In the drawer, they found a letter opener with a slender white-shell handle. The blade was small, but it looked like it had been sharpened recently. It wouldn't stab through an enemy warrior's flesh, but it was sharp enough to slice through Eti's long, dark strands.

Swallowing hard, Eti took a seat at the writing desk. She didn't look at Ariel as she thrust the letter opener into his hands. For a mournful second, she ran her fingers through her hair. It would grow back, she reminded herself. Hair meant nothing to her—not if Eti evaded the Kulaws long enough to rescue her family.

Roughly, she brushed her hair over her shoulders so it hung straight down her back where she couldn't see it.

"Cut it," she told Ariel in the crisp, blunt tone she'd learned from Laya. "Now, Ariel, before I change my mind."

To Eti's surprise, she rather liked how the cool night air felt against her nape when she and Ariel stepped back outside. The man's shirt Ariel had found for her fit comfortably over her slight frame, a welcome change to the fine silk dresses she'd worn over the feast days. Dusk had fallen over the city, and the area around the inn was too quiet. If they wanted to learn anything about the Kulaws' plans, they needed to roam the crowded quarters of Mariit.

They ventured deeper into Mariit than Eti would have dared when she looked like a princess. Garbed as a humble serving boy, she faded into the throng. No one spared her a second glance. She and Ariel walked a few blocks north, rounding the corner onto the busy street leading to the heart of the city. It was easy to follow the noise. Distant shouts and jeering drew them all the way to the base of the sword-fighting tournament platform.

The feast-day festivities were long over, but a crowd had gathered. Two people stood at the crowd's center—a man and a woman—arguing at the top of their lungs. The woman appeared around the queen's age, with eyes that burned with anger and a simple green sash draped over her right shoulder. The sash shone in the light of torches above their heads in stark contrast to the stripe of scarlet hanging from the man's heaving chest. Eti scanned the crowd, picking out scraps of green and scarlet all around her. From where she stood, almost a head below everyone else, it was impossible to determine which color outnumbered the other.

"The gods blessed Maynara with the Gatdulas. When the westerners came, they fought and bled and died for us. They're the one thing standing between us and annihilation," the woman cried, stabbing a disparaging finger in the man's direction. Her voice rang loud and clear over the tournament pit. "You, sir, forget who really protects this kingdom. You forget where true loyalty lies."

Murmurs of agreement rose from the crowd, quieting a second later when the man roared, "Loyalty? And whom do you think the Gatdulas serve? Not the servants who scrub their tiles, I'd wager. Nor the men who build their ships. No, the Gatdulas care only for those who can fill their strongboxes with gold. Generations of waste and negligence—and so it will continue, as long as cowards like you beg for scraps at their feet like starving pups."

Eti stiffened at the man's harsh words, and Ariel laid a hand on her shoulder. Tension cut through the pit. The other half of the crowd yelled in the man's favor.

But the woman did not back away. She took a threatening step toward the man. She was taller than him, and she looked down at him with an unwavering glare. At Eti's side, Ariel leaned over her shoulder. He whispered, "I don't like the sound of this. We should—"

The woman let out a sharp laugh, drowning out the rest of Ariel's warning. "And what did the Kulaws do to deserve your loyalty? Half their rulers, cruel puppet masters, eager to enslave any subject who dared defy them. The other half, greedy beast-kings, who didn't hesitate to pick this very island to the bone. If it is their mercy you seek, brother, I pity you. For that is the true mark of cowardice."

A deafening crack split the air as the man struck her smartly across the face. At once, the spectators surged forward in outrage. Several lunged to hold back the man from striking her again. Others tried to appease the woman to no avail. She leaped from their arms and clawed at the man's cheeks. Dozens of smaller brawls broke out between Kulaw and Gatdula supporters throughout the crowd. People banged into Eti as they rushed back and forth across the pit. She let out a cry as someone jammed into her left side. She might have fallen had Ariel not hoisted her to her feet. Arm in arm, they fought through the sea of flailing limbs. Eti struggled to push through, but she was too small. Cursing in Orfelian under his breath, Ariel half carried, half dragged her to the edge of the crowd.

"We need to leave!" he shouted over the rising noise.

Unsteadily, Eti nodded. She grabbed his hand and made to follow him. Then a booming voice echoed across the tournament pit, freezing everyone where they stood.

"Enough!"

An imposing man in heavy armor was standing atop the platform. Eti recognized him, the warrior Vikal, head of Imeria Kulaw's private guard. At his orders, royal guardsmen swarmed into the pit below. They pried apart the brawlers. Those who refused to stop fighting, even those with scarlet fabric pinned to their clothing, were taken away in chains.

"Rioting in this city will not be tolerated," Vikal declared as the guardsmen subdued the crowd in the pit. "This will be your final warning. Anyone caught fighting will face imprisonment, with bail of up to one hundred gold pieces."

A chorus of agitated grumbles rippled across the tournament pit.

"Yeah? Under whose orders?" one spectator yelled. Eti searched the crowd. It was the woman in the green sash who spoke out, a thin line of blood trailing from her swollen lips. Her remark sent a defiant spark through the crowd. Shouts of indignation exploded from the pit. They cursed Vikal, pointed fingers at him, and called him a traitor. The guardsmen couldn't subdue them all. Another riot would break out any minute. Ariel tugged at Eti's hand, desperate to slip away, when another figure joined Vikal on top of the tournament platform.

"Under my orders," barked a crisp, familiar voice that fused Eti's feet to the ground. She stared at the newcomer, half-concealed by the torchlight's wavering shadow. Eti's gut churned in protest. She didn't want to admit that she recognized the outline of the woman towering above them on the platform.

But everything, from her brisk gait to her slender stature, was undeniable.

Laya came to stand at the edge of the tournament platform, sending a shocked hush through the throng of rioters. She already looked like a queen, with blinding rings of gold hanging from her head and neck. It looked as though she'd descended upon them from the heavens. A force equal parts divine and terrible.

Hara Duja's heir wore not Gatdula green, but the scarlet silk of her captors. Laya held her head high. But the torchlight caught on the angry tears bubbling up at the corners of her eyelids. Tight brass shackles encircled her wrists. Eti's mouth dropped open at the sight of them. If she could only get close to Laya—get one finger against the brass—then she could snap the shackles in two. But the crowd separated the Gatdulas like a yawning cavern. Laya was too far. Instinct told Eti to lie low. To reveal herself now would be too risky.

Silent rage built at the base of Eti's throat. She started to tremble, helpless and indignant. Was she truly meant to do nothing while the Kulaws paraded her sister about Mariit as if she were their puppet, chaining her up like a lowly prisoner?

"If you will not listen to my guardsmen, listen to me, your future sovereign. *The violence must cease.* Remember that it is a crime to lay a hand upon your brother. And we are all brothers and sisters here." Laya's voice shook as she addressed the crowd. Not once did their attention waver. They stared at her in tense silence. She went on, more forcefully than before. "You fight over divided loyalties, when your allegiances are one and the same. When I take my place on the throne, I will not be alone. Luntok Kulaw, heir to the kingdom of Thu-ki, will rule at my side."

At Laya's announcement, cries of outrage and confusion rang out across the pit. She raised her bound hands. Nothing she said would calm them. If Eti hadn't been so transfixed by her sister's reappearance, she might have missed the rest of Laya's message.

"Our reign will bring peace and prosperity to the realm," the future queen declared with crushing finality. Her words carried over the mounting turmoil. "It will begin with our marriage in three days' time."

Bleak understanding shivered down Eti's spine. The Kulaws were forcing Laya to marry Luntok, their family's sworn enemy. And they claimed it was in the name of peace.

Wait! Eti wanted to cry out as Vikal took Laya's arm and led her down from the platform. Her sister hadn't caught sight of her in the crowd. Even if she had recognized Eti, with her baggy clothes and black hair snipped short, what good would that do? Laya couldn't save anyone while they towed her away in shackles. Already she was on her way back to the palace that had turned into a prison. Already she was leaving Eti behind.

In Laya's wake, the brawl threatened to start anew. If the Kulaws thought sending Laya out would appease the capital dwellers, they were wrong.

Ariel clasped Eti by the shoulder. "Now we really have to go," he insisted.

Eti didn't budge. She stared at the edge of the tournament platform, where Laya had stood mere seconds before. She had blown back into Eti's life so quickly, only for the Kulaws to whisk her once again out of reach.

Anger pulsed around them, threatening to sweep them off like a tidal wave. The mob had grown in number, their energy rivaling Laya's fiercest storms. A small voice chimed in Eti's head, ringing above the noise. It dimmed the pandemonium that raged around her. It whispered an answer that tied her safely to the ground. Let the tide come for her. This time, she would not be swept away.

Unknowingly, Laya had given Eti the key to their rescue. Her announcement left no room for ambiguity; she was marrying Luntok. *In three days' time.*

"Eti," Ariel whispered, pleadingly. "We have to go. Please."

She shook her head as a plan took form in her mind. She knew how royal wedding ceremonies worked. Wedding ceremonies were ten times more demanding than the feast days. Wedding ceremonies required an army of servants and shamans and seamstresses. Wedding ceremonies spelled a certain amount of chaos, even when the palace had months to plan them.

This was the distraction they needed.

Eti's revelation hit her with a shock that nearly sent her tumbling down again. She stared at Ariel with a feverish gaze. "I know," she whispered, her thoughts moving too fast to wrangle into words. "I know how we're going to save them."

Twenty-Eight

IMERIA

One week had passed since Imeria had wrested control of the palace. She stood in the courtyard where she and Duja used to play as children. The floor had been wiped clean of the broken glass and bloodstains left over after their attack. The courtyard buzzed with activity. Save for the conspicuous absence of Hara Duja, one might assume the feast days had yet to end. Servants flooded past her in all directions, bearing brooms and rags and pails that sloshed with soapy water. Imeria had enticed several new workers to come to the palace with the promise of obscene amounts of pay, twice what they would have earned under Hara Duja. Royal weddings took weeks to plan in normal situations, and she needed the extra labor to expedite the process.

The marriage ceremony itself was a logistical nightmare. Maynaran custom required it be held at sundown on the edge of the Black Salt Cliffs. It was among Maynara's most sacred grounds, nestled at the base of Mount Matabuaya, far away from the palace on the edges of the city. Imeria did not understand the significance of the place, nor did she care to. All she knew was that they had to follow the royal customs precisely in order to ensure the datus accepted the marriage as legitimate.

After Luntok married Laya, they were to host yet another

midnight feast, which would conclude with a reprisal of the vow ceremony. Instead of bowing before Hara Duja, the Council of Datus would assert their fealty to their new sovereigns in blood. Then at last, Imeria could rest in her chambers, their claim to the Maynaran throne officially sealed.

Yari hurried past Imeria, Laya's wedding gown scrupulously bundled in her arms. Imeria had ordered her to have them laundered. The poor girl was managing her new duties with surprising grace, considering she had no prior experience as a lady's maid. Imeria knew she'd chosen her allies well. She would have to think of how to reward her after the ceremony.

"Yari," she barked.

"Yes, my lady?" Yari rushed to her side, her head lowered in respect.

"Is Dayang Laya almost ready?"

"Yes, my lady. The other girls are tending to her hair. Shall I bring her to you when she is finished getting dressed?"

"No, that won't be necessary." Imeria didn't have time to speak to Laya before the ceremony, but she wanted to be ready should Laya decide to do anything rash. "How would you describe the princess's temperament this morning, Yari? Did she seem restless? Excitable?" she asked.

"I would say she seemed agreeable, Your Majesty. I believe your son spoke with her last night."

Imeria bit back a laugh. The last word she would have used to describe Laya was *agreeable*, but the princess wasn't heartless; she wouldn't dare defy Imeria, knowing her family's lives were at stake. "Very well, Yari, I'll leave you to attend her."

"Yes, my lady," she said, and scurried into the main building.

As long as Imeria had Laya under control, she could deal with the other loose ends later. According to Vikal, the Royal

Maynaran Guard had yet to track down Eti. The girl's disappearance was a nuisance, but Imeria needed to worry about the wedding first. To quell the riots in the city, she'd consumed more precioso than she'd anticipated. The drug left her with growing cravings, a lingering headache, and little energy to think of anything else. In the hours following each use, its absence grew harder to ignore. It didn't help that the vial of precioso shifted along her necklace at the slightest movement. The tiny shards of crystal whispered in her ear like naughty spirits—*more, more, more.*

Imeria banished the thought with a sharp exhale. She gazed past the bustle of servants in the courtyard, her eyes landing on the eastern wing. The alchemist was not hiding there, as she had hoped. She remembered the last time she had been inside that building, the same day the eastern wing went up in flames. The memory returned to her in a billow of smoke, crashing into Imeria before she could push it away.

She could still feel the weight of the air inside the guest chamber pressing up against her skin. Beyond the Untulu Sea loomed the threat of a hurricane. The midday sun had baked the tiles in the courtyard outside. The shell-paneled window screens did little to block the wet-season heat, and young Imeria had wanted to open them to filter out the thick, resinous incense the old queen liked to pump into the eastern wing, but they needed to keep the screens drawn for fear of being seen.

Despite the boiling heat, Imeria awoke curled up alongside Duja's sleeping form, her cheek pressed against the princess's bare shoulder. Duja was far softer than the earth she wielded. Imeria couldn't help but nestle closer, even though the princess's skin felt hot enough to burn.

Beside her, Duja stirred. "Imeria?" she called, her voice sluggish from sleep.

Imeria's heart leaped at the sound of her name. "Yes?"

Duja yawned and stretched her arms over her head, arching into Imeria's embrace. Slowly, she rolled onto her side. For a wild moment, Imeria feared what she would find on the princess's face when she turned around—apathy? Or worse, disgust? Instead, Duja gazed at her tenderly, her dark eyes free of their usual shields.

"That was foolish of us," she said, smiling shyly.

Warmth crawled up Imeria's neck and spread across her cheeks. "Do you regret it?" she asked.

"No," Duja said. She sounded sure of herself for the first time. "Truly, I don't."

Imeria wanted nothing more than to accept Duja's reassurance, but she couldn't quell the doubt that continued to simmer deep within her gut. "What about the—the others?"

Duja frowned. "What others?"

"You know," she said, tearing her gaze away. "*Them.*"

She couldn't bring herself to name a single one of Duja's growing band of suitors. Their numbers had doubled since the previous season when the princess had turned eighteen, an endless parade of arrogant men who deigned to think themselves worthy of Maynara's beloved princess. Imeria glowered each time a guard interrupted her walks with Duja to announce yet another gentleman's visit. These men thought they could win Duja's heart by regaling her with overblown tales of their own excellence. Only one had come close—the young and beguiling Aki Tanglaw, whose gift for storytelling constituted a magic of its own. At first, Imeria had dismissed Aki as an unremarkable boor, no different from the stream she watched strut through the halls of the palace. Then she noticed how Duja's eyes sparkled when she looked at him—the same way Duja was looking at her from the opposite side of the bed.

The princess softened when she reached out to cup Imeria's face. "Who else could I possibly be thinking about right now?"

Imeria fought the urge to melt against Duja's touch. Instead, she leaned in and kissed her gently on the lips.

Duja sighed in contentment. She ran her fingers through Imeria's hair and pulled her closer. Imeria's stomach fluttered—Duja had never reached for her before. The princess was too hesitant, too inhibited, too afraid of her own wanting. It was always Imeria who had to reel her in.

They folded into each other, skin flush against skin. Duja's fingers trailed from Imeria's hair to the swell of her breast. They continued their journey downward, pausing at the apex between her thighs. Out of instinct, Imeria parted them. Duja slid her hand into the wetness there, teasing Imeria with slow, languid strokes.

Imeria moaned wantonly at the princess's touch. Her hips bucked against her hand. Duja didn't need to guess what her companion wanted. Imeria made her desires abundantly clear; she wanted anything Duja was willing to give her. She wanted *more*.

Lovingly, Duja complied. She slipped a finger inside Imeria's slick channel. Then a second. Then a third. Imeria closed her eyes. Her back arched off the pillows. Duja's hand began to pump inside her at an exquisite rhythm. Imeria drew in a sharp breath before losing all sense of restraint.

"Please," Imeria chanted over and over, like the prayers of a blessed shaman. *Please, please, please.*

Duja buried her face in the crook of Imeria's neck. She

continued her ministrations. The angle of her hand shifted. Her fingers plunged deeper, hitting a spot inside Imeria that sent her over the edge. She climaxed with a strangled gasp, wave after wave of pleasure surging through her body.

Moments after Imeria floated down from her high, Duja leaned over and pressed her mouth to hers. Imeria sighed against her warm, tender lips. To lie with Duja was to steal a slice of divinity from the gods. If loving her was an offense in Maynara's eyes, so be it.

This, Imeria thought as she coiled into Duja's embrace. *This is why they want to keep us apart.*

As Imeria deepened the kiss, footsteps thudded from down the hall. Both girls froze. Faint laughter echoed through the thin walls of the eastern wing—the queen. Duja's mother was making her way upstairs. It sounded like she had just returned from her trip to the southern provinces, and, judging by the deep male voice Imeria could hear all the way from the guest chamber, she had brought her consort with her.

They shot up from the bed, scrambling to find their clothes in the tangled sheets.

"I thought you said she wasn't coming back until tomorrow evening," Imeria hissed as she forced her arms through the long, cumbersome sleeves of her blouse. The old queen had accepted Imeria as a member of the royal household, but the terms of the Kulaws' surrender were painfully clear. Imeria remained the daughter of a traitor. She could never marry Duja. She could never know her this intimately. The only reason they ended up in the eastern wing was because it was supposed to be empty.

"She must have returned early," Duja whispered, tight-lipped, as she pulled her skirt up over her hips.

When they were both dressed, Duja crept over to the door. It gave a loud, condemning creak when she opened it. Imeria leaned heavily against the wall, her heart hammering as they exchanged a nervous glance. They remained still for one agonizing moment, waiting to be discovered. But the queen's light, unhurried footsteps continued to resonate from the upper floor. The consort was still with her. He called out to the queen, his voice muffled through the floorboards so that Imeria couldn't understand him. He must have said something clever, because the queen laughed once again. Imeria let out a sigh of relief. No one was coming for them.

Duja grabbed her wrist. As quietly as they could, they darted across the corridor and down the stairs. The hard soles of their sandals clacked against the smooth tile, but they managed not to call any attention to themselves. Imeria followed Duja to the lower level, and they snuck out the way they had come—through an oft-forgotten side entrance reserved for scullery maids and armored guardsmen.

With enough distance between them and her mother, Duja let out a sigh of relief. "We ought to be more careful next time," she said, patting down her mussed hair as she cast a wary glance over her shoulder.

"Next time?" Imeria's lips stretched into a knowing grin.

Duja turned red as a beet. "No—I mean, I didn't mean to presume—"

Before the princess could talk herself into a stupor, Imeria kissed her again, pressing her against the cool stone of the outer wall. But rather than sigh against Imeria's lips, Duja stiffened. She braced her hands against Imeria's collarbone and pushed her away.

"You can't do that," she said sternly. "Not here."

Imeria's throat clenched. "Yes. My apologies, Dayang." She

could not keep the bitterness from seeping into her tone as she stepped back, shame heating her ears. Roughly, she brushed past Duja and made a beeline for the courtyard.

Duja groaned and ran to catch up with her. "Imeria, wait," she said, and grabbed her hand.

Imeria wrenched her hand back as if burned. "You can't be like this, Duja—loving one moment, hateful the next," she said, tears threatening to spill out from the corners of her eyelids. "You're cruel to me. It's not fair."

Duja pursed her lips. "Please, Imeria, be reasonable. There's nothing cruel about my wanting to exercise a bit of discretion—"

"Discretion?" Imeria let out a high-pitched laugh. "You and I both know it's more than that." She barreled around the corner with Duja close on her tail.

"What do you want from me, Imeria?" Duja called after her, her voice strained. "Tell me, and I shall give it to you."

Imeria froze in her tracks. They were standing in the courtyard now, mere steps away from the entrance hall of the eastern wing. The sun, still high in the sky, beat down on the nape of her neck. Sweat beaded along her back, likely soaking through the thin fabric of her blouse. She could hardly breathe. How did capital dwellers stand it? The air in Mariit was thick as tar, stifling.

"I want you," Imeria murmured, hands clenched into fists at her sides. *All I could ever want is you.*

Over her shoulder, she heard Duja steer to a stop. She refused to turn around. She imagined the princess's face, her soft lips contorted into a confused frown.

"Imeria," Duja said, a throaty whisper that sent a bolt of longing down the column of Imeria's spine.

Nasty snickers erupted in the courtyard. Both girls whipped around. To their right, the crown prince emerged from the shadows of the arcades. He slouched against one of the pillars, a vile smirk on his face.

"Pangil," Duja snapped. "How long have you been standing there?"

"Long enough," he said, crossing his arms in front of his chest. His black eyes flitted over to Imeria. "Didn't think you were the type to wear your heart on your sleeve, Kulaw."

Anger boiled in Imeria's veins. She took a menacing step toward the prince, but Duja laid a hand on her shoulder to stop her.

"Leave her alone, Pangil," Duja said. "This doesn't involve you."

"Oh, it does," he shot back. "How do you think Mother will feel when she hears about this little affair?"

"I don't know what you're talking about." Duja's eyes flashed red as her cheeks. Beside her, Imeria grimaced—the princess was a terrible liar.

Pangil's eyes narrowed. "I think you do, Sister. The moment Mother returns from the south, I'll let her know exactly how you've carried on with your little traitor tart, Duja, then you'll see—"

The ground lurched before he could finish his threat. Imeria fell, scuttling back several feet. She cried out as her side collided with rough stone. A bright red glow flared up at the edge of her vision as heat, stronger than a thousand suns, flooded the courtyard. She rolled over to see Pangil, his palms raised above his head. A fireball the size of a small planet blazed between them. He aimed it straight at his sister.

"Duja!" Imeria screamed.

A column of earth shot up in the center of the courtyard. Duja ducked behind it. The fireball collided with the column in a mighty blast that shook the entire palace.

Pangil conjured a long fire whip, which he unfurled against

Duja's weakened column. It crumbled to dust at the impact. Duja scrambled to her feet. The ground between her and her brother split open with a deafening crack. She erected a jagged wall that spanned the courtyard, reaching nearly twice her height. Pangil didn't relent. He bombarded her with an onslaught of flame. The wall groaned but absorbed most of the impact. It would hold—but not for long.

Duja turned, chest heaving, and met Imeria's gaze. "What are you doing?" she cried. "Run!"

But Imeria couldn't run. Her eyes locked on the wall over Duja's shoulder. Pangil had lobbed a fireball directly at the crisped earth at its center. "Duja," she screamed again as the wall exploded into a thousand bits.

Guards and servants flooded the courtyard at the sound of tumult. Their terrified shouts filled the air.

"Your Highness. Oh, Your Highness, please!" they shrieked at Pangil. But the crown prince could not be appeased.

"Don't you dare stop me!" Pangil spat, stabbing a finger in Duja's direction. "Not when she would choose *her* over her own blood—this filthy Kulaw *traitor*."

With a snarl, he charged toward his sister, both hands ablaze. Duja didn't have time to wield. She dived, dodging the streak of flame by inches. The fireball soared into the eastern wing. It gobbled up the front door, the antique giltwood sputtering as it burned to ash.

"No!" Duja's terrified cry rang out over the sound of crackling flame.

The fire fanned out from the door with breathtaking speed. Within seconds, it leaped all the way up the eastern wing's facade to its tall, sloping roofs. Imeria watched the flames spread, helpless to stop them. The scorching heat warped her vision.

She opened her mouth to call for Duja, but her lungs filled with smoke.

"Your Highness, don't!" It was the booming voice of General Ojas. Beyond the flames, Imeria recognized his towering silhouette. He had emerged from the main building and was running toward the royal siblings. A wall of flame fanned out across the courtyard, blocking Duja off from all who could save her.

Pangil stalked toward Duja. Imeria saw the flash of madness in his eyes, as though he had been possessed by malevolent spirits.

"Pangil, please!" Duja cried.

He ignored her and wrenched her up by the collar with one hand. With the other, he conjured an arc of flame. Its shadows danced across his dark cheeks, and his lips curled into a sneer. He raised his hand, ready to cast the flame down toward his sister.

"Stop!"

The second his fingers flexed, Imeria shot to her feet. She launched herself at the prince's back. He hit the ground with a groan. She pressed her hands to his forehead. The power she had long struggled to hide burst through her fingertips, hungry to be unleashed. *Take him*, it screamed in her head, and Imeria complied. She clawed deep into the rageful threads of Pangil's mind and pulled tight.

"You won't touch her," Imeria said between ragged breaths. "You won't touch her ever again."

Beneath her, Pangil stilled. His head lolled back. He stared up at the smoke-filled sky, unseeing. Inky pools seeped out from his irises, blotting out the whites of his eyes. Only then did Imeria release him. She fell back on her hindquarters as the power that roared in her ears quieted to a dull whisper.

"Imeria—by the gods." Duja's terrified gasp jolted Imeria

back to her senses. She looked up in a daze. Her nose stung with the caustic scent of ash. The facade of the eastern wing crackled as Pangil's flames leaped to the upper floors. Thick clouds of smoke rose from the broken windows, smothering the sunlight. Agonized screams reverberated across the courtyard.

Imeria barely heard them. Her eyes darted between her hands and the black-eyed prince, still trapped under her curse. Her entire body quaked when she realized what she had done.

"Duja"—she croaked out a response—"I can explain." She reached for her, but Duja scuttled back.

The princess shook her head in disbelief. Beneath the streaks of soot, her cheeks had gone gray. "No," she said in a strangled voice. "It can't be." When she stared back at Imeria, her face twisted into a look of horror.

A hundred half-formed apologies fought their way to Imeria's mouth. No time to utter a single one. More shrieks for help rang out from the eastern wing. Her heart plummeted in her chest. She recognized that voice. The queen was still trapped somewhere between the mounting flames.

"Mother," Duja whispered. She charged toward the burning building, leaving Imeria in her wake. An armored guard stepped into the princess's path.

"Don't come any closer, Dayang. It's too dangerous," the guard yelled, his voice carrying over the sound of snapping timber.

Imeria turned to find the courtyard flooding with servants. Water sloshed across the tiles as they thrust buckets from one hand to another, transporting them all the way from the palace kitchens. As quickly as they could, they tried to douse the fire leading up to the staircase. Anything to clear a path up to the queen.

Guards barked orders from all directions. More water, they cried. But the fire was moving too fast.

General Ojas emerged from the eastern wing, ash smeared across his face. "The staircase is collapsing," he choked out between coughs. "There must be another way."

Imeria's eyes stung as she gazed up at the blackened sky. She knew the eastern wing and all the corners where she and Duja used to play. If another path to the queen existed, it had already been lost to the inferno.

The palace staff worked tirelessly for what felt like an eternity to put out the fire. By the time the flames started to die down, much of the eastern wing's facade had been reduced to smoking rubble, and the screams coming from inside had long quieted.

At last, Imeria crept toward Duja. "Dayang," she called tentatively, breaking the deathly silence.

But Duja didn't budge. She studied the embers that remained of the eastern wing. Tears carved a trail through her soot-stained cheeks.

"Mother is gone." A rare, wild spark flashed in the princess's eyes. She turned around, her gaze falling on Pangil, still lying unconscious several feet behind them. The black pools in his eyes had just begun to fade. Moments after, his eyelids drifted shut. He looked like he was sleeping. "Mother is gone," Duja said again, this time with fatal certainty. "And *he* killed her."

Ojas approached Duja with red-rimmed eyes. For a long, painful moment, the general struggled to find the words. "I . . . I'm sorry, Dayang," he finally said. "We did everything we could."

"I know you did. Thank you." Duja's words came out steady, even as her bottom lip trembled.

Ojas gave a stiff nod, then hesitated. Imeria realized that he was awaiting orders.

Duja also came to this realization at the same moment. She glanced once again at her brother, sprawled out in the middle of the courtyard. Her next command caught Imeria by surprise.

"Take the prince down to the prison hold. We struck him down with a blow to the head. You must shackle him before he awakens. He's too dangerous to leave to his own devices," Duja said in a brutal, guttural voice Imeria didn't recognize.

The general's expression hardened into one of grim acceptance. "Right away, Your Majesty," he answered without question.

Imeria's eyes widened as she witnessed the exchange. The queen was dead. Pangil was a murderer. Which meant—

"Duja," she called as she reached for her once again. She wanted to hold her. To comfort her. To promise her that everything would be all right. In the blink of an eye, their destinies had changed. The world they once knew had crumbled beneath Pangil's fire. The queen was dead, and only one could take her place.

Duja Gatdula was to be the next queen of Maynara.

But the second Imeria's fingers brushed against her wrist, Duja recoiled. *"Don't."*

Imeria's entire body went rigid from her icy rebuff. She stared at Duja as a renewed wave of hurt wracked her body. It was too late. The princess had seen what Imeria Kulaw was. She'd never let Imeria touch her again.

"General." There was no hint of tenderness in Duja's tone as she called Ojas back to her attention. "Have someone escort Imeria Kulaw back to her chambers. Keep a guard posted in front of her door. I fear she is in shock and may need some time to recover."

The apologies turned to bile in Imeria's throat. Distantly, she felt a guard's hand closing around her elbow. She opened her mouth to protest. No words came out. How could she deny the Maynaran sovereign? She prayed for Duja to relent, but her mind was already made up. The new queen gazed impassively at Imeria, her face cooling into a mask of stone.

"Don't look at me like that. Duja, please!" Imeria pleaded as the guard led her away.

The hand on her elbow gave it a comforting squeeze. "Her Majesty is occupied. She will attend to you soon," the guard murmured in her ear. But Imeria couldn't be reassured. She craned her neck to meet Duja's eyes a final time. She wanted to cry out: *I saved you. I protected you. I love you. I—*

"Enough," Imeria hissed to herself, blinking away the memory. When she opened her eyes again, she was still frozen in the middle of the courtyard, caught in the sea of servants rushing with the wedding preparations. She tore her gaze away from the eastern wing and leaned against one of the marble pillars on the edge of the courtyard as she caught her breath.

The pain from that wretched day, would it ever end?

Above, the sun dipped beneath the palace roofs, the jaw-shaped finials casting long shadows across the tiles. Dusk crept in over the horizon. They needed to depart for the Black Salt Cliffs soon. With little time before the ceremony, Imeria didn't visit Luntok's chambers. Nor did she go upstairs to dress. Instead, she headed for the winding staircase that led down to the prison hold.

The staircase emptied onto a long, narrow corridor lined with cells, each of them filled with the Gatdulas' closest allies. Duja was being kept in the largest cell all the way at the end. Cool sweat dripped down Imeria's spine as she swept through the corridor. She stopped at Duja's door. Imeria kept the key to the queen's cell in her pocket because she didn't trust any of the guards with it. Through the barred window, Imeria spied the outline of Duja's sleeping body on the cot at the back of the cell. It was the first time Imeria laid eyes on her since the coup.

Her hand hovered over the doorknob. She couldn't bring herself to open it.

"Imeria Kulaw," a familiar voice rang out. "Have you come to flaunt your victory?"

Imeria whipped around. The king was being held in the cell diagonally across from Duja's. His face peered out from between the thick metal bars. His tone had been jovial, but his gaze was hard.

"Hari Aki," she said, raising her chin. "How do you find your new accommodations?"

"I must say, I prefer my old chambers." The king held her gaze, his fingers curling around the bars. "But I'm pleased to see you, Imeria. I was wondering when you would grace us with your presence."

Imeria didn't like the knowing way he was looking at her. "I couldn't deny my old friends a visit," she said curtly, turning to leave.

"She loved you too, you know," Hari Aki said.

Imeria froze. She let out a shallow breath. "What did you just say?"

"Duja," he whispered. "You know it's true."

She squeezed her eyes shut. "It was never love," she spat. "If she loved me, she never would have—"

"A mistake," he said. "It was all a terrible mistake. You must forgive her, Imeria. Please. It doesn't have to be this way."

Imeria shook her head furiously. "You don't know of what you speak."

"But I do," Aki protested. "I was the one who stood by Duja's side all these years. I saw how she wept after she banished you from the palace. The decision to push you into another man's arms destroyed her. She regretted it every day."

"No," Imeria spat. "Duja never—"

"Duja never told me how she truly felt for you," he said, his mouth twisting into a bitter frown. "Because that feeling never went away."

Hope fluttered in Imeria's stomach, but she refused to give in to it. The king was merely feigning hurt. He was trying to win her over with his honey-coated words, the same way he won over the rest of the court. The same way he stole Duja from her all those years before.

"You're wrong, Aki. Duja never loved me," she said. "This is how it was always meant to be. And in a few years' time, I'm sure Laya will thank me for it."

At the mention of his daughter, the blood drained from Aki's face. His knuckles whitened against the bars. "What have you done to Laya?"

Imeria's lips curled into a cruel smile. "I'm giving her what she's always wanted. Thanks to me, Luntok is all hers. Thanks to me, she'll be queen of Maynara."

The king's eyes widened in panic. "No. This isn't Laya's fault. Imeria, please—"

"You should be satisfied, Aki," she said, cutting him off. "I found your daughter a suitable match—a way to thank Duja for finding mine."

His voice lowered to a desperate whisper. "For Mulayri's sake, don't drag my daughter into your personal vendetta. Punish me if you wish, for I was the one who took Duja away from you. I knew you loved her. I was the one who convinced Duja to marry you off. I wanted Duja for myself. Don't you see, Imeria? The fault is mine. I beg you. Leave Laya out of this."

A lump formed in Imeria's throat. The king was babbling now. He didn't mean a word of this. He was only telling her what he thought she wanted to hear. She tore her gaze away. "I'm sorry, Aki. It is done."

The king pounded the bars in terror, and the hall filled with the echoes of clanking metal. "Imeria, wait!"

Imeria ignored his pleas as she turned toward the exit. She ran up the stairs, nearly stumbling over her skirts on the way. Servants bombarded her when she emerged at the courtyard level. They needed to leave for the wedding ceremony in a mere hour's time, and the palace was still in chaos. Imeria swept past the servants, dismissing their questions with a wave of her wrist. Let Vikal or Gulod deal with it.

Imeria didn't stop walking until she locked herself into one of the guest chambers on the upper floor. She slammed the door shut and sagged against it. Frustrated tears threatened to spill over her eyelids. No time to dwell on the smoke-filled memories. She wiped her eyes on the back of her sleeve and pushed the tears away.

After drawing in a deep breath, Imeria headed for the nearest water closet to bathe before the wedding ceremony.

A personal vendetta, the king called it. So be it.

Soon, Imeria would have her vengeance. Soon, her dance with Duja would come to an end.

Twenty-Nine

DUJA

Duja's brother joined her in her cell. She saw him as the handsome young man he'd once been. Tall and slender, with dark-brown skin and a sharp, mocking gaze. It startled her in that moment just how much he resembled Laya. The outline of his profile blurred in the dim bar of light that streamed through the narrow window. She should have known he would come to her in this miserable prison cell, appearing only when she was at her lowest.

"Poor sister," he said, sighing as his dark eyes fell on the brass shackles encircling her wrists. "How on earth did you wind up down here?"

"Brother," she said in a low voice. "You know better than to return."

None of this was real. Pangil had not come back to Maynara. *I watched you,* she thought. *I watched you sail away.*

"You look well, Duja," he said, smiling sadly. "Did you enjoy my gift?"

She laughed to herself. The sound echoed across the slime-coated walls of the prison hold. Pangil was talking about the precioso.

"Your gift—fat lot of good that would do me now," she said, waving her hand at the gray walls of the cell around them.

Pangil let out a weary sigh and inched closer to her. "Duja—"

"*Don't.*" She recoiled. He was a ghost, but she still feared him. His eyes dropped to her neck, to the tail of the scar that peeked out from under her ceremonial sash. "I know I hurt you. My own sister. Know that I am a changed man. I will never harm you, or anyone else, again."

Lies. Pangil would not fool her with his empty promises. Not this time.

Duja shook her head, backing away from him. "How can I believe you? You are the reason Mother is dead," she said, her voice cracking. "All of this is your fault. Now Imeria has my family, and I can do nothing to save them."

Pangil fell to his knees before her as she sobbed into her hands. "Don't cry, Sister," he said in that smooth, velvet voice of his. "I am here now. All is not lost."

"It's too late, Pangil. I bet you're satisfied with the mess I've made of my reign," she bit out through her tears. "You were always telling me I was never meant to be sovereign. I should have listened to you. Now I'm about to lose everything."

Perhaps she should have never ordered her brother's exile. Becoming queen—perhaps that had been her first mistake.

Guilt creased her brother's face. "I was cruel and immature. I would have made a pitiful king. In a time of turmoil, you brought stability to the realm. You were the queen Maynara needed."

Duja sniffled in disbelief. She had prevented Maynara from falling apart, but she'd never made her country anything more than what it had been during her mother's reign. Pangil had been the rightful heir—not her. She'd been too preoccupied with appeasing the datus. She wanted to prove that she was nothing like her brother, that she was worthy of the crown. Her caution veered too often into cowardice. Any vision she had for Maynara's future had gotten lost somewhere between the politicking and the posturing and all the court games she'd been forced to play.

"In a few decades, Maynara will have forgotten all about me," she said, for once giving voice to her fears. "I have no legacy of which to speak."

"You have your daughters. You have Laya."

Pangil's words hit her like a punch to the stomach. She did have Laya—an heir she failed to prepare in time. A daughter who wanted nothing but her mother's unconditional devotion. But Duja had been too afraid of turning Laya away from her. Of turning her into Pangil. Even in exile, her brother had cast a shadow over their relationship. She couldn't love Laya in the way she needed.

"It's too late," Duja said again. "If Imeria gets her way, Laya is already lost." She could already see her daughter's future mapped out before her, etched into copper like a Maynaran epic. Imeria would use Laya to solidify her family's claim on the throne. If she couldn't wear her down, she'd contain her by any means necessary. She'd wait for Laya to produce a new Gatdula heir—one whom Imeria could mold as she pleased. Imeria had no problem biding her time. The second the rest of Maynara had their backs turned, she'd dispose of Laya. And she'd be clever about it too.

Duja swallowed a frustrated scream when she thought about her former lover. "I should have killed her," she muttered to herself. "I should have killed her when I had the chance."

"Imeria?" Pangil cocked an eyebrow at her. "But you loved her."

Reluctantly, she nodded. It was true. "I did love Imeria. And she made me weak."

In the shadows, her brother flashed her a sly grin. "No, Sister, she did not."

His claim made Duja take pause. What had loving Imeria

Kulaw gotten her, other than an adversary who threatened to destroy everything she held dear? Memories flooded back from their shared childhood. Imeria's long, inky hair spilling down her shoulder. Her unguarded laughter echoing across the palace courtyard. Always urging Duja to speak louder, run faster. A lump formed in the queen's throat when she remembered.

Imeria had been the first person to make her feel brave.

"Why are you here?" Duja cast her brother a wary glance.

Pangil leaned toward her. "I vowed to Aki that I would help you. This is a promise I intend to keep."

She tore her gaze from him. "Help me," she said bitterly. "How do you plan to do that?"

Pangil's ghost sighed. He laid a hand atop her head. "First, you will take care of Imeria. Then, when you both are gone, I shall handle the rest."

When I am gone. What did he mean by that?

Duja's head jerked up. Her brother had disappeared. The cell before her was empty. She opened her mouth to scream.

Pangil. Pangil, come back!

"Duja . . . Duja, wake up!" Another man's voice called her back to her cell. Her husband.

Aki.

Duja's eyes flung open. She shot up in the cot with a strangled gasp.

She wasn't alone in her prison cell, but Pangil's ghost no longer accompanied her. The king was hovering over her in the cot, his brow furrowed in concern.

"Duja, are you all right?" he asked.

She sat up and tried to speak, but the inside of her throat had gone as dry as sandpaper. "Water," she croaked, and a cup was thrust into her hand.

"Here, Mother. Drink." It was Bulan. She was staring at Duja, a broad smile on her face.

Duja blinked. Was this another hallucination? When she reached out and touched Bulan's shoulder, she wanted to sob in relief. "Darling! I don't understand. How did you—"

"Mother! You're alive!" A serving boy barreled through the open door of the prison cell, straight into Duja's arms.

The queen looked down in surprise. It wasn't a serving boy at all, but Eti, her black hair cropped above her chin. Duja would recognize her daughter's round cheeks anywhere.

"Oh, darling," Duja said, cupping Eti's face in her hands.

"We've come to rescue you," Eti said as she gazed up at Duja happily.

"Eti snuck back into the palace disguised as a servant. Clever little thing—she's the one who broke the locks on all these doors. In fact, General Ojas and the others are waiting for you just out there," Bulan said, nodding toward the corridor that cut across the prison hold.

Duja felt as though her heart couldn't be any fuller as she stared at her daughters. After Imeria had locked them down there, she feared she would never hold them in her arms again. But one was missing. She turned to Aki as a cool wave of dread trickled down her spine.

"Where is Laya?" she asked.

Aki's lips tightened into a thin line. "She's heading to the Black Salt Cliffs with Imeria," he said gravely. "They plan to marry her to Luntok at sundown."

Duja's expression hardened. "We cannot allow that to happen."

Imeria must have thought she could wrest control of Maynara without waging a bloody war. A ruthless takeover thinly disguised as a blessed union. Duja could concede that it was a cunning strategy. Maynaran law was uncompromising when it came to marriage pacts. Once Laya and Luntok exchanged their vows on the Black Salt Cliffs, they could never take them back. And without the Gatdulas' aid, the datus were too weak—too terrified of Imeria—to stop the marriage from happening.

All of them assumed the Gatdulas were already defeated. That was their mistake.

Duja thought back to the cold smile she'd seen on Imeria's face when her people had stormed the throne room. *Foolish queen. Now do you see what I am capable of?* her eyes seemed to say.

It was true. Duja had underestimated Imeria for twenty-two years. *Very well, my heart,* she thought, her jaw squaring in determination. *Let us see what happens when you underestimate me.*

"Come, Duja. We must leave at once," Aki said.

We? Duja turned to her husband. "You will stay here," she told him. "I will not have you fight the Kulaws."

"Stay safe behind the palace walls while my family heads straight into battle? I think not."

Rarely did Aki defy her orders. She wanted to shake the sense back into him. "I bid you stay. You are not a fighter," she cried.

"But I am a father." The king raised his voice. His words echoed off the cool walls of the cell, alarming everyone inside. Softening, he took Duja's hand. "Have you forgotten the vows I made to you? I am your husband. Through triumph and adversity, my place is by your side."

Duja's heart swelled, and she swallowed her objections. She pressed her lips to his—a hard, fleeting kiss. She loved him. Oh, how she loved him. There was so much more she wished to say, but now was not the moment.

The king held out his arm to help her to her feet. But Duja stood too quickly. She stumbled, and Aki caught her before she fell. He eased her back onto the cot.

"They must have put something in the wine with my meals," she muttered, grabbing his arm to steady herself. "Something to sedate me. It's muddled up my head—and now my hands . . . I cannot fight, Aki. Not like this."

"But we don't have time to wait for the drugs to wear off. If we want to make it to the cliffs, we need to leave now," Bulan said, her eyes darting between her parents.

Bulan was right. The Black Salt Cliffs were far outside the city, and judging by the long shadows that slanted across the floor of the cell, Laya would have just left.

Duja wanted to scream in frustration. "By the gods," she cried, wringing her wrists, "how can I hope to stop Imeria now? My daughter needs me, and I do not have the strength."

"Um, Your Majesty?" Duja looked up to find Ariel Sauros standing before her in the prison cell. His lanky stature and wire-framed spectacles were unmistakable.

She stared at him. "How did you—"

"With all due respect, Your Majesty, we don't have time for explanations," Ariel said. He reached into the pockets of his trousers, digging out a handful of crystal bars and a rusty pipe. Cautiously, he knelt before her and laid the objects in her lap.

Duja's heart raced as she stared down at them. "I don't believe it. It's—"

"Precioso," Ariel said, nodding. "I believe it's exactly what you need."

Thirty
LAYA

Laya's neck ached as she leaned out the window of her carriage. It was the damned headdress with wide gold plates that weighed a pound each—the same one her mother had worn during the closing ceremony. Behind her stretched a string of royal attendants and the spineless nobles who had already capitulated to Imeria, eager to win the new sovereign's favor or to spare their families from her wrath. She glanced at the lone girl sitting across from her and would have allowed herself a dark, humorless chuckle at the laughable size of her retinue for such a momentous occasion, if she weren't leading her country to its doom.

They passed through the heart of Mariit on their way to the ramparts that protected the city. The entire population had gathered around the canals—ruddy fishermen, finely dressed merchants, mothers with crying babies swaddled against their chests. If this were like royal weddings past, there would have been baskets of coconut-flaked sweets passed around and paper lanterns launched into the air and rice wine flowing into the streets. From every footbridge, minstrels would have serenaded them with warbling love songs. Children would have chased behind her carriage, waving banners, cheering.

Instead, the people watched in silence as the procession cut through the throngs. Their faces were somber, resigned, as if they were bearing witness to a funerary march.

Save me, Laya thought as she met their gazes through the carriage window. *Save your future queen.*

In spite of her gods-given power, Laya could not save herself. Before she left the palace, the brass shackles had been fastened to her wrists anew. The marriage ceremony was too important, Imeria had told her, for things to go amiss. Laya cast a bitter glance over her shoulder. The Kulaws rode in the carriage directly behind her. If she were to try to escape, they would be the first to see.

"You look lovely, Dayang. Your betrothed will be more than pleased."

Laya flinched. It was that dreadful, simpering serving girl Yari, whom Imeria had assigned to her carriage. That morning, she had clothed Laya in her wedding gown, a gorgeous dress of bloodred silk. It was sleeveless, pinned together above her right shoulder with a filigree brooch in the shape of a dragonfly, its wings carved from vitreous jade. A thick belt strung together out of golden disks cinched her waist. Her hair, which Yari had rubbed with jasmine oil until it shined, was twisted into a knot at the top of her skull. Laya looked lovely, but not at all like herself; she looked like Imeria's puppet.

Ignoring Yari, she stared straight ahead. Over their driver's shoulder, the jagged mouth of the Black Salt Cliffs loomed. The cliffs stretched out from the base of Mount Matabuaya, enveloping the bay like shark teeth. Laya thought about the story Maiza had told her about the first Gatdula king, the daughter of Mulayri, and their blood-soaked marriage atop those cliffs.

The high shaman used to regale her with Maynara's founding myths during their lessons. But on this day, as a bride herself, the story gave her no comfort. How could she feel like the mother of her nation when she'd been brought to the Black Salt Cliffs in chains?

"We have arrived, Dayang," Yari muttered as their carriage rolled to a stop at the end of the rocky path. A footman dismounted and hurried to open the door. As Laya tried to balance on the carriage step without the use of her hands, the footman held her arms to steady her and help her to the ground.

Swallowing the knot in her throat, she continued down the path.

The wind was stronger along the coast, and her skirt caught between her legs. At the mouth of the cliff, the witnesses had already gathered: Datus Luma, Tanglaw, Sandata, and Patid. Rows of nameless servants hung behind them. Over two hundred guards flanked them on either side, scarlet sashes draped around their waists. Imeria had summoned an even bigger battalion than Laya expected. Her palms grew clammy as she passed them, line after unbroken line. Even without the shackles, she couldn't fend them off single-handed. All watched in silence as she approached, their faces as somber as the ones she had passed in Mariit.

Maiza stood alone all the way at the edge of the cliff. She looked frailer than usual. After the coup, she must have fought back. Laya's blood boiled when she saw the purple bruise that streaked across Maiza's narrow chin. The Kulaws dared strike a high shaman.

With a pained expression, Maiza took Laya's arm and had her kneel before her on the windswept grass.

"What a shame, my child, to be wed beneath such cruel skies," the shaman murmured. She brushed her leathered knuckles against Laya's cheek—a rare display of affection, which caught Laya off guard.

A whimper escaped from her mouth. "Maiza."

"You are doing your duty, Dayang," Maiza said in a gravelly voice. "As shall I."

Imeria arrived a moment later. Luntok was at her shoulder, handsome in his gold-trimmed vest, his eyes soft and hopeful.

"You look beautiful," he whispered as he knelt beside her.

Laya's gut clenched. She cast her eyes forward to avoid looking at him. Beyond the cliffs, the sun was just touching the horizon. Its orange rays skated across the Untulu Sea.

"Sundown," Imeria said, as she gave Maiza a curt nod. "The ceremony may begin."

A hush dispersed through the crowd. Laya stilled, listening to the soft rumble of the sea as it lapped against the rocks and the cackling of terns overhead. Maiza began to chant blessings in Old Maynaran, a language as ancient as the gods themselves, abstract words that lost all meaning in translation. Laya recognized a few from her studies. The words for *devotion, compact,* and the most useless of them all, *promise.*

As she chanted, Maiza beckoned to a serving boy, who brought forward a bowl of uncooked rice and laid it in the grass. Desperately, she met Maiza's gaze. *Save me. Stop the ceremony. Please.* But Maiza shook her head as she reached forward and entwined Laya's fingers with Luntok's above the bowl. Her hands were clammy. Luntok, unaware of the depths of her suffering, gave her fingers a tight squeeze.

Maiza called again for the servant, who presented a goblet and ceremonial dagger—the same objects that had been used at the midnight feast. When she lifted the dagger, Luntok leaned forward. Maiza made a shallow cut across his chest no larger than a dimple, then dripped his blood into a goblet. She did the same to Laya. She hardly felt the blade pierce her skin. Maiza mixed their blood, diluted it with blessed water, and handed the goblet to Luntok to drink. He took a sip and passed the goblet to Laya. With bound hands, she lifted it to her lips. Their combined blood tasted bitter—tainted, like the rest of them.

How many times had Laya dreamed of this day, praying Luntok would be the man kneeling beside her on the cliffs? She wondered, If Hara Duja had let them marry, if she were the one standing by her side, would this moment have tasted any sweeter?

More chanting, more blessings followed. Maiza nodded to the serving boy, who came forth once again with a cord. The boy brought Laya's hands to Luntok's and wound the cord around their shoulders and wrists. As he wrapped the silken threads around Laya's shackles, his hands snagged around her fingers, and he gave them a light tug. Too intimate. Too familiar. Her gaze snapped up to meet his.

Laya nearly gasped. *Eti?*

Her sister's long hair had been snipped short, her knobby knees concealed by baggy, threadbare trousers—but her round cheeks and light footsteps were unmistakable.

Laya tore her gaze from Eti for fear of calling attention to her. Her eyes flitted between the Kulaws and Datu Gulod standing next to Imeria, convinced they would register her sister's presence at any second. But Imeria remained fixated on the goblet resting between the high shaman's hands. And Luntok—Luntok only had eyes for her.

Maiza drew Laya's attention back to herself. This time, she caught a sharp glint of defiance in her eyes. In a thin, scratchy voice, the shaman announced, "I bring together this man, Luntok Kulaw, and this woman, Laya Gatdula. They are now one. May we all bear witness to their union, and to the start of their enduring reign as sovereigns of Maynara and Thu-ki."

Behind them, a discontented rumble spread across the crowd. Luntok's gaze locked on hers. His eyes burned with a love that Laya suddenly knew was genuine—it always had been.

"Laya..." He hesitated, waiting for her to speak.

Out of the corner of her eye, she saw Eti shuffling toward her. Neither Luntok nor Imeria had noticed her. So consumed were they by the marriage ceremony—and the victory it would bring them—they could think of little else. But the ceremony was drawing to its farcical end. Eti was standing so close to them; anyone might recognize her if they gave her a second glance.

Laya forced her eyes to soften when she returned his gaze. "I suppose that makes you my husband," she said.

"And you, my wife."

She saw the question in his eyes and gave him a small nod to encourage him. He exhaled sharply, like he had been waiting his entire life for this signal, and leaned in.

As Luntok pressed their lips together, Maiza barked out, "Boy, the marriage cord!" and motioned Eti over.

Laya barely registered the heat of Luntok's mouth on hers. It was no more than a brief peck, but any softness from Laya sufficed to distract him. When he pulled back, he did not spare a glance at Eti, who was hovering over them. Laya held her breath as Eti reached between her and Luntok. Her sister kept her head bowed, her cropped hair spilling over her cheeks. With nimble fingers, Eti untied the cord binding Laya to Luntok. The young girl's hand lingered on the shackles for a long, pregnant moment. The short chain linking her wrists together snapped with a metallic click, and the marriage cord fell to the dirt between them.

Laya flexed her fingers. She couldn't hear her own thoughts over the swell of the waves and the blood pounding in her ears.

A nervous tingle seeped throughout her body. She was free. Eti had rescued her—and neither Luntok nor his mother appeared to notice.

"Come," Imeria announced to the awaiting crowd. "It's time to return to the palace for a celebration feast."

Gently, Luntok helped Laya to her feet. He made to lead her to the carriages, but she held him back. "Luntok," she called breathily, as though flustered by the beauty of the cliffs, by the weight of their nascent union.

"What is it?" He looked at her worshipfully, lovingly, in spite of everything he had done.

But Laya finally understood that to love a Kulaw was dangerous. And she would not yield herself to him.

Laya grabbed the collar of his shirt and yanked him close. He didn't have time to react before she pressed a harsh kiss to his lips. He kissed her back hungrily. *Foolish boy.* She planted her palm flat against his chest, right above the wound where the dagger had pierced him.

Luntok looked down and, finally, noticed the broken chain between her wrists. His eyes narrowed. He opened his mouth to yell—but not fast enough.

"Goodbye, Husband," she sneered and raised her other palm to the sky, then heaved him back with a jet of wind. Luntok flew high above the heads of the datus and the Kulaw guards. He crashed to the ground several feet away, skidding to a stop near the carriage path with a groan.

Imeria whipped around, nostrils flaring. She threw her hand in Laya's direction. *"You stupid bitch!"*

Roughly, Laya shoved Eti behind her. She closed her eyes, readying herself for the inevitable onslaught of pain, when the ground beneath their feet rumbled with tremendous intensity.

Laya would have fallen had Eti not grabbed her arm and jerked her upright.

Over her shoulder, Maiza cried out, "Hara Duja. By the gods!" Barreling down the path on a great floating slab of earth was the queen. She wasn't alone. Hari Aki and Bulan stood beside her. Laya counted about a hundred warriors at their flanks, including the towering figure of General Ojas.

"Ariel and I," Eti whispered excitedly, "we got them all out. And then we—"

"The Orfelian?" Laya let out a startled laugh. "Really?"

Hara Duja released the earth she had been wielding. It sank down, shuddering, onto the flat face of the Black Salt Cliffs. Inches away, Luntok had only just begun to come to his senses.

"Imeria," Duja cried. A gale from the coast swept over the cliffs, whipping back her wild hair. She stalked toward the other woman. The Kulaw warriors clustered behind Imeria, their hands poised on the hilts of their weapons.

If Imeria was afraid, she didn't dare falter. "You cannot defeat me now, Duja. The ceremony is finished, and I have double your men."

"Have you?" The queen gazed at the rows of warriors the Kulaws had amassed. Her dirt-streaked face was hard and unrelenting. Impressive as Imeria's numbers were, the vast majority had either been intimidated by the Kulaws or paid off. Laya realized that her marriage was no longer the only alliance in question. She watched, rooted where she stood, as her mother addressed the traitors gathered before them.

"Brave warriors. Each one of you has pledged your sword to the rightful ruler of Maynara, and yet you fight beside our greatest enemy. Maybe you think I have failed you as sovereign. Maybe you're afraid. If that is the case, I can forgive your transgressions.

But if you throw your support behind Imeria Kulaw, I cannot rectify the mistakes I've made.

"In my reign, I may not have been the perfect queen—but I am a daughter of Mulayri. The throne is my birthright, and this land is mine to defend. So I ask again: To whom do you pledge your sword? The true queen of Maynara? Or a dangerous usurper, who, at any second, can claw her way inside your head?"

Imeria uttered a cry of indignation. "No one is interested in your lectures, Duja. Your reign is over. The people have already decided."

But judging by the chorus of agitated murmurs rippling through the Kulaws' ranks, nothing was decided. A tense silence overtook the cliffs. And then—

"Have mercy, Your Majesty." A lone figure broke away from the Kulaws' ranks. He was a senior officer around Ojas's age. Laya recognized his steady gait from the countless times she'd seen him patrolling the halls of the palace. He staggered across the grass, shame clouding his features, before throwing himself at Hara Duja's feet. "I have broken my vows. I allowed fear to stand between me and my duty. I owe my service to your family, for your sacrifice and your protection. I cannot undo my errors, but I can offer my sword to you—the true queen of Maynara."

His words echoed in the salt-sprayed air. Then, all at once, the mass of warriors crowded behind Imeria began to shift. Dozens followed the senior officer to the other side of the cliff, where the rest of the Gatdulas were waiting. One by one, they begged for forgiveness and pledged their swords to Hara Duja. A smirk spread across Laya's face as she reevaluated their numbers. By the time the warriors settled into their new positions, nearly half of Imeria's forces had defected to the Gatdulas. Imeria could no longer be certain of her victory—the size of their battalions were suddenly even.

Seeing that the odds had shuffled in their favor, Hara Duja opened her arms to the rest of the Kulaw faction. She raised her chin and spoke with renewed confidence. "Come. You need not fear my wrath if you step forward. I promise to grant each one of you clemency if you stand down. Now."

Then a moment of uneasy hesitation. A fleeting stillness swept over the Black Salt Cliffs. When no one else crossed over to the queen's side, Imeria threw her head back and laughed. "Oh, I've had my fill of Gatdula clemency." She turned to her remaining warriors and roared, "Guards! Attack the queen."

Laya scarcely had time to register Imeria's abrupt order. But the Kulaw forces didn't hesitate. In a menacing swell, they advanced. Their stampeding footsteps thundered across the cliffs. They swarmed Hara Duja, the steel of their weapons burnished with the pink-and-orange cast of twilight.

"Hurry," Ojas yelled from the queen's side. The terse quiet of the cliffs broke as his men surged forward to engage them.

Laya steeled her shoulders and ran after them.

She had never known battle before. The war songs and sweeping epics could not have prepared her for the chaos of clashing metal, the sickening squelch as blades penetrated flesh. No training could have steeled her soul to withstand the shrieks of men struck down in a flash of silver. Bodies darted past her, bolts of green and scarlet and flailing limbs. The sea wind stung the corners of her eyes. Her nostrils filled with the smell of rust as blood soaked the grass atop the cliffs.

In the tumult, she struggled to orient herself. She skirted past slashing swords and walls of breastplates until she arrived at the center of the fray, where the fighting was fiercest. A flash of gold drew Laya's focus to the front line.

Imeria Kulaw stood shielded by a ring of Kulaw warriors, their swords raised as they deflected the Gatdula offense. Their assailants came at Imeria from all sides, and they did not relent. As the Kulaw warriors closed in to protect Imeria, Laya glimpsed the older woman's face. Her brow was furrowed in concentration. Both her hands were directed at the lines of Gatdula guards advancing toward them. With a pang, Laya realized what she was doing. Instinctively, she raised her palm. The threads of power braided themselves through her fingertips. If she calculated the angle just right, she could send a blast straight down the front line without taking down too many of her mother's men.

The second before Laya launched her attack, Imeria swore at the top of her lungs. For once, she sounded panicked. "It's not enough. I cannot get a hold of them," she barked to the group of warriors shielding her. "I need more cover. Get me to the rear."

Laya refused to let her slip away. She sucked in a breath, ready to strike her down, when a metallic gleam caught her eye. Three Kulaw warriors were charging toward her. Reflexively, she flung out her arms. She sent them hurtling across the grass with a violent blast.

"Laya!"

She ducked as a rock hurtled from behind her, narrowly missing her brow. A Kulaw warrior had his sword posed above his head, ready to strike her down, before the rock crashed against his chest. With a nauseating crunch, he fell back, crumpling beneath its weight.

Hara Duja ran over and grabbed her face in her hands. She gave her a harsh shake, a savage spark in her eyes. "You have to be more careful."

More and more Kulaw guards advanced toward them. The queen grabbed Laya's arm with one hand and with the other, raised the earth beneath their feet. They shot up to the sky on a limestone pedestal. On the flat face of the cliffs, there was no higher ground from which to fight, so Hara Duja made her own. When she raised her palms, four gigantic chunks of earth broke off from the cliff face. They rose to orbit the pedestal, ready to crash down on any who dared attack her.

Laya could not help but gape at her mother. Had the queen wielded such power all this time? Her thoughts flitted to the substance Imeria had boasted about back at the palace. The secret Hara Duja had been keeping from her. *Precioso.*

"They're too strong. We must act fast," a voice bellowed from the ground—Vikal, who'd trained Luntok in the art of war. Imeria had managed to join him behind the Kulaws' defenses. He stood, pleading, at her side. Luntok and Datu Gulod were with them. They stared up at Hara Duja, frozen in anticipation.

Imeria held herself still as the battle raged around them, but Laya could see the color drain from her cheeks. She was shaken. From high up on the pedestal, Laya watched as the woman groped for something around her neck.

"Mother," Luntok pleaded, his cry carrying over the sounds of battle. "You need to hurry."

Laya frowned, trying to decipher Imeria's next move. Behind her, a familiar voice boomed.

"Duja!"

She turned around and spied her father, a borrowed sword at his side, shouting to them from the base of the pedestal.

Hara Duja's eyes bulged in their sockets. "What are you doing?" she snapped. "Get back to the rear."

The king ignored her command. "I tried to warn you from

back there. You must stop Imeria as soon as you can. I couldn't get a good look, but I fear she has her hands on precioso."

To Laya's shock, her mother let out an ungainly curse. Then her gaze locked on the Kulaws. With a grunt, she hurled a chunk of earth in their direction. It missed them by mere inches, smashing into the dirt at their feet. Imeria stumbled back to avoid it. Vikal dragged her and Luntok bodily from the fighting, barking out orders to retreat. Their surviving soldiers and loyal attendants raced for the carriages.

"Don't let them escape!" Duja yelled, her voice echoing across the cliffs. She knelt low, the ground rumbling as she erected a great wall to block Imeria from the carriage path. Ojas and his men rushed forward to detain them.

With a frustrated growl, Vikal plunged back into the fray. He headed straight for Ojas, who was limping, a blood-soaked bandage hanging from his side. Ruthlessly, Vikal dug his knee straight into his injury. Ojas yelled and toppled to the ground. Vikal raised his sword, ready to plunge it into his gut.

"No!"

Bulan threw herself in between them. Vikal was twice her size. It took all of her force to deflect his blade. She lunged, but Vikal blocked her easily. He flicked her onto the grass as if she were nothing but a fly. She yelped in pain, her weapon tumbling from her grip. He took a step toward her, his body dwarfing hers, and raised his sword once more.

"Bulan!" Hara Duja gasped. The earth cracked open as she flattened the pedestal back into the dirt. She sprinted toward her, dodging the Kulaw warriors in her path, but her husband got there first.

"Don't you dare," the king gritted out, swinging his sword over his head.

Hari Aki was a man of wit, not a fighter. He was no match for Vikal and his warrior's instinct. In one sweeping motion, Vikal disarmed the king and plunged his blade into his gut.

"Father!" Laya screamed.

Time slowed down. In the moment before she blinked, her father floated, suspended in midair. His head tilted skyward, his back curved in a graceful crescent. The king was no god, but rimmed in the dying sunlight, he became a creature that did not belong to this earth. He was not falling, no, but rising to meet Mulayri in his mountain kingdom. As though the gods had called him by name. As though they had already claimed him.

When she opened her eyes, her father had crumpled onto his back. A bolt of scarlet seeped through his rumpled court silks and dripped onto the dirt. Hara Duja and Bulan huddled around him. One of Ojas's guards fell to his knees at their side, offering his sash. They pressed it into the wound. The dirt beneath his body turned to mud where the blood continued to pool.

Weakly, he looked up. "Duja," he said. When he opened his mouth, rivers of blood rippled down his sharp, clever chin.

And Laya could only watch. Her vision warped and seared at the edges. The Black Salt Cliffs folded in around her. The battle waging around them faded. She could only hear her father gasping for breath. She saw nothing but the light fading from his eyes.

"Maiza," Bulan yelled, a sob caught in her throat. "Maiza, he needs a healer."

Out of the corner of her eye, Vikal was backing away. His sword hung limply at his side, drenched with the king's blood. He looked stunned, ashen-faced.

"We must leave," Datu Gulod hissed. "Now."

No. Laya tore her gaze from her father. Her eyes closed in on Vikal as waves of anger wracked her core. They weren't going anywhere. She raised her palm, feeling the threads of energy tauten around her fingers, when a body tackled her from the side.

"Run!" Luntok screamed to his mother. He struggled to hold her down, but Laya elbowed him hard in the ribs. He groaned and she shoved him off, scrambling to her feet.

"I'll kill you for this," she said, her chest heaving. "I'll kill you all."

His expression hardened as he rose, retrieving the horned, ceremonial dagger from his belt. He held it in his fist. "You would kill your lover? The man you've just wed?" Luntok spat. He was taunting her. He wanted to distract her while his mother and the others fled. Laya didn't care.

She hurled a blast of wind toward him. It hit him square in the chest. The dagger flew from his grip. He hurtled several feet backward, rolling to a stop inches away from the cliff's edge, winded. On shaking arms, he struggled to push himself upright.

Laya ran over and grabbed the collar of his shirt. His hands shot to her fingers, but he didn't fight to free himself from her grip. He stared up at her, and for a wild moment, she thought he might try to kiss her again.

Instead, he shook his head. His lips parted in disbelief. "Laya. You wouldn't."

She glanced over her shoulder to where her father was bleeding out on the grass. She could hear Ojas's deep voice booming for more bandages. The datus flocked to the king, offering strips of cloth torn from their shirts and clean pairs of hands. But they couldn't give the king what he needed most—more time.

Amidst the chaos, she saw her mother. The queen had folded herself over her husband's bloodied chest. She was sobbing, brutally, brokenly, because she already knew the truth. Hari Aki was beyond saving.

He was dying, Laya realized. A sharp stab of pain pierced her soul. Her fingers clenched into fists, threatening to rip through Luntok's marriage vest. At her beckoning, black clouds gathered overhead and the cool, coastal air crackled and sparked. Her vision cleared and a strange calm washed over her, the quiet that preceded a typhoon.

"Laya," Luntok whispered from where he knelt. "Please."

Laya looked down at him. For a moment, the fear melted from his handsome face. In her mind, an old memory flickered, where their positions were reversed. He was bowed over her naked body, dragging his lips between her breasts; when he met her gaze, his eyes burned. It was not love, but obsession.

She let out a ragged breath. He was the reason for all of this. Her family's undoing, her father's downfall, was all because of him.

"For anyone who dares harm my family," she said as her gaze frosted over, "let this be my message."

Farewell, my love.

Without hesitation, Laya drew her palm back. An arc of wind rushed forward to meet it. She cast it down at the man who loved her, pitching him headfirst over the Black Salt Cliffs.

Thirty-One
LUNTOK

Beautiful, he thought, the moment before she cast him to his death. He caught a glimpse of her face. He marveled at the storm brewing within her eyes, at the dirt and blood that marred her lovely cheeks. In her desperation, in her grief, Laya had become the wrathful god Luntok always knew her to be.

His neck snapped forward when Laya pushed him. The wind swept through his thin marriage silks and sweat-slicked hair. It roared in his ears, bitter as the woman who summoned it.

Laya's storm clouds swirled in the blazing sky. The last rays of the sun shone from below the horizon, scattering orange up through the spaces between the clouds, and the glow of their underbellies blinded him.

The wind whipped the water below into violent peaks, threatening to swallow him whole. The sharp rocks that punctured the bay grew closer and closer as he fell. Soon, his bones would shatter like glass against their jagged tips.

No time—the rivers of death drew frighteningly near. Their waters washed over him, his body swept up in their unrelenting currents. He wasn't afraid. He could hear the eternal music of the underworld and the grumbling giants who awaited him.

I'm coming, he told them.

He closed his eyes, bracing himself for the impact. His fate had been sealed from the first day he climbed the white stone walls of the palace. This was no different. A pleasant numbness hummed through his body. He knew this well, this feeling of weightlessness.

The wind whirled past him in a dying gasp of breath. He thought of Laya's lips, soft against his—a final earthly ache.

Thunder erupted in the sky above. Then the bay sucked him in as the underworld beckoned to him. The waves kissed his eyelids, his cheeks, the faint line across his back where his mother had healed him. Darkness enveloped his body, the warm embrace of an old lover. If this was death, it was but a mere shadow of mortal pain, and he felt none of it.

Luntok had spent years climbing to precipices beyond his reach. He was ready. He wasn't afraid.

The gods called his name, and Luntok was ready to meet them.

Thirty-Two

IMERIA

No.

Imeria watched, open-mouthed in horror, as her son flew over the edge of the cliffs. She had watched Luntok fall countless times before: sparring with Vikal at sunrise, barreling down the streets of Mariit to answer Laya's beckoning. He stumbled often, but never without grace, and always—*always*—within Imeria's reach.

Her breath caught in her throat. *I can reach him. I can save him.*

In the split second before he fell, she lunged for him. But Imeria was too slow, too feeble. By the time she blinked, Luntok was already an ocean away.

"My lady." She heard it as a low, distant whisper. *"My lady, please!"*

Dimly, she became aware of a pair of strong arms holding her up. Holding her together. Vikal pressed her face to his chest, shocked tears spilling down his blood-splattered armor. He held Imeria no longer than a heartbeat before he took her hand and started pulling her away.

"We must leave now," he said, choking back a sob. "And Luntok—gods help us. If we wait any longer, they won't let us get away."

Panic gripped the base of her throat. She jerked her arm back. "No," she said. "We're not going anywhere." Her stomach twisted in grief. *Not without him.*

Datu Gulod darted toward them from the other side of the cliffs. He was ashen-faced, his waxy features stretched wide in terror. "Are you insane?" he hissed at Imeria. "What are you waiting for? *Run.*"

She cast her gaze at the flattened grass where her son had been lying mere moments earlier. Laya was kneeling at the cliff's edge. The last orange tones of twilight glinted dimly off the golden plates radiating from her temples, her head bowed as if in prayer. Her right arm hovered above her head, cupping the air she'd used to strike Luntok. Her fingers trembled. The rest of her remained hauntingly still.

Monster, Imeria thought, clenching her hands into fists. "No," she said again, as white-hot rage flooded her veins. *Not before I kill this bitch.*

She thought only of Luntok's face as she barreled toward the edge of the cliffs.

"My lady!" Vikal yelled, his desperate cry piercing the shocked silence.

Metal flashed at the corners of Imeria's vision. She glimpsed green sashes, stained scarlet at the hems—the threat of Gatdula warriors closing in. She paid them no heed. She charged forward, thrusting her hand out in Laya's direction.

I will make her hurt. I will make her pay—

"*No!*" A broken voice rang out.

A muddy chunk of earth jutted out of the ground. Her foot caught on its ragged edge. She slammed into the grass with a scream. When she looked up, the queen was hovering over her. Bright-red blood coated Duja's fingers, her arms, the torn silk of her dress. Salty tears dripped down her jaw, squared in sorrow, in rage. She stared down at Imeria, her tight lips trembling.

"Duja—" Imeria gasped.

Duja's fists closed around the collar of Imeria's dress. She had become monstrous in grief. Her hands did not shake when she wrenched Imeria to her feet. "Touch my daughter and I'll kill you," she said, her voice lowering to a growl. "I'll kill you like your people killed him."

Imeria glanced over Duja's shoulder, where the king lay in a patch of bloodied grass, lifeless. Her vision clouded with shame and anger and pain. He was gone. They were both gone. An excruciating pang wound through her when she thought of her son—her beautiful, broken boy—waiting for her at the base of the Black Salt Cliffs. *My son, my son*—she couldn't bear it.

One strike by Duja's hand would end it. And for the first time in her life, Imeria craved Gatdula clemency more than anything. "Go on," she said, staring Duja in the eye. "Kill me, then."

Doubt flickered in the queen's gaze. For a moment, Imeria saw the young girl she'd once been—afraid of her brother's shadow and paralyzed by second guesses. The mirage faded as quickly as it appeared. Duja's face hardened into a mask of steel.

"No," she said again, and pointed to her fallen husband. "Not before you heal him."

Imeria froze. She looked beyond Duja's shoulder at the crowd of people clustered around Hari Aki's body, their heads bowed, their clothes soiled by royal blood. The old hag Maiza had already stepped away, muttering ancient prayers under her breath. Bulan was kneeling beside the king's chest, her shoulders shaking with violent sobs. General Ojas stood straight-backed at her shoulder. He was watching Imeria with cold eyes, his weapon drawn.

The king was dead. Imeria could do nothing to change that.

She looked back at the queen. In spite of Imeria's bitterness, in spite of the pain that threatened to cleave her in half, she ached for Duja. *Look at what we've lost.*

"I-I can't, Duja." Imeria's voice cracked. "I can't bring back the dead."

"You don't know that." This time, it was Laya who spoke. She came to stand at her mother's side, her bright eyes oddly blank, as if she were caught in a trance.

Laya. Imeria's fingers twitched. If she tried, she could sink her claws into Laya's mind and make her throw herself off the cliffs. Duja must have seen the vengeful gleam in Imeria's eye, because she stepped protectively in front of her daughter, her hands clenched into fists. All three women stumbled as the cliff face gave a menacing lurch.

But Imeria didn't strike Laya. The princess was heartless and vile, but her words made her take pause. Laya was right; Imeria *didn't* know if she could bring back the dead because she had never tried. At this realization, a faint glimmer of hope burst in her chest.

"Luntok," Imeria said, her voice hoarse.

Duja frowned. "Luntok is—"

"Dead." She nodded, her mind spinning, and met Duja's gaze once more. "*Please.* Let me save him. Give me this, Duja, and I'll save your king."

For all anyone knew, it was a hollow promise, but Duja hesitated. "If I allow this, you will begin by saving Aki," she said, choosing her words with care. "And if this works, you will not linger. You will take your men and get out of Maynara. I never want to see you here again."

"And if I fail?"

Duja cut her a sharp look. "You will pay for your treason. With your lives."

In her grief, Imeria still found it in her to let out a dry laugh. "This is the choice you give me—execution or exile?"

"Only if you save my husband's life."

Imeria fell silent as she weighed her bargain. These were the words of a desperate queen, but Imeria's situation was no different. "Very well, then," she said, and lifted her chin. "I accept your terms. But you will let me save my son first."

Disgruntled murmurs rang out from the watching crowd. Duja shook her head in disbelief. "Now, Imeria, you overstep."

"Is that what you think?" Imeria snarled. She took three swift strides to the edge of the cliff, stopping in the same spot where her son had been kneeling moments earlier. "I will save Luntok first or no one at all. If you refuse me now, I will not simply overstep. I will jump straight to the rocks below. So if that's your decision, make it fast. But think twice before denying me," she declared, followed by an eruption of horrified gasps.

The queen didn't lunge for her. At Imeria's threat, she stood still as a statue. "You wouldn't," she answered in a deep, throaty voice.

Imeria stared at Duja, biting her lip to keep it from trembling. "I will be reunited with my son. One way or another."

The queen didn't dare tear her gaze away. She knew Imeria—knew that it wasn't a bluff. Bitterly, she conceded. "You shall get your wish, Imeria. We will begin with Luntok—but you must remember my terms. If you fail, or if you betray me again—"

"I know." Imeria stared back as the ache in her chest grew impossible to ignore. "First Luntok, then the king. Afterward, our attack will cease. We will withdraw from Maynara. You have my word."

Once again, the queen could not know if it was a hollow promise, but what choice did she have? Duja set her jaw. She looked like she wanted to say more. But then she turned to the guards still clustered on the cliff, unsure of their next move. "Everyone, stand down," she said. "And General Ojas."

"Yes, Your Majesty." Ojas rushed to Duja's side, still tracking Imeria out of the corner of his eye.

"Go with Imeria's men to the rocks at the base of the cliff. Take your strongest divers."

The general's mouth twisted into a frown of uncertainty, but he kept his doubts to himself. "Right away, Your Majesty," he said. Then he turned around, limping, and started barking orders.

The eerie quiet on the cliffs broke as the onlookers sprang into action. Imeria watched, filled with a different kind of grief, as Vikal accompanied Ojas down the steep path that led to the base of the Black Salt Cliffs. The two men took a handful of Kulaw and Gatdula warriors with them, their imposing figures disappearing over the cliffside in a flutter of scarlet and green.

She glanced at Duja, who had returned to Hari Aki's side. Eti and Bulan flocked to her. Laya held back. Seeing her father's body up close had shaken her. Laya stared at the king in wide-eyed horror, her hands balling into fists. The air above their heads began to thicken once more into storm clouds. Then Bulan held her hand out to her sister. With a gasping sob, Laya took it. Grief made allies of them. The clouds cleared, and together, they held their mother tight. The ache swelled in Imeria's heart at the sight of it. She steeled herself and turned her gaze toward the horizon, swallowing the pit that had formed in the back of her throat.

This was supposed to be her son's wedding, gods help them. She wanted to scream. She couldn't shake the sense that she had been robbed of something glorious.

What could have been.

The moment she turned around, Gulod appeared at her

shoulder. "Do you . . . Do you truly think you can . . . ," he asked before trailing off. His shoulders were tense, and his eyes were darting toward the carriage path. But the window to escape had long closed; not even Gulod could smuggle his way out.

"I have no idea if it will work," she admitted, her fingers tracing the thin glass vial hanging from her neck.

His gaze trailed down to her necklace—to the precious remains of their precioso. "I'm sorry about your boy, Imeria, but this"—he shook his head, his mouth hardening into a line—"this is a risky gamble. I hope you know what's at stake."

He didn't need to tell her. Imeria knew what she was risking—her life, and perhaps the lives of those who had followed her into battle. She didn't care. She would risk everything—her title, her wealth, even her grip on the throne. She would surrender it all to save her son's life.

"None of that matters now. I have to *try*," she said in a quiet voice.

Gulod let out a desperate sigh, but he didn't try to convince her otherwise.

It seemed as if an eternity passed before the divers returned. By the time their heads emerged over the side of the cliff, the sky had lost all warmth and was painted in purple and blue, like a bruise above the Untulu Sea. Vikal approached her first, his wet hair plastered against the side of his face.

"We have found him, my lady," he said, the muscles in his jaw stretched taut.

Imeria didn't understand the tremor in his voice until Ojas and the other men sidled up behind him. They were carrying what looked like a bundle of bones wrapped up in a bloodied fisherman's tarp.

"*Oh.*"

They were gone for so long, she thought she would be prepared for this moment. But Imeria was too weak to withstand the wave of pain that coursed through her at the sight of Luntok's body. A fractured wail escaped from her mouth. She fell to her knees.

A strong hand squeezed her shoulder—Vikal. "If this is too much, my lady—" he said softly.

"It's not." Imeria shook his hand away and squared her back. She looked up to find that Duja was on her feet, watching her, a shadow of pity on her haggard face. The tight coil of pain in her heart unfurled once again—*oh, what we've lost, what we both have lost*—before Imeria shoved it back down.

She thought once more of Luntok's young, handsome face and braced herself before she reached for the edge of the tarp. With a sharp breath, she peeled it back. Her stomach turned. Behind her, she heard the nobles on the Black Salt Cliffs gasp. A rumble of dread tore through the crowd. The grisly assemblage of muscle and flesh was unrecognizable.

This is my son, she reminded herself. Imeria shook her head and squared her shoulders. She thought of Laya and the ruthlessness with which she threw him into the water. The anger focused her. *I won't let you kill him.*

Imeria reached for the glass vial around her neck with one hand and for the pipe in the pocket of her skirt with the other. She filled the bowl with precioso, nearly using up the entire vial. It was a precious resource, but she would waste all of it if it brought her son back.

"A match," she said in a harsh whisper. Gulod retrieved one for her, holding it to the pipe. Imeria inhaled deeply and let the poison flood her system. Several times, she repeated the motion until she felt the power swell within her like a seismic wave. It surged through her blood, stronger than it had been during their attack on the palace. It morphed into a creature of its own volition, too great for her mortal body to contain.

She held her hands to Luntok's battered corpse. She closed her eyes and dug deep, past his exposed muscles and broken bones, and found the sliver of life buried there. Her body convulsed as the power ripped through her, coursing through her fingers and pouring into her son's remains. Deftly, the threads of energy wove through the bloodless veins and torn flesh. A cacophony of gasps rose from the crowd. Imeria looked back down. Luntok's body glowed, white as a comet, as she stitched him back together.

Tears spilled out of the corners of her eyes. With a strangled moan, she pressed harder, dug deeper. *Live,* she screamed in her head. *Live, live, live.*

Behind the glow, shadows shifted. Imeria watched, wide-eyed, as Luntok became whole again. His ribs, which had protruded from his chest, disappeared beneath a layer of unmarred skin. His left femur fused together with a sickening crack.

On the ground, Luntok's eyes shot open. The white glow dimmed. Below the roar of precioso in her ears, she could have sworn she heard him gasp for breath.

"By the gods," Vikal cried out beside her. "Luntok. He's—"

Alive.

A spark of triumph burst in Imeria's breast. She let out a sob of relief. She had done it. She had saved him. She tried to lift her hands to stroke his cheeks but found them mired to his chest. She looked down in alarm as her hands glowed anew. The power shot through them once again, this time beyond Imeria's control. She cried out in shock.

"Imeria!" Duja shrieked. But Imeria could barely hear her. A strange, foreign voice filled her head.

I've been waiting for you, Imeria Kulaw, wielder of mind and flesh, it whispered. It was the voice of power, older than Maynara, maybe older than time itself.

No. Imeria straightened in panic. She squeezed her eyes shut, willing the voice to quiet. But the moment she resisted, it grew louder, impatient.

Fight me not, Imeria Kulaw, the voice told her. *Mother of Luntok. Maker of gods.*

Images flooded her mind. She saw her son tearing through Laya's letters. She saw him falling from the palace walls. One blink, and she saw the shadow of a raptor gliding across the open sea. Sunlight rippled across its glossy plume. It dived low, dipping a sharp talon into the water. When it craned its neck, Imeria caught a glimpse of the raptor's face. Deep in the amber pools of its eyes, she could make out the silhouette of a young man. She recognized the broad shoulders, the sharp edge of his jawline.

"Luntok?" she gasped.

"*My lady!*" Vikal's deep voice pulled her back to earth.

Imeria's eyes flew open. She was kneeling on the Black Salt Cliffs. Dozens of eyes were on her, but only one pair mattered.

"Duja," she whispered, unable to ignore the sinking feeling in her chest.

The queen pressed her lips together. "It didn't work," she said flatly. She tried to appear strong, but Imeria knew Duja's stony resolve was about to crack.

"Impossible." Imeria looked down, dumbstruck. She had healed Luntok's body. He was lying beside her, young and handsome and whole. But when she laid her hand once more on his chest, her fingers free of the power's glow, she could detect no heartbeat within. "Luntok," she whispered, resisting the urge to shake him awake. But his eyes were sealed shut. He wasn't breathing.

"Imeria." It was Gulod. He knelt beside her and placed a hand on her arm. "He's dead," he said in a low voice. "I'm sorry."

"It can't be." She shook her head in disbelief. "You saw him. He was awake. He was looking at me. He—"

She hadn't imagined it. Luntok was not merely alive. Luntok was *flying*.

Gulod frowned. Imeria looked around and saw the same confusion stark on everyone else's faces. A pit of dread formed in her stomach.

They had not seen what she had seen.

"It didn't work," Duja said again, jolting Imeria from her haze. The ground shook as the queen took a step toward her. Imeria hadn't forgotten—execution or exile. Those were the queen's terms.

Gulod groaned. "I told you," he hissed. "We should have run when we had the—"

If I had more time. If I could try again—

Imeria shoved Gulod to the side and scrambled to her feet. She ran for the queen. "Wait—"

Duja raised her hand to the sky, erecting a stone pillar from the ground.

Panic gripped Imeria's throat. "Duja!" she screamed.

But Duja didn't relent. With a great cry, she lifted the pillar from the ground and hurled it straight at Imeria.

Thirty-Three

DUJA

A chorus of surprised shouts rang out across the Black Salt Cliffs the moment Duja delivered the first strike. Merely an hour earlier, the king had been at her side, desperate to pry their daughter from Imeria's clutches. Now his blood soaked the sunbaked grass. For her entire life, Duja had taken great care not to succumb to fits of rage. She was not her brother, nor was she like the generations of wrathful Gatdulas who'd come before them. But when she looked at the other woman, she could see nothing but the joy Imeria had stolen from her. And when Duja's gaze fell on Imeria's quivering lips, all she could taste was vengeance.

Courage. This in Pangil's voice. His ghost was right; it was time to end Imeria Kulaw once and for all.

The last remnants of precioso pulsed in Duja's veins. The pillar soared through the air at her summons. It struck Imeria square in the chest, knocking her to the ground with a resounding thud. The next time Duja blinked, the other woman was lying sprawled across the cliff face like a broken doll. She drew in a shaky breath. Tears sprang to the corners of her eyes as shocked cries tore through the crowd. From the ground, Imeria didn't budge. Had Duja killed her at long last? She ought to scream in triumph or crumple in relief. But all that filled her was a weary and bone-deep sadness.

No time to examine Imeria's unmoving body. From the sides of the cliffs, Kulaw and Gatdula warriors readied their weapons.

"Your Majesty!" Ojas was at Duja's side in moments. He tightened his grip on his sword, awaiting her order. Imeria Kulaw might have fallen, but her people wouldn't surrender without a fight.

Duja stole a glance at her husband's body lying several feet away. *My love, my love, my love.* She steeled herself against the renewed rush of pain and nodded. "Charge."

The ground shook, not from her beckoning, but from the stampede of royal guardsman rushing to meet their foes. The air filled with cries of pain and clanking metal as the clash resumed with unrestrained fervor. The fighting earlier had already taken large chunks out of both battalions, leaving dozens of bodies strewn across the Black Salt Cliffs, but Imeria's allies had suffered the greater blow. Those who remained would fight to their dying breath. Without Imeria Kulaw's infernal powers, they were hopelessly outmatched. If they were lucky, the Gatdulas' forces would make short work of them.

Duja sucked in a breath, readying herself to reenter the fray, when a head of curly hair darted past her.

"Bulan, stop!" she cried, grabbing her by the shoulder.

Bulan jerked back in surprise. "But General Ojas. He needs—"

Duja shook her head firmly, swallowing the lump in her throat. *I cannot lose you too.* "Fall back," she told her. "Go to the palace. Take your sisters and—"

She faltered and spun around. Chaos had broken out all around her. The rage that had overcome her mere moments before faded to blind panic. Her eyes widened in fear as she searched for her daughters. Amidst the mass of clashing bodies, she could not see Laya or Eti anywhere.

When she opened her mouth to call for them, booming thunder rolled overhead. She looked up. Black clouds blew in from across the Untulu Sea, shrouding the cliffs in darkness. The air above them cracked and sizzled. At last, Duja's gaze fell on Laya. She was standing at the cliff's edge once more. Harsh winds swept her hair from her face. When she raised her palm, lightning exploded in the sky behind her head. Its blue light flashed across the gold plates of her headdress.

"Your men are outnumbered, Imeria. You've lost!" Laya taunted, her voice echoing over the clamor of the battle raging on the cliffs.

Duja's heart hammered. How was Imeria still alive? Desperate, she whirled around. Imeria was back on her feet, and she was making her way to her daughter. Duja lunged in Laya's direction. She was too far. Imeria got to her first.

"Stupid girl." Imeria let out a sharp, hollow laugh. "You know nothing of loss." Before Laya could blast her back, Imeria grabbed her by the throat.

Laya fell to her knees with an earsplitting shriek. Duja stared, helpless, as Imeria sent tides of pain surging through her daughter's skull. At the sound of the princess's screams, the battle ground to an abrupt halt.

"Dayang!" a deep voice yelled—Ojas. Duja saw him standing several feet away, not far from the edge of the cliffs. He thrust his sword into the belly of his opponent. The Kulaw warrior fell to the ground with a moan. Ojas leaped over his body as he rushed to Laya's aid.

Across the cliffs, several other royal guardsmen followed suit. They ran to Laya, but before they could reach her, each and every one of them froze in their tracks.

Duja's stomach knotted in dread. Imeria hadn't kept her word. *The precioso.*

An eerie quiet overtook the cliffs. Laya's storm clouds dispersed across the horizon. All around, the Gatdulas' most loyal guardsmen froze where they stood. The whites of their eyes turned black as they fell prey to Imeria's curse. The silence broke as swords thudded against the blood-soaked grass. One by one, they surrendered their weapons.

Duja met Imeria's eyes. The other woman's palms were raised to the heavens. A breeze swept in from the sea and ruffled Imeria's skirts. She stood there calmly, a buoy drifting amidst the rolling chaos. She returned the queen's gaze, head cocked to the side, as if she were inviting her to make the first move.

"What will it be, Duja? I have your daughter," Imeria called to her. But Duja could hear no wrath in her voice. Imeria sounded tired.

"Not Laya. *Please,*" Duja pleaded, desperate.

"She killed him." Her voice cracked. "She killed Luntok."

Duja looked around helplessly. Laya was stock-still at Imeria's right. Beside her stood Ojas, his sword arm frozen midstrike. Dozens of the Gatdulas' allies were caught in Imeria's curse. And Duja could do nothing to save them—nothing except run.

"She killed my boy," Imeria said, her shoulders shaking with repressed sobs.

A stone dropped in Duja's stomach. "The fault is mine. Take me," she begged.

Imeria's fine features contorted in pain. She didn't say a word. She stood as frozen as the guardsmen flanking her.

Duja let out a shallow breath and held out her hand. "Come," she said. "Too many have died. I am the one you want."

"No," Imeria whispered, shaking her head.

"Take *me*," Duja said again, her voice carrying in the wind. "Please, my heart."

The other woman swayed on her feet. A gentle gale sailed over the cliffs, whooshing through the blades of grass. Duja could still peer into Imeria Kulaw's heart, even after all this time. She may be a monster, but not even she could stomach mindless bloodshed. Not when her victory had been stolen from her. Not when both families had lost so much. If she wanted to avenge her son, so be it. Out of the hundreds of souls frozen on the Black Salt Cliffs, there was only one life she wanted.

After a moment of tortured deliberation, Imeria lowered her hands. She steeled her shoulders and straightened her back. "If that is your wish," she said, her voice constricted.

Imeria limped toward Duja in slow, measured steps. She clutched her side, wincing; she may have survived Duja's blow, but not without a couple of broken ribs. As she approached, she freed the men she passed from her power. They pitched forward, falling to their knees, groaning as they regained their senses.

"My lady!" Vikal called from across the cliffs. His blood-drenched sword fell limply to his side. He stared after Imeria in shock. "What on earth are you doing?"

But Imeria didn't answer him. She took Duja's arm. "Let us end this," she agreed.

At her side, Bulan let out an indignant cry. "Mother, where are you—"

"Take care of your sisters," Duja said, her throat tightening. She tore her gaze away from Bulan's questioning eyes. Then she flexed her fingers and clawed deep into the earth. It rose beneath her and Imeria's feet, before shooting off into a rippling wave that carried them away.

Duja transported them far from the Black Salt Cliffs. Paths so high above Mariit were scarce, but she didn't need them to ascend to the mountaintop. She wielded the earth over the rolling foothills, weaving between the moss-coated boulders and whistling riverbeds and flowering pine trees, all the way to the summit of Mount Matabuaya. At the top of the mountain, several hundred feet above the capital city, lay a lake. It was small, not even a mile wide, and it was born from the crater below the rugged gray ledges that formed the mountain's jawlike peak.

She released the earth at the edge of the lake, where it settled back beneath the surface with a shuddering groan. Imeria, who had been clutching Duja's arm tightly, fell to her knees. She lay there, panting, as she caught her breath.

Duja didn't look at her. She stooped low and laid her hand atop the lake's smooth, glass-like surface. Her fingers trembled as she dug deep, the precioso thrumming dimly through her veins. The summit vibrated as she carved out a tiny island at the center of the lake. She gave a last tug, and a slender strip of land sprang out from the island to the lake's edge, sending ripples across the water's surface—a footbridge.

"What on earth . . . ," Imeria murmured.

Once more, Duja ignored her. Carefully, she stepped onto the bridge. The earth didn't crack beneath her weight. She followed it, one step at a time, until she made it to the island. Then she turned around and waited for Imeria to join her.

"Oh," Imeria said. "I think I understand now." Gingerly, she planted one foot on the bridge, moving cautiously so as not to upset her injured ribs.

The narrow outline of Imeria's figure wavered in the silvery fog. She glided toward Duja like a fevered fantasy that Duja had dreamed up when she'd been too young to know any better. A hallucination. A mirage. Neither of them spoke; the only sound was the dull pad of Imeria's footsteps as they echoed across the water. Duja shivered as a zephyr breezed through the summit, rustling her tangled, dirt-ridden hair and the bloodred hibiscus flowers that poked through the rocky ledges of the crater. For a brief moment, it lifted the veil of mist hiding Imeria's face from view. She stared at Duja, her slender jaw squared and her fine eyebrows arched in anger.

Duja's chest tightened. Imeria had always been the braver, the lovelier, of the two.

She was the reason Aki was dead.

"To die alone. Is this what you wanted?" Imeria called, her voice a delicate saber that pierced through the blanket of fog. She lifted the hem of her skirt and stepped onto the island, which was almost too small to shelter both of them. If she leaned in, her breath might have danced across Duja's hollowed cheeks.

"I am not alone," Duja said, unable to quell the ache blossoming in the pit of her stomach.

"We're both alone," Imeria said with a firm shake of her head. "You shouldn't have come all the way up here. You shouldn't have abandoned your men." Her nostrils flared as if she were chiding her, but Duja thought she heard a quiver of remorse in her voice.

"You were the one who should have stayed on the cliffs. You shouldn't have followed me here," Duja said.

"I'd follow you anywhere. I've been chasing you since the moment we met." Imeria's voice quaked. Duja fought the urge to reach for her.

As the queen stood across from Imeria, the harrowing battleground at the base of the mountain faded to a distant nightmare.

This lake was the only universe that had ever mattered, all because Imeria Kulaw stood at its quiet center.

"You knew long before I did," Duja told her. "It was always meant to be you and me."

The corners of Imeria's lips curled into a pained grin. "Then why do you sound displeased? I allowed you to draw me away."

Duja shook her head bitterly. "Too many people have died," she said again. "We must end this."

"I agree." Imeria's hand shot out. Without warning, she cupped Duja's face. Her fingers were gentle—a clever mimicry of a lover's caress. Duja knew better. She jerked back, but it was too late.

A wall of pain struck her body. Duja keeled over. She felt as if a thousand knives had sliced through her skull and lodged themselves into her brain. She tried to beg for mercy, but her mouth hung open in a silent scream, unable to form words.

In her agony, Duja grew acutely aware of the battle's toll on her body. She felt every tear in her muscles, every pang in her limbs. The ache flooded her all at once—along with the full weight of the previous twenty-two years. Since that fateful day in the palace courtyard, everything she had feared had come to pass. Strangely, Duja found freedom in it. She stopped struggling. Let her body fall limp. It was easier to lean into Imeria's palm. Easier to offer herself up to her tormentor like a boar on a spit.

Imeria's hard voice pierced through the burning haze. "What are you doing?" she demanded between labored breaths. "Fight me. *Fight back.*"

She relented long enough for Duja to let out a tired chuckle. "This once, Imeria, I wish I could indulge you. But I'm afraid I have no fight left within me."

"That's it, then?" Imeria gritted out. Once again, the queen had disappointed her. "You've decided to forsake your family. Your people. The same way you have forsaken me."

Duja allowed her eyes to close for a brief, arduous moment. She barely felt the passing wind as shame heated her cheeks. Atop Mount Matabuaya, there was nothing to shield her from the honesty in Imeria's words. For the first time in two decades, they were truly alone. Isolated from their families, their armies, and the court that had kept them apart. What brought them there—a child's yearning? A god's wrath?

Their love was once a secret whispered in a young girl's ear. Perhaps, in another life, they could have remained princess and companion, rather than queen and enemy. But their bloodlines had sealed their fate long before. A Gatdula and a Kulaw, drawn together for no longer than a heartbeat in history. Reunited miles above the capital, they left nothing but destruction in their wake. No declaration of love, no promise of mercy, could have altered the outcome. They should have known their path would lead there, in the end.

Duja's heart filled with hollow acceptance. "Haven't we been punished enough for our youthful errors? Or is more violence to follow? More senseless death?" she wondered aloud.

Bitter recognition flickered in Imeria's expression. At last, she released her. Duja fell to the ground, trembling, her chest slicked with sweat. She looked up. Something had broken in Imeria's gaze.

"I don't wish to hurt you, Duja," she said in a ragged voice. "I didn't wish for any of this."

Duja saw her own torment reflected in the other woman's eyes. The thick fog blurred the harsh lines of her face. In the dusky light, Imeria almost looked like the girl she'd been when she'd arrived at the palace. She hadn't harbored such hatred inside her then. Duja looked at the vessel of destruction and pain she had become, and her heart filled with grief.

I created this.

"You must forgive me," Duja whispered. "If I had been kinder to you back then—"

"Duja, don't." Imeria turned away. Her shoulders shuddered. She was crying. "I was loyal to you. I defended you when your miserable brother threatened to burn you to a crisp," she said as the sobs wracked her body. "I loved you, Duja, even though I knew you would never love me back. I told myself it didn't matter. I thought it an honor just to serve you. I never would have harmed you. By the gods, Duja, I was your *heart*. How could you not see that?"

Duja's soul cleaved in two. For a long moment, she said nothing. She listened to Imeria's cries as they echoed across the crater—the sound of Duja's mistakes.

"I'm sorry, Imeria," she whispered as she reached for her.

Imeria folded into her embrace. Her hands clung to Duja's filthy hair. Her touch was gentle. This time, no pain came.

"I'm sorry," Duja said again. Her arms tightened around Imeria's shaking shoulders. The other woman's long, ink-black hair tickled her collarbone. A spark of the decades-old yearning burst in Duja's chest. She leaned in and pressed her lips to hers.

Imeria gasped in surprise. Duja reeled her close by the neck, deepening the kiss. Imeria's lips tasted like soured feast wine, but they were warm and full and softer than orchid petals. Softer than Duja remembered.

I'm sorry, my heart.

"Duja," Imeria sighed, crumpling in her arms. By the time she noticed Duja withdrawing slightly, thrusting one hand to the ground, it was too late.

The delicate island below their feet gave a violent lurch. The ledges of the crater began to crumble. Giant chunks of rocks chipped away and tumbled into the clear water of the lake. With her free arm, Duja reached deep into the earth and yanked with all her might. The mountain peak groaned, and the tremors escalated.

"Duja," Imeria gasped. She tried to pull away, but Duja held her tightly to her chest. The crater started to cave in on itself with a deafening roar. Duja sucked in a breath. A shallow calm washed over her.

Together.

This was how it was always meant to end.

Imeria tried to press her hand to Duja's temple, but Duja drew back, shaking her head. "My power has already penetrated deep into the mountain. You cannot stop it now."

"No." Imeria shook her, digging her nails into her arms. "Duja, please. Think of your children," she begged.

But Duja did not relinquish her hold on the earth. She steeled her jaw and pulled harder on the invisible threads. The trembling intensified.

"It's for my children that I must do this," she said.

She dug her fingers into the energy thrumming at the heart of the mountain and turned her wrist. Tremendous mounds of earth gave way from the walls of the crater. Faster, the rocks tumbled down, down, down. The ground beneath them sank deeper, swallowing the lake. Imeria cried out in fear and clung to her. Duja met her eyes. This time, Imeria stared back at her with resolve—both women had accepted their fate.

Lower and lower, they sank. Imeria's fingers curled around the nape of her neck. She pressed her forehead to hers. Vaguely, Duja remembered the promise they had whispered to each other as girls: *until the end.*

Rocks tumbled over and around them, jagged shapes that devoured the sky. She could no longer hear her own heartbeat. She could no longer hear Laya's thunder. She felt only the heat of Imeria's breath as they descended into the darkness together. A moment of quiet, and she thought she heard Aki's deep, hearty laugh resonate from the other side.

The last glimmer of light faded. The island, reduced to a delicate sliver of ground, cracked open beneath their weight. Duja's heart leaped from her chest, too heavy with grief and tenderness and pain. Images flashed before her eyes. She saw her daughters, the round-faced girls they'd once been and the women she watched them become. She saw her husband looking up from his book to gaze at her. He awaited Duja. He was standing alone across a luminous river that sang as it coursed around the bend. He was holding out his hand, inviting her to cross over to the next life.

Around her, the jagged rocks continued to fall. She had broken the delicate balance that held the crater together. The entire summit vibrated, and she could do nothing to stop it.

I'm coming, my love.

Hara Duja closed her eyes and allowed the mountain to swallow her whole.

Five

A DAWN FEAST

A CORONATION PRAYER

All hail Hara Laya
Our kingdom's chosen steward
Summoner of the sky's might
And daughter of Mulayri
Whose blood flows through her veins.
All hail Hara Laya
Daughter of Duja
Bearer of the Gatdula legacy
And defender of Maynara's glory
For many years may she reign.

Thirty-Four

LAYA

At dawn, people flooded the streets of Mariit by the thousands to catch a glimpse of their new queen. They gasped in awe when the palace gates opened and Laya emerged. Her dark skin glowed with an unearthly essence. She appeared like a goddess, descending from her mountain kingdom. The dull morning light glinted off her headpiece, a half circle of gold plates that radiated like sunrays. She wore a coronation gown of viridian silk, its long train slinking along the marble steps like a water serpent. She glided to the riverboats, where her retinue was waiting.

General Ojas offered Laya his arm and helped her onto the largest boat from which the Gatdula banner waved. Bulan followed, a ceremonial sword at her belt and a green sash tied over her gleaming breastplate. Eti and the rest of Laya's retinue joined them.

Laya leaned on Ojas's arm as they strode across the deck of the riverboat. The battle against the Kulaws had shaken the aging warrior. Although he still stood upright at her side, he had come to Laya alone earlier that week. He'd told her it was time to think about choosing his successor. Laya didn't hesitate to name Bulan. In fact, her first directive as queen would be to announce her sister's new rank as general and head of the Royal Maynaran Guard.

It was one of the most important roles in the palace, and it suited Bulan more than high counselor or any other empty title. If anyone dared question Bulan's experience or level of swordsmanship, the queen would refuse to hear it. Laya could think of no one better to protect her than her own blood.

A member of the royal guard gave the order to start the engine, and they chugged down the main canal. Along the sides of the water, the entire city had gathered. They sang as the royal procession passed. Children reached into baskets and showered their boat with fistfuls of jasmine rice. At the bow, Laya laughed in delight as the rice scattered across the deck.

"Your kingdom, Your Majesty," General Ojas murmured as Mariit unwound before them. Its spires and sloping roofs rippled across the water, twisting into patterns of red and gold. Even though Laya had lived in the city her entire life, it didn't cease to entrance her. She wanted to fall asleep amidst the spirits of the mangrove trees. She wanted to sail along its network of canals, which branched through the capital like arteries.

Around her, Mariit's citizens hummed and rejoiced. "All hail Hara Laya," they chanted.

That was the heart of Maynara. Laya's mother had surrendered everything to give it to her. Despite all the secrets between them, all the tensions between mother and daughter, Hara Duja had loved Laya and loved her people. But she'd left behind a hole in Laya's heart, along with a thousand unanswered questions. In darker moments, Laya allowed that hole to fill with anger and bitterness—that is, until she remembered the weight of her mother's sacrifice.

A determined spark coursed through Laya at the reminder. "I will not waste this," she told Ojas in a tight whisper.

And Ojas nodded because he understood.

A distant echo of drums rang out over the cheering crowd. The beat started at a slow, steady pace before it picked up and grew riotous. On top of the footbridges, the people of Mariit continued to dance and drink. Platters of food passed from hand to hand: steamed pork buns and squid balls and batter-fried quail eggs. The sounds and smells overwhelmed her as the boat drew closer to the heart of the city. The feast wouldn't last forever. Were the Kulaws truly gone? Did Laya's reign mark a new era of peace?

She wanted to believe that was the case, but she couldn't deny the voice in the back of her head that whispered otherwise.

Over Ojas's shoulder, Laya caught a glimpse of sunlight glaring off a pair of spectacles—Ariel Sauros. The growing fondness she felt for him aside, she owed him for protecting Eti. When any self-seeking man would have fled, Ariel had stayed in Maynara and helped the Gatdula family. He was part of Laya's retinue because she needed him and his priceless alchemy skills—more than she cared to admit.

The previous evening, Laya had summoned Ariel to her chambers. She waved before him the letter she had stolen from his desk all those weeks before. Although she had finally deciphered it, the words left her with more questions than answers. "I think it's time you told me about this," she said.

Ariel stared at her, dumbfounded. "How on earth did you find that?" he demanded.

"I'm queen now. And it's my duty to get to know my guests," she said, giving him a wry grin. "It's your own fault, you know. If you didn't want me to read it, you should never have taught me that dreadful alphabet."

Ariel had sighed in half-hearted defeat, because Laya was right; Ariel was under her protection as queen and had no right to lie to her. Thus, the story came out. Parts of it, Laya already knew—what precioso could do, and why her mother had sought his services. As for Pangil, the man who'd sent Ariel to Maynara in the first place—

"I wish to speak to this man," she said. "Can you contact him for me?"

"Certainly, Your Majesty," Ariel told her. He met her gaze before bowing his head in deference, his lips curling into a hesitant grin.

On the riverboat, Ojas drew back so Laya's family could join her at the bow. Eti leaned against Laya's side, her cropped hair tumbling over her eyes in the breeze. Bulan placed a reassuring hand on Laya's other shoulder, keeping her steady gaze trained on the canal ahead.

Laya tightened her grip on the brass railing. The three Gatdula sisters, left to fend for themselves in the land of gods. The land of monsters.

At the end of the tour of Mariit, the riverboat circled back to the balete tree. Laya could hear the wind rustling through its twisted vines, the whisper of spirits—the dead who awaited her on the other side. With a heavy heart, she stepped onto the platform. The whispers quieted as she walked past the ring of spirit houses and into the sacred grove. Her parents slept together in the same rosewood tree. Hari Aki's remains rested in the tree, tucked into a limestone sarcophagus. Over the nine days following his death, Maiza's shamans sang funeral dirges as they cleansed his skin with blessed water and betel sap. They had hollowed out a space for Hara Duja's sarcophagus beside him earlier that week, even though they never recovered her body.

Laya reached out and laid her palm against the bark. If she could have wielded the wood, she would have reached straight through and tugged her parents' spirits from the resin. But they were gone, roaming a distant realm, and not even Maiza could call them back.

"I will not fail you," she murmured. She wanted her mother to hear this more than anyone else. Her mouth flooded with all the questions she would never get a chance to ask her. Hara Duja had left her too soon, and Laya was not yet ready to bear the mantle. How could she govern a country that had scarcely healed from its recent scars? She had coveted the throne her entire life, but the reality of taking her mother's place terrified her.

But she wouldn't be alone. Her ears perked up at the light tread of footsteps. Laya looked over her shoulder. Bulan and Eti hung back to give her a moment alone with their parents. The small act of deference caught Laya by surprise—the first of many changes. She beckoned to them, and they joined her. They linked hands as they stood before the sacred rosewood tree.

"They're still with us," Bulan said softly. She squeezed Laya's hand. A deep trust had blossomed between them in the hole their parents had left behind. After everything they had lost, they put aside their unspoken grievances. They agreed to be kinder to each other. To lean on one another, as sisters should. Their past arguments, the hurtful insults they had exchanged over the years—all of that seemed so petty. Laya's cheeks burned with shame when she thought about how awfully she had treated Bulan before.

Eti sighed and pressed her forehead against the bark. Ever since the battle on the Black Salt Cliffs, she had fashioned herself into a little adult. She changed her mannerisms and even adopted a lower timbre to her speaking voice—all to appear older than her thirteen years. But Laya knew better. She could see the scared child underneath, and her heart ached for her. Eti was the youngest of them, and she had known their parents the least.

Hara Duja and Hari Aki were gone. No one but Laya was left to protect her sisters. A fierce desire flooded her heart as she gazed at them. *I will protect you,* she vowed. *Both of you.*

Laya vowed to be an even better queen than her mother had been. She was not the foolish girl she had been before the start of the feast days. And she would learn from Hara Duja's mistakes, same as she would learn from her own. Laya realized, with a dull pang, how much she had changed over the previous few weeks. Her heart had led her wrong before, and she vowed to ignore its nagging whispers. She had learned to trust no one but her family—for Laya had not understood loyalty until she was betrayed.

Wisdom bore a terrible cost, Maiza once told her. And Laya had paid a steep price for the knowledge and the throne she had desired for so long.

At the edge of the sacred grove, someone cleared their throat. Laya turned around. General Ojas was waiting, his shoulders level and his hands clasped behind his back. That was his signal.

"Come now," she said to her sisters. Ojas led them back to the riverboat. By the time they emerged from the grove, the sun had risen on the horizon, marking the end of their tour of Mariit. That afternoon, Laya had her first meeting with the council following her coronation. She imagined them gathered around the council table—Datu Luma with his wispy white hair and somber gaze, Datu Tanglaw with his thick black eyebrows and groveling tone.

Out of the six highborn families, four loyal datus remained. They wouldn't think to cross her like the Kulaws had. Laya vowed to make them cement their fealty to her in blood. They were probably at the palace already, awaiting their next set of orders. Like the rest of Maynara, they were waiting patiently for Laya to steer them.

Well. They need not wait for her any longer. Laya smiled as the riverboat rounded the corner onto the main canal and the white stone walls of the palace came into view. The palace's tiered roofs peeked up above the walls, sunlight glaring off their gold-encrusted finials. At the sight of the riverboat, one of the guardsmen barked the orders. A moment later, the gates swung open for their new queen, revealing the marble staircase that rose up to the palace's great giltwood doors. Over Mariit, the day broke with a blinding fervor.

Hara Laya had arrived.

Epilogue

YARI

Yari shivered inside the creaking hull and pulled her shawl snug around her shoulders. Over a month had passed since they'd escaped Mariit on a stolen ship. They were racing through choppy waters into the eye of a storm.

A violent wave crashed into the hull, turning Yari's stomach. She vomited into the bucket beside her bed.

"That's disgusting," snapped the young man with whom Yari had been sharing her cabin. He was one of Datu Kulaw's sword-trained serving boys. Before they attacked the palace, he had sung Imeria's praises to whoever would listen. The Gatdulas had never cared for a nobody like him.

Yari left the cabin, hauling the bucket with her. She climbed the ladder to the main deck and tipped the bucket over the railing, spilling its contents into the Untulu Sea. She didn't regret throwing her lot in with the Kulaws. While Imeria hadn't thought of Yari as more than a tool she could sharpen for her own gain, at least she had learned her name. That was more than Yari could say for Hara Duja.

She set the bucket on the deck and leaned against the railing. The fresh air whipped her hair from her face and cleared her head. She drew in a deep breath, the scent of brine filling her nostrils. The water stretched for miles, with no land in sight.

Angry shouts echoed from down in the hull. Vikal and Datu Gulod were arguing again. Vikal wanted to rendezvous with the Kulaws' allies in the south. Gulod kept telling him that the war for Maynara was already lost.

Yari didn't care where they went. Her sole request was that they dock somewhere where Hara Laya could not chop off her head.

She headed to the bow of the ship, where Luntok's remains lay beneath a threadbare tarp. Vikal had insisted on taking the dead boy with them when they'd escaped from the Black Salt Cliffs.

With Imeria gone, no one dared touch Luntok. But several weeks had passed since that awful wedding. Surely, the bow should be tainted with the sickly-sweet smell of decaying flesh at this point.

Curiosity got the better of Yari. She leaned over Luntok. Gingerly, she peeled the tarp back from his face. Luntok's body remained intact, with no sign of rot. With his eyes closed, he looked like he was sleeping. She pulled the tarp lower, her hand brushing against his wrist. Luntok's eyes shot open.

Yari screamed.

Footsteps thundered across the deck as dozens more joined Yari on the bow. Luntok's skin emanated an unearthly glow. He rose to his feet. Yellow threads of life snaked up his arms and legs before winding themselves like a silken noose around his neck. He threw his head back with a howl, and his torso arched up toward the sky.

Light exploded from his body, and Yari squeezed her eyes shut. Luntok's screams went quiet. A deathly silence swept over the ship. Cautiously, Yari raised her head.

A dark figure hovered above her, casting its shadow across

the warped boards that lined the deck. In Luntok's place stood a raptor, twice as tall as any man. It possessed a beak that could snap through Yari's spine as if it were nothing but a twig, and sharp talons that could pierce through thick layers of armored skin. It flexed its wings, which spanned the entire width of the ship.

Yari gazed up at the raptor, her mouth open in disbelief. Its—no, *his*—glorious plume rippled in the sea breeze. Soft thuds echoed in the air as the Kulaw men fell to their knees.

"My lord," Yari whispered, and held out her hand.

The raptor leaned forward and let her caress his feathered cheek. A shiver crept down Yari's spine when she realized what she had witnessed.

When Imeria healed her son on the cliffs, she had not merely stitched together his wounds. She did far more than breathe life into his shattered bones. No, Imeria had breached the realm of possibility. For a brief time, she had become mightier than any Gatdula, as powerful as Mulayri himself.

"My lord," Yari said again, folding her body at the raptor's taloned feet.

And so Yari understood what it meant to kneel before greatness. For the Luntok they knew back in Maynara was gone. Standing before them was a *god*.

Acknowledgments

If writing a novel is like scaling a cliff, writing a *debut* novel is like scaling a cliff during a thunderstorm, your fingers slipping against the holds, rain streaming down your face and clouding your vision. I owe my gratitude to those who saw me through to the summit, without whom *Black Salt Queen* would not exist.

To Chelsea Hensley, my rockstar agent and biggest champion. Thank you for believing in me and my words. Your faith has kept me going through the rough storms of "trad pub." Thanks to you, I'll see my debut in print (and, hopefully, many books to come).

To Kevin T. Norman for making my author dreams come true. I don't know where I'd be without your passion for this story, its universe, and its characters. I couldn't have asked for a better partner in getting *Black Salt Queen* out into the world.

To the Bindery team—Matt Kaye, Meghan Harvey, Charlotte Strick, and CJ Alberts—for your hard work and inspiring vision. Thank you for including me in Bindery's journey. I'm truly honored to have a place in your growing catalog.

To the Girl Friday team—Sara Addicott, Katherine Richards, Paul Barrett, Wanda Zimba, and Tiffany Taing—for all the time and care you've poured into this book. Getting this book to print has been perfectly seamless, thanks to all of you.

To my developmental editor, Zhui Ning Chang, whose insights and guidance made my manuscript stronger than ever.

To my cover artist, June Glasson, who captured the beauty of Maynara in ways I never thought possible.

ACKNOWLEDGMENTS

To Brittani Hilles at Lavender Public Relations, for your commitment to getting *Black Salt Queen* to its most devoted readers.

I'd be remiss if I didn't acknowledge my writing village as well. Before *Black Salt Queen*, I was scaling the metaphorical cliff alone. They say creativity is the reward—but so are the connections you make along the way. A huge thanks to the following people for making trad pub feel less lonely.

Most of all, to AM Kvita. There are no words to express my gratitude for your mentorship over the years. Thank you for your edit letters and for holding my hand in the query trenches. You were the first person to see this story's potential, for which I'll be eternally grateful.

To the rest of the Raft—Casey Colaine, S. Hati, Amanda Helms, Shay Kauwe, and O.O. Sangoyomi—for your feedback and friendship, which have been keeping me afloat.

To the incredible AMM R9 family and the broader writing community, of which there are too many wonderful souls to name. Thank you for sharing your talent, advice, and boundless support.

To my first readers, especially Kim and Zach, who saw but the barest bones of *Black Salt Queen* and cheered me on, nonetheless.

To Philippe, for staying true to your vows and taking on my share of the chores whenever I'm on deadline. You've taught me the true meaning of partnership. Thank you for supporting me while I chase my dreams. *Je t'aime à la folie.*

Last but not least, to my family, who raised me on good books and home-cooked Filipino food. Thank you for showering me with encouragement, no matter the endeavor. Your love is the one thing that transcends time and distance. *Mahal kita,* forever and always.

Thank You

This book would not have been possible without the support from the Violetear Books community, with a special thank-you to the Associate Publisher members:

dannyjladd
Ashley Odriozola
Jeffrey Tristan Thyme
BecosIRead
Holly Blakemore
TiffanyWangAuthor
williampdozier
Courtney Doerr
Dani Paez
Fairiedancr
Cristina Rowe
Christian Bellman
MalunkeyReads
MAMARia

About the Author

© 2024 Thomas Dossmann Photographie

SAMANTHA BANSIL is a Filipino American fantasy author. She studied sociology and French at Boston University before earning a master's degree at Institut d'études politiques de Paris. After trying on many a professional hat, she found her way back to her one true love—writing. Her stories often feature big feelings, lush settings, and unlikable protagonists. A jet-setter at heart, she lives to travel worlds both real and imagined. When she's not writing, she can be found wandering bookstores and ricocheting between continents. She works in Paris, France, as a content marketer.

Violetear Books is an imprint of Bindery, a book publisher powered by community.

We're inspired by the way book tastemakers have reinvigorated the publishing industry. With strong taste and direct connections with readers, book tastemakers have illuminated self-published, backlisted, and overlooked authors, rocketing many to bestseller lists and the big screen.

This book was chosen by Kevin T. Norman in close collaboration with the Violetear Books community on Bindery. By inviting tastemakers and their reading communities to participate in publishing, Bindery creates opportunities for deserving authors to reach readers who will love them.

Visit Violetear Books for a thriving bookish community and bonus content:

violetear.binderybooks.com

KEVIN T. NORMAN is a Latinx creator from Los Angeles, California, who combines humor and his love of reading to create content focused on education, social justice, and all things bookish. He has a combined TikTok and Instagram following of over 370,000. In 2022, Kevin was chosen as an LGBTQ+ Trailblazer, a title awarded by TikTok to only twelve creators from the US for their work with the LGBTQ+ community. He has been featured on *The Kelly Clarkson Show*, Spectrum News, and NBC News, and in *Forbes*, *Teen Vogue*, the *New York Post*, *Rolling Stone*, and more.

TIKTOK.COM/@KEVINTNORMAN

INSTAGRAM.COM/KEVINTNORMAN